THE PRESIDENT'S WEEKEND

VIVISPHERE PUBLISHING

Cover design by Jay Cookingham
Printed in the United States of America
President's Weekend is a paperback original publication of Vivisphere Publishing.

ISBN 1-58776-110-6
Library of Congress Catalogue Number: 2001094913

www.vivisphere.com
1-800-724-1100

VIVISPHERE PUBLISHING

To 'Jennifer'

— for what was and what might have been

EPTEMBER 7, 1901, THE NEW YORK TIMES:

PRESIDENT SHOT AT BUFFALO FAIR

Buffalo, Sept. 6—President McKinley, while holding a reception in the Temple of Music at the Pan-American Exposition at 4 o'clock this afternoon, was shot and twice wounded by Leon Czolgosz, an Anarchist, who lives in Cleveland.

MR. ROOSEVELT EN ROUTE

Burlington, Vt., Sept. 6—The first news of the attempted assassination of President McKinley reached Vice President Roosevelt at 5:30 PM this afternoon. President Clement of the Rutland Railroad placed a train at the disposal of the Vice President and make arrangements to take him on it to Buffalo.

SATURDAY, SEPTEMBER 14, 1901, THE NEW YORK TIMES:

MR. MCKINLEY DIES AFTER A BRAVE FIGHT

MR. ROOSEVELT SUMMONED

Buffalo, Sept. 14—President McKinley died at 2:15 o'clock, this morning. He had been unconscious since 7:50 o'clock last night. His last conscious hour of life was spent with his wife to whom he devoted a lifetime of care.

UNDAY, SEPTEMBER 15, 1901, THE NEW YORK TIMES:

MR. ROOSEVELT IS NOW THE PRESIDENT

"Life and death are all part
of the same great adventure.

—Theodore Roosevelt

THE PRESIDENT'S WEEKEND

Chapter One

February 1993

Driving the hundred or so miles from Fairfield to New Paltz, New York, in a February blizzard, especially along the section of the New York Thruway from Newburgh north, was not Jamie's choice of how to spend a leisurely Saturday morning. The latest weather report was ambiguous both as to amount of snow expected and to whether the Connecticut coastline and upstate areas would escape the full blast of the yet-indeterminate cold front.

Wet, sticky snow flakes, not yet heavy but threatening, were beginning to pile up on the windshield as Jamie approached the Connecticut Turnpike bridge over the Saugatuck River in Westport.

Damn wipers, when was he going to take the time to change them. Since November, he had been carrying around new replacement blades; "guaranteed to last the life of the car," stated the promo on the package. Yeah, he thought, especially if you keep them in the back seat all wrapped up.

Jennifer would not be too happy about driving to Mohonk with her side of the windshield providing about as much vision as advanced cataracts. Never mind, he thought, serves her right for postponing departure.

"Jamie, honey, don't be upset," she had told him that morning over the phone. "I have to drop off some paperwork at the office. I'm really sorry. Bear with me? Pick me up at 10:00 instead?" 'Instead' was supposed to have been 8:30. Jamie had felt a tinge of annoyance, particularly in view of the unpredictable weather, but Jennifer had too many great things going for her.

Bloody Hell, I hope this eases up, he muttered to himself as slush splashed against the windshield from a passing vehicle.

Jamie still subconsciously attached 'bloody' to describe things, the residue of his marriage to Glena and all that time he had spent in southwestern England.

Bloody was wonderfully descriptive for all occasions—a verbal condiment the English used to season the banquet of life. Food, the weather, sex—all could be described as either 'bloody great' or 'bloody awful.' American idioms were no match for the verbal economy and wit of cockney speech which had woven its coarse but colorful threads into the fabric of English society all the way up to the House of Lords and Buckingham Palace.

Although things English still punctuated his mind at unexpected moments, such reminiscences were leavened by the time and geography that separated him from the broom-clean little village of Portishead in Southwestern England where Glena now lived. And Glena—well, it was nearly eight years since the divorce, and the once razor edge of pain had finally dulled. He had discovered there was life beyond Glena. Meeting Jennifer, of course, had helped.

Snow was falling heavier now as he passed a long tractor-trailer rig with huge initials G-O-D on both sides and back of the box. The driver, oblivious to the not so veiled sacrilege, was busy down-shifting to avoid braking too abruptly on the increasingly icy roadway.

Jamie Stanner had always been Jamieson to his mother, but the pragmatism of school days had soon distilled Jamieson to 'Jamie.' He had slowly been acclimatized to a name that seemed to evoke a tinge of effeminacy. He had countered this by developing a very physical and somewhat aggressive personality that demonstrated itself in a proficiency in high school sports and girl-baiting. Slightly built during his high school years, even as a senior he tipped the scales dripping wet at no more that 136 pounds. However, his match-stick size was well proportioned and no football heavy-weight was better at charming the socks off the prettiest cheerleader at Charles Evans Hughes Academy than Jamie.

His once wiry, red hair had faded by 1993 to an almost golden blond, thinning out on top but curling down yet over his forehead in a boyish wave that could still evoke envy in younger men and draw occasional lustful stares from younger women as well. His waistline had expanded and contracted during his marriage and later single years in direct proportion to the emotional imbalances of several roller-coaster relationships.

At 48, he was now a fairly trim 170 at 5'10, about ten pounds above a good ring weight; but his girth had stayed constant at 34inches, his belt truly around his middle and not sagging under a beer belly as many men his age sported. Dark brown eyes that narrowed to knife slits when he laughed complimented a ruddy complexion and freckles, still in evidence after youthful summers working on a dairy farm. Thin, firm lips curled into dimpled cheeks when he smiled, which was often. A chisled profile could have, in younger days, subbed for Robert Taylor's, except for a high school football tackle that reshaped his nose into a duplicate of the one sprouting from the face of Uncle Sam on the well known recruiting poster from World War I stating, 'I want you!' Still, Jamie Stanner was not unhandsome and few facial wrinkles belied his true age.

Jamie's attention shifted to the highway ahead. It appeared that a car had, not long before, skidded and collided with the steel guard rail in the median strip. Nothing too serious, he noted. Two other cars had already stopped and a man was waving traffic around the site. Another mile, and the Kings Highway exit in Fairfield loomed off to the right.

Please, for God's sake, Jennifer, be ready, Jamie exhorted. If things were par for the course, Jennifer's being ready meant two suitcases almost but not quite packed, at least three garment bags to be placed around several enticing, sexy dresses, the cat's litter box to be emptied and the dog to be walked briefly. 'Pepper' would be picked up later for the weekend to be cared for by a friend. All of this would likely take 40 minutes or so without sex in the offing and if there were no hitches, such as the cat sneaking out an open door and having to be hunted down in the snow.

Jamie turned into Strathmor Terrace, a cul-de-sac off the street of the same name in Fairfield's north end and pulled into

Jennifer's driveway with an expectant, hopeful sigh. Snow flakes dusted across the large living room picture window framing Jennifer's smiling countenance as she appeared and waved to him.

Pepper's bark coming from the kitchen, loud and insistent, seemed hostile, but Pepper was a complete fraud—at least to those who knew him. A small, short-legged, fluffy black and white terrier mix of unknown ancestry, Pepper had as much venom in him as a cup of hot chocolate. To a stranger, though, his bark gave the appearance of a mean little mutt that would as soon leave an imprint of his teeth in your hand as he would take a proffered doggy bone.

Jennifer greeted him with a wrap-around hug as he stepped into the living room, the shoulders of her bathrobe slipping sensuously down to her waist.

"Jennifer," Jamie felt almost uncontrollably aroused, "you know I'd be the first one, if the sun was shining, to suggest a delayed departure, but we've just got to get going. I don't want to wind up straddling the guard rail on the median divider of the N.Y. Thruway. Can we please save it for Mohonk?"

Jennifer pretended a pout and put on her Sunday School teacher face—prim, proper, stand-offish. "All right," she said as she hiked up her robe, "class dismissed—we'll play 'after-school' at Mohonk and you get extra homework tonight."

Strangely enough, Jennifer had a sort of reputation with her business associates as being a bit school marmish in manner. Although she had certainly never taught Sunday School, she had taught High School French during her early years in Cleveland, Ohio.

But for all her teacher-like, somewhat sedate appearance to others, at least at first meeting, Jennifer Dickson possessed a striking sensuality.

It was not because she was particularly beautiful. She had a rather small mouth with thin lips which were subject to a pouty look when she became annoyed. Although only 38, Jennifer's eyes were already offset by tiny crow's feet which, while extremely appealing when she flashed a quick smile, suggested a woman of some later years. Jamie suspected those tiny wrinkles were the result of Jennifer's peculiar habit of wincing as she closed her eyes very tightly upon being kissed—a reflexive action of which she seemed completely unaware.

Before Jamie, there had been another man, after a painful

divorce and nine years of no relationship. During that hiatus, Jennifer had given her full attention to raising her daughter. An only child, Ellen was both pretty and gifted. At seventeen, she had just entered the Ivy enclaves of Yale University.

Jamie's 'predecessor' had played upon Jennifer's vulnerability and desire for some kind of a relationship, although at the time she wasn't at all certain of what she wanted in the long run.

There seemed to be something unresolved in Jennifer's past that prevented her, at this point in her life, from considering a total commitment to a relationship.

Then came Jamieson Stanner, tripping into her life so unexpectantly. Jamie loved her and sooner or later the day would have to come for commitment to him or separation. Right now, Jennifer expressed no wish for either. Whenever Jamie had pushed too hard, she would feel closed in and would decide to date other men. Jamie would back off and they would reunite. Now, in February, 1993, Jamie had decided to play it Jennifer's way—at least for awhile, convinced he could eventually break the symbiotic hold the phantoms of the past held over her. A romantic weekend at Mohonk might advance the cause, he thought. It was worth a try.

As he walked into the bedroom, Jamie was amazed at how far along Jennifer actually was with her packing. Only one suitcase was left open and that one was filled, a daring little bit of nothingness from *Victoria's Secret* draped almost artfully on top. That had, of course, been left for his benefit. He almost succumbed to the temptation, but drawing upon the tattered remnants of his fast-waning resistance, he firmly closed and locked the cover. Jennifer shouted from the bathroom, "Do you like it Jamie?"

"Yes, sweetheart, but I'll like it better at Mohonk. Can we go, please?"

"Go load up the car, Jamie, honey, I'll be down in a minute. I promise."

Jamie dutifully and quickly loaded up the Subaru. Thank God for four-wheel drive, he thought. The snow was thickening, but it seemed wetter. The temperature was on the rise. That could mean that it might not be sticking on the road surface on Route 84 or the Thruway.

True to her word, Jennifer came skipping out the front door

with an additional garment bag in her hand. "You forgot one, honey."

"Jennifer, my God, we're only going for one night." Jamie shook his head in wonder as he placed the garment bag over the suitcases and closed the hatchback.

"You won't regret that last one, Jamie. You would have been sorry if we had forgotten it."

Jennifer babbled away like a little mountain brook, tinkling away over rocks, trickling towards verdant lowland valleys.

"Won't if be fun to dress up tonight in our Victorian outfits—or I guess I should say 'Edwardian,' since we're supposed to be in the early 1900's, aren't we?" Jennifer said with a starry-eyed look.

Jamie wasn't at all sure he would enjoy spending an evening dressed in tails he would have to flip up behind him every time he wanted to sit down, but if the evening included Jennifer, it didn't matter if he was going to be dressed like Liberace or G.I. Joe.

"Looks like a fun evening," he agreed as he backed the Subaru out of the drive and turned toward Main Street and the Merritt Parkway to pick up Route 25 north to Route 84 west. The snow was not collecting too heavily on the Parkway. The rising temperature was alleviating some anxious moments.

A short while later and they were headed west on 84, crossing the Hudson on the Newburgh-Beacon Bridge. It was just an hour and a half drive from Fairfield to Mohonk, and they had gotten off at a reasonable time, after all, not withstanding Jennifer's wiles to sabotage the schedule.

Jamie grabbed the toll ticket thrust at him at the Newburgh toll station entrance to the Thruway, relieved to see that the new wet snow that had fallen and was still falling, but more lightly, had mostly melted on the roadway surface, no doubt due to the rising temperature and salt spread earlier by the Teutonic snowplows of the N.Y. State Highway Dept.

Several miles of gently rolling fruit orchards, blanketed in snowy drifts, bordered the Thruway. In one place, twenty or thirty deer had herded together and, like woods phantoms, browsed gingerly among the orderly rows of bare-limbed trees.

From the Thruway, just before New Paltz, the Shawangunk Mountain chain could be seen looming up from the west through the clearing mist. Stretching from north to south, the dull gray and silver ledges and cliffs of over a thousand feet in height, threatened to break like a titanic tidal wave over the lowlands and valleys in a torrential flood-tide of cataclysmic proportions.

Jamie down-shifted in the approach to the off-ramp and the Thruway toll station at New Paltz and pointed toward the western horizon. About five miles distant in the clearing winter haze, the Smiley Memorial Tower could be seen, a landlocked lighthouse crowning the highest promontory overlooking the expanse of the Hudson lowlands to the east and, to the west, Lake Mohonk and the Mohonk Mountain House, not yet visible.

Beyond the little college community of New Paltz, they drove toward the escarpments of the Shawangunks. The road steepened as it pitched toward the aged rifts, winding precipitously upward and narrowing as it swung around in several horseshoe curves before flattening out in the last hundred yards as it reached the turn-off for Mountain Rest, the gatehouse at the base of the final sloping ridge before the summit of the Mountain House.

"There you are, sir," the gatehouse attendant handed Jamie his reservation confirmation. "Just leave the tag for your car keys on the dashboard. Guest services will park your car for you. Just follow the road right up to the Mountain House."

"Thank you," Jamie replied as he shifted and steered the Subaru toward the entrance to the drive.

How many times had he made this trip up this beautiful, cliff-carved roadway, always fascinated by the scenic wonderment presented at every turn as the narrow lane snaked through corridors of ancient hemlocks, gracefully swaying now in the winter breeze, and ambled past gnarled, wind-twisted pitch-pines clutching steep embankments.

At certain places, the sometimes ungenerous passage hewed tightly to huge blanket-like layers of bedrock overhanging and rimming the right of way, leaving little margin for driving error, especially in the navigation of several spiral curves that offered up, for unwary chauffeurs, uncompromising cliff edges and steep plunges to wooded slopes far below.

Here and there, on occasion, due to the more recent attention to conservation measures, wild turkeys gingerly stepped through the thick cover of dead falls, and almost always, gentle, nearly tame whitetail deer pranced across the roadway, ears turning sharply to root out alien sounds, black noses sniffing wind currents and large brown dewy eyes, alert and all-seeing, looking for any strange motions not compatible within their familiar environmental vision.

As the car completed the final S bend in the road, the great storied Mountain House slowly emerged from the light snowy haze and mist, an awesome superstructure of balconies, porches, verandas, towers, chimneys, stone ramparts, gables and roof top perches—a whimsical architectural confection designed to delight and enfold its guests in 19th century tranquillity—albeit enhanced with 20th century plumbing.

Jamie always felt as if he were coming home in the moments when the Smiley House first appeared through the rim of trees which skirted the gardens and surrounding grounds.

Having visited the Mountain House again and again over the years from the age of about nine, he had developed such a sense of belonging to Mohonk that each time he found himself once again in the great house's embrace, all of his life and time beyond Mohonk's borders felt strangely subordinated—mute and gray, a monotone of existence that seemed to fade away even as the valleys surrounding Mohonk disappeared in the encroaching shadows of twilight.

It would be only hours before Jamieson Stanner would come to realize just how subordinate his life beyond Mohonk would become.

Chapter Two

Jamie turned off the main road onto the approach driveway, a half-circle leading to the hotel's west entrance. The west side of the Mountain House faced the Catskill Mountains. An early afternoon mist enshrouded the farmlands and forests of the Rondout Valley far below and was beginning to spread to the mountains some fifteen miles westerly.

The west entrance was distinguished by a porte-cochere of ponderous rock slabs forming three huge archways, two of which framed a passage over the driveway. The third arch connected the other two and, normally, weather permitting, presented to guests emerging from the entrance a stunning vista of lowlands and mountain heights.

Above the arched entrance area was an open porch connecting with a sweeping, covered verandah along the west front of the hotel which opened into the first floor lobby and parlors. JFK rocking chairs lined the verandah like sentinels awaiting their marching orders.

Jamie checked his watch. It was just 1:00 PM. They had made good time despite the threatening weather.

Two alert and extremely polite bellhops clamored around the car as Jamie pulled to a stop and shut off the ignition. He opened his door as one of the bellhops assisted Jennifer in exiting.

"Hi, guys. I'm afraid we're going to need your largest luggage trolley. My friend here could fill a Madison Avenue Boutique with what she brought," Jamie teased. Jennifer looked askance.

"The trouble with you men," she retorted, "is that you want your women to be fashion plates for every occasion and expect us to pack everything into a briefcase when we go away."

Jamie smiled and whispered out of earshot of the bellhops busily unloading, "As far as I'm concerned, you could pack everything I'd like you to wear in a briefcase."

Jennifer feigned a glance of disapproval but the tiny crinkles around her eyes gave her real feelings away. She loved Jamie to refer to her sexiness. They played a constant game of sexual taunt, each baiting the other, throwing little darts designed to excite and press in a hundred sort of ways their separate advantages.

The luggage trolley was in overload as one of the bellhops hustled the towering pile of suitcases, garment bags, coats and two down pillows through the lobby door. Jamie and Jennifer always brought their own pillows. They didn't like to take unnecessary risks with the average hotel pillow, which seemed to be stuffed with a combination of turkey feathers and hard-packed sand.

Jennifer took Jamie's arm and snuggled up close as he ushered her through the immense oak portal separating the outer entrance lobby from the inner corridor leading to the reception area and front desk.

"We have some time to make up for, Jamie. School is out for the day, remember?"

Arm-in-arm, they sauntered along the corridor with its muted beige walls and dark-beamed, paneled ceilings. Near the reception area, they found themselves dodging a group of small children following a Mohonk recreation assistant as if she were the Pied Piper of Hamlin.

"Children," the young lady instructed, "after our hike, we'll have some hot chocolate in the Lake Lounge. But that's only for those who stay together. Everybody, take your partner by the hand now and away we go."

The group lunged forward with one mind, each child seeing how close he or she could get to the leader before they bounded out a side entrance, looking, in their colorful winter garb, for all the world like little gnomes out to spread mischief in snowy forest reaches.

"Jennifer," Jamie said as they approached the front desk, "what do you say to an old fashioned sleigh ride?"

"You mean like a belly-flopper?"

"I mean behind a horse, sitting under a warm blanket with sleigh bells jingling as in 'Jingle Bells, Jingle Bells'!" Jamie tweaked Jennifer's nose. It was a dusty rose, as were her cheeks, acclimating to the colder mountain temperatures of Mohonk.

"That is," Jamie continued, "if your nose can stand the wind bite."

Jennifer laughed. "Sounds wonderful. Maybe we could play some games under the blanket."

"Behave yourself, you wanton woman," Jamie chastised, delighted, of course, at the prospect.

"Ah, miss," Jamie inquired of the desk clerk as he registered, "we'd like to arrange for a private sleigh ride for later, maybe around 3:30?"

An attractive girl with long blond hair that nestled gracefully around her shoulders turned to answer Jamie.

"Oh, I'm really sorry, sir. We don't book individual rides any more. They only keep a few horses now in the winter season for the large sleigh rides. If you'd like to check with guest services, I believe there's a ride scheduled for tomorrow morning at 10:00."

"Hmm, doesn't sound too romantic." Jamie was disappointed. He turned to Jennifer. "I was really looking forward to getting you into a genuine one-horse open sleigh, as the song goes." He turned back to the clerk, "We'll give it some thought. In the meantime, our room is ready, is it?"

"Yes, sir, room 353, third floor left, down the hall from the elevator." She handed Jamie the keys with a big cheerleader smile. "Have a happy Mohonk weekend! I'll have your luggage sent right up."

Jennifer gave Jamie an intimate nudge as they walked to the elevator. He could feel his pulse quicken as they stepped into the empty elevator and the doors closed.

"How about if we make love right here and now, make everybody use the stairs for the next twenty minutes—I'll push the emergency stop button, okay?"

Jennifer squealed in response as Jamie breathed heavily in

her ear. She placed Jamie's hands on her breasts and drew him close to her.

"Cool your hot blood, darling, but leave your hands where they are—we'll be in the room in a twinkling." Jennifer kissed the words into Jamie's mouth as her lips sought his, softly but insistently. The elevator stopped and the doors swished open silently.

They uncoupled for the short walk to the room. Jamie fumbled with the key while Jennifer, peering both ways down the corridor and seeing it empty, stepped up behind him and reached with her hands around his waist, slowly allowing her fingers to creep downward.

The door swung inward. "Jennifer," Jamie whispered hoarsely, "we may have to include the bellhop in a *menage-a-trois* if we don't wait for the luggage."

He stepped through the door, pulling Jennifer across the threshold, and kicked the door shut with his foot. Almost instantly, there came a soft knock at the door. "Good God, he must have been right behind us," he uttered as he unpeeled Jennifer's arms and opened the door.

A towering luggage trolley, seemingly unguided, crossed the threshold. Almost hidden from view, the bellhop entered and hastened to the door on the opposite side of the room leading to the small outside balcony.

"Quite a view from here, folks," the bellhop cheerfully started his orientation piece. "You can see Slide Mountain, twenty miles west, the highest peak in the Catskills."

The bellhop expertly unloaded the luggage trolley and hung the garment bags in the closet. "If you need more wood for the fireplace, just call guest services."

Opposite the bed, the quaint fireplace, with a hand-carved oak mantel, framed by miniature Romanesque columns and topped by a wide cut-glass mirror, looked inviting.

"Yes, well thank you, son." Jamie ushered the bellhop to the door. "Thanks again for your help—hope your trolley isn't too badly damaged from the load." He closed the door and faced Jennifer who was already stripping off her blouse and stepping out of her skirt.

"My God, Jennifer, you are the most . . ." Jamie moved toward her expectantly. Their tongues merged in a deep kiss, Jennifer's darting in and out, wet against Jamie's lips. Jamie's hands slipped to the clasp on Jennifer's bra. The soft curves of her breasts broke free. Jennifer's knees were trembling. She leaned on Jamie heavily, barely able to stand any longer. Her voice was low and throaty, breaking into tiny gasps. Words failed now—just breathy sounds, rising in pitch, giving over to soft squeals reflecting Jennifer's increasing excitement. She fell back weakly against the bed. Clothes were discarded in ritual succession. Jamie's arms coupled Jennifer tenderly, hands grasping gently. Their bodies moved rhythmically to ignite, once again, the inevitable climax they would share at the final heights of their merging. As minutes passed, short, sharp spasms forced child-like cries from Jennifer, and then came deep, long sighs from Jamie as he gulped his breath and panted, spent from the ultimate ecstasy.

It was complete. The fulfillment they both had sought had arrived. Now, an afterglow of rich but quiet sensations permeated them for passive moments as they snuggled closely under the creamy folds of the Mohonk blanket they had so rudely thrust aside in their earlier passion.

Chapter Three

"Let's go down to the Gazebo Shop, Jamie, before we go out." Jennifer's eyes sparkled as she contemplated browsing through the little gift shop on the first floor corridor just off the central stair landing. Jamie shuddered inwardly as he envisioned Jennifer let loose against the poor defenseless sales clerk who would, undoubtedly, if Jennifer's normal track record prevailed, be requested to show for 'closer inspection' every piece of antique jewelry on display.

"Now look, my sweet—if we're going on a hike to Sky Top, we really don't have a lot of time for rummaging in boutiques."

Jamie put his arms gently around Jennifer and kissed her lightly on her forehead. "After all, our unbridled passion of the last hour came at a slight price. Didn't you say we had to be ready by 6:15 to meet our dinner mates?"

"Oh, yes, but it's only 2:00—just 10 or 15 minutes, okay? I promise I'll be good. I only want to look at some earrings. I'd really like to find some silver and pearl pendants. They might go better with my gown for tonight than the plain pearl rings I brought with me."

It was no use, really. Jamie knew that right from the start. "Okay, love—elevator or stairs? But remember, 15 minutes or I'll pull the fire alarm."

Jennifer laughed in that low, sensuous, almost inaudible

throaty style that always left Jamie weak with desire for her. She kissed him softly with wet lips and darting tongue tip. Sensing his immediate arousal, she broke away. "Come on, honey—we do have a schedule, don't we?"

Their room, 353, was close to the third floor landing and elevators. "Let's take the stairs." Jennifer bounded happily down the two flights of the wide, lushly carpeted stairs. Jamie followed in hot pursuit, artfully side-stepping like a football player running broken-field, several small children playing 'peek-a-boo' through the beautifully turned chestnut spindles of the stair railings that boxed in the square shaft of the central stairs as they opened on each floor level.

The Gazebo Shop had once been a small library lounge or alcove which at one time had opened directly to the outside on the wide, covered expanse of the first floor verandah immediately over the quintessential porte-cochere and west entrance to the Mountain House.

A mannequin dressed in a lacy Victorian gown stood, like a cigar store Indian of old, in the hall by the door to the shop, advertising the wares within and enticing unwary husbands and lovers passing by to enter—at their own risk.

The former alcove opening from the corridor had been glassed in, providing a quaint Dickensian store window effect. Old stair railing spindles had been set in two rows, one above the other within the glass frame, providing unique niches for the display of silver vases, cut glass and odd pieces of china.

Jennifer entered the shop, all ohhs! and ahhs! as her eyes darted around the tiny room absorbing the myriad delights—cloisonné vases, fine old English bone china, demitasse cups in intricate wildflower designs, tea sets, dinnerware from Staffordshire, luncheon plates and colorful coffee mugs of every description.

From the entrance, the right hand wall was fitted with shallow shelves placed on either side of a typical Mohonk fireplace. Such shelves held scores of brightly colored bows, ribbons, perfume bottles, assorted bric-a-brac, more English bone china, cut-glass bowls, more cloisonné vases and tiny porcelain pill and jewelry boxes.

Against the opposite wall, on what were formerly built-in book shelves, were neat piles of women's cotton blouses, sweaters and casual women's knits, fronted by a rack of silk blouses,

Victorian-styled dresses, chemises and frilly night gowns. There were even a few old books left on the shelves, notably: a three-volume set, in mint condition, of James Whitcomb Riley poems, a copy of *The Blue Flower* by Henry Van Dyke and Oliver Goldsmith's *The Vicar of Wakefield.*

Jennifer flitted from one object to the next, transfixed by the delights. But, as she had promised Jamie, she soon focused on the large glass display case to the left of the entrance which she decided held the most promise. Antique silver and gold earrings, brooches, pendants, bracelets—enough jewelry to bedeck the Metropolitan Opera cast and full chorus in an authentic production of *La Traviata*—sparkled from the black velvet trays within.

Jennifer's eyes almost immediately picked up the soft luster of a silver and pearl pendant earring set. "Look, Jamie—just what I had in mind."

The clerk opened the case and brought out the earrings. Jennifer quickly tried them on. Oddly enough, they were designed for pierced ears, which Jennifer thought cast in doubt their authenticity as antique pieces.

However, the clerk explained, "Many women at the turn of the century did have pierced ears, but these, I'm afraid, are reproductions of some of Mrs. Cornelius Vanderbilt's favorite pieces."

Jennifer yelped with delight. "That means I might be able to afford them then if they're fake. They're really beautiful."

"Actually, they're sterling silver. Just the pearls are imitation," the sales clerk pointed out. "They're really quite reasonable, though, only $125 for the pair."

Jamie interjected, "Well you can have an early birthday, this year, Jennifer." He looked at the clerk. "Wrap them up—unless Jennifer wants to eat them here," he quipped.

Jennifer was bubbling over. "Now, you see—that didn't take long, did it?" She brushed Jamie's mouth with a soft kiss. "Thank you, darling, you're so good to me."

As the clerk wrapped the earrings, Jennifer's gaze, once again, turned back to the display case. Jamie, following her line of vision, said, "Uh-uh, no more, love—your fifteen minutes"—he looked at his watch—"were up two minutes ago."

"Oh, Jamie, look." Jennifer tuned out Jamie's admonition—her eye had caught something. "Look at that beautiful gold signet ring, Jamie—I can't quite make out the initials, but it looks like one could be an 'S'."

"Would you like to see it, miss?" The clerk smiled eagerly—she was on a base salary, but she received a 10% commission on sales as well.

"Oh, please, yes." Jennifer took Jamie's hand. "Jamie, maybe those are your initials."

The clerk removed the ring and handed it to Jennifer. "Oh, Jamie," Jennifer squealed happily, "look, 'J.S.', isn't that wonderful? What a coincidence. What a really lovely ring."

The ring was artfully crafted, no doubt about it. The initials 'J.S.' were cut in a distinctively styled script, deeply entwined with one another but in such a way as to provide clarity without sacrificing artistry. It was a very special ring, that was obvious—lovingly made for the original 'J.S.', whoever that might have been. Jennifer turned the ring over and peered inside the band.

"Jamie, there's an inscription—no, it's a date, a year." She squinted; she wasn't wearing her contacts. "I think it's—it looks like '1900.' Some woman gave this to her lover, or husband, in 1900. Isn't that romantic, Jamie? Maybe it was on New Year's Eve."

Jamie sighed. "You're hopeless, Jennifer—it's just a ring. How do you know it wasn't a birthday present or graduation gift?"

"Jamie, try it on—I'm going to buy it for you. It's perfect—you know I've been wanting to buy you a ring. See if it fits."

With that, Jennifer took Jamie's left hand and ring finger, slipping the ring over his knuckles. It was a perfect fit.

"See—that ring has been waiting for you all these years." Jennifer glowed with pleasure. Even Jamie had to admit he liked it.

"It does look nice," he said.

"All right, how much?" Jamie looked at the clerk and reached for his wallet.

"Oh, no, Jamie, I'm buying this, put your wallet away."

The clerk replied, "Well, it is an antique piece and it's 14-karat gold. The appraiser set a price of $475."

"Just out of curiosity, miss, do you know anything about the history of the ring or how it got to the Mountain House?" Jennifer said as she held up Jamie's left hand, the gold reflecting brilliantly the light from the overhead chandelier.

"It's believed it was part of an estate that was willed years ago to Mohonk, but nobody seems to know just where it came from. It had been tucked away with some other jewelry that was only just discovered recently in the Smileys' family quarters in the Rock Building when the builders were doing some renovation." The clerk smiled as she continued. "The Smiley families, Albert's and Daniel's in particular, had many friends who often made contributions to further the causes of the many charities the Smileys sponsored. Jewelry was a popular commodity for that kind of thing."

"Oh, so we have a mystery, Jamie." Jennifer raised her eyebrows quizzically. "Well, maybe it'll be more fun, not knowing but guessing about it. That's more romantic, anyway, don't you think, honey?"

"Of course, Jen," Jamie replied indulgently. "Nothing like a little mystery to spice up a romance, I always say."

Jennifer turned to the clerk. "Do you take checks, miss?"

"Oh, yes," replied the clerk. "You're staying at the Mountain House, aren't you?"

"Yes, room 353." Jennifer took out her check book from a knapsack-size pocketbook.

"Would you like to wear the ring, sir, or would you prefer to take it in the box?" The clerk handed Jennifer a pen and placed a small, square ring box on the counter.

"Oh, please wear it, Jamie, but take the box anyway so it won't get lost when you take it off." Jennifer handed the clerk her check and picked up the box, slipping it into the 'saddlebag.'

"All right, now, are we finally ready for Sky Top?" Jamie looked at the ring as he took Jennifer's hand and ushered her to the door. Yes, he had to admit it. He liked the ring. He seemed to feel a strange contentment in seeing the ring on his finger. Funny, he thought to himself, he had a sort of feeling that something was completed by wearing the ring—like a link that had once been broken had now been reforged.

Jamie straightened his shoulders as he stepped out into the corridor, "Okay, let's take the path up over the labyrinth to Sky Top, Jen. I'd like to get a picture of the Mountain House."

Jennifer nodded happily and they scampered down the central stairs into the main lobby where the small fireplace near the entrance to the Winter Lounge and library was crackling away, warming the toes of several cross-country skiers curled up on the floor about as close to the fireplace hearth as you could get without inducing self-immolation.

Jamie and Jennifer waved at the happy and contented skiers and walked out on the Lake Lounge porch, down the wide steps to the carriage drive bordering the ice-covered waters of Lake Mohonk, and turned up the path leading past the Council House to Spring Path and the trail to Sky Top.

Chapter Four

The footpath leading up to the trail had been cleared of snow. However, at the trail entrance, a chain stretched across from which dangled a bright red sign with white letters that announced:

SORRY
PATH CLOSED

"Oh, Jamie," Jennifer sighed disappointedly, "I guess that eliminates Sky Top." Jamie took Jennifer's hand as he nimbly stepped over the low-hanging chain.

"C'mon, Jen, I just want to get a picture of the Mountain House where the trail opens up over the lake. Don't worry—we'll just go a few hundred feet." He put his arms around Jennifer and lifted her over the chain.

"Jamie, that trail looks awfully icy. We shouldn't be doing this."

"Jennifer, good Lord, it isn't as if we're cramponing up the face of a glacier. C'mon."

Jamie jumped ahead, pulling Jennifer into the middle of the trail.

Jennifer relented and shimmied up behind him, putting her arms around his waist. "You win, darling, but promise we'll stop at a gazebo on the way up for hanky-panky?"

"Jennifer," Jamie turned to face her and touched her mouth with a finger while holding her close with his arm around her back. "Do five minutes ever go by without you thinking about making love?"

He kissed her gently—her lips were cool and moist, her breath warm as she returned his kiss. He broke away and smiled. "Don't answer that—it's rhetorical and we both know the answer, anyway."

Again, that husky, low, almost inaudible whisper of a laugh from Jennifer. "Do you want to wait five minutes more to find out, darling?"

"C'mon, love, up we go." Jamie leaped ahead, kicking up the snow from the trail into the wind, which had begun to flow down from some upper slope. Jennifer caught up and they continued, hand-in-hand up the narrow trail, trading insinuations of affection, exchanging unveiled glances of desire, occasionally stopping for an embrace and a gentle touch.

To the left, about 100 yards along from the trail entrance, a grove of century-old hemlocks and white pines rose majestically from the forest floor.

Further on, slim, tapered white birches bent in graceful arcs over the giant palisade-like rocks jutting up from the lake edge. The silvery bark, tattered and torn, was peeling off in short strips, giving the appearance that the trees wished to shed themselves of their constrictive outer layers, as if in some primordial, instinctive desire for renewal.

Jamie and Jennifer reached an opening in the trail as it branched out to the right over toward the top edges of the rock formations. Below, in deep crevasses, frigid air and dark shadows merged and swallowed whatever hapless sunlight managed to pierce such hidden recesses.

On top of a great pinnacle that had split away eons ago from its original hillside anchor against the face of the conglomerate cliff, perched a gazebo known as 'Landmark Rock.' A short, rustic cedar bridge connected the mainland cliff to the island-like plateau.

"That's almost the view I'm looking for, but not quite," Jamie said as he stepped over to the edge of the little bridge, unslung his camera from his shoulder and aimed it at the Mountain House across the lake.

"There's a gazebo just up another hundred yards or so—

Eagles' Nest—remember, Jennifer? We stopped there last summer for a breather."

They had both wanted to linger there a little longer at the time, but the gazebo was too exposed to view for proper 'lingering.' They had searched and found another gazebo on up toward Sky Top that suited their lingering much more appropriately.

"Okay, Jamie, but please be careful. There are icy spots under all this snow." Jennifer's cheeks were rosy from the sharp, frosty air and the slight breeze that felt like pin-pricks against her face. "It's getting colder, Jamie—let's hurry."

Jamie shouldered his camera, caught Jennifer's hand and together they lurched up the trail toward Eagles' Nest.

"That should do it, all right." Jamie once again unlimbered his camera. "You see, there won't be any tree tops in the way of a nice panoramic shot of the Mountain House if I get out there beyond the bridges." He was referring to two short, narrow cedar bridges just below the gazebo that stepped over two separate crevasses, deep and gloomy, from which reached up several sparse, contorted hemlocks in a perpetual striving for air and sunlight.

From such a promontory, one had an unobstructed view of the Mountain House, which was now at a somewhat lower elevation. Above and far beyond to the west was a breath-stopping visual embrace of the Catskill Mountains, ranging from north to south for more than one hundred and fifty miles.

The Mountain House roof was also more visible from the height of Eagles' Nest. Numerous stone chimneys of various heights pierced the hotel roof like tombstones, suggesting a bizarre cemetery effect, except for the tiny wisps of wood smoke that sifted upward from the chimney openings of well over a hundred working fireplaces in rooms and parlors.

"Jamie, those bridges look dangerous with all that snow. Nobody's been out there. God, it's a long way down to those rocks if you fall." Jennifer's alarm had often bumped up against Jamie's risk-taking. "Why don't you take it from here, please? We're not supposed to be here anyway."

Her pleading had no visible effect on Jamie as he smiled and tried to reassure her. "Jennifer, the bridges have railings. Don't worry—I'll only be a minute."

She had been holding tightly to Jamie's right hand with both of her hands. Gently, he loosened her grasp, kissed her cheek and turned to negotiate the slight slope leading down to the first bridge.

Jennifer watched him go. She wanted to shut her eyes until he came back—why does he do such dumb things? He had no idea of fear.

Jamie had reached the edge of the rock slab that anchored the land end of the first bridge. It had a slight pitch and slanted downward more sharply than he remembered from last summer.

He didn't see or feel the ice under the snow that had drifted close to the bridge end until it was too late.

His right foot hit the slippery surface first, giving way in a sickening slide toward the opening under the bridge railing. In a reflexive action, he tried to correct for his slide by reaching out his left hand as he pitched toward the railing on the left side of the little bridge. It was too much correction. He hurtled forward, his left hand missing the railing, his right leg slipping through the opening under the railing on the right, causing him to strike his head in a glancing blow against the railing. As he fell forward, his right hand clenching the camera strap fell heavily and useless ahead of him against the bridge deck, the camera nearly dropping off the edge to the chasm below.

There was ice under the snow on the bridge as well, and he felt himself sliding, his body about to slip completely under the railing where his right leg already hung in empty space. He clawed for any kind of a grip with his left hand, ending up face down, his fingers grasping the edge of a splintery deck plank just barely keeping him from sliding over—a forty foot plunge to jagged rocks below.

He could hear Jennifer screaming, "Jamie, Jamie, Jamie," her voice slowly fading away in what seemed to him like a sudden rush of air—a high pitched wind sound akin to a stiff breeze passing through tree tops on a summer day.

Although it lasted only seconds, to Jamie, his falling seemed endless. Actually, it was more a sensation of floating than falling. He felt trapped in a moving current or vortex against which it was useless to struggle. It seemed as if someone or something was reaching up for him from the dark shadows of the chasm. Something—not a voice, but some alien inner presence, foreign to his own psyche—was trying to persuade him to hang on. The effect was tranquilizing. He felt himself slowly drifting beyond physical perimeters. There was no pain, no sound. There were just darkening visions, fragments of unfamiliar images as might be reflected in the shards of a broken mirror—distortions, bits and pieces of objects—even faces and figures, but nothing recognizable.

But now there was another presence that sought to break through his muddled psyche. It was a high-pitched voice, "Hold on, Jamie—hold on—oh, God, please hold on, Jamie!" The fuzzy edges of the echoing tones faded away. The voice became clearer, sharp, penetrating. Jamie felt a tugging on his left leg as he slowly surfaced from the mindless bog of a semi-conscious state.

"Oh, God, Jamie, please say something." Jennifer's initial screams had had little connection to her actions as she had watched Jamie fall and slide toward the awful oblivion awaiting below the little bridge. She had fallen to her hands and knees as her faculties had instantly sensed the terrible threshold he appeared about to cross in his headlong thrust toward the bridge deck and under the railing of the bridge—a rustic span that, just moments before, had seemed so innocently picturesque.

Half crawling, half sliding herself on the icy surface Jamie had so unsuccessfully traversed, Jennifer had sprawled full length in a desperate lunge to reach his left foot and leg that projected back toward the anchor rock of the bridge end.

Her voice, pleading, tearful, suddenly turned into a loud sigh as Jamie raised his head and opened his eyes, his left hand gripping the edge of the deck as he pulled himself into a kneeling position.

"Jennifer," Jamie smiled brightly, just as if he were in her front yard on his knees weeding the flower garden. "If you'll let go of my foot, I'll get up."

He appeared to have absolutely no memory of the strange images or thoughts that had streaked through his midnight mind only moments before. He deftly grabbed the bridge railing and hopped back up the sloping snow bank to the safety of level ground.

"Are you all right? My God, you scared me." Jennifer couldn't decide whether to berate him for his recklessness or throw her arms around him in relief. She decided to do both. She threw herself at him, clutching him around the waist, nestling her face against his snow-covered chest and then leaned back slightly to peer up at his face. "Damn you, anyway. If you want to kill yourself, I wish you'd do it when I'm not around. I feel like Mrs. Knievel watching her husband trying to jump the Grand Canyon on a motorcycle."

Jamie leaned down and kissed Jennifer's pouting mouth. He could feel her lips soften and accept his unspoken apology for causing her concern. As he gently held her very close, he whispered in her ear, "It's sweet that you worry so. I have to stage little incidents like this every once in awhile, you know, to assure my ever-doubting mind that you care on Tuesdays for me as much as you do on Sundays."

Jennifer broke away. "Jamie, if you keep on with these little suicidal stunts, I'm going to kill you myself and then find a nice rich couch potato whose only jeopardy will be going from the TV to the refrigerator and back again!"

"Well, I'll be honest with you, Jennifer." Jamie paused, his face darkened. "For a second there, I really thought I was on the way out. The sensation of sliding into an abyss is not a thrill ride I intend to repeat any time soon, not even in Disneyland."

Jamie shivered, his body involuntarily reflecting the vestige of his near miss with death on the bridge. Fragmented images, clouded and unfocused, flashed once again for a moment out of the corners of his subconscious—like the flame of a candle flaring abruptly, as when caught in an unexpected breeze.

"Look, Jennifer, let's forget Sky Top for today. I agree, it's pretty icy. Why don't we go back to the Mountain House, have a quick cup of tea—it's just about tea time—and take a short walk up to Pine Bluff before we have to get dressed for dinner? That'll be easy going, and most of those crazy cross-country skiers will be out of our path by that time." Jamie reached up to rub his right temple. It was sore and a bit of an ache had emerged on the right side of his head.

"Jamie, did you hit your head on the railing? Does it hurt?" Jennifer's voice reflected a new alarm.

"I'm all right," Jamie replied. "It's just a little tender. I must have given it a good whack when I went down, but I'll be damned if I remember hitting anything."

"Jamie, you're going to see the house doctor, right now." She reached up to touch his temple. He winced slightly, not wishing to admit that it did hurt. Jennifer noticed that his head was not bleeding, probably due to his cap protecting his head from an abrasive collision, but there was an ugly red welt alongside his temple. "You might have a concussion. You may have hit that railing harder than you think. C'mon, it's almost 4:00. We've got to get to the doctor before he leaves."

Jennifer grabbed his hand and yanked him down the trail toward the Mountain House. Jamie knew he'd better cooperate or else he'd be on short rations in the love department later on. They bounced along, kicking and sliding along the tracks of skiers that followed the middle of the trail, until they reached the path to the porte-cochere and east entrance to the Mountain House.

"Jennifer, I'm all right, really. We're not going to have enough time to walk up to Pine Bluff."

Jennifer growled, "Don't start, Jamie—unless you want to sleep in the Lake Lounge tonight. It'll only take a few minutes if you stop grousing and cooperate. God, men are such children."

Jamie decided compliance was called for and presented his wrists to Jennifer in a mock posture to accept handcuffs. "Okay, take me away, officer. Don't bother reading me my rights—I lost those the first time I kissed you."

Chapter Five

The doctor's office was on the ground floor at the end of the corridor in the first Stone Building, conveniently adjacent to the ski shop where skis could be easily traded, if necessary, for sturdy crutches in all sizes.

Jennifer's knock on the door of room 57 brought an immediate response. The door was opened by an attractive, dark-haired forty-ish woman, smiling pleasantly and garbed in a doctor's white service jacket. Instead of the traditional stethoscope which did not hang around her neck, she had an extension cord in her left hand.

"Oh, hi, C'mon in." She placed the electrical cord on the table. "My Mr. Coffee is on the fritz. I think I need a new cord, or a 'coffee machine doctor' might be more like it." She smiled and offered her hand, "I'm Dr. Fairchild." Jennifer shook her hand followed by Jamie.

"Hello, I'm Jennifer Dickson and this is my friend, Jamie Stanner."

"Welcome to my little office of hope and healing," said Dr. Fairchild. "It's not the Mayo Clinic but we do what we can."

The 'little' office, like many of the one-time guest rooms on the ground floor of the Mountain House, had been pressed into use as the need for more staff and services arose. The room still showed many distinctive signs of the grace and charm it had once possessed in abundance when 19th and early 20th century ladies and gentlemen promenaded up and down the corridors and through the parlors of the Smiley brothers' 'household.'

The typical Mohonk fireplace, with a green tile surround and oak-carved mantel and mirror, was centered on the wall to the left. Next to it was an open door to an old fashioned bathroom stuffed full of crutches, a wheelchair and several tanks of oxygen, no doubt for the recovery of cross-country skiers who roamed too far and too wide, forgetting they did not enjoy the assistance of ski tows and chair lifts.

Dr. Fairchild adjusted her granny glasses as she said, "Now, I'm sure that you didn't come for a social call, although it has been rather dull around here. It's been a ten aspirin and one sprained ankle day so far. How can I help you?"

Jennifer began, "Jamie fell down a little while ago on one of those little rustic bridges over on Sky Top trail and he hit his head on the bridge railing." Jennifer pointed to Jamie's right temple while Jamie smiled benignly at Dr. Fairchild.

"Oh, my," said Dr. Fairchild, "let's have a look then, shall we?" Dr. Fairchild assumed a clinical but friendly expression that made it clear that she was not seeking any response to the 'shall we?' from Jamie.

"Would you like to just hop up here on the examination table, Mr. Stanner, and we will see what's what." It wasn't really a request—it was more like a carefully-worded command from a mother to an errant child.

Jamie offered no resistance—better to get it over with as quickly as possible, he thought, otherwise he would never hear the end of it from Jennifer. He climbed up on the edge of the black, vinyl covered, cushioned table which was more like a bench with foot stirrups on the end, placed there to provide for more practical and, assuredly, more embarrassing examinations of sorts. The table was covered with a stiff paper sheet which immediately slid backwards over the vinyl cushions, making Jamie feel awkward, like a small boy who had just tipped over a glass of milk.

"Don't worry about that, Mr. Stanner. Those paper sheets are only important when the patient's wearing a hospital gown." The doctor moved in and with an instrument like a tiny flashlight, peered into each of Jamie's eyes.

"Um—okay there, no pupil dilation. Do you feel any dizziness at all?"

No, he didn't feel dizzy, and he didn't have any double vision, and he really felt just fine except for the slight soreness over his right temple, he explained, sequentially, to Dr. Fairchild.

"Just follow my finger tip with your eyes as I move from left to right, okay? . . . All right, well, you don't appear to have any symptoms of a concussion." Dr. Fairchild smiled and turned to Jennifer. "Just see he gets a good night's rest tonight."

Jennifer breathed a sigh of obvious relief. "I'll see he gets some TLC and an early turn-in."

"Hey, hold on—we have a dance after dinner tonight. I'll take the TLC but I don't think it's going to be beddy-bye time just because I got a conk on the noggin." Jamie hoped off the examination table and faced the doctor. "Clean bill of health, yes? I don't even have a headache."

"Well, yes, but you never really know with concussions. This gray matter of ours can take a lot of punishment, but sometimes—just sometimes, symptoms may show up later, like a day or two. So don't fly any airplanes or do any drag-racing for awhile, okay?" Dr. Fairchild joked. "Seriously, you should be careful and do get enough rest. These kinds of things have a way of creeping up on you from behind."

"Okay, Doctor—I'm all out of apples, but thanks for the vote of confidence."

Dr. Fairchild smiled and held out her hand. "If you need me, I'll be around for the entire weekend. Now, have a good afternoon, what's left of it anyway, and a very good, *peaceful* evening. I don't want to see you two here again. Next time, let's do it over tea in the Lake Lounge."

"Thank you, Doctor, you're very kind. I know Jamie likes women doctors, though he'd never tell you." Jennifer smiled in return as she took Jamie's hand and whisked him toward the door.

"Good-bye, Doc. She's right, you know, and I like them even better after today," Jamie imparted as he was pulled out the door by Jennifer in a motion that verged on a cross between a sharp yank and a tug of war.

"Dr. Fairchild is entirely too attractive to be a doctor, at least your doctor, Jamie," Jennifer said as she guided Jamie down the corridor to the double doors opening onto a terrace that led to Eagle Cliff Road. "Five more minutes of the Stanner charm unleashed in there and I'd probably have to go and call an escort service for a partner tonight."

Jennifer wasn't really jealous. She knew she had Jamie in a box, but she liked to let him think that she fumed if he looked sideways at another woman. It was, again, part of the continuous game they played with each other.

"She's not really my style," said Jamie, offhandedly. "I like long hair, and you know how I feel about breasts. She was a little flat-chested, actually." He paused, tantalizingly. "Of course, she did have beautiful legs."

Jennifer swung on him with a mock-hay maker. "I guess I better put a monitor on you tonight with a buzzer that goes off if you move more than ten feet away from me."

Jamie laughed. "I bet you could really pack a wallop in the ring!" His voice became that of a ring announcer. "The most pulchritudinous fighting female in the annals of the ring! Get her mad and see her swing! But don't forget to duck or you'll need a wake-up call in the morning!"

Chapter Six

The late afternoon sun was due southwest, causing Jamie and Jennifer to squint as they walked along the trail heading from the Mountain House in a generally southwesterly direction. Patches of blue sky had appeared and the cloud cover, so ominous and threatening just a few hours ago, had dissolved for the most part into wispy filaments.

Sunlight flickered down through the hemlock woods bordering Eagle Cliff Road. In the light breeze, tree limbs rustled and cast shadowy tentacles across the snow-covered, gently sloping hillsides falling away toward the woods and farmlands of the Rondout Valley far below.

"Oh, Jamie, we should come up for an extra long weekend the next time." Jennifer whirled around in a full circle, arms outstretched, breathing deeply of the crisp mountain air as she embraced the heights of Pine Bluff overlooking the lake.

Pine Bluff, in its natural state, could have served as the archetype for a thousand Japanese gardens. Clumps of mountain laurel interspersed among the wide, flat, lichen-coated conglomerate slabs, jockeyed for position with stubby pitch pines, grotesquely bent in their ceaseless struggle to maintain stature against the prevailing winds while drawing meager sustenance from the sparse soils among the cracks and rifts of the huge layers of bedrock.

"Jennifer," Jamie called out. He had been standing on Eagle Cliff Road near the picnic area called the 'Granary' watching a woodpecker attack a tree trunk just down over the hillside near a dense hemlock grove. Jennifer had bounced up to the left for a view of the lake, distancing him by about twenty yards.

"Hey, Jennifer, what do you say we take the Lake Path back?"

No answer. She seemed lost in some sort of introspection and had, apparently, tuned him out.

He was about to repeat his suggestion when from the lower hillside the sound of sleigh bells, faintly at first, drifted up the slope. He turned in the direction as the sleigh bells jingled and jangled, louder and louder. From beyond a dense stand of hemlocks and mixed hardwoods, a sleek, shiny black sleigh with bright red runners, drawn by a spirited appaloosa with a full mane and flowing tail came flying along an old wood road that would not normally have been visible from Jamie's vantage point.

The sleigh held two people. A man with a fur hat and black fur coat with a white scarf trailing behind in the wind, snapped a long whip that curled over the horse's heaving flanks without touching him. A woman sat next to the driver dressed in what appeared to be an ermine shawl with matching cap and muff. Both were tucked in with a scarlet lap robe. Altogether, the sleigh and passengers poised a startling study in red, white and black, hurtling through the woods in a lively 3D rendition of a popular Currier and Ives lithograph.

Jaime was spellbound. "Jennifer, look down there. See the sleigh?" Jennifer was in plain sight but for some unknown reason her attention to him was completely overshadowed by whatever it was she was looking at as she knelt beside a little cedar bench. She turned toward Jamie for an instant but did not respond or show the slightest sign that she had either seen or heard him.

The sound of the sleigh bells diminished abruptly as the sleigh and its occupants merged with the dark fringes of the forest growth through which the old logging road wound its way. Jamie jogged up to Jennifer who was engrossed in studying a weather worn brass plate on a cedar bench.

"Jennifer, didn't you hear me just now? Didn't you hear the sleigh bells or see that sleigh?"

Jennifer turned to Jamie as she stood up, a puzzled look on her face. "Sleigh bells?—I didn't hear any sleigh bells, Jamie."

"You didn't see me standing on the road when I shouted to you? You turned to look at me." Jamie was incredulous.

"Jamie, I honestly didn't notice you. You must have been standing behind a tree." Jennifer stood up. She had a curious expression on her face as if to say, what game is this we're playing now?

"How could you not see me?" Jamie didn't know whether to be annoyed or dumbfounded. "You had to hear the sleigh bells. God, they were loud enough!"

"Jamie, I didn't hear any bells—not sleigh bells, not church bells. Did you really see a sleigh?"

"Right down there, through the woods—two people all dressed up like a couple of Victorian swells," he answered.

"Sounds romantic, maybe we'll see them later on tonight at the dinner."

"But you heard the desk clerk when we got here," he reminded her. "She said they didn't offer one horse sleigh rides anymore."

"Well, Jamie, maybe they were members of the Smiley family. After all, the owners are entitled to a few privileges for themselves, don't you think? The clerk merely said the hotel doesn't offer sleigh rides for the guests. She didn't say the Smiley family didn't go sleigh riding. I sure would if I owned the place."

"Well," Jamie shrugged, once again bowing to Jennifer's logic, "you're probably right. Whoever it was looked like they were born to it. I couldn't believe the speed that sleigh was going. Even the horse seemed to be enjoying it."

Jennifer checked her watch. "Oh, Jamie, we have to travel. It's after 4:30 and you men don't have to do what we girls have to go through to keep your eyes from wandering to pretty female doctors and the like."

Jennifer picked up a large handful of snow and stuffed it down his open shirt, turning to dash down the trail to the Mountain House.

"Argh!" Jamie sputtered in full pursuit. "You're going to get a bra full of snow, you little minx."

She was fast, even with boots, and Jamie only caught up to her as she tripped up the three steps to the west portico entrance of the Mountain House. She artfully dodged between two guest service staffers unloading luggage from several cars of late arrivals and slipped like a wraith through the heavy lobby doors nearly knocking an elderly lady into the arms of a surprised and obviously unrelated guest just emerging from the foyer entrance.

"Oh, I'm sorry, miss." Jennifer, half laughing, half gasping for breath as she herself lost her balance, tilted toward Jamie, who had managed to close the gap. He caught her as she nearly tripped up a couple of other elderly ladies following close who looked to be friends of Jennifer's first near-victim.

"Jennifer," Jamie took over, "we better retreat to our room before you turn this place into a bowling alley."

Hand-in-hand, they moved to the elevator, Jennifer nearly out of breath and Jamie breathing hard himself.

"Jamie," Jennifer teased, "it's a good thing we don't have time for sex right now. I do believe you'd fade out on me half-way through."

"Oh, you think so, do you?" Jamie retorted as he opened the door to 353 and swept Jennifer into the room.

"Okay, I take it back," Jennifer giggled as Jamie greedily began to disrobe her. "But, honestly, this time we really don't have time, Jamie, but I'll take a raincheck. C'mon let's see how your outfit looks on you." She put her finger into her mouth and traced the moisture on his forehead.

Jamie relented. "Don't ever underestimate my capacity for old-fashioned lust when it comes to you." He kissed Jennifer fully, feeling her body melt under his embrace. She sighed and kissed him back, her hands roaming toward his belt buckle.

"Uh, uh, remember what you just said? Something about a raincheck?" He stepped back.

Jennifer was wilting fast, but she caught herself. "You're right, Loverboy. It's a good thing one of us has will power, at least part of the time. Go take your shower before I do damage to you. I'll lay out your tails, if you'll pardon the expression."

Jamie showered and shaved and with loving assistance from Jennifer, he quickly segued into the early 1900's with his period dress suit she had procured at a local costume shop in Westport, Connecticut, replete with 'tails,' white tie and wing collar.

"You're beautiful, darling. I could positively eat you alive. Now, go get lost while your mistress gets ready. I don't want you to see me until I'm completely dressed and coiffured like a lady of the night right out of the pages of the Police Gazette."

Chapter Seven

JAMIE STEPPED OUT into the corridor. The sound of the shower and Jennifer's squeal as warm water unexpectedly turned cold was muffled as he pulled the heavy oak paneled door closed. He glanced at his watch—a little after 5:15. If Jennifer was dressed and ready by 6:00, it would be no less a miracle than if it snowed in July. There was plenty of time for a little wander.

Although the halls at the Mountain House certainly could not be characterized as antiseptically bright, even in daylight, in the early evening when the windows at the end of the corridors and in the adjacent parlors were shuttered by the setting sun, the halls darkened perceptibly. Illumination, more akin to 19th century gas light, was provided by small ceiling fixtures placed about every twenty feet. Each was shaded by a dainty tulip-shaped cut-glass bowl or encased in a translucent milky globe the further the distance from the central foyer areas.

Victorian gloom, thought Jamie as he strolled down the third floor corridor toward the oldest wing of the Mountain House known as the 'Rock Building.' A wooden frame structure of five stories, the building was constructed by the Smiley brothers in 1879, replacing an old Tavern built on the ascending rock ledges stepping up toward Pine Bluff over-looking the lake.

Jamie's eyes ranged along the walls of the corridor. On both sides, the walls were studded with pictures of European cathedrals, scenes of old Venice, Madonnas and other rather forgettable religious images, including shepherds, cherubs, angels, and the like. Some figures uttered pious declarations—others looked heavenward, arms outstretched awaiting the sublimity of the Divine.

All such subjects were very popular in the earliest days of the Mountain House. That had been a period embroidered in religiosity when Sundays were for preaching and a guest artist at Mohonk was more often than not known as the 'Reverend' So-and-So.

Jamie's and Jennifer's room was located in that section of the Mountain House known as the 'Stone Buildings.' These consisted of two distinct buildings constructed side by side, one completed in 1899, the other in 1902.

An army of stone masons from the Rondout valley had labored mightily to cut, shape and fit together in precise and articulate fashion the iron hard conglomerate blocks which formed the ramparts and turrets of the Stone Buildings.

Rising majestically seven stories above the lakeside, the buildings were distinguished by rows of filigreed iron balconies. Each room was graced by its own balcony, providing a stunning selection of landscape views at every point of the compass. Guests on the west side of the building enjoyed visual panoramas of the spreading, checkerboard farmlands of the Rondout Valley and the undulating Catskill Mountains beyond.

On the east side of the building, guests could view from their balcony vantages overlooking Lake Mohonk, great jumbles of giant rock ledges thrusting upward at impossible angles on the opposite shoreline of the lake.

Huge slabs of conglomerate sandstone, in perfect but precarious balance, leaned dizzily upon one another in preposterous poses, jutting arrogantly from their stations, successfully disputing and defying the laws of gravity for millions of years. Hoary hemlocks and hardwoods sprang upward through cracks and fissures, mindless of their tireless territorial leasehold. It seemed a tenuous occupancy which one could imagine would end at any moment, given the possibility of even a slight earth tremor in the region.

Over the years, through the chiseled, multi-storied rock

fissures formed by the ancient upheaval that left such a geological disarray, so rugged and yet so beautiful, a trail had been fashioned that wound through dark, deep crevasses, over jagged stone platforms, under tilting ledges and along sheer rock faces ever upward toward the cliff edges that beckoned high above from the carriage road leading to the promontory known as Sky Top. From such a vista, the Hudson River and five neighboring states could be viewed. Known as the labyrinth, the trail for decades had tested the endurance and will of any such hardy hiker daring enough to face off against the trail's obvious challenges and sometimes unpredictable hazards.

Jamie continued down the third floor corridor. The hallway stretched on, seemingly endless in the pervading shadows, which threatened to smother the feeble illumination of the piteously inadequate ceiling lights.

Jamie remembered his forays of yesteryears when as a nine-year old during his first visit to Mohonk he had gingerly explored the dark recesses of these very halls. In his boyish imagination he had conjured up demons and ghosts from the shadowy shapes lurking in the dark corners and at the head of the long iron staircases that ascended and descended into unknown murky reaches.

Now, years later and with a more or less adult mind, Jamie's pulse still quickened as he turned at the end of the long hallway and gazed once again at the same iron staircases that led to the nether regions of upward floors and appeared to descend to the very bowels of the Mountain House.

He marveled at the turn-of-the-century industry and skills of the iron workers who had placed such enormous and yet so gracefully designed staircases in their appointed niches. The polished black slate stair treads showed no sign of wear whatever from the abrasive soles of thousands of visitors to the Mountain House over some ninety years.

As he started up, his hand glided along the elegantly shaped and polished oak railings, sensuous to the touch, like the soft curves of a marble figurine.

Reaching a landing halfway to the floor above, he paused and looked back toward the darkened hall below. A barely perceptible flash of light, bluish in caste, had caught his peripheral vision, but as he turned to view the phenomenon, there was nothing. As he turned back to continue upward, however, a faint rumble, like a heavy table being trundled across a floor, echoed for a brief second or two. It seemed to his straining ears to come from both above and below.

Thunder? Strange weather, he thought, appropriate for the Mountain House, though spooky—must have clouded up again.

Jamie shrugged and moved on quickly to the floor above. He reached the fourth floor landing where, at the head of the stairs, the corridor turned at an abrupt right angle and led off as if arbitrarily designed to break the monotony of a straight-line.

Another left turn along walls hung with more views of Japanese pagodas, Grecian shores and temples, cascading waterfalls, and Hudson River School paintings brought him to the end of the corridor.

On the left side, he noted a storage room and a bathroom quaintly designated by a sign: *Water Closet.*

On the right were two fire doors marking the entrance to the Rock Building. A sign, neatly lettered in white script on a shiny oak plaque, suggesting more of a memorial or a historical moment, warned simply and straightforwardly:

CLOSED FOR SEASON—DO NOT ENTER

Another, less permanent-looking sign on white cardboard stated rather contradictorily, *Water turned off for winter, do not use toilets.*

Jamie pondered the admonitions briefly and tentatively pushed the heavy brass latch on the right hand door. A blast of arctic air issued from within the dimly lighted hall. Jamie guessed it had a wind chill factor of minus ten degrees as he swung the door inward, stepping through but carefully checking to see that no latch would prevent escape through the left hand door which opened from within the corridor.

As the doors closed behind him, shutting off the warmth and comfort of the occupied portion of the Mountain House, another bluish caste of light, which seemed to come from nowhere and everywhere, filled the hall for a millisecond. This was followed by a rumble and a distinct quiver in the floor boards beneath his feet. Momentarily startled, Jamie, in an almost reflexive action, pushed against the panic hardware bar of the fire door to the main corridor.

Hold on—what's made you so nervous? You're not nine years old anymore and the evil witch in the attic can't get you at Mohonk.

Jamie's recurring dream from childhood seeped back into his conscious mind. Where he grew up, in the small but prosperous farming community nestled in the Catskill Mountains in upstate New York, the church his father had served had provided the Stanner family with a veritable mansion of twelve rooms and a huge attic. To Jamie, the attic seemed large enough to hold a herd of rampaging elephants. There were two gables on each side of the attic with wide Palladian windows matching the front or street side and rear gable end windows. But even with all the bright sunlight admitted by the windows, there were dark corners in the attic and ominous shadows that caused Jamie to shiver if he dared to venture up the back stairs to that cavernous space all by himself.

One autumn night, following a Halloween party staged in the attic by his older sister for neighborhood children, Jamie, who was a second grader at the time, had a dream in which he found himself walking up the stairs to the attic. It was a very dark night and the only light came from a blue light bulb left over from the Halloween party. As he approached the landing halfway up, the light seemed to glow brighter and a single ray emerged from the bluish haze hitting him directly in the eyes. This was accompanied by a rush of cold air and the sound of someone sighing deeply. Jamie was frozen, powerless to move up or down. He would try to speak, but only soundless gurgles came from his throat. There was a dark silhouette that emerged from the light, almost blocking it out, a black blanket-like force which enveloped him until he could not draw a breath. He would struggle against the force but his feet would remain glued to the stairs and his arms, paralyzed, would have no feeling or connection to the rest of his body.

At that point, Jamie would awaken to the sound of his own voice—a half scream, a half cry—his small bedroom adjacent to the back stairs leading to the attic slowly emerging from distant shadows to become, once again, an enclave of comfort and security as his consciousness returned.

The dream had recurred through the years, even into adulthood. Sometimes the attic would become a huge ballroom and Jamie would find himself floating up a wide flight of stairs.

Ghostly music wafted down from above, bluish light always at the upper reaches of the staircase. His feet would be moving without his direction, the rest of his body like an automaton, executing the motions of ascending, heedless of his resolve to fight the strange force moving him inexorably toward the piercing blue light. It always ended with the black shape materializing, smothering the light, suffocating him as he awoke.

Jamie felt a childhood shiver as he continued down the corridor of the Rock Building. He sensed a disturbing similarity of the light in his dreams to the bluish light that now flickered unmistakably through the partially open doorway to a room on the left side of the corridor, fronting on the lakeside of the Mountain House.

Lightning, that's all—a freak inversion of warm and cold air, Jamie reassured himself. Thunder storms aren't all that unusual in winter weather.

Approaching the door to the room, Jamie noted how new the painted woodwork appeared, even in the faint light of the quaint ceiling fixtures which held clear glass light bulbs with sharp points on the ends. The light filaments were clearly visible and glowed with a soft but intense yellow light. Also, the wallpaper on the corridor walls, a sprinkling of wild flowers interspersed with soft pastel stripes, seemed very bright and fresh, as if the paperhangers had just finished and had gone off to wash out their brushes. The hall carpet, a central pathway over a beautifully planked and polished pine floor, was a rich plum color, soft and yielding to the step. Must have just finished renovating—getting ready for the spring season, thought Jamie as he pushed lightly against the partly opened door.

Expecting a creaky swing of 1879 hinges as the door opened wider, he was surprised at how smoothly and silently the door swung inward, revealing a fully furnished bedroom.

The first thing he noticed as he stepped inside was the warmth of the room. There was no fireplace, just a cast iron steam radiator against the outside wall between the window and the door to a small balcony overlooking the lake. He walked over to the radiator. It was warm, very warm. The room was downright comfortable and cozy, given the announcement out in the main corridor that all the heat had been turned off and the plumbing drained for the winter.

He walked into the small bath which opened off near the

door to the balcony. He noted the 1900 vintage cast iron bathtub perched on clawed feet. Just like Grandmother Stanner's, he reflected. He reached for the brightly polished chrome and ceramic faucet handle labeled hot affixed to the seductively curved marble rim of the washbasin, uncommonly new looking. Hot water gushed out in a torrent as he turned the handle, splashing over the rim and falling on the spotless, oyster-tiled bathroom floor. So much for the water being turned off, he thought. And what about the heat?

Jamie's mind searched for various scenarios that might offer rational explanations for what he was experiencing as he stepped back into the bedroom.

He glanced at the room's furnishings—two lovely white wicker armchairs sat at the end of a double bed with an oak bedstead, the top edge of which sported an intricately carved garland design. An oak dresser and matching bureau shared the wall space to the left and right of the door from the hall, all quite typical farmhouse American, circa 1880. The bed was made up with the covers neatly turned down as if expecting imminent use. An assortment of cosmetics, a woman's comb and brush and a pair of dainty white elbow-length dress gloves graced the dresser. Over the back of a small white wicker chair drawn up to the dresser was draped a long black dress or negligee of obviously Victorian style.

"Someone's been to Victoria's Secret," he said aloud. He began to feel intrusive, realizing that the room was obviously occupied and that the present residents might show up at any time, closed off wing or no closed off wing.

His mind devised a soap-opera scenario which unfolded with his sudden discovery by an angry husband bursting into the room, accusing him of a clandestine affair with his beloved.

He turned to go, but another bluish shaft of light, this time from outside the window overlooking the lake, flashed into the room, projecting jagged bits of silhouettes against the opposite wall.

He stepped to the window. A ring of flaming torches circled the lake just in front of the main parlor and porch. The lake surface had been cleared and there, pirouetting and waltzing, were skaters in Victorian dress, the men with tall silk hats or fur caps and trailing scarves, the women in fur wraps and billowing long skirts and muffs. Strains of *The Blue Danube* drifted faintly on a light breeze toward the Rock Building as Jamie curiously opened the balcony door.

As in his childhood dream, he half expected another flash of blue light and the emergence of some black shape out of the flickering tongues of firelight the torches cast from the lakeside.

Nothing—just a picturesque scene of winter skating, albeit embellished with gentlemen and their ladies in period dress and manners.

The next sensible thing that crossed Jamie's mind was: how in God's green world did the hotel staff clear all the snow from the center of the lake in such a short time. He and Jennifer had been up on Pine Bluff not much more than an hour and a half ago. At that time the snow on the lake appeared glacier-like, very crusty and deep. None, as yet, had made any effort to clear an area for skating. The enormity of the task, Jamie thought then, would not lend itself to a very high priority, given all the other chores the staff had to deal with in providing for over three hundred guests and their whims.

Chalk one up for Mohonk efficiency, Jamie reflected as he checked his watch, 5:45. He ought to be getting back to Jennifer, as a matter of fact. They were scheduled to greet their table companions—three other couples whom they had not yet met—at 6:15, before dinner at the west parlor known as the Grove Circle.

He was abruptly jarred out of his reverie by the sound of approaching footsteps coming from the corridor. "Mother Cabrini, here it comes," he murmured to himself as he scooted toward the door, hurriedly fabricating some lame excuse to explain his unauthorized presence.

"Sorry, folks—guess I have the wrong room." No good. "Gee, thought I smelled smoke coming from your room, folks." Better—might work—no time for elaboration.

As he reached the door which had nearly closed on its own while he had been perusing the scene, a quick but somewhat soft knocking from the corridor side edged the door slightly into the room.

Jamie grasped the handle, opening the door. Sheepishly, he began his flimsy greeting, "Hello there. I know you're wondering just what I'm doing in your room—you see I smelled smoke—"

He was interrupted by the woman who faced him from the

hall, who seemed not to have heard or understood his half-uttered preamble.

"Mr. Sommers, I must talk to you. I have only a moment." She was attractive, probably 40 or so—long auburn hair done up in Gibson girl style. She was dressed in a low-cut forest green satin gown that just brushed the tips of her silver dress slippers. A choker of exquisite pearls highlighted her ivory neck and a large cameo brooch discreetly, but pointedly, emphasized the ample cleavage of her bosom, made even more ample by artfully camouflaged whale bone stays.

Definitely a very classy lady, thought Jamie as he stood helplessly, glancing up and down the hall, wondering if and when her consort would most assuredly make his entrance.

"Mr. Sommers, please. I know you will think it strange, but I have no time to explain now. You must listen to me."

She was agitated and her voice quivered, reflecting a nervousness that alarmed Jamie. She appeared to be on the verge of collapse.

"Hold on, ma'am, first of all you have the wrong man. My name is Stanner, Jamieson Stanner, and I want to apologize for being in your room. You see—" Jamie was cut off again.

"Mr. Sommers, you really must listen to me—there is no time for pleasantries." Again, the woman looked furtively up and down the empty corridor as if expecting a very unwelcome arrival of some third party at any moment. With hardly a break, she continued, completely ignoring Jamie's attempt to identify himself.

"I have something I must tell you of the utmost importance," she hastened on, "but not here, not now. After dinner and the program following, you must meet me in the little parlor, just next to the main dining room—12:30—by that time everyone will have retired."

"Wait a minute—ah, Mrs., is it? Since you don't seem to want to acknowledge my name, perhaps you'll tell me yours?"

"Mr. Sommers, please, did you hear what I said? Please, you must not take this lightly. I cannot urge upon you enough the seriousness of what I have to report to you."

"But," Jamie started, his next few words obliterated by the woman's exasperated admonition.

"Please, no more, Mr. Sommers, we can talk later. Please do not fail to meet me—12:30—the little parlor off the main dining room. You have no idea what fate hangs upon the news I have for you and of such consequences as shall surely occur upon your actions thereafter."

With that and a swish of satin folds, the woman flew down the corridor toward a set of stairs on the opposite end of the hall from the entrance to the Rock Building.

Jamie bolted after her, this time shouting. "Wait a minute! What's going on here?" There was no sign of the woman as Jamie reached the head of the stairs.

God, he thought, the walls have swallowed her up—how could she disappear so fast? Which way did she go, up or down?

Jamie tried down but after one flight he knew it was useless. The stairwell below was dark. It appeared unlighted except for a faint glimmer of reflected light from the snow outside stealing in from the window on the landing. Nothing else moved in the shadows further down. There was no sound—no creaking floor boards to indicate a passage, not a remnant of life in the cold shanks of the lower floors.

Jamie was fairly certain the woman had not gone up, although he now glanced up as he reached the hall landing. Nothing up there except a cold draft of air that streamed down the open stair well from frigid hallways in upper regions.

He walked back toward the room of the encounter. There was something different—he sensed it even as he had been engaged in the puzzling, one-sided conversation with the mystery woman. What was it?

He approached the room. Everything, as before, seemed fresh and new. The hall lights glowed softly, bathing the corridor and the room to which the door was wide open in a gaslight ambiance. That wasn't it.

Wait. The hall was warm now, just like the room. That was very cold air seeping down the stairwell from the upper floor, but somehow it didn't pervade the fourth floor corridor. The entire corridor was warm and toasty—just like the mystery room.

If Jamie had had hair on the back of his neck beyond the conservative limits of his somewhat conventional haircut, it would have been straight up. As it was, he could feel a shiver beginning in his shoulders, spreading down his arms.

"What in hell is going on here?" he spoke softly to himself. It was as much a statement as a question. He felt a sudden urge to leave the Rock Building.

A quick parting glance in the mystery room—everything the same, Jamie noted. The room's residents had not materialized. Maybe they're skating—or gone down to dinner, although it's a bit early for that, Jamie speculated. There certainly had to be a rational explanation for all of this. What about Mrs. X? How do you add that up to make four?

Jamie, his cool not altogether intact, was still sufficiently operational to place one foot ahead of the other without outward signs of panic as he retraced his steps toward the fire doors and the entrance to the corridor to the Stone Buildings.

He pushed against the door latch on the right hand fire door but something or someone seemed to be pushing on the door from the corridor side. He could not budge it. He tried again—the latch again resisted his effort as he put his shoulder to the door, at the same time shoving hard with his right hip against the panic bar. But this time, there was a whooshing sound—no, it was more like someone on the other side releasing his or her breath at the end of a strenuous exertion.

Could the strange woman be on the other side of the door trying to prevent his exit? The door burst open as Jamie gave an almost violent shove, causing him to nearly lose his footing as he stumbled into the corridor. There was no one visible. If someone had been pushing on the door from the opposite side, there was no way such a person could have escaped the path of Jamie's lunge.

Puzzled, Jamie examined the door hinges and swung the door closed, re-opening it immediately. The door's operation was smooth and free of any object or hindrance that might have jammed it in a closed position.

He gauged his pulse rate at about 140/minute as he slammed the fire doors shut and breathed in the musty, faintly perfumed air tinged with slightly stale cigarette smoke which revealed the recent presence of fellow hotel guests of 1993 vintage.

His comfort level increased as he passed along the corridors of the Stone Buildings, down the iron steps, free now of the bluish caste of light, precipitative of his earlier exploration.

As he approached room 353, Jamie reached into his pocket for his room key and realized he had left it on the bureau as he had changed into his early 1900's evening dress assigned to him by Jennifer.

Jamie's soft knock on the door and a whisper, "Jennifer, I hope you're there," triggered a yelp on the other side.

The door opened. "Jamie, my God—where have you been? Do you know what time it is?"

Jennifer was regal in a black velvet evening gown that, for all its Victorian style and elegance with its tightly cinched waist, its bouffant shoulders and deep-cut bodice which presented Jennifer's bosom so temptingly, it still would have looked perfect at any New Year's eve gala all the way from 1900 through 1993.

Jennifer, beautiful as she was, her cheeks glowing, her lips the color of wild strawberry, was not smiling. She was not at all happy.

"Jamie, it's nearly 7:00. What in God's name have you been doing for the past two hours? You know we were supposed to meet our dinner companions at 6:15."

"Hold it, hold it—your watch is fast, love. I just left the Rock Building a few minutes ago. It was only 5:45."

Jamie, although certain that the episode with the mysterious woman had not taken more than about five minutes or so, at the most, remembered just before her appearance he had checked the time. He held up his watch for Jennifer. It read 6:50.

Jennifer glowered. "Honestly, Jamie, sometimes you are so absent-minded, it's a wonder you can find your way to my side of the bed. Come on—let's go."

With that, Jennifer swished out the door, clutching Jamie's right hand, his left snatching the door knob, slamming the door closed with a thunderous bang that reverberated up and down the corridor, raising the eyebrows and smiles of two nearby young housekeepers just stepping off the elevator. Jamie tried a lame smile as Jennifer pulled him past. "You should see her when she gets mad."

Jennifer growled ominously, "Jamie, you'd better have a good story when you apologize to our tablemates for being late." They stepped into the elevator. Jennifer, taking charge, pushed the first floor button.

"Jennifer, that's one thing I have—a story, maybe even a ghost story." He began to tell her of the strange events in the Rock Building as they left the elevator hurriedly and trotted as fast as their costumes would allow down the long wide corridor toward the main dining room.

"Oh, please, Jamie, wait till we sit down—we haven't got time. You always slow down when you begin to tell me anything."

It was true. Jamie became so engrossed in trying to tell Jennifer of his perplexing exploration of the Rock Building, she was reduced to very nearly dragging him along the last fifty feet or so to the graceful arched portal of the immense dining room.

Chapter Eight

The main dining room of the Mountain House, like all of the other features of this wonderfully anachronistic hotel, exuded old world charm and new world efficiency.

The lofty hall—it could hardly be called a room—was completely paneled in long leaf pine, walls and ceilings contiguous in rich, orangy warm hues. Such wood, once abundant in 19th century America, was in rare supply in 1993.

The west side of the hall, with its circular exterior wall, provided panoramic views of the distant Catskill Mountains.

In the center, walls soared upward two and a half stories to a veritable firmament in which there seemed to float countless black wrought iron chandeliers with curlicue brackets set at flower-like angles and tipped with blossoms of light-bulbs, each of which was ensconced by a tulip-shaped frosted glass shade.

Directly across from the arched portal through which one entered the hall from the main corridor, a great red brick fireplace of proportions matching the immensity of the hall, rose to the highest arches of the ceiling. The towering chimney, with its monolithic dimensions, constituted an overwhelming presence. The fire chamber could accommodate timber with girths as thick as the huge Yule logs often pictured on Christmas cards of 'Old English' Yuletide scenes. Indeed, at that celebrated moment, a roaring blaze crackled and sparked behind the hearth, voraciously consuming within its flames as much forest tinder as it was safe to present without encompassing the very dining hall itself in total conflagration.

The dining area was dotted with tables of all shapes and sizes to ensure romantic intimacy for couples as well as camaraderie for large families with children. The sturdy, well built oak tables and chairs were typical 'American Farmhouse' style of the later 19th century, satisfying in workmanship, enduring and surprisingly comfortable.

A sea of white tablecloths with artfully folded forest green napkins, sparkling water goblets, long stemmed wine glasses and polished silverware surrounding gleaming white dinner plates, completed the scene.

Bustling waiters and waitresses—the men in dazzling white shirts, set off by black vests and black bow ties, the girls, all very pretty, in starched white pinafores—played a pleasant symphony of sorts in their servings as glasses tinkled, plates touched and tableware struck musical tones.

That Jamie and Jennifer were late was obvious. The dining hall was full, every table encircled by guests in turn-of-the-century dress, as all had been requested to provide in the promotional brochure advertising the special 'President's Weekend.' The degree of cooperation by participants was a hundred percent. Not a single dress, suit, jacket or, God forbid, sweater of 1993 vintage was in evidence.

Most of the men were in black tails and white ties, some with chesterfield jackets, others in cut-aways, still others in less formal light-colored linen jackets, colorful ascots and plus-fours.

The women were all literally fashion statements from early 1900's magazines such as *Harper's Weekly* or *The Ladies Home Companion*. Evening gowns of velvet, taffeta, satin and silk in deep tones of wine, plum and earthen colors such as chocolate brown and green or creamy confection shades, as well as many in basic black, were complimented by pearl and diamond necklaces, ruby and emerald pendants and matching earrings.

Most of the gowns exhibited daring décolletage and alluring bosoms enhanced, if need be, by secret stays. Long gloves, in abundance, accentuated sensuous snowy white arms. Hair styles were mostly up in the popular 'Gibson girl' fashion, which emphasized long neck lines and graceful shoulders. Diamond tiaras caught the candlelight and flashed tiny sparkles in every direction. Shiny, laughing eyes, glowing cheeks and parted lips, ruby red and slightly moist in happy anticipation of the evening's pleasures, seemed to universally characterize all the women present—both the beautiful and the not so beautiful.

Did it matter that much of the jewelry on display, if not most of it, was paste? Not really, for this was an evening of fantasy. Reality for this special evening was in the mind and not the object and all things of 1993 relativity were to be placed in abeyance.

The dining room hostess smiled beneficently on Jennifer and Jamie as Jamie announced his presence and apologized for their tardiness.

"That's quite all right, Mr. Stanner, I don't believe you're the last ones, as a matter of fact. Let's see, I believe you're at table 3C." Jamie thought she was just being polite. He could not see a single empty chair throughout the entire place except for two seats at a table to which the hostess was directing them.

Jennifer, alluring and poised, was smiling as they arrived at their assigned table. Six people were seated and were already at work on the first course, a lobster bisque that enjoyed a reputation far beyond Mohonk but could only be found on the Mohonk menu, its recipe so jealously guarded by the head Mohonk chef, a graduate of the famous world-renown American Culinary Institute.

"Thank you, miss," Jamie nodded at the hostess as she, having performed her duty, turned and retreated to her station.

Three men, as if triggered by a small explosive charge, rose simultaneously to initiate introductions.

"Sorry we're late folks," Jamie apologized, wanting instantly to blurt out the strange incidents in the Rock Building that had delayed their arrival. Jennifer gave him a veiled warning look which said, "Don't start, Jamie!" Instead, he said, "I'm Jamie Stanner and this is my friend, Jennifer Dickson."

Intros went clockwise around the table. First there were Peter Hardy and his wife, Carol; next, Niko Shimomurai and his wife Timeko; and last, John Harrigan, Jr. "This is my wife, Betty," said Harrigan.

Jamie felt a sudden rush of adrenaline and a sharp, almost electric-like shock in his chest as he faced Betty Harrigan.

On approaching the table a moment ago, Jamie had given a summary glance at everyone, not really seeing individual persons, just granting an acknowledgment of their presence. Now he was face to face with Betty Harrigan. There was no doubt about it. Betty Harrigan was the mystery woman from the Rock Building.

She was not wearing the green satin gown he had seen her in earlier, nor did she wear the pearl choker around her neck. Instead, she was dressed in a royal blue taffeta gown, off the shoulders, deeply cut, again revealing cleavage that, alone, would have qualified her for a centerfold. A single strand of cultured pearls graced her neck, emphasizing the almost luminescent ivory tones of her bosom.

Jamie struggled to regain his poise. "Very glad to know you, Mrs. Harrigan." There was absolutely no sign of recognition from her—no furtive glance as if to say, "All right, don't act surprised. I'll tell you about this later." Mrs. Harrigan, in eye-to-eye encounter with him, gave no indication in any way that Jamieson Stanner was anyone she had ever seen before in her life or any other—let alone met, let alone confused with another man by the name of 'Sommers.'

Jamie, the incident in the Rock Building so fresh in his mind, could not believe Mrs. Harrigan was anyone other than the mystery woman, sans the present gown she was wearing.

He tried something as they all took their seats. "Mrs. Harrigan," he began.

"Oh, please call me, Betty," Betty Harrigan broke in.

"Yes, by all means," John Harrigan added, "let's put formality aside—first names okay, everyone?' There was a murmur of assent around the table.

"Yes, well, Betty," Jamie continued in a headlong approach, "didn't I see you in the Rock Building a little while ago? You know, in the corridor on the fourth floor?" Jamie was just short of being abrupt.

"The Rock Building? Where's that?" Betty replied.

"The building beyond the Stone Buildings, way over on the south end of the hotel," Jamie answered. "You had me confused with a Mr. Sommers."

Betty looked blankly at Jamie. "I haven't the foggiest notion of what you're talking about, I'm afraid. I've been with my husband all afternoon. We went cross-country skiing—great fun, by the way. Boy, I've some firming up to do—found muscles I didn't know I had. Tomorrow we're going skiing to Eagle Cliff. Why not come along? Let's make a party of it." Betty Harrigan prattled on, smiling at everyone around the table in a sort of sequential invitation, oblivious to Jamie's inquisition.

It was time for Jennifer to take control. "That does sound like fun. I haven't been on skis for donkey's years."

Jennifer's remark was accompanied by a not-too-hard kick to Jamie's shin under the table. Jamie knew what it meant, but he wasn't going down all that easily.

"Are you sure you don't have an identical twin running around here, Betty? I could swear—"

"Ah," Jennifer interrupted, "Jamie, we have some catching up to do here. Um—try this bisque, it's delicious."

The waiter had just deposited silver bowls of the highly appraised bisque before them. Jennifer shot Jamie a warning glance which clearly stated, "Please, no more. You're mistaken about Betty. Don't be difficult."

Jamie surrendered to Jennifer's tack and dipped a spoon into the bisque, returning a look to Jennifer which clearly said, "This isn't over yet."

"Well," came a buoyant exclamation from John Harrigan. "I don't think names alone are sufficient for this evening. What do you say to us giving a little background on ourselves?" Another murmur of assent. Everyone seemed content to acknowledge John Harrigan's self-chosen role as interlocutor.

"Why don't you start off, Jennifer?—to give the age of feminism its proper due." Polite smiles encircled the table as Harrigan motioned Jennifer to the starting gate.

Jennifer beamed, enjoying the role of initiate. "Well, I'm an appraiser—you know, that's the person who comes around from the bank and tells you your house isn't worth what you think it is." Jennifer's self-deprecatory humor raised smiles around the table and a groan from Philip Hardy.

Hardy spoke up. "Next to lawyers—anybody here a lawyer, by the way? I hope not. Next to lawyers," he repeated, "and possibly bank loan officers—appraisers probably should be put on the hit list, though I believe we should make an exception for you, Jennifer."

Hardy then proceeded to tell a horror story of how the

house he and Carol had purchased in 1988 had dropped in value, according to the appraiser, by $50,000 by 1993. The appraiser who had down-valued the property wept crocodile tears with the Hardys before cheerily moving on to his next doomsday assignment.

Carol interjected. "You'll have to excuse Philip. He still has his first piggy bank. I think he's waiting for it to get pregnant." The table erupted in spontaneous laughter.

"Well, to get back on track," Carol continued, "I'm a Jr. High School teacher in Rhinebeck, and yes, I know, everyone thinks teachers are overpaid and underworked. What do I think? This weekend isn't long enough to give you even my short answer."

She turned to Philip. "Do you want me to tell everybody you're an antique dealer or do you want to?"

Philip, like Jamie, knew when acquiescence was called for. "Thank you, darling, for the in-depth exposé."

John Harrigan took the reins again. "Since we started with Jennifer, how about you, Jamie?"

"Oh, I just build houses, that's about it." Jamie was distracted, he couldn't accept that the mystery woman wasn't Betty Harrigan. There were serious pieces missing. His mind was etched with the image of the woman as she flew down the corridor of the Rock Building. There couldn't be two people who looked that much alike—to say nothing of being in the same hotel together. He was getting a slight headache trying to fit square blocks into round holes. He had to leave this alone for awhile, or Jennifer would lobster *his* bisque.

"Jamie builds beautiful expensive homes for spoiled rich people," Jennifer was saying, "and they're worth every penny he charges—even I say so. But then I don't appraise his houses. That's not conducive to a . . . relationship." Titters from the women were accompanied by a guffaw or two from the men around the table, except for Jamie who simply smiled appreciatively.

"Okay, that brings us to you two," Harrigan smiled and gestured to Niko and Timeko Shimomurai.

"Thank you." A slight trace of Japanese accent configured Niko's speech. "I teach Japanese and Far Eastern History at SUNY in New Paltz. That's, as you know, the State University of New York. So, at least, Timeko and I don't have to worry about a long snowy drive home tomorrow afternoon." Niko chuckled quietly. He was referring to a rather iffy weather report projecting a possible 6-10 inches of snow for Sunday throughout southeastern New York and New England.

Timeko smiled demurely, as only a beautiful, shy Japanese woman could do. "My only job is to try to keep Niko happy and content."

Everyone took an instant liking to Timeko. Jennifer thought she had the most beautiful complexion she had ever seen—true 'peaches and cream.' Timeko also had stunning soft, black hair, beautifully glossy in the candlelight of the dining hall. Her hair style was up, almost, but not quite, in a geisha style. It was reflective of the cultural mix of far east and west in the 1900's, a cross link which influenced the creation of the 'Gibson Girl' hairdo so popular in America in those years.

"That leaves Betty and me, I guess," John Harrigan spoke up. "I just retired from the Air Force as a Brigadier General. I was an air controller in Vietnam and am now in the midst of organizing an independent airline in the Caribbean with linkage to Europe." Harrigan smiled proudly, although his tone was not braggadocio. It was more like a matter-of-fact press statement from a military spokesman commenting on a routine body count used to measure the success of a military maneuver. "Betty helps me with the paper work."

Betty smiled subordinately, obviously proud of her husband's demonstrated leadership and get-things-done personality.

Jamie came back to life. "Not to get personal, but I hope you weren't responsible for the forward observer we shot at after getting napalm dropped on us at Phnam Penh in '69."

Jamie had been an infantry Captain in the 25th Division in Vietnam in the late sixties and had nearly been cremated along with his entire company by a shortfall drop of napalm about a hundred yards from a V.C. underground supply dump his combat team was attacking. The invective let loose by the GIs with singed eyebrows was nearly as lethal as the .50 caliber slugs fired at the U.S. spotter plane they blamed for the mishap. The tiny aircraft had eluded the lead storm and luckily, no one was seriously burned or injured. But there had been other incidents in such close encounters where U.S. casualties by 'friendly fire' sometimes numbered nearly as high as the V.C.

body counts.

"No, it wasn't me," Harrigan, a bit defensive, replied. "Of course, that kind of thing did happen—from the ground as well as the air. I'd hate to have to count up the short rounds our artillery dropped on our own forward positions."

Betty Harrigan decided that was enough war talk. "Timeko, I must compliment you on your beautiful hair style."

Jennifer and Carol joined forces. "Oh, yes," Jennifer agreed, "I love your tiara."

"God, I always wanted beautiful black tresses like yours," Carol said enviously. "When I was eight, I rubbed coal dust in my hair. I hated blond hair, especially dirty blond. Well, my mother—I'll never forget her face—she thought I'd been run over by the school bus."

Laughter erupted all around the table. Jamie decided to get into the spirit of things. "Has anyone got a clue as to what particular year we're supposed to be celebrating tonight?"

"Aren't we supposed to be honoring the Presidents' birthdays?" Jennifer inquired from no one in particular.

"Washington and Lincoln—thank God, both had February natal days. Makes for a nice winter break," Carol replied. "I guess we have them to thank for tonight."

"How come we're dressed in turn of the century outfits, then?" Philip said.

"Somebody rightly decided you wouldn't look very promising in blue satin knickers and a 1780 hairpiece, darling." Carol responded lightly to Philip as she leaned over to straighten his bow tie.

"I'd say we all look about 1900," Philip offered as he gave his wife a tweak on her cheek. "Except you, dear—you're ageless." Philip kissed Carol ceremoniously.

"Yeah, I know—like the Sphinx." Carol came back.

"Let's decide on the last day in 1899, the eve of the century," Jennifer said happily as she clapped her hands, caught up in the romantic imagery of Edwardian moments.

"Perfect," Betty Harrigan said. "What a time that surely must have been."

"I wonder what Times Square was like on that night," Philip speculated.

Jamie answered, "Well, they didn't drop a ball from the Times building, but I bet they popped enough champagne corks to float the Statue of Liberty in the East River."

"By the way, wasn't McKinley President on New Year's Eve in 1899?" Philip asked.

"He was. He was reelected in 1900 and Teddy Roosevelt became his Vice-President," came Jamie's staccato reply. After Geology, American history ran a close second in Jamie's panoply of interests.

"And McKinley was assassinated," said Jennifer. She was beginning to feel quite contemporaneous with the early 1900's. Maybe it was the dress or the general milieu of the dining hall. It was almost like a scene straight out of Delmonico's Restaurant in New York, gathering place for America's most famous literati at the turn of the century.

"McKinley was shot by a self-styled anarchist, name of Leon Czolgosz," Jamie explained, "on September 6, 1901. The weapon used was a .32 caliber Iver-Johnson revolver. The assassination took place at the Temple of Music at the Pan-American Exposition being held at Buffalo, New York. McKinley died on September 14th and Theodore Roosevelt became the 26th President of the United States at the ripe old age of 42 years, the youngest man ever to assume that high office. Czolgosz was tried, convicted and executed in the electric chair six months later at the Federal Penitentiary at Auburn, New York."

Jamie's recitation received a round of applause from his admiring table mates. He rose and bowed melodramatically.

"God," said Carol, "I ought to have you lecture to my 8th graders. Half of them never even heard of *Franklin* Roosevelt, never mind Teddy."

"Gosh, it's really beginning to feel like 1900, all right," Jennifer warmed to the occasion. "I can't get over this wonderful atmosphere! Isn't it great what the right clothes and candlelight will do to set the mood?"

"I'll tell you one thing," said Carol. "Walk into our house any day of the week and you'll swear you were back in 1900. It's a regular time warp with all those damn antiques Philip insists on dragging home all the time." Carol sighed, "God, what I'd give to have a living room furnished with chairs that didn't once belong to Grandma Moses. I'd even settle for Bronx modern."

Philip responded, "Yeah, we cry all the way to the bank

with what I eventually sell those pieces for."

"I just get used to a nice barrel-style armchair that looks like it came out of Abe Lincoln's bedroom, and a week later I'm sitting in a wicker porch chair you'd swear Philip stole off the porch of the old Hotel Saratoga."

As the easy-going laughter subsided, Niko spoke up, almost apologetically. "Japan in 1900 was full of Western capitalists. They were showing us how to make money." He allowed an almost inaudible chuckle to escape from his lips which were drawn in a very broad smile, displaying perfectly white teeth. "As you see from the number of Hondas and Toyotas in the Mohonk Mountain House parking lot, we learned our lessons well."

Jamie chorused. "Bravo, my Subaru just passed 154,000 miles. It should be good for at least another 100,000 as long as I don't forget to change the oil. That I have trouble with, I admit, but then I have Jennifer to remind me. She's very good at that sort of thing." Then he added, "She's good at a lot of other things, too."

Jennifer accepted Jamie's sidelong wink and intimation of brooding lust, but toyed with him. "By the way, where are you sleeping tonight, darling?"

Carol counter-pointed. "Aw, Jennifer, aren't you lucky to have a man whose every waking moment is how to keep you warm in bed without an electric blanket? Take me now," she continued. "Philip brought home this big old Franklin stove one day—you know, the kind that burns coal with doors that open up and all? Well, he insisted on setting it up in our bedroom and poked a big hole through the wall for a chimney. Never mind we have steam heat in these big old cast iron radiators in our house even if they were new when Edison invented the light bulb—or maybe it was the phonograph? I dunno—anyway, Phil hooks up the damn thing, throws on a load of coal, lights it up and the goddam thing pours out smoke like the Con Edison power plant at Indian Point! There we are with a bucket brigade from the bathroom trying to put out the damn fire before the house burns down. I'm just about to call 911 when Philip picks up the damn stove and throws it right out the new bay window we just had installed, telling me at the same time not to goddamn panic."

The table was in stitches—Betty Harrigan was laughing so

hard she had tears in her eyes. Both Niko and Timeko were giggling like two children who had just been told they could have a gallon of chocolate ice cream to eat for desert. Jennifer and Jamie found each other's hands under the table, squeezed and laughed along with the rest. John Harrigan was the most composed, as retired General officers might be expected to be, but even he wiped away a tear as Carol continued to regale everyone with the hilarious tale of how she and Philip coped with their near disaster.

"I told Philip," Carol went on relentlessly, "the next time he brought home anything that remotely resembled a Franklin stove, I'd throw him out the window first and then the goddamn stove after him."

Everyone was gasping for breath as Carol finished her tale. Each was trying to retain some outward composure or a portion of dignity which was hard to do when overtaken by a case of the giggles out of control.

The antics at their table had caught the attention of other nearby diners who began to succumb to the hi-jinx in effect at table 3C. A ripple of laughter, like a stone thrown into a quiet pond, spread throughout the hall. People had no idea at all what they were laughing at—they were simply caught up in the contagion. You would have thought everyone was at the Sands Hotel in Las Vegas listening to Rodney Dangerfield.

The raucous laughter at table 3C gradually subsided to murmurs as their waiter deftly removed the empty first course dishes and presented the menu and wine list.

Chapter Nine

Somewhere between the main course and the desert, musicians had begun to infiltrate the dining hall, unpack their instruments and occupy an area previously reserved for them on a small stage that had been set up just to the right of the landmark fireplace.

A large section of the dining hall immediately in front of the orchestra had been left free of tables and was obviously to serve as the dance floor. Toward the very center of the area, two waiters began to wheel in a remarkable ice sculpture—a large replica of the Nation's Capital. The diners closest to this action began to applaud as the waiters positioned the Ice Capital in its appointed stand.

Hidden lights from below the crystal structure provided a luminescence that radiated upward and outward from the miniature dome, capturing in a golden hue the fringes of a large American flag being lowered from the lofty recesses of the dining hall ceiling. The flag unfurled just above the Ice Capital as a strategically placed spotlight faded in to catch the 'Stars and Bars' in a flood of light. Everyone arose as the musicians, who by now had taken their positions, began to play the National Anthem.

As the last strains of 'the land of the free and the home of the brave' floated up to the lofty ceiling and reverberated around the walls, every guest, every waiter and waitress, even a cordon of cooks and workers who had magically appeared for that special moment from the bowels of the Mohonk kitchens and galleys, joined in a thunderous applause. Window panes rattled in sympathetic vibration to the overt response of over 300 people caught up in the patriotic surge of the moment.

From the area just behind the bandstand which masked an inconspicuous doorway to the Mohonk kitchens, there emerged, to an accompanying fan fare from the orchestra, a smiling, debonair young man, immaculately dressed in tails and white tie.

In a Fred Astaire like movement, he swept up a vintage megaphone and announced to the still standing diners, "Good evening everyone and welcome to the President's Weekend. Please be seated." He turned to the bandleader standing to one side. "Thank you, Roger Thorpe, for that splendid rendition of our National Anthem. As President Theodore Roosevelt might have said on an evening such as this when he visited the Mountain House so many long years ago, 'That was just bully!'"

Applause and polite laughter rippled across the dining hall as the guests took their seats in happy anticipation of the evening's program.

"My name is Gary Hopkins," began the emcee, "and on behalf of the Smiley family down through the years from 1869 to the present, I'm happy to welcome all of you to the Mohonk Mountain House for a very special weekend."

Polite applause from the diners rippled across the hall.

"Since we usually celebrate the birthdays of George Washington and Abraham Lincoln during the month of February at Mohonk, we thought we'd add a little more drama to such a celebration by honoring tonight the four Presidents of the United States who actually visited the Mountain House during their lifetimes. All of us, of course, are very proud that four distinguished Presidents have been guests at Mohonk. But, for those of you who don't already know which Presidents visited Mohonk and just when they were here, I will enlighten you with such trivia information that may help you one day if you ever have a chance to get on the TV show, *Jeopardy*.

"Roger, if you will, please—" Hopkins gestured to the band leader who raised his baton and, with a great flourish, swept the band into a vibrant rendition of *Hail to the Chief.*

A star spangled drop, revealing large portraits of four United States Presidents, slowly unrolled from the ceiling heights above the fireplace to a position beside the American flag.

Jamie, who had been watching the rather campy staging process with some amusement, leaned over to Jennifer and whispered, "I feel like I'm at a Chinese Peoples' Party banquet waiting for Chairman Deng to make an entrance."

"Jamie," Jennifer nudged him with her elbow, "behave yourself."

As the drop completed its descent, a spotlight, trimmed to pick up the portrait of Chester A. Arthur, faded in.

"Ladies and Gentlemen, I give you the 17th President of the United States, Chester A. Arthur, who visited Mohonk in 1888."

Diners applauded vigorously as a spotlight picked up the next portrait. Hopkins continued. "The 18th President of the United States, Rutherford B. Hayes, who visited Mohonk in 1889 and again in 1892."

The applause continued as a spotlight illuminated the third portrait.

"And now, the man known as the rough rider, the hero of San Juan Hill, the 26th President of the United States, Theodore Roosevelt, who visited Mohonk in 1892 and again in 1904."

The spotlight that picked up Roosevelt's portrait reflected off the wide-brim smile of T.R. Whoever had painted the likeness had taken particular delight in exaggerating the toothy grin of the President, giving him the appearance of a western range rider about to devour a great chunk of buffalo steak.

A fourth spotlight focused on the fourth portrait as Hopkins gestured upward. "Finally, we have the 27th President of these United States, William Howard Taft, who was a guest at Mohonk in 1916."

As the last President was named, Roger Thorpe led the orchestra's rousing conclusion of *Hail to the Chief*, punctuated by a crescendo of drums and traps. At the finish, the tables all but lifted off the floor in a tornado of clapping hands, whistles and stomping of feet.

Hopkins lifted his arms to quell the demonstration. "You might be interested to know that we're working on President Clinton to visit Mohonk to close the long gap since President

Taft's stay at the Mountain House. We're thinking of dedicating a new jogging trail beyond the garden, to be called 'Bill's Hill.'"

If there were any Republicans among the numbers of diners that evening inclined to hold back their approval of Hopkins's partisan levity or Democrats offended by the reference to Clinton's proclivity for jogging, the response of the assembled guests did not show it. The hall shook once again in an upheaval of appreciative applause.

"And now—the magic moment has come," Hopkins's voice lowered and took on an almost reverent hush as he waved a hand toward the band leader.

Roger Thorpe lifted his baton and the orchestra began to play a haunting medley—a drifting current of dream-like notes that flowed through the hall, hypnotic in its affect upon the attendant guests. The hall lights dimmed to a soft candlelight and a spotlight picked up Hopkins as he continued over the musical chords.

"Step with me this evening across the threshold of time, through the decades that wind beyond the years of our lives and our parents and grandparents back to the very turn of the century. It shouldn't take too much for us to imagine ourselves back in those days—for tonight, the very walls which surround us in this great hall are the same walls which have echoed to the voices of Mohonk guests ever since 1893."

Hopkins paused as the orchestra music swelled to a dramatic crescendo and then softened and continued as a silver projection screen descended silently from the rafters just to the right of Hopkins. A video projector, hidden away behind the opposite wall, lit up the screen with a panorama of images and old newsreel clips that synchronized perfectly with Hopkins's narrative as he resumed.

"What would life have held for us in those years? Well, in 1900, the horseless carriage was described in the Literary Digest, a leading periodical of the day, as strictly a luxury for the wealthy, never to come into common use as the bicycle. Of course, that was a prophecy that had to be seriously modified just four years later when Theodore Roosevelt took the oath of office as President in his own right in 1904. At that time, more that 78,000 horseless carriages were careening down country lanes, stampeding horses, cows and chickens."

Hopkins's recounting of the emergence of the gas eating buggies and the fateful contest for control of the roads between automobiles and farm animals was accompanied by a sequence of screen images and offstage sound effects—sputtering gas engines backfiring, horses whinnying and snorting, chickens cackling and background shouts of "Get a horse!" from angry carriage drivers.

"In the beginning, the automobile gave a definite, if temporary, romantic edge to handsome swains in pursuit of beautiful damsels. However, that edge faded when the gas eating buggies bogged down on muddy roads where service stations were as non-extant as Democrats at a Lincoln Day dinner."

At this point in Hopkins's narrative, as he paused, the screen showed a sequence from an old silent movie depicting an open touring car, vintage 1904, sunken to its hub caps in ruts. The frustrated, mud covered, totally disheveled driver attempted to crank the inert machine back to life while his lovely passenger sat, not so patiently, berating her hapless companion mercilessly with wide gestures and angry looks. Appropriately, Roger Thorpe's orchestra burst into a lively rendition of the old favorite of that time, *Get Out and Get Under*. The meaning of the song was made quite clear by the vocalist, a 'whiskey tenor,' who sang of the travails of early drivers and inconstant autos prone to breakdown every second mile of country roads.

The diners, none of whom were old enough to have experienced such 'olden days' first hand, nevertheless, showed their approval with much clapping and a bit of hooting.

The screen images continued their parade as Hopkins, once again, took to the microphone to enwrap his audience in further 1900's happenings of note.

"Those were also the days when two bicycle building brothers named Wright put a flying machine aloft for all of twelve seconds.

"Thomas Edison's devices to show motion pictures were installed in nickelodeons all over the country, and for a nickel you could see *The Great Train Robbery*.

"On Broadway, Maude Adams starred in *Peter Pan*, William Gillette played *Sherlock Holmes* and Victor Herbert's, *Babes in Toyland* was the biggest musical success in American stage history.

"Baseball grew up to be a world series event in 1903. And the distaff side, with apologies to the feminists present, had just obtained the right to vote in Wyoming, Utah, Colorado and Idaho.

"Oh yes, great revolutions were on the way. But the emancipation of women was slow in coming, both in votes and clothing styles. The bustle was on its way out, but skirts were still within one inch of the ground—never mind the weather, wet, dry, hot or cold.

"In the great metropolis of New York City, the barons of industry were building palaces. The Vanderbilt Mansion fronted on six city blocks. Andrew Carnegie's New York townhouse boasted fifty rooms and a miniature golf course. The millionaire, Charles Schwab, built a cozy little Riverside Drive domicile that contained 75 rooms, 40 bathrooms and a refrigerator capable of holding 20 tons of beef.

"Mrs. William Astor was the empress of New York society, and the term '400' was coined to describe the number of persons who could be comfortably accommodated in her ballroom. Those lucky enough to be invited made up the register of 'Who's Who in New York Society.'

"And so, for this evening, let's pretend. Let's play we are there. The year?—1904, the month?—November. President Theodore Roosevelt has just been reelected, and the nation is forging ahead on all frontiers.

"There is no income tax, no war, no television, no computers. But there is the Mohonk Mountain House with all the delights and conveniences of that age that Mohonk had to offer—electricity, indoor plumbing, yes, even water powered elevators. Things haven't changed much around here since then. They've just gotten better."

Hopkins turned and gestured to Thorpe.

"So, Roger, give us the music of the 1900's, the waltzes, the songs of romance and adventure. Let us dream for awhile of things past when our grandfathers and grandmothers were young and foolish, when sleigh rides with jingle bells and horseless carriages and steam trains took us everywhere we needed to go through a world where the words nuclear and holocaust were still unknown. And although the horizons were darkening with the storm clouds of the first World War, that was the future. For tonight, we journey to the past.

"So—on behalf of the Smiley family and all of the staff of the Mountain House we welcome you on this magical evening back to the gateway of the 20th century.

"Hit it, Roger!" Smiley waved to Thorpe and executed a sweeping bow as the orchestra swung into a rousing finish. Over three hundred pairs of hands signaled the approval of their owners in a swirling syncopation of sound that curled around the diners like tongues of fire.

As the musicians broke into a refrain from Johann Strauss's *Gypsy Baron*, the applause softened and gave way. Couples rose to their feet to join in the first waltz of the evening.

At Jamie's and Jennifer's table, after-dinner coffee was topped off and conversation centered on Hopkins's entertaining introduction.

"Boy, that's show biz," Carol remarked. "You know, he really makes you feel like you're there, or here, or wherever the hell we're supposed to be tonight".

"And what about that ice sculpture," Jennifer chimed in. "Isn't it beautiful?"

The two waiters who had brought the ice capital in were now wheeling it over to a new position against the front center of the bandstand to clear the dance floor. A number of couples were beginning to leave their tables to waltz to Roger Thorpe's swelling rhythms which now swept sensually through the dining hall turned ballroom.

"C'mon, Jamie, like the man said, 'It's let's pretend time,'" Jennifer said as she rose, taking Jamie's hand and guiding him toward the dance floor. Both were excellent dancers, having honed their dancing skills at several swing dance weekends held at Mohonk over the past three years.

"Jennifer, now that I've cut you out of the herd," Jamie swung Jennifer out and in again very close, whispering in her ear, "there's something very strange going on around here. I've gotten this far in life without believing in ghosts and I don't intend to start believing in them now. The woman in the Rock Building was no ghost. She was Mrs. John Harrigan Jr., wife of one U.S. Air Force Brigadier General Harrigan, Jr., retired, and somebody is playing games here."

Jennifer, stepping to the measure and trying to follow Jamie, who had momentarily lost the beat, said, "Watch my toes, darling, I bruise easily. Why would Betty Harrigan lie about being in the Rock Building? You heard what she said—she and John were skiing this afternoon."

"I wouldn't care if they said they were ice fishing for the Loch Ness monster. I know what I saw and who I talked to. It was Betty Harrigan." Jamie crunched the words into Jennifer's ear, making her wince.

The music stopped and the dancing couples applauded Roger Thorpe and the orchestra as he stepped up to give some background to the music that was popular in the 1900's.

"Here's a little number called *After the Ball.* It was waltzed to at the turn of the century in ballrooms across the nation and recorded on player piano rolls to be found in family parlors from New York to San Francisco."

Jamie led Jennifer into the waltz and continued theorizing as the orchestra picked up the cue. "Jen, Betty Harrigan called me Mr. Sommers. Of course, she hadn't yet met me at that time so she could have mistaken me for this guy Sommers, who ever he is, but when we met at dinner, well you saw what happened. I'm telling you, no two women could look that much alike. She's the mystery woman of the Rock Building."

"Wait a minute, Jamie. She called you Mr. Sommers?"

"Yeah, Sommers. I guess I must look like him. I wonder where he is right now." Jamie peered around the hall. "If I look like him, he must look like me."

"Jamie, I've got it, I know the answer." Jennifer's face lit up and she gave a little bounce and clapped her hands. "Betty Harrigan was the mystery woman, all right. It's an act. She's playing a part. Somebody has put together a little mystery program here. You know, like the mystery weekends Mohonk has every year? Betty Harrigan must be a professional actress. She's chosen you as part of the cast in some kind of skit that is going to unfold tonight and tomorrow. Didn't you tell me she wants to meet you later around midnight in the little parlor down the corridor here to tell you more?" Jennifer was positively glowing with insight.

"Yeah, that's right," Jamie smiled. The light of reason turned his face bright. "By Jove, I do believe you've got it." Jamie started to tango to *The Rain in Spain*, a number from *My Fair Lady*, as he took Jennifer by the waist, somewhat in conflict with the orchestra's theme of *After The Ball*, sung by a young handsome male vocalist. Jamie and Jennifer shifted back to a waltz.

"Jen, you are totally brilliant—God, to have such great looks, body and brains all in one package. It's absolutely frightening. There's just a couple of things, though. First, how did she know I would be in the Rock Building? And how did she get changed into the dress she has on now? Remember she was already at the table when we came in late."

"Simple, she was following you. She didn't know you were going to the Rock Building. She was probably assigned to you to make contact. She might have caught you in the elevator or the corner of the gift shop or just in the hallway somewhere. She is very clever. She must have picked you up when you left the room and sort've just meandered after you, knowing you were probably daydreaming anyway and wouldn't notice as long as she stayed far enough behind. You made it easy for her by going into the Rock Building. All she had to do was wait a few minutes and follow you in."

Jennifer is getting to be a regular Mrs. Markel, Jamie thought. "All right, so she followed me, that was easy enough, okay. What about the room, all made up warm and cozy? How did anyone know I would stumble into that room? The sign at the entrance of the Rock Building certainly didn't encourage trespassing. 'Closed for winter,' 'do not enter,' 'water turned off,' etc., etc."

"It was a setup, Jamie. Somebody would have found it sooner or later. It just happened to be you. Whoever wrote the script for this probably thought up a half dozen ways of getting somebody into that room."

"Okay, that sounds logical, but what about her dress? How could she change that fast and get down to the dining hall?"

"Jamie, when a woman wants to get dressed that fast, or undressed, she'll do it. Besides, she's most likely a professional actress and has probably had plenty of experience on and off-stage in quick costume changes. Look, all we have right now is one instance and a few clues that something is going on that we are not yet supposed to know about. That's what makes it fun. We'll find out as we go along. Oh Jamie, it's exciting, isn't it? I love mysteries. I wonder what's going to happen next?"

"I'll tell you what's going to happen next. We are going to change partners with one John Harrigan and one Betty Harrigan. I want to talk to her, see what I can find out—see if she gives anything away. Meanwhile, you grill John Harrigan,

See if you can find out if he is in on this. We may as well go along with the gag."

Jamie swept Jennifer toward the far right of the dance floor where they intercepted John and Betty Harrigan.

"Hi, General, Betty," said Jamie. "What about a trade? Jennifer's been after me for the last five minutes—says she always wanted to dance with a General."

"Jamie, you're fresh," Jennifer's face reddened slightly as she gave Jamie a glare.

"I'd be delighted," said Harrigan. "I'm flattered, Jennifer."

Jamie bowed and handed Jennifer over to Harrigan with a flourish and at the same time reaching over for Betty Harrigan's hand.

"Shall we, Betty? Let's pretend we don't know them."

Jamie whisked Betty Harrigan away as the orchestra began another round. He maneuvered her toward a less crowded corner of the dance floor near the main entrance. "Betty, c'mon now, level with me. That was you in the Rock Building this afternoon, wasn't it? You called me Mr. Sommers. Who is he, by the way?" Jamie inquired disarmingly.

"Jamie, you really do amaze me. I told you. John and I went skiing this afternoon. We only just got back in time to get dressed for dinner. I thought we were going to be late. One of my skis kept falling off. John was getting quite impatient with me, but we made it all right. The trails were really quite crowded. All those children—I think they really should set up separate ski trails just for the families with children. They do hold things up."

Betty Harrigan prattled on and on. Jamie marveled at her ability to totally disconnect from his questioning. She was good all right; she certainly wasn't going to give anything away. A real pro, she was going to play out whatever script she was working from. Looking Jamie straight in the eye, she smiled and bubbled away about the beauty of Mohonk—the invigorating winter air, how she and John had looked forward to this weekend and how she intended to enjoy every minute of it with even more skiing tomorrow. Jamie realized it was no use. He wasn't going to crack her. She was too well rehearsed. Well anyway, he thought, the next twenty-four hours were certainly going to be interesting.

Jamie was not keen on these kinds of games. He really hated charades or any other after-dinner parlor activity that eliminated intelligent conversation. He had to admit, though, there was a gnawing intrigue associated with the happenings in the Rock Building that afternoon—and the strange meeting with the fascinating woman he was now dancing with who was pretending there had never been any encounter with him earlier. She was so convincing that if Jamie hadn't, with Jennifer's helpful explanation, been swayed that she was an actress playing a role, he would have been bored out of his skull with her.

She was now rambling on about her husband's work, starting up a new airline. She seemed oblivious to the fact that Jamie wasn't listening. God, he had to get rid of her. He much preferred the mystery woman to Betty Harrigan. He was beginning to look forward to the midnight meeting.

Jamie wheeled them over to Jennifer and John Harrigan just as the orchestra completed the round and Roger Thorpe stepped up to the microphone to announce a short break. John Harrigan spoke first as the foursome came together.

"Jamie, I think Jennifer needs a break after enduring my assault on her toes."

"Not at all, John, you are very graceful. He is a very good dancer, don't you agree, Betty?" Jennifer gave a snide little smile to Jamie. A quick passing glance that said wordlessly, that will teach you to cozy up to female doctors.

"Oh, John's a smoothy when he concentrates," Betty replied. "Like when he flies airplanes. Trouble is he thinks he's flying airplanes when he dances. Now Jamie, he's really smooth—a regular Fred Astaire."

"Hey, John, maybe we should extend the exchange. I like what I hear. How about you?"

Jamie winked at Jennifer and made a feint toward moving Betty back to the dance floor, but the music had stopped as Roger Thorpe left the dais and the musicians stacked their instruments preparing for their break. The two couples moved back to their table, Jennifer giving Jamie a little pinch on his bottom as she maneuvered herself behind him. Carol and Philip Hardy, hand-in-hand, appeared from behind several couples who were meandering slowly to nearby tables.

"Boy, that Roger Thorpe," said Carol. "He may not be Sammy Kaye, but he sure plays like him. Looks like the 'Big Band' sound is still alive and well at Mohonk."

Jennifer smiled at Niko as he returned to the table. "Hi, you two looked pretty good out there." Niko smiled and bowed slightly.

"Ah yes, Western music has definitely conquered Japan. I learned to Lindy while singing karaoki. 'Don't sit under the apple tree with anyone else but me.'" Niko gave a restrained but comic rendition of the Andrews Sisters' famous tune. Timeko placed her hands over her mouth in the traditional Japanese posture designed to sustain dignity in such an outrageously mirthful situation which Niko was at the moment providing with his karaoki-style performance.

"Niko," Jamie spoke up, having decided to put aside the business of the Rock Building for awhile. "Not to get too serious, but how do you see the trade situation shaping up between the U.S. and Japan?" Jennifer frowned, the conversation once again was verging on the edge of heavy.

"Ah yes," Niko replied, "well, in Japan we observe the ways of nature and try to apply these ways in our daily life. We have a saying in Japan that comes from bird-watching." He paused, smiling, then said. "The bird that flies into the wind may catch rain on its feathers."

Jamie smiled. "Inscrutable, Niko—are you saying the more the U.S. pushes Japan toward opening its markets to U.S. products, the more resistance we'll encounter?"

Niko nodded politely. It was not so much a positive acknowledgment in response to Jamie's pointed question as it was a traditional Japanese posture indicating that a certain position, once articulated, might encroach unfavorably upon another's views. Hence the exaggerated politeness of Japanese businessmen and politicians in expressing disagreement, often accompanied by much apologizing and the wish not to offend.

"In Japan, business and industry take the long view as you know from the, ah, collisions of the United States and Japan in electronics and car production," Niko strove to explain. "Americans are always in a hurry. Don't get me wrong, Jamie. I've been in America for ten years now and I have, as you say, jumped on the bandwagon too. But during the 19th and early 20th centuries, Western nations controlled the Far East. The British were in India, Malaysia, Singapore, Hong Kong, Shanghai—the French in Indochina—the Dutch in Indonesia—Spain in the Philippines—Russia in Manchuria and Korea. The U.S.

had a little piece of everything by controlling the banking system in China and Japan and the economics on every street corner everywhere. Japan, without natural resources, was in a constant squeeze play, struggling for resources and markets, never able to call its own shots for its own welfare. All the Western World carved up China with the 'Open Door Policy' under the Manchu Dynasty.

"Everybody was playing volleyball in Japan's back yard, so when Japan took down the net and said, 'Go home, you foreign devils,' beginning with Russia in 1904, everybody got mad, but nobody went home, except Russia, and we had to sink their navy before they would listen to reason."

Niko's micro-lecture on Far Eastern affairs and his slightly-veiled hand slapping might have come across offensively to right wingers and families of servicemen lost at Pearl Harbor, but he was so charming and pleasant in his presentation, it was almost as if he was apologizing for Hiroshima being in the path of the atomic bomb.

"So you see, Jamiesan," Niko addressed Jamie, but was aiming his diplomatically blunted barrage at everybody, "this is, after 90 years or so, Japan's turn at the bat. All we want is three outs and a chance to hit a few home runs. We don't want the game called because of rain."

Jamie, with a side long glance at Jennifer as if to say, 'Ok, I'm almost finished with this, hang on,' said instead, "A good analogy Niko. I can see why we don't want the World Series played in Tokyo," Jamie grinned. "You'd soon have us playing extra innings.

"Actually, you are right," Jamie continued, "the Western World first proselytised and then exploited the hell out of the Pacific nations. I had two uncles who spent their lives in the Far East—one with the system, a New York Banker who operated out of Shanghai before World War II—the other, outside the system, a medical missionary in China. One healed bodies and saved souls. The other made sure the bottom-line year-end report was in the black and that good old American dollars flowed east faster than west."

"President Theodore Roosevelt, whom we honor tonight, brought to Japan a great white fleet in 1907," Niko countered, "as if to say to us, 'don't get uppity, the Pacific is our swimming pool too.' Can you really blame Japan for wanting to build its own fleet when Tokyo Bay was filled with foreign warships from most of the western world?"

"No," Jamie agreed, "as a matter of fact, Teddy Roosevelt subscribed to a double standard. He used the Monroe doctrine to warn German and British ships to stay out of the Caribbean in a dispute with Venezuela over non-payment of a debt but endorsed the 'Open Door' policy in China, creating a giant flea market for Europe and America."

"Theodore Roosevelt liked the Japanese, though, and he was admired in Japan. He helped settle the Russo-Japanese war," Niko pointed out, "but there were many Japanese that disliked him, even hated him, because they thought he sided too much with Russia and wouldn't agree to Russia giving Japan reparations for losses suffered."

"Roosevelt didn't want Japan to get too big for its britches," said Jamie. "He wanted a balance of power in the Pacific."

"Yes," said Niko. "That meant for Roosevelt and America, keeping Japan with a Boy Scout Troop Army and a bathtub-size fleet that didn't threaten the U.S." Again, Niko smiled disarmingly and placed the palms of his hands in a supplicating posture.

Jennifer finally prevailed. "Okay, that's enough world history for tonight, you two. I want to dance, not fight a trade war."

"I agree," said Timeko as she took Niko's hand, a decidedly Western feminist gesture, and drew him to his feet as the orchestra struck up a lively number from *Babes in Toyland.*

"What do you think of Niko and Timeko, Jen?" Jamie queried as he maneuvered Jennifer toward a quiet corner of the dance floor.

"Timeko's really sweet. Niko must treat her well. She looks like she adores him."

"And Niko?"

"Very sure of himself—a gentleman, great manners, but I wouldn't want to be on the other side of him in a debate."

"Or a war. You're right—superior intellect and charm. He was blaming us for World War II and making fun of us at the same time for letting ourselves believe we beat them. He knows Japan really won the war, and the war isn't over yet. That's what he was warning us about. To Niko and his generation, war is business and business is war. There is only one bottom line and that is winning. For losers, it's disgrace and *hari-kari* in one form or another—not much in between. We may think Japan functions like a democracy, but the Samurai class are still alive and well. They just wear black Western-style business suits instead of kimonos."

"All right, lover," Jennifer tightened her hold on Jamie and whispered in his ear. "No more politics, history or world view discussions tonight or someone I know is going wish he committed *hari-kari.*"

Jamie responded with a playful nibble on Jennifer's ear. "I can't decide whether I want to finish my dessert or cover you with whipped cream for a midnight snack."

"Hmm—sounds tasty, darling, but I want to be the main course." As the music slowed, Jennifer snuggled even closer to Jamie, wrapping her arms around his neck, maneuvering her right knee between his thighs. Jamie could feel his stomach muscles tense involuntarily, nerve endings in legs and thighs sensate with the feather-like touches of Jennifer's words.

"Jen, it's after 11 o'clock, and I think it's time for a little of that TLC that Dr. Fairchild prescribed. What do you say?"

"Sounds good to me as long as we have a little quid pro quo." Jennifer's voice was husky, anticipating. She took Jamie's hand as the music stopped and guided him back to the table. Niko and Timeko were seated talking to Carol and Peter Hardy. The General and Betty Harrigan were talking to another couple still on the dance floor. Jennifer gave apologies.

"Folks, Jamie's supposed to get some extra rest tonight. He had a little fall on the ice on the trail at Sky Top this afternoon and the doctor thought he should take it easy for awhile."

Niko rose. "Ah, Jamie, sorry to hear that. I hope you're all right. What ever happened did not impair your reasoning—I enjoyed our East-West discourse." Niko smiled broadly, gave a little bow and held out his hand.

Jamie smiled in return. "Thanks, Niko. Goodnight, Timeko, and Peter, Carol—I haven't laughed so hard since a fast-talking Colonel tried to get me to reenlist in the Army."

Carol quipped, "You should be married to Peter, 'My Life with an Antique Dealer.' I could write a book."

"I got a book of my own in mind, Jamie," Peter responded. "How do you like this? 'Life on the Edge with Carol Hardy,' or 'Do I Jump Now or Wait until Somebody Pushes Me?'"

Carol gave Peter a playful cuff and a facial expression that rivaled that of a Maori warrior.

Jennifer laughed. "You two are a barrel."

"Goodnight, Jennifer, Jamie," said Peter.

An overlapping flurry of goodnights ensued as John and Betty Harrigan arrived back at the table. Jamie and Jennifer made their way across the floor as the orchestra began another round. "One more dance before we get down to carnal matters, Jen?"

"Ordinarily, I would say yes, Jamie, but right now I feel like tearing off your clothes. They must have put something in the creme brulee. Let's get out of here before I get arrested for molesting you. Besides, you have to meet the mystery woman in not much more than a hour and that doesn't leave much time for preliminaries."

Jennifer smiled and looked hungrily at Jamie. Both quickened their step as they started up the long corridor from the dining hall to the lobby area and the elevators.

A slight shiver stabbed Jamie's shoulder blades unexpectedly as they reached the Grove Circle Parlor. The tremor traveled down Jamie's left hand holding Jennifer's.

"You okay, Jamie?"

"Sure," he said, without much conviction. Meeting with the mystery woman was beginning to hang on him.

Chapter Ten

"Rendezvous time, Jen." Jamie tenderly extricated himself from Jennifer's child-like embrace, sat up and looked at his watch. "This time, let's synchronize our time pieces. I still don't know what happened this afternoon—how I could have lost an hour in the Rock Building? Either my watch needs new batteries or I do."

Jennifer stretched her legs and wiggled her toes as she sighed and rolled over on her back.

"Darling, your watch was correct. Remember? It showed 6:50 when you got back. And you definitely don't need new batteries, not after the performance you just gave." She reached up and kissed Jamie. "Now if you don't get out of here and down to meet the mystery woman, or should I say Betty Harrigan, I won't be responsible for my actions. Of course, if I didn't know you better I might think you seduced Betty Harrigan in the Rock Building, or she you. A lost hour would be just about right for that, don't you think?" Jennifer teased. She was not comfortable about Jamie's obvious lapse of memory, but she attributed it to a momentary mode of disorientation caused by his fall, not to a *tête-à-tête* with Betty Harrigan.

"I have it at 12:20, Jen."

"12:20 it is. Now behave yourself, lover, and try not to undress Betty Harrigan with your eyes, or in any other way, for that matter."

Jamie turned to the door, opened it and peered out, both up and down the corridor. "God, for a hotel with 300 guests, it's more like the Egyptian wing of the British Museum after closing time. There is nobody around."

"Off you go, Jamie. I'm dying to hear about your meeting. Remember, go along with the game plan. Let the mystery woman do the talking. Try to forget she's Betty Harrigan, okay?"

"Right. I wonder if she'll change back into the dress she wore in the Rock Building." A soft whistle escaped his lips. "What a number that was." He smiled slyly and deflected a pillow aimed at his head as he opened the door to the corridor.

"You'll be numbered among the missing if you don't behave yourself, Jamieson Stanner. Now get."

Jamie blew Jennifer a kiss and stepped out into the corridor, closing the door behind him.

The corridor seemed much darker now than when he and Jennifer had walked back to the room just an hour ago. What was it anyway? he thought. Are the hall lights on a dimmer? Did some staff member go around about midnight and turn all the lights down to save electricity? Or did someone change the light bulbs? Crazy. He shrugged and began to walk down the dim corridor towards the Grove building and the parlor rendezvous. He decided not to take the elevator. The elevator doors seemed barely discernible in the murky shadows of the third floor foyer. It was almost like looking through smoked glass.

Jamie's recollection of when he walked the Mountain House halls as an eight year old was disturbingly renewed as his eyes searched hidden corners and dark recesses. Chairs, tables and desks tucked away in the corners of parlors and along the halls—objects which in daylight were comfortable and familiar now suggested sinister forms that might at any moment metamorphose into nightmarish shapes, waiting to creep up from behind and cast any unsuspecting guest, foolish enough to be about at such an hour, into some bottomless purgatorial pit.

A frigid breath of air suddenly settled like a mantle around his shoulders as he trotted down the central stairs to the first floor. Some windows or doors left open somewhere, he guessed. He passed through the Grove Circle—a darkened parlor of wicker chairs and reading tables, now unaccountably threatening in its midnight reclusiveness.

The rows of portraits of distinguished past visitors to Mohonk covering the walls along the final length of corridor leading directly to the dining hall seemed to evolve as he walked along, into greenish-tinged holograms, grossly distorted images with ghoulish eyes and faces fixing and following him in malevolent stares. He quickly looked to his left and right. The portraits assumed their natural poses; happy smiling faces of eminent gentlemen from around the world who had visited the famous Mountain House. But as he turned back to proceed along the corridor, the pictures, once again he noted in his peripheral vision, assumed cadaverous shapes—baleful, bulging eyes staring at him, following him as he proceeded down the hallway.

He turned back, suddenly, for another look in the direction of Grove Circle from where he had just come. The corridor was perfectly peaceful and, if not bright, certainly not uncommonly murky as it had appeared to him only moments ago. The effigies of the world famous personalities, past friends and guests of Mohonk, were all in proper place behind glass and frames, hanging in regimented order along the ochured walls.

Jamie ran his fingers through his hair, touching the still slightly sore side of his head which had struck the railing of the little bridge up on Sky Top trail. Could these weird images and hallucinatory effects be the result of his fall?

The doors to the dining hall were closed. No light from within the vast chamber escaped through the black panes of glass set midway in the doors. Something decidedly unorthodox here, he thought. How could they have cleaned up after the dance so fast and shut everything down? Everybody must have been anxious to clear out. That was explainable when it came to lovers impatient to consummate romantic trysts within the comfort of their cozy Victorian rooms, warm and bright with glowing fireplaces. But what about the workers, waiters, security people, etc.?

He pushed against the doors to the dining hall. They were locked. He tried looking through the door windows—nothing, blackness. It was almost as if someone had pulled down opaque shades over the windows from within. But he remembered what the doors were like from the inside. There were no shades. Queer, he thought. Not a light in that huge hall; not even emergency lights could be seen as he leaned up close against the door. There was not the clatter of a single dish, not a footstep, not a voice, nothing. It was as if that part of the building had ceased to exist—had been obliterated with some kind of black graffiti-like paint.

Turning toward the right, he faced the little parlor adjacent to the dining hall, the designated meeting place selected by the mystery woman. The door was closed, but there was a dim light shining through the transom casting a small square of illumination toward the hall ceiling. He tried the doorway. It was not locked.

The door opened inward to reveal a room of about 12 by 14 feet illuminated solely by a typical Mohonk ceiling fixture—two brass tendrils reaching out, opposite to one another, like wisteria vines searching for a new anchor. At their ends, petal-shaped, etched-glass shades shielded the low watt bulbs. Bright orange filaments, plainly visible, cast a soft candlelight glow over the room's furnishings.

Jamie looked around the room. To the right of the entrance door was an oak, farm-house style china cabinet with curved glass sides and shelves holding ribbons and certificates of awards from New York flower shows presented to Mohonk gardeners for winning displays.

On the right hand wall was the ever present Mohonk fireplace. The black, iron-framed fire box was surrounded by orange colored ceramic tile bricks which blended into the hearth of the same material, reaching out about two feet from the finely wrought andirons on which rested several pieces of dry kindling, well aflame, resting on dying embers from other less recent replenishments.

In the center of the room was an oval-shaped mahogany table with scrolled legs and marble top, upon which had been placed, rather recently it would seem, a flourishing bougainvillea plant with profuse red blossoms.

Two more-or-less nondescript oak, cane-bottomed chairs and a maple rocker with a cushioned seat covered with a fabric of small flowered patterns encircled the center table.

A Victorian chaise lounge, worthy of the style on which one might imagine the reclining Lillian Russell, one of the most beautiful and voluptuous of America's leading actresses of the 1900's, rested against the left hand wall.

Pictures of the Smiley family decorated three walls. Albert and Daniel, in smiling portraits, offered their good will and salutations to all who would pause to view the turn of the century photos.

Jamie walked over to the window, turned about and looked at his watch, 12:30 AM, exactly. He felt awkward. He was uneasy due to his unsettling walk down through the darkened corridors which had prompted such strange hallucinations. It *must* have been the knock on the head. He rubbed his temple as if to alter whatever body chemistry was effecting his cogitative processes.

He was beginning to hope the mystery woman—that is, Betty Harrigan—would not show. He really did not want to play this game. How did he get sucked into this? Why couldn't he have minded his business and stayed out of the Rock Building?

Of course, if Jennifer was right, Betty Harrigan might have figured some other way to nail him. If he had seen her coming he could have slipped into a men's room. Although sensing her determination, she probably would have followed him in there as well.

He didn't like the disorientation he felt. The warm comfort of the Mountain House in which he had always basked had been dispersed by cold, menacing shadows in dark corners, much as a blanket of fog drifting across open water might dissipate, exposing treacherous shoreline rocks.

Stark fragments of unpleasant memories reared up in Jamie's mind—in particular, his afternoon encounter with near tragedy at Eagles' Nest on the trail to Sky Top. He could almost feel himself falling again, floating in that awful vortex—hearing that alien voice crying out to him, "Hang on—hang on." Where the hell were such thoughts coming from? Maybe he did suffer a concussion.

He had to leave, he had to get back to the comfort of his room, to Jennifer's soft embrace—to the warmth and security of her arms around him, curled up behind him in the womb-like familiarity of bed and blankets.

To hell with this game, he muttered to himself. He moved to the door, his decision made to depart the discomfort and oppression he felt in the little parlor.

As he reached the doorway, she seemed to materialize out of the corridor walls. One moment he was looking down the gloomy corridor towards the Grove Circle, about to leave, closing the parlor door behind him. The next, she was at his right hand—as close as when they had danced together earlier in the evening.

"My God, Betty, you startled me." She seemed not to notice his sudden shock.

"Mr. Sommers, I'm grateful you've come. Please, we don't have much time. Come into the parlor and I shall try to explain the circumstances that have necessitated this meeting."

Jamie nearly stumbled as he reentered the room. The mystery woman—of course, it was Betty Harrigan—pointed the way to the chaise lounge. She was dressed exactly as she had been in the Rock Building—stunning forest-green gown, silver slippers, pearl choker and cameo brooch accentuating white shoulders and bosom even more beautiful and seductive than he remembered from their earlier encounter.

There was something about her speech though. It seemed stylized, like the dialogue in a Jane Austen novel—stilted, that was it. Certainly not the casual way she was speaking at dinner earlier.

Jamie settled down on the chaise lounge next to her. All right, let's get to it, he thought. At least we're going to find out something about this charade—might as well play along.

The mystery woman began, "My husband, General Sidon, is not aware of my meeting with you at this moment, and he must not know of it. Dire circumstances would most assuredly follow if knowledge of my conversation with you were to be revealed."

She is really good, Jamie thought. Here she is, the woman I danced with not two hours ago who was talking about cross-country skiing, now looking me straight in the eye and telling me nobody is supposed to find out about this meeting.

"Okay, Betty, oh, sorry, Mrs. Sidon. I don't know who the hell this guy Sommers is, but if you want to make believe I'm him, be my guest. Now what's next on this scenario? Go ahead, give us the clues."

Mrs. Sidon continued, completely oblivious to Jamie's not-so-veiled sarcasm. She stared intently into his eyes. He was almost beginning to believe he was Sommers, her concentration on him was so intense, her words so emphatic and certain.

"Mr. Sommers, I shall speak directly. You will appreciate, I'm certain, the delicacy of my position, due to your responsibility in such matters I'm bound to address."

Jamie nodded in dumb assent, although totally at sea as to Mrs. Sidon's train of thought. "Of course, Mrs. Sidon, please continue."

Actually, Mrs. Sidon's slight pause allowing Jamie's short exclamation seemed to have little to do with any desire she might have entertained in providing him an opportunity to reply.

Her mind seemed fixed on presenting to the particular space Jamie was at that moment occupying, a non-stop monologue of incidents and events laced with bizarre implications that both astounded and amused him as he politely listened.

It seemed to Jamie that he might stand up and walk around the little parlor without affecting in the slightest Mrs. Sidon's urgent recitative. Several times he moved his head and broke eye contact with the woman, purposely.

Her eyes never moved to follow him. She was relentless in pursuing her exposition, not in the least either distracted by his shifting attention, nor responsive to his frequent efforts to comment or interject a question from time to time. She hardly paused in her script, except to cast an occasional furtive glance over her shoulder toward the door to the corridor, as if expecting a third party to appear.

"Mr. Sommers, information has come in to my possession of a diabolical scheme to undermine the pinions of our government and to destroy the very essence of order and authority upon which our nation rests. Indeed, it is not an exaggeration, I dare say, to imagine that should such an evil scheme meet with success, international conflict must surely result, casting America into a veritable maelstrom of violence and strife.

"I speak, Mr. Sommers, of a conspiracy, a plot if you will, to assassinate the President."

Wow, Jamie thought, that is one hell of a script. Where do we go from here with only half a weekend to uncover a 'Presidential' assassination attempt? People are going to be busy tomorrow. Jennifer will love it.

"Excuse me, Mrs. Sidon, are we talking about Theodore Roosevelt here?" He supposed it was Theodore, since the evening had been devoted to the early 1900's.

"A short time ago," Mrs. Sidon continued, completely ignoring Jamie's question, "there came to our home in Washington, several strange men of rather dark and forbidding features. I would say, possibly, of Turkish or Greek extraction, although in all honesty, I cannot speak with certainty of their origin.

"My husband, heedless of my wish to offer hospitality and greetings, ushered them without ceremony into the library, announcing to me that they were not, under any circumstance, to be disturbed." Mrs. Sidon paused. A frown crossed her face.

"Mr. Sommers, I must interject here that, as of late, my husband has displayed a penchant for somewhat unpredictable behavior. A man, who in his performance of duty as an aide de camp to President Roosevelt, has always prided himself on his impeccable observance of protocol and form, suddenly begins to come and go at all hours of the night with no announcement to myself or our servants.

"I must tell you, it has been of no small concern of mine as to such comings and goings. Upon my inquiring into such matters, the General admonished me to keep my peace; that, in effect, such matters had to do with affairs of state and should not be the province of wives or idlers.

"I should inform you, Mr. Sommers, if you are not already aware of such, General Sidon enjoys a reputation for acidity and brevity in his dialogue. His Scottish ancestry has, I fear, endowed him with a taciturn manner that is not at all designed to accommodate or encourage familiarity. In a word, Mr. Sommers, the General does not suffer fools gladly.

"Knowing this of my husband, I was not so offended by his dismissal of my person as I was taken aback by his marked departure from such ordinary routines as was his wont to observe in his daily life." Mrs. Sidon's eyes lowered for a moment and then refocused resolutely on Jamie's. "However errant I observed his behavior to be over a period of recent weeks, there was an occurrence following the late night visit of the dark strangers that cast me into a state of alarm and left me in a total quandary as to what my further actions should be."

"Hold on, Mrs. Sidon," Jamie found it difficult to address Betty Harrigan as some fictitious character, but he played out his role, impressed with the unswerving veracity this mystery woman projected. Mrs. Sidon paused as he spoke, but he once again had the impression that his interruption had little to do with her pause. She seemed on a different frequency. She appeared to be intently focused on him, but he could not shake the notion that if he moved or got up and walked around the room, Mrs. Sidon would still be addressing the space itself which he had occupied, rather than follow him with her eyes as he changed his position around the tiny parlor.

He decided to test his theory. Mrs. Sidon had just looked over her shoulder at the door during her momentary pause and had raised her right hand to her forehead as she returned her gaze to where he was sitting. She lowered her eyes in a gesture which indicated further thought before starting again. At that moment, Jamie rose from the chaise lounge and walked briskly to an e'tagere between the two windows turning to look back at Mrs. Sidon. Her gaze had returned to exactly where he had been sitting. She focused on where his eye level would have been if he hadn't moved.

"Mrs. Sidon," Jamie said. "Yoo hoo, Betty, here I am." He waived in her direction. No change, no response from her. She continued her monologue, for that was now what it had become. Jamie had, in fact, no apparent interplay in the scene what ever. He felt he could have left the room and Mrs. Sidon would still be talking to the space on the chaise lounge, as if he, or somebody, was still there.

This is getting very weird, he decided. Why in God's name did this woman, whoever the hell she was, ignore his presence? Who the hell was he supposed to be in this crazy script? She called him Mr. Sommers, but he might as well have been the abominable snowman for all the attention she was now paying him. What in hell was going on anyway?

He decided to replace himself on the chaise lounge. He moved into Mrs. Sidon's perimeter and sat down heavily on the end of the reclining chair, searching for her eye level and contact.

Just before he resumed his position, she had been talking about the discovery several days prior of a short note tucked into one of her husband's shoes. The note had fallen out on the floor as she had picked up the shoe to place it in her husband's shoe caddie.

"Mr. Sommers, I truly could not stop my hand from trembling as I read that cryptic prescription for the President's murder. And to think my husband is a participant in such conspiracy. Oh, I tell you, I have endured palpitations from that night to this. I have been fearful that the General will look upon my face at some moment and see revealed my knowledge of this affair, although I confess I know nothing of the details of such plot. The note bore little for further discernment. It simply stated, 'November—Mohonk—best conditions—Roosevelt—'"

Mrs. Sidon became suddenly distraught and broke off reciting the rest of the note. It was as if she abruptly sensed the unknown conspirators had instantly become aware of her sharing such incriminating evidence that might, at any moment, reveal their identity.

She cast a frantic look over her shoulder toward the parlor door. "Hark, Mr. Sommers, do you hear footsteps? Oh dear, I must leave. The General may return at any moment. He left after tonight's program in a carriage with two other gentlemen, neither of whom have I seen before—nor are they in attendance here at the Mountain House. He said only, as he left, that he would return in a short while, with not another word as to his destination or business."

Mrs. Sidon rose swiftly. "Thank you for coming, Mr. Sommers. I shall endeavor, within my means, to learn more of this event. I shall contact you tomorrow. The President, as you well know, arrives in the afternoon. You no doubt will be busy with your preparations. We must stop this terrible plan. President Roosevelt must not be harmed. I must rely on you, as you on me. We are the only two persons who at this moment can avert such a tragedy."

Casting a last harried expression toward Jamie, she paused and then turned, scurried to the door and slipped out into the darkened corridor. Jamie, off balance by her sudden departure, rushed to the door to try to catch the direction she had taken, knowing full well, as in the Rock Building earlier, she probably had already disappeared.

Indeed, she had. In the brief seconds it had taken him to reach the door and peer down the corridor, Mrs. Sidon had vanished.

Jamie caught his breath as he stepped out into the hall. The entire length of the corridor was once again bright, at least Mountain House bright, given the normally diminished lighting throughout all the corridors, hallways and parlors in the hotel.

He also became suddenly aware of unmistakable noises

coming from the dining hall—dishes clattering, chairs and tables being shuffled across bare wooden floors, muted voices of the dining hall staff in the process of cleaning up and preparing for the next meal time.

Jamie moved quickly to the dining hall doors. He could see clearly through the glass door panels now. There were no shades. Nothing blocked the illumination of the profuse ceiling fixtures, all of which sparkled as brightly as they had during dinner earlier in the evening.

He pushed on the right hand door to the dining hall. It swung open easily. Bus boys were busy shuttling dishes to and from the kitchens. Waiters and waitresses bustled back and forth setting table cloths and preparing place settings.

Jamie was both shaken and relieved. What strange prompting had caused him to believe the dining hall, a short while earlier, was a shadowland—empty, devoid of any activity and certainly of all life? Hadn't he looked through these very windows into pitch blackness? There had been no sounds, no lights, no life of any kind. And what about the corridors and alcoves on his way down here—menacing, brooding alleys of unspeakable, unknown dread? Had he been sleepwalking from the time he left Jennifer? Had some fearful spirits taken possession of him and shrouded his reason in clouds of stygian fantasies?

Jamie had never known true terror in his life beyond that of his recurring childhood dream that had continued to haunt him into his adulthood. Now, however, he sensed that he had finally touched the clammy surface of unseen horrors that seemed to lie in wait beneath the familiar edges of everyday reality. The night world his childhood imagination conjured and called into being—was it real, after all?—hidden away beneath the conscious perceptions of the day world in which form and structure could be so easily measured? His mind was struggling to make sense out of phenomena that defied dimension. It was too much. He had to shut off this morbid train of thought, get back to the world he could touch, feel, sense—maneuver within. He had to be able to count on objects to be exactly what his senses described to him—lighted hallways, chairs, tables, pictures with real people, not shades or holographic images.

Perhaps he did suffer from a concussion, as Jennifer feared and the doctor warned. What in hell else could account for the horrific sensations he was having? It couldn't have anything to do with the mystery woman, i.e. Mrs. Sidon, i.e. Betty Harrigan. She was a character in a script, a weekend charade that would continue to unfold even more so tomorrow. Besides, he told himself, she was definitely Betty Harrigan. She was convincing. She had a great story line, but she was still Betty Harrigan—no doubt about that.

The sounds and lights from the dining hall faded as Jamie allowed the door to close and turned to retrace his steps back down the now normally lighted corridor of the Grove building toward the Grove Parlor and the adjoining Central building.

Around the corner, up ahead from the direction of the Grove Parlor, came a young security guard with a hand-held walkie-talkie, whispering some sort of instructions into the mouth piece. He smiled and gave Jamie a hearty "Good evening," as he passed on his way toward the flight of stairs at the end of the corridor opposite the little parlor where Jamie had just finished his clandestine meeting with the mystery woman.

Jamie felt, once again, the comfortable, familiar atmosphere of the Mountain House he had known and loved for forty years. The shadows in his mind, just as the murkiness of the corridors, began to dissolve.

He passed through the Grove Parlor, now warm and inviting in the soft glow of the overhead ceiling lights. As he approached the central stairs, the brighter lights of the hotel reception area and central foyer reached up from the ground floor, bathing the chestnut stair spindles and railings in warm earthy hues, raising his spirits even more.

Although he didn't expect anyone would be ice-skating at such an hour, he decided he would slip down to the Lake Lounge, which led off the central hallway and reception foyer, to take a look out on the water. He waved at the youthful night duty desk clerk busily tending a computer, which was neatly spitting out what appeared to be an endless paper-trail of room billings. The clerk, a pretty, blonde wisp of a girl, tore off about two yards of spread-sheets from the computer printer and gave him a wave and a "Have a good evening," a rather ritual expression that belied the true hour of the early morning.

Jamie strolled briskly through the Lake Lounge to the front side overlooking the lake. He relished the enticing smoky aroma of a snapping wood fire still burning cheerily in the inglenook-style fireplace, although radiating comfort and warmth to not another single guest in the entire lounge.

He checked his watch—2:30. God, where did two hours go? On the outside, he couldn't have spent more than twenty minutes with Betty Harrigan—add another fifteen minutes, maximum, back and forth to the parlor. Jennifer is probably having a not so mild conniption fit. Better get back, he thought, ruefully. But first a quick look at the lake.

He pushed opened the heavy French doors to the balcony deck of the Lake Lounge and stepped out into the sharp, clear but cold air of the Mohonk winter night.

He was not prepared for what he saw—particularly after the preceding events surrounding his encounter with the mystery woman.

The surface of the lake was totally obscured by glacier-like drifts of snow and ice, just exactly as it had been upon his and Jennifer's arrival. There was no surface area cleared, not even an area big enough for an ice fisherman to cut a hole through to angle for the famous Mohonk rainbow trout wintering under the ice layer.

There were no torches around the lake edge, which was clearly visible in the bright light of a more than three-quarter moon.

Impossible, he almost shouted aloud. That damn lake was clear this afternoon. People were skating out there. The lake edge had looked like a torch light parade. But now—he could not ignore it. The lake hadn't seen a shovel—never mind a party of Victorian-garbed ice skaters. He staggered back into the Lake Lounge and made a bee line for the desk clerk in the reception area.

"Miss, the lake, wasn't that supposed to be cleared for skating earlier? Has anybody been out there skating?" He knew it was a silly question before he even got it out. He felt stupid and confused. The desk clerk gave him a puzzled look.

"Gee, I don't think they're going to be clearing the lake for skating anytime soon, sir. The heavy snow we had last week sort've melted in the warm spell that came after, and then it froze up again. They're going to have to wait until the cold stays for awhile so they can get a snow plow out there. The ice isn't thick enough yet for that and the snow is too frozen to move by hand." The young clerk smiled patronizingly at him as she gave her answer.

Very logical, thought Jamie, but it doesn't match with my printout.

"Okay, miss, thanks, I guess we'll have to let the skating go till the next trip." The desk clerk tried hard to offer a happy alternative.

"Sorry, sir. Lots of good skiing though, if you like to ski."

Chapter Eleven

The elevator doors opened to the third floor corridor. Jamie stepped out hesitantly, half expecting to be swallowed up in the same, nearly impenetrable shadows that had obscured his earlier passage down the corridor on his way to meet the mystery woman. However, the hallway was devoid of all but its normal Victorian gloom, just like the reception area in the Lake Lounge he had just left—no dark overlays, ceiling lights clear, if not bright.

A few muffled, indistinguishable vocal sounds came from behind the door to room 355 next to Jamie's and Jennifer's room. The young couple occupying 355 were obviously in an advanced state of rapture, never mind the hour.

Jamie knocked softly on the door to 353 as he inserted his key in the lock and gently pushed the heavy door inward, feeling it suddenly give way as from inside Jennifer assisted the effort.

"Oh, Jamie, honey." Jennifer melted into Jamies arms, her face pressing against his chest. "God, I'm glad you're back. I've been so worried."

"Jen, where's the Jack Daniel's? I have a lot to tell you but my nerves are twanging like an out-of-tune calliope."

Jennifer reached for Jamie's favorite drink, an unopened liter of Tennessee mash, strategically placed on the oak bureau, ready for both social and therapeutic use. She poured a stiff measure into a tumbler, dropped in several ice cubes and handed it to him. She then poured herself one, adding a little orange juice. Jen didn't like J.D. straight.

"Jamie, I was so worried. It was getting so late. I finally walked down to the parlor a half hour ago thinking you would or should be finished by then. The parlor was empty. You were gone. I thought maybe you'd gone outside for a walk. I had visions of you collapsed in the snow somewhere. As the doctor said, I thought you might have had a delayed response or something." She kissed him impulsively—the taste of Jack Daniel's, sharp and aromatic on both their lips.

"Jen, let me tell you what happened. You won't believe it, but then I don't know whether I believe it myself. I have the feeling I've been sleepwalking. Are you sure I really left here tonight? This whole thing feels like a weird dream."

Jennifer, was down right solicitous. "You look so drawn and tired. Come on over on the bed and lie down while you tell me."

Jamie took a belt of J.D. and sat down on the edge of the bed kicking off his shoes. "God, I am tired."

He sighed and stretched out on the bed. Jennifer puffed up the pillows and placed them behind his head and shoulders. She sat down on the edge and leaned over close to him. Relieved that he had returned, tired, but apparently no worse for the wear, Jennifer, with the help of an ounce of J.D., was beginning to relax.

"Jamie, you were gone for almost two hours. Either Betty Harrigan is a hell of a conversationalist or you've been in a catatonic state since you left her. I'll rule out hanky-panky. You just don't look like a man that's come from a midnight jump in the hay."

Jennifer was striving for lightness. She had never known Jamie to be in such a mood. His face, normally ruddy at all hours of day and night, had a grayish cast, but his eyes shone strangely bright, almost as if illuminated from within. Jennifer had the feeling that if she turned off the lights, Jamie's eyes would glow in the dark like a deer's eyes caught in the glare of headlights on a country road. She wrote the strange sensation off to the flickering firelight.

"Tell me what happened, Jamie. Are you feeling better

now? Here, have a refill." Jamie had nearly downed his drink. Jennifer reached for his glass, topping it off with another ounce or so, ice cubes tinkling as he took the replenished liquor and swallowed a large swig.

"Jennifer, when I left here, this place seemed to turn into a setting for an Edgar Allan Poe story. *The Fall of The House of Usher* comes to mind. Remember that one, with Vincent Price?"

He began to describe his odyssey through the darkened corridors of the Mountain House and the strange caliginous voids into which the hallways had seemed to coalesce.

"I felt as if at any moment the floor would dissolve and I would find myself falling into some bottomless pit surrounded by phantasmal shapes, shrieking and moaning." He shivered involuntarily.

Jennifer nestled closer, touching his cheek with her hand. "God, Jamie, you do look like you've seen a ghost."

"Then as I reached the Grove building and the corridor to the dining hall," he continued, "it really got creepy. You know all those pictures along the hallway?"

Jennifer nodded, her expression rapt.

"Well, as I passed them, I swear they turned into holograms—3D, greenish, monster-like faces with eyes that turned to follow me as I walked along. I could just see them out of the corners of my eyes, but when I turned to face them directly, they were just pictures again."

"You're putting me on." Jennifer looked at him disbelievingly. "Come on now, you almost had me believing you. What really happened? What about Betty Harrigan? Did she show up?"

"I swear to you, Jennifer, I'm telling you exactly what happened. I know it sounds crazy." He went on to relate how the dining hall had been non-existent except for the doors, locked and impervious to any effort to breach their threshold and allow passage into whatever unknown space or continuum lay beyond. "The dining hall was gone, Jen—no noise, no lights, no life—a black hole, that's all—nothing but two doors to nowhere."

Jennifer was trying hard to absorb Jamie's account. She believed that he was teasing her, making up a story in line with his meeting with the mystery woman—just to get her all keyed up—something like children around a camp fire listening to a ghost story. At the climax of the tale, the story teller would raise up suddenly and shout BOO!—scattering scared children back to their tents to dream of goblins and ghosts the rest of the night.

Jennifer kept waiting for the *gotcha!* But there was no change in his manner. He seemed mesmerized—his mind's eyes transfixed by some object or happening, unidentifiable to Jennifer.

He related how the mystery woman materialized out of nowhere. "She must have walked right out of the wall, Jen. I still haven't figured that one out. All I know is, I'm looking left down the hall past the stairwell and the rest rooms opposite the parlor where the dining hall was supposed to be on my right and, presto, there she is—as close to my right shoulder as when we were dancing earlier. I must have jumped a foot."

He then told Jennifer how they settled in the little parlor and how the mystery woman revealed herself to be a certain Mrs. Sidon, wife of a certain General Sidon, an aide-de-camp to President Theodore Roosevelt—of how she, Mrs. Sidon, had discovered her husband to be involved in a plot to assassinate the President at the Mountain House—of how he, Jamie, who was supposed to be a certain Mr. Sommers, was, according to Mrs. Sidon, the only one that could uncover the perpetrators and thwart the assassination attempt.

"It's a great script for a mystery weekend," he said, "but the thing is, Mohonk's mystery weekend isn't scheduled until March the 25th. Don't you think they're getting a little ahead of themselves?"

"God, Jamie, that is some story," Jennifer said. "But it fits right in with the President's Weekend, don't you think? Betty Harrigan really sounds convincing. What happened next?"

"Well, that was about it except for something really strange I noticed while Mrs. Sidon—there, I've got myself almost convinced Betty Harrigan was really Mrs. Sidon. Anyway, while Betty was talking to me, I had the eeriest feeling that she was really talking to someone else—as if someone else was actually sitting where I was. Crazy, right? Except, when I purposely stood up and moved to another part of the room to see if she would react, she didn't follow me. Her eyes never moved from where I had been sitting. She never gave me a glance—went right on talking as if I was still sitting on the chaise lounge. I finally waved at her and said, 'Hey Mrs. Sidon.' I even called her, 'Betty, here I am, over here.' She kept on talking to empty space. I might as well have been in Saskatchewan for all the attention she gave me once I moved out of her line of vision."

"Golly," Jennifer interdicted. "Sure sounds strange, all right. Go on, Jamie."

"Well, I moved back and sat down again. I could feel her eyes lock on to mine and she suddenly became very nervous. She looked over her shoulder toward the door and asked me if I heard footsteps. And before I could answer, she said she had to leave—get back to her room before her husband got back.

"According to her, he had left some time earlier with some dark characters. She explained that she knew he had some kind of late meeting scheduled for after dinner and the evening program. That was why she was able to meet with me—excuse me—meet with Mr. Sommers. She said she'd contact me tomorrow, that she would try to find out more. Then she was up and out the door in seconds. I ran to the door and looked down the corridor. She was gone—melted away, evaporated—just like she did in the Rock Building this afternoon."

Jamie paused, taking a deep breath, and swallowed more J.D. Jennifer started to speak, but he swallowed and continued.

"That's when I noticed the corridor was lit up again—and the dining hall, I could hear dishes clattering and I looked through the windows of the dining hall door.

"Everything was just the way you'd expect—everybody rushing around trying to get the place cleaned up and get out of there. I walked back to the lobby area and the Lake Lounge. It was all absolutely normal—even met a security guard in the hallway. Everything was the way it should be, except for one thing." He gave Jennifer a puzzled look. His eyes narrowed as he continued. "I walked into the Lake Lounge to look out at the lake. Even though it was late, I figured I'd check out the conditions in case we wanted to go skating tomorrow." He paused once again, breathing very shallow. He drained the rest of his drink, caught Jennifer's eyes and spoke. "Nobody had ever been skating there today, Jen. The lake surface hadn't been cleared. The snow was as thick and heavy as it was when we were on our way to Sky Top. Nobody had been out on that lake and there was no sign of any torches stuck along the edge of the lake, either." He stopped. His voice had dropped to a whisper. "What did I see this afternoon, Jennifer? I mean, I know what I saw on that lake. Am I losing it? What about my midnight walk down to the parlor to meet the mystery woman? What the hell is happening to me, Jen? Tell me who I am. Is something or somebody haunting me and why me, for God's sakes? Why can't this be happening to some other Mohonk guest? God, I wish I had stayed out of that Rock Building."

"Oh, Jamie now you know there's nothing here that can't be explained." Jennifer's voice was soothing. She could always be counted on for rationality except where it applied to her own feelings toward men.

"First of all, we know the mystery woman is Betty Harrigan, no matter how strange she may have appeared to be. And there is certainly some kind of script unfolding here which we will know more about tomorrow." Jennifer took Jamie's hand and held it to her face, gently kissing his fingertips.

"As for what you thought you saw on the lake, maybe you did see skaters, in your mind's eye anyway. This place can certainly work on the imagination. Remember how you imagined all kinds of dark happenings when you were only nine years old, traipsing around these corridors in the evening? Well, all those memories are still there, buried. Today some of them surfaced and underwent a little embellishment, that's all. The mind is tricky, Jamie. Look at all the wild dreams we have when we're asleep. You were caught up in a little night-dreaming during the day. I'm more worried about that blow on the head. God knows that could cause some hallucinating. You heard what the doctor said." Jennifer paused and smiled reassuringly at Jamie. "You'll be all right. You just need a good night's sleep next to my warm body. Tomorrow we'll see how you feel. But, any more hallucinating and you are off to the doc, lover, even if she is a female."

As always, Jamie felt relieved by Jennifer's irrefutable logic. She always made everything sound so sensible, as when she pointed out to him why she needed a dozen changes of clothes, filling two suitcases and three garment bags for a simple two-day weekend. It all sounded so reasonable when she explained it.

Jamie was too accustomed to dealing with life as a series of postulates and equations. Not that he was scientifically minded. On the contrary, he had hardly gotten past high school math. But, that was more due to his preoccupation with sports and an over-attentive attitude toward girls.

A voyage into some macabre world of fantasy or make believe, appealing when he was an eight-year-old, had suddenly, in the last several hours, suffered a very diminished rating in his list of frontiers to conquer.

Prior to his meeting with the mystery woman, Jamie had dressed casually in slacks, shirt and sweater. Jennifer now cuddled up close to him and, in a cross between seductive finger play and a nurse's tender attentions to assisting in removing an incapacitated patient's clothing, she gently stripped him down to his briefs. She herself, in a magic of maneuvers, simultaneously slipped out of her all-purpose terrycloth robe, revealing a white, lacy see-through 'Merry Widow' negligee that looked as if it had been sprayed on her body. She snuggled close to Jamie, managing to both switch off the small bedstand lamp and pull up the creamy wool blanket from the bottom of the bed over their closely merged forms. She kissed him on his shoulders, moving slowly up to his chin and finally, as he turned to accept her enticing overtures, her lips moved to his—her tongue in a gentle but urging probe that signaled her desire to join once again in that symphony of sensations that so totally consumed them in their ascendance of the love act.

In the afterglow, they both fell asleep. The wood fire still flickered, hot coals and embers crackling and occasionally sparking—tiny, white hot meteors arching against the fire screen.

The flames slowly died down as the fire made a last frenzied effort to renew itself—until all that was left reflecting against the walls and the sleeping couple was a faint rosy shade of light that could no longer hold at bay the intrusive shadows of night.

Chapter Twelve

Jamie was the first to awaken to a burst of morning sunlight through the windows and door leading to the little balcony. The light was quite bright considering the room faced the west and only received direct rays of the sun in mid to late afternoon through the windows facing the Rondout Valley and Catskill Mountains.

Wait a minute, he thought as he struggled to shift his sleepy mind into a conscious state, that light should be coming in from the right of the bed. There aren't any windows to the left. He sat up sharply looking at the bright sunlight streaming in through the windows and balcony door. There was no doubt about it. The windows were on the left side of the bed.

He looked toward the fireplace at the end of the bed. There was no fireplace. There was a door in the wall, left of where the fireplace should have been. It was slightly ajar. He could see into the adjoining room. It was a bath. A wash basin was just visible beyond the door on the right. And opposite, the white porcelain surface of a bathtub was awash in sunlight coming into the bathroom from a window overlooking the tub.

Cold chills began in Jamie's arms and shoulders, moving in a reflex of ripples down his trunk and legs. He could feel perspiration stimulated by some glandular alert trickling down the small of his back.

He was dreaming—dreaming that he had awakened in the bedroom of the Rock Building where he had wandered yesterday afternoon. That was it, of course—there could be no other explanation. God, he needed to wake up. He didn't need this kind of nightmare.

He closed his eyes, slumping down in the bed, and pulled the covers up to his chin. The woman lying next to him stirred slightly.

He felt wide awake. There was no drowsiness or stupor that often accompanies a half-awake, half-dreaming state. Nevertheless, he kept his eyes closed, counting slowly to himself until he reached a full minute. When he opened his eyes he would be looking right down the end of the bed at the fireplace and to his right he would look out the window to the morning haze over the Catskill Mountains.

He opened his eyes. There was no fireplace—just the open door to the same bathroom that he had tried to erase in his mind just moments earlier. This time he noticed the white wicker chairs at the end of the bed and a woman's cosmetics on the dresser between the windows that offered a gateway to the early morning sunshine. The wallpaper was blue pastel stripes interspersed with patterns of wildflowers, exactly the same as in the room in the Rock Building.

There was no denying it. He was in a bed in a room in the Rock Building—the very same room he had stumbled into yesterday in his explorations.

He tried again to shake the dream. It was so real. Yet his rational mind, awake or sleeping—whatever loose state it was in—told him it was an illusion. It could not be real.

He was Jamieson Stanner at a weekend at the Mohonk Mountain House, the date, February 26, 1993. That was all there was to it. The dream would soon fade, somehow. Jennifer would wake up and shake him awake and he would take her in his arms and make love to her as they often did in the morning and he would look out the windows to the west and see those lovely Catskill Mountains rising from the early morning mists hanging deep in the Rondout River Valley.

Once more he shut his eyes. It would be all right this time. He'd wait a couple of minutes before he opened his eyes again. He counted slowly this time, 120 seconds—118 . . . 119 . . . 120.

He opened his eyes. Damn, where the hell was the fireplace? Why couldn't he shake this nightmare? The woman stirred again. He decided he would draw Jennifer into his dream. Maybe when she answered his call, it might shatter the dream world and its tissue of false images. He leaned over the woman, who was on her side turned away from him.

Softly, he called out her name—at least he did so in his mind, forming the words with his lips, pronouncing and articulating the sounds he had voiced thousands of times.

His ears, however, did not report the name, his mouth did not form it. What he did hear himself saying was not at all, Jennifer. It was very clear, however, what name he did pronounce.

It was "Helena."

Where the hell did that name come from? he thought. God, he was losing it fast. Why couldn't he wake up? He tried calling Jennifer again, several times in succession, "Helena, Helena."

Each time, his mind called Jennifer but he could hear his voice saying only "Helena, Helena, for God's sake, Helena."

It was as if someone else controlled his voice, someone speaking through him. The third time he leaned over to shake her. The woman next to him was finally aroused, albeit, sleepy-eyed and yawning. She turned to him, stretching her arms as she moved herself into a half-sitting position.

"Yes, Joseph," she answered. "My goodness, dear, are you quite all right? Did you have a bad dream? You look quite peaked."

His face was ashen. Why did she call him Joseph? Who the hell was this Joseph?

He looked at Jennifer, disbelieving what he saw. This woman next to him, with whom he had made tempestuous love only hours before, was not Jennifer. She certainly looked like Jennifer. But her hair was very dark brown, long, very long, silky with threads of gray. He couldn't help thinking how attractive it was, but it was not Jennifer's hair. Her face was certainly Jennifer's—her voice, Jennifer's—no difference there. There was something else different about her, though. She was wearing a very Victorian nightgown—demure, but quietly sexy. Jamie did not recognize it. It definitely was not one of Jennifer's selections from Victoria's Secret.

He still could not understand why he couldn't wake up. What does it take to snap oneself out of a dream state anyway? Again, he tried to say "Jennifer." Again it came out "Helena." The woman looked at him. Her face showed distress.

"Joseph, dear—it's all right, I'm here. You're awake. You're not dreaming anymore."

She took his hand gently and touched his brow with her other hand.

"My poor Joseph, you're feverish."

He couldn't take it anymore. He had to break out of this terrible dream trap. He had dreamt plenty in his lifetime, of course, and there were a number of times when he could tell he was dreaming and was able to will himself awake without effort, but this—this was like nothing he had ever experienced.

All his senses were working. He could detect the faint scent of an unfamiliar perfume. He could feel Jennifer's cool hand on his forehead—hear the distant rattle of steam in the radiator—see the sunlight and feel the warmth of the sun's rays penetrating the sheer curtains over the windows and balcony doors.

Enough was enough. He bolted from the bed. Maybe if he dashed cold water on his face the shock would wake him up.

His logic was disjointed. He didn't reason that it would probably take cold water thrown at his face from outside the perimeter of his dream world to awaken him. Nevertheless, he literally leapt into the bathroom, reached for the cold water faucet and turned it on full. A torrent of water gushed from the opened tap. He scooped up handfuls and doused himself. For the first time he noticed he was wearing a nightshirt. The water soaked his garment and dripped to the oyster tile floor. He could hear the woman, whoever the hell she was, scrambling out of bed behind him.

"Joseph, whatever is the matter? Oh my dear, are you trying to drown yourself?" He paused, the cold water obviously not having any effect upon ushering him from the madness of his dream state. The only result was a deluge, a minor flood covering the tiled bathroom floor, threatening to overflow on to the plush bedroom carpet.

As the woman who answered to the name of Helena rushed to the bathroom in alarm, he glanced in the mirror over the wash basin. It was the final shock. He was looking at a man with reddish sideburns and mustache, long reddish brown hair, rather unkempt from a night of sleep. It was a man with a face and features of one Jamieson Stanner. But nothing else computed.

He felt a sudden wave of vertigo as he stared at his image. He could feel himself beginning to sink into a whirlpool of images now beginning to surround him, enveloping him—the bridge at Eagles' Nest, the chasm below with its jagged rocks, the horse and sleigh dashing through the woods of Pine Bluff, the mystery woman looming over him in the little parlor—for some reason now grown strikingly grotesque, disproportionate in her visage, frightening in every aspect.

Skaters on the lake, wheeled and waltzed in ever increasing speed, torches flaring along the shore, casting surrealistic shadows against the stone facade of the Mountain House. He could feel himself sinking into a void, disembodied hands and arms reaching, snatching for his body parts. Out of the corner of his mind, his last, unvoiced but conscious thought before he hurdled through some unseen horrific veil was,

"Oh God, at last, maybe I'll finally wake up from this bloody nightmare. Be there, Jennifer, please be there."

The woman whom he had found impossible to address just moments before as any other than Helena leaned over the man sprawled on the bathroom floor.

"Joseph, my darling, my poor dear, oh please, Joseph, please say something. I'm here, Joseph." She cradled his head in her arms and slowly and tenderly rocked him as she might an infant fallen asleep. The man mumbled something unintelligible and breathed deeply. His shoulders stiffened and his eyes opened. He looked at the face of the woman who held him so gently as he regained his consciousness.

"Helena, my sweet Helena. What? where am I? In the name of heaven I seem to have been bathing with my nightshirt on."

There was not the slightest vestige of Jamieson Stanner, not a remnant of Jamie's conscious or unconscious mind, not a shred of his personality apparent in the man that now stirred himself and rose unsteadily from the bathroom floor.

Jamieson Stanner was gone. In his place was a man who answered to the name of 'Joseph,' a man who knew exactly who he was and knew exactly who the woman was who administered to him.

"Oh Joseph, you did startle me. You flew out of bed into the bath and commenced to shower yourself with cold water from the tap and then you collapsed. I must say you did give me a fright. Are you sure you're all right?"

Joseph looked into her eyes, smiled and said, "Helena, I just had the strangest dream. I must tell you about it while I remember it. What an episode it was. Give me a moment to assemble myself, and I shall tell you at least as much as I can remember."

The man reached for a towel to dry himself and took the hand of the woman he addressed as Helena as he strode back into the bedroom.

"Sit down for a few moments." The woman reached for a silk wrap that beautifully matched her black negligee and took her place on one of the wicker chairs at the foot of the bed. The man took the other wicker chair and began his tale.

"Helena, I dreamt last night that you and I were living in a future time. The year rings in my mind as 1993, the month, February.

"We were living in Connecticut and traveled to the Mountain House here in a very strange vehicle. A kind of automobile, actually, but unlike any of these stuttering, smoky, noisy contraptions of today. We traveled at a very fast rate along a very wide and straight carriage way on which there flowed endless numbers of these remarkable horseless carriages.

"We ascended to the Mountain House by virtue of a paved road. There were no carriages to be seen. Upon our arrival, we were greeted by a veritable host of attendants who whisked away our valises and the strange vehicle as well. It all seemed quite real and natural to me. Strange how we convince ourselves our dreams are real."

Joseph Sommers smiled vaguely and gazed at Helena, studying her features in the early morning sunlight. He reached for her hand. "Helena, I must say you were quite a lovely woman in my dream. Your hair was quite light, reddish in color and cut short. It was also very curly. I can even remember how your tresses bounced lightly around your shoulders as you walked."

Helena smiled. "My Joseph, I am relieved to know that it was I that accompanied you and not some hussy you were perfectly at liberty to conjure up from some dark side of your libido. I never would have known otherwise, would I?"

"Helena, there is no woman under the sun who could replace you, either in my life or in my dreams. Waking or sleeping you occupy every moment of my mind and heart." Joseph Sommers slipped out of his chair to settle on the floor in front of Helena, taking her hands and resting his head in her lap. She responded by running a hand through his thick reddish hair.

"My darling, I married you because you were so romantic. I never tire of your adoration. Your manner and attention to me leaves no doubt as to who rules your heart."

"And so it shall always be. Besides, my profession leaves me little time to trifle with the vagaries of clandestine love. Although, I must say, protecting the President of the United States does afford one the contacts and occasions to meet many beautiful young women, married or otherwise. Mr. Roosevelt takes great pleasure in the affairs of state that bring about, indirectly, shall we say, the opportunities to indulge in fields of other affairs."

"I'm sure it must be so, Joseph, although, I doubt if the President would countenance such goings on if he were to discover either members of his staff or his cabinet quaffing the wines of secret pleasures." Helena smiled mischievously at Joseph. "Now then, on with your dream tale, Joseph. Do you remember more?"

Joseph Sommers drew his knees under him seeking a more comfortable position as he continued,

"Well, the visions are fading, but I remember you and I taking a walk up to the Sky Top. Along the way, I cannot remember exactly, but I seem to have met with an accident while crossing a little bridge overlooking a deep chasm. Indeed, I slipped on some ice and nearly fell off the edge of the bridge, but you apparently caught me by the foot and saved me from an inevitable encounter with the Almighty. I surely would have been killed if I had crashed onto the rocks below.

"By the way, I must thank you for that, my sweet. You know what they say about falling while in a dream. If nothing stops you, you do indeed meet with such a demise in real life."

"Oh, how horrible, Joseph. That was certainly not a pleasant dream. Indeed, you were quite beside yourself when awakening. Well, it is all over. The sun is shining, and it's a lovely Saturday morning in November 1904, not 1993."

Helena Sommers slipped to the floor beside her husband, her lips seeking his as she let fall the silken wrap to her waist.

Joseph lifted her to the bed, removed his damp nightshirt and enfolded her in a gentle embrace—prelude to the more vigorous attentions that would soon follow as they began the rhythmic cycle of their love play.

Afterward, as they lay together in wordless reminiscence of their joining, a bugle sounded from the lakeside—sharp and intrusive in the November morning.

"Good Lord, Joseph," exclaimed Helena as she turned toward the windows overlooking the lake. "Are we to be invaded by some foreign army or has the Mountain House suddenly become a military post?"

Sommers laughed and sat up, swinging his feet over the edge of the bed. He moved to the dresser and put on his robe as he spoke. "It would seem that General Sidon's adjutant has been carried away in his zeal to establish discipline among the President's staff on field duty. That bugle call, however, is actually a quaint custom of the Mountain House. This morning, it is serving additional duty, a reminder notice from the adjutant that all members of the advance staff preparing for the President's arrival are to meet for a final briefing on the half hour following that obstructive blast." Joseph Sommers's smile suddenly turned to a frown. "Before I answer to duty, Helena, there is something of substance that I feel I must reveal to you."

Helena looked perplexed. "Is it something to do with your meeting last evening with Mrs. Sidon, Joseph? You came back to the room so late, and you seemed not to want to discuss it." Sommers did not answer but stared out the balcony door toward the shimmering surface of the lake.

"Of course, I well remember your admonishment to me when we were married," Helena continued, "how I was not to question you about your work—that you could share most of your life with me but certain aspects of your duties for the President must remain secret." Helena gathered her gown from the floor where it had been hurriedly cast off in the love heat of prior moments and moved to Sommers. She placed her hands on his shoulders.

Sommers turned to her, taking her hands in his. "Helena, normally my duties in protecting the President are of little interest and would bore you or anyone to learn of the nature of such routine responsibilities I face every day. But, occasionally an incident occurs that, on the surface at least, would indicate a possible jeopardy for Mr. Roosevelt. Mrs. Sidon informed me of such an incident last night."

Helena gasped involuntarily.

Sommers continued. "I don't really place much stock in the matter. The whole thing is of such a bizarre and fanciful content, it hardly seems possible that it could be implemented and carried out successfully."

"What on earth are you talking about, Joseph? Are you at liberty to include me in your confidence?"

Sommers broke his contact with Helena and moved across the room. He turned abruptly and spoke very evenly. "Helena, I'm talking about a conspiracy, disclosed to me by Mrs. Sidon, last evening, that, if indeed it has its basis in fact, is so horrendous that its execution could result in chaos for this entire country. It might even precipitate a war which could engulf all the major governments of the world."

Sommers paused and breathed deeply. He turned away and, for a moment, gazed distractedly out the bedroom window, as if the announcement he was about to make to Helena was too unbearable to voice aloud and the words, once articulated, would assume a dimension and a life of their own, giving a kind of wild credence to the possibility of the event. He turned back to Helena. "Mrs. Sidon has informed me of a plot to assassinate the President."

Helena gasped and sat down on the edge of the bed.

Sommers continued. "Indeed, according to her it is an action already initiated and well under way at this moment." Sommers sat down next to Helena on the bed and took her hands. "Now I have no way of knowing at this juncture if there is any truth to such a wild tale. I must tell you, Mrs. Sidon is very shaken by the turn of whatever events placed her in the middle of this. She told me that she might be able to discern more details before the day is out.

"In the meantime . . ." Sommers, in a sudden restless movement, stood up and walked to the balcony door. The morning sunlight flooded across the heights of Sky Top across the lake and splashed in through the glassy portals. Sommers winced in the bright light. He turned back to Helena. "In the meantime, we have little to go on until we have more information. I can hardly report unfounded suspicions to the President upon his arrival this afternoon. Nor having any direct evidence of who might be involved, it would be unwise to share Mrs. Sidon's apprehensions with my men, whom, nevertheless, I believe to be completely loyal to me and to the President."

Sommers moved back to Helena as she stood up.

"I've told you this, Helena, precisely because I have so little to go on. There simply is no one else I can confide in for the moment. If there proves to be merit and substance to Mrs. Sidon's supposition and if, in the unlikely circumstances I become incapacitated, well, there will be at least one other person who is aware of whatever scheme may be afoot—a person I could trust with my life, if necessary."

Helena shuddered as the import of his words penetrated. "Oh, Joseph, what a terrible burden for you, my darling. I'm so afraid for you." She impulsively embraced Sommers, her eyes searching his, anxious, fearful.

"It's more than likely that this will turn out to be a false alarm, Helena. Mrs. Sidon's imagination may be fabricating surmises that are groundless. She is undoubtedly having difficulty with the General. And perhaps this is one way she may feel she can inspire to discredit him, for whatever of her own reasons, who knows. Perhaps she intends to pressure him to release her from her marriage vows.

"A sad business, but I have no choice but to pursue the woman's forecasts, either to unmask the alleged conspirators and thwart whatever attempt might be made on the President's life or, in the alternative, to clear the air of a vindictive woman's false intrigues."

Sommers gently withdrew from Helena's arms, kissed her on the forehead and placed his hands on her shoulders.

"Now, I must dress and report for my meeting. If you hear from Mrs. Sidon while I'm gone, do not of course divulge your knowledge of this matter."

He made his way to the bathroom and addressed himself to preparing for his imminent staff meeting. Lathering his face and chin, he then skillfully proceeded with a surgically sharp straight razor to remove a day's growth of beard, carefully detouring around his bristling sideburns and mustache.

Helena Sommers laid out her husband's riding clothes—

tweed jacket and jodhpurs, white shirt with detachable celluloid collar and a handsome purple-colored ascot. She placed on the vest a shiny gold pocket watch similar to the style carried by rail conductors, the face of which displayed large black numerals and hands that could be read at a distance of at least ten feet.

"It's 8:15, Joseph. That bugle invocation gives you fifteen more minutes till assembly. By the by, where is the meeting to be held?"

Joseph exited the bathroom wiping a slight accumulation of suds from his face. "In the main parlor. I shall have to postpone my bath till I return, Helena, since it is late, although the dousing I gave myself upon waking up has provided some measure of ablution, a custom I hope will not characterize future awakenings." He winked at Helena. "I should think we should be finished by 9:30 unless General Sidon and his adjutant, Major Hertzog, decide to indulge in some rhetoric on the President's election success. I dare say, both of those men excel in currying up to the President." Sommers buttoned his vest and slipped on his coat.

"My, such a handsome fit, Joseph," purred Helena. "No more dazzling member of the Secret Service will be in evidence today, I warrant. Those young ladies in New Paltz who are bound to be on hand at the President's arrival will, I declare, have no eyes for Mr. Roosevelt if you are close by."

Sommers smiled and chuckled softly. "Helena, you are not going to be jealous, are you? I promise you I shall not be moved by flirty eyes and well-turned ankles, not today, anyway." He paused, his smile melding into a look of distraction—his eyes suddenly reflecting a shimmer of inner disturbance. "I must look for signs of anything unusual around the President, Helena, and I am at a loss as to know where to begin."

Helena touched his cheek softly in a gesture of comfort.

He shrugged his shoulders as he moved toward the door. "No doubt, Mrs. Sidon's indictments will be found to be frivolous—we shall see." He composed himself, smiled and kissed Helena as he prepared to make his departure. His voice failed to suggest the nonchalance he tried to impart to his wife in the face of ugly prospects he might soon be forced to confront. "Well, I'm quite sure I should be back before 9:30 and we shall go to breakfast. That should give you enough time for such gilding as will assist you in out-shining any other woman who dares to challenge your beauty by standing too close to you."

Helena broke into a radiant smile that moved Sommers to additional verbiage in which he excessively compared her visage to the brilliance of the morning sun now spilling into every corner of the quaintly styled bedroom. Helena laughed softly. "Joseph, I doubt there is a woman alive who would not agree that you are the king of blarney. But I do revel in your worship, and your elocution overwhelms me. You are indeed a man of style. It is a good thing the Democrats did not have you running against Mr. Roosevelt this time around. I daresay, the President might well have been turned out of office."

"Thank you, my good wife, for your flattery. But beneath this facade, I am but a simple man with simple objectives. I desire not to build canals or fight wars. I desire only to wake up every morning for the rest of my days with your warm body nestling in my arms."

Sommers swept Helena into his arms and a nearly suffocating embrace that seemed to suggest a prelude to a long and sad parting. Strange, unfocused premonitions had lately bothered him every time he had said good-bye to Helena—as if one time in the unforeseen, but not distant future, one such parting would be their last.

Chapter Thirteen

Moving quickly down the fourth floor corridor of the Rock Building, Sommers glanced at his watch. The bold black hands against the stark numerals indicated 8:25. Rather than taking the elevator, he advanced his pace, deciding to descend to the first floor and main parlor by way of the ornate iron staircase of the newly constructed Stone Building.

A technological sensation when installed in 1893, the water-powered hydraulic elevator could be slow and temperamental, and it was not unheard of for a fish from the lake, from which the water source was derived, to get sucked into the hydraulic system, causing the car to get stuck halfway between floors.

Sommers reached the first floor corridor and walked quickly to the foyer area in the Central building from which the main parlor was entered. There was a small group of men, several in military dress, standing near the central staircase. General Marcus Sidon was nowhere to be seen. Sommers concluded the General must have other business. He thought uncomfortably about Mrs. Sidon's revelations. Two men, civilians, upon noticing Sommers's arrival, separated themselves and approached him.

"Good morning, sir," the younger of the two spoke first. He was not tall but muscular. His frock coat, well-tailored as it was, barely camouflaged what must have been, at least, a forty-eight-inch chest. Sandy-colored hair framed a round, boyish, rather handsome face which seemed to grow directly from square, thick shoulders without benefit of a neck. The obviously physical attributes suggested that the man was not to be trifled with in a close encounter. With the aid of a full darkish brown beard and a thick mustache, the man's general appearance suggested a maturity somewhat beyond his actual 26 years.

"Good morning to you, Malcom," Sommers responded and turned to the second man. "Good morning, Jerry."

"Good morning, sir."

Jerry Kenner was obviously an older man, perhaps forty or so. His hair was thin and graying but carefully groomed to cover as much of his gradually balding pate as was possible. He too sported a beard, almost black in contrast to his receding hair. It was clipped short and did not mask but distinctly emphasized a very square jaw that gave the owner the appearance of a prize fighter. Such a visage was augmented by a somewhat pock-marked face, the right cheek of which was distinguished by a clearly visible scar running from the bridge of the nose almost to the corner of the mouth. Every nuance of the man's stature and presence suggested street experience and previous armed combat. In the lapel of his coat there was pinned an emblem of such experience—a medal attesting to meritorious service during the Spanish-American War with the then Colonel Roosevelt's Rough Riders.

Sommers did not serve with Roosevelt's Rough Riders during the war. His experience and his first meeting with the President had occurred during his fifteen years with the New York City Police force, part of which time had been under Roosevelt during the President's tenure as Police Commissioner of New York, beginning in 1895.

After McKinley's assassination in 1901, Congress had instituted, under the U.S. Treasury Deptartment, a new five-man Secret Service detail, charged with exclusive responsibility to protect the President. Both Sommers and Jerry Kenner had been requested by the President to serve as the first agents of the new unit. Neither man had given second thoughts to turning down what amounted to a Presidential summons and had reported to Washington forthwith.

"Gentlemen," Sommers addressed his fellow agents. "It seems

we precede the Major." It was 8:45 and Major Hertzog was uncharacteristically late. Sommers was about to expound further on the subject when the Major himself made a hurried and harried appearance from the elevator just off the central foyer.

A flurry of "Good mornings" ensued from the knot of men standing by the parlor entrance. They were acknowledged summarily by the Major and an army captain in his company.

"Yes, yes, very well. Come into the parlor, gentlemen. That new-fangled elevator needs some working on. The damn thing got stuck between floors—should have taken the stairs."

Sommers shot a smile and a wink toward his men as they all trooped into the gracious confines of the Mountain House main parlor.

The adjutant's voice rang out, high-pitched and nasal—not a voice to listen to out of choice. "Please take your seats, gentlemen, and we will try to make this as quick as possible."

A rather thin man of short stature with not a superfluous ounce on his ramrod straight frame, Major Hertzog, always impeccably tailored, sometimes displayed a pinched expression that belied his confidence and capability as an officer.

On this morning, the pressures of the impending Presidential visit had resulted in a distinct petulance in the Major's behavior at not having total control over the processes of such a visit. Every time the President left Washington, the overall logistics of such trips had come to fall within the disciplines of the Major working in conjunction with the President's official military attaché, and Joseph Sommers, the Chief of Presidential Security. More often than not there were a myriad of details Hertzog had to farm out to alien and sometimes unreliable agencies, whose resources for administering such responsibilities gave some pause.

In short, the Major often felt like a man charged with the task of extinguishing a brush fire with gasoline. Usually, things worked themselves out, but schedules were often warped out of shape, and it frequently fell to the Major's lot to organize new arrangements that would strain the ingenuity of the General Staff, the Cabinet and Congress, itself, were such to be called upon.

The hardest part was getting the President to stop making speeches on every street corner or shake hands with every constituent within a hundred feet of his landau after alighting into a crowd of well wishers, an occupational frustration also shared by Joseph Sommers, but for a different reason—that of ensuring that the President not supply too ready a target for an assassin's bullet.

In the instance of this Presidential trip to Mohonk, however, Major Hertzog had been usurped of the office of accompanying the President by train from his home at Oyster Bay, New York, where he had voted in the election the previous Tuesday—a task he would have much preferred to his present one.

Hertzog had been assigned responsibility for seeing to the numerous arrangements of the Mountain House in conjunction with the Smiley family and to welcome and care for more than two hundred friends and supporters of the President, all influential, mostly wealthy contributors and Republican party faithful.

Also in attendance would be an important, as yet unnamed, foreign diplomat who was scheduled to meet with the President on a critical international matter. Such preparations had occupied the Major since the advanced party arrived early on Friday.

It was not the practice for guests to arrive and depart on Sunday since the Sabbath at Mohonk was observed as a quiet day of meditation with morning worship services. So those that had not arrived on Friday would be arriving today, along with the President, making for somewhat hectic maneuvering on the part of the adjutant.

"Gentlemen, the President is due to arrive at New Paltz at 3:00 PM. He will be accompanied, of course, by Mrs. Roosevelt and two of the Roosevelt children, Archibald and Quentin.

"The Presidential party, after a brief welcome at the New Paltz station, will repair by carriage to the Mountain House. The President is due to arrive hence at approximately 5:00 PM. As you are aware, the President's itinerary and schedule, as well as can be anticipated at this time, will include a formal dinner this evening for all guests, beginning at 8:00 PM, to be held in the main dining hall. Dinner will be followed by a musical program here in the main parlor.

"The President will, on the morrow, embark on an early morning hike with personal friends of his choosing and a contingent of Mr. Sommers's unit. Later in the morning after a brief meditation and Sunday service in the main parlor, the President will take saddle in the company of Mr. Daniel Smiley for a trail ride to Eagle Cliff and environs. Those of you who have been invited to accompany him on the trail ride will, of course, be bound to observe the protocol that is attendant upon such an outing. No rider shall advance beyond his position in the train, nor allow his mount to cantor or strike a pace at a rate so as to disrupt the discipline of the troop. President Roosevelt will not very kindly tolerate any rider advancing or altering his position on the trail unless welcomed to do so.

"Following lunch, the President will meet privately in the Smiley's family parlor with undisclosed individuals on matters of State. In the evening, beginning at 8:00 PM, the Smileys will host a private dinner for the President and Mrs. Roosevelt and selected party faithful.

"The President will continue his stay at the Mountain House through Tuesday morning. He will then depart in the afternoon, following lunch, for Washington, leaving New Paltz at approximately 3:00 PM. Remaining segments of the President's schedule are open as of this moment and will await the pleasure of the President as to his further interests and priorities.

"Now then, gentlemen, if there are no questions"—Major Hertzog hated questions and didn't leave a lot of room for asking them—"I'll turn this meeting over to Mr. Joseph Sommers, Chief of Special Detail, Secret Service, who will briefly address certain items of security."

Agitation consumed the adjutant's demeanor as he looked stonily at Sommers, who imagined him thinking: 'you people should be reporting to me in matters of security; what right do you have to operate independently? How can I keep order and proper communications when there are five men hovering around the President not subject to my jurisdiction and command?'

Sommers mounted the dais, turned and smiled warmly at the group of men. "Gentlemen, I believe you are familiar with my fellow agents, Mr. Jerry Kenner and Mr. Malcolm Yost." Sommers gestured for his agents to rise and acknowledge his intro.

"I will be brief, as the adjutant indicated. Security for the President of the United States is not a subject for open discussion, naturally. Those of us directly responsible are always around but, supposedly, not too visible, although in the case of Mr. Yost's sturdy athletic frame, it's quite difficult to ignore his presence. Mr. Yost finds this particularly true when it comes to young lady admirers, of which I have no doubt he has many."

The group of men, who had been sitting stiffly during Major Hertzog's rhetoric, chuckled lightly and shifted positions in their seats, relieved that the adjutant's strict and humorless indoctrination had given way to Sommers's casual manner and self-indulgent humor.

"Actually, gentlemen, although only I and my agents have direct responsibility for the President's security, my admonition to you, as you are all indirectly subject while here at Mohonk to some measure of responsibility, would be to stay alert to unusual circumstances as might be observed, such as a wheel about to fall off the President's carriage or, better yet, over-attentive ladies strewing roses in the President's path."

The men listening to Sommers seemed to be uncertain as to whether he was serious or making light of the task of protecting the President.

"Actually, I am being facetious, gentlemen. You may smile if you care to. I suppose what I am trying to say is that in my department, simple observation and common sense, along with a slow trigger finger, are the rules. We think we know what to look for in determining a potential threat as the result of our training, but we could be ably assisted by the eyes and ears of other intelligent observers not directly charged with the responsibility we face in protecting the President.

"We are a small force of men, only five—three here today and two more with the President on the way.

"President Roosevelt, as we have all become aware, is not without his detractors. Also there seems in recent years a growing penchant for doing away with U.S. Presidents, for whatever the reason. We have an unenvious record of three Presidents down in less than forty years. We joke about it sometimes, but it is a deadly serious business. You can help us best to do our job by ignoring us, pretending we're invisible if you will, and we will try to stay out of your way as well. Thank you, gentlemen."

The group politely applauded Sommers's brief talk as he retreated to the rear of the parlor with his fellow agents. Major Hertzog sputtered one final directive. "Thank you, Mr. Sommers, I'm sure. Now, hear this, gentlemen. There will be a directive as to the remaining schedule issued at a meeting in this parlor thirty minutes following reveille tomorrow. Gentlemen, you are dismissed."

Sommers directed his men to a quiet corner in the main parlor as the other men, including Major Hertzog, dispersed. He reached for his watch as he began to brief his men regarding the afternoon arrival of the President. "It's 9:15, I just have a few instructions and then you men run along to breakfast. Malcolm, I suggest you familiarize yourself with the trail to Sky Top. I have little doubt that the President will wish to ride up to the fire tower on Sky Top for the view—if not tomorrow, then most likely Monday or Tuesday morning."

Yost nodded assent.

"As we know, the President is already scheduled to ride up to Eagle Cliff. He wants to get a look at the bald eagles that soar over the escarpment, a place called the traps. Malcolm, you should have time for a trot up to Eagle Cliff after Sky Top. You'd best get a fresh horse though. Then I want you to follow on down to Lakeshore Road and meet us at the Spring House on our way back from New Paltz." Sommers turned to Kenner.

"After breakfast around 11:30, Jerry, you and I will saddle up and escort the carriages down to New Paltz to meet the President's train. Albert Smiley will have the lead carriage. Daniel Smiley will ride Sunshine, his favorite mount, at the head of the train.

"The trip down with empty carriages will be somewhat faster than the trip back up. As for our duties at the railroad station, we will be joining forces with the Ulster County Constabulary. They have assigned four men to us for the arrival. I expect we'll have a large local turnout. Chief Gordon of the constabulary is busy this morning having his men set up barriers to control the crowds.

"In discussing arrangements yesterday with the Chief, Major Hertzog and I were pleasantly interrupted at one point by a very lovely delegation of lady students from New Paltz Normal College. They wish to present a bouquet to the President on behalf of the students, friends and colleagues.

"I suspect from observing Chief Gordon's inordinate attention to several well-turned ankles, made coquettishly visible by two or three of the more forward ladies, that these women will be reserved for the very front rows so that their swooning and sighing upon glimpsing the President will not go unnoticed."

"I must say, even the Major's eyes wandered floorward, hypnotized by the forbidden fruits of those ankles—the first time I've seen him speechless. I do believe he might have been prepared for a little dalliance, if the occasion had been presented to him. Unfortunately, the young ladies were only laying on a bit of a tease and flitted on out of Chief Gordon's office like a flock of butterflies." Sommers winked and grinned licentiously at Yost and Kenner.

"Don't get any ideas, gentlemen. Anyone of those future teachers will hog tie you faster than any range rider can throw a bull calf. These days they learn a lot more in college than you and I picked up on the streets of New York.

"So, to get on with it, the President is scheduled to make a short speech upon debarking from the train. Major Hertzog's people have provided for a small speaker stand at the station platform. The whole business should take no more than about thirty minutes, providing the mayor of New Paltz is not unduly carried away with flaming rhetoric while basking in the reflected glory of a United States President.

"Of course, from experience we know the President, who has stated that he merely wants to acknowledge the best wishes of the assembly, a feat he has informed me should take no more than five minutes, will, upon hearing the cheers of the multitudes, no doubt respond with vigor. Nevermind that he has won the election and has no further need to campaign, particularly since he has resolved his intentions not to run for another term."

Having accompanied the President on campaign trips, Yost and Kenner smiled knowingly—amused at Sommers's capsulation of the forth-coming events and his reference to the President's oratory, which always tended to expand in style, force and length in direct proportion to the size of the populace he addressed.

"Very well, gentlemen, we have our assignments. The Mohonk chef awaits your pleasure in the dining hall."

With a shake of hands, the men parted. Yost and Kenner proceeded down the first floor corridor to the dining hall while Sommers bounded up the central stairway on his way back to the Rock Building and room 490. It was just 9:30. Helena would be patiently awaiting his return.

As he started up the iron staircase to the corridor that joined with the Rock Building on the fourth floor level, he felt a peculiar sensation in his hands and feet—a tingling—almost a vibration.

He stopped halfway up on the stair landing, wondering if some sort of malady was about to overcome him. Then, as quickly as the odd sensation had afflicted him, it disappeared. He clenched and unclenched his hands and lightly stamped his feet while rather abstractedly peering down at the hall below.

That's odd, he thought. He distinctly remembered the corridor walls as being wall-papered, a stenciled-like pattern of thin, light green fern leaves. He was now looking at painted walls—a light beige color.

Coming around the corner was a young woman pushing a pram with a small child. She was dressed in strange clothes—a colorful jacket and blousey pants. The woman was saying something to someone behind her who had not yet appeared,

"Darling, do you have your American Express card with you? I want to stop at the Gazebo Shop for a minute. I think I'll buy that demitasse set with the Royal Dalton teapot for your sister. After all, we don't fly to California for her birthday every year. She hasn't been to Mohonk since she moved to San Francisco."

A man dressed in tan trousers, tucked into bright red socks and wearing a pair of red and white boots had appeared around the corner. He sported a green long sleeve sweater-like shirt tied around his neck. The garment displayed a picture of a Mohonk Gazebo and a date—1993.

"My wallet's in the room," the man replied. "I'll get it. You go on ahead, I'll see you at the shop in a minute."

With that, the two people went their separate ways, leaving a stunned Joseph Sommers standing on the stair landing, remembering vaguely the peculiar nightmare he had experienced the night before, wondering if by some inexplicable turn of the screw, he had once more been thrust into the dream realm of a future world—a world from which that very morning he had escaped by awakening in the arms of his beloved Helena.

Before his muddled mind could reason further, the walls began to circle around him as if he were in the center of a carousel madly out of control. The stairs dropped beneath his feet. Pierced by stabbing bright lights, strange faces and shadowy forms appeared and disappeared like jagged, kaleidoscopic fragments tumbling in a myriad of geometric patterns. Abruptly, he felt himself sinking, falling like a stone into a gray colorless dreamscape of hills and valleys, slowly darkening, merging into a black abyss that offered no anchor points for his weightless body and reeling mind. He collapsed on the stair landing.

The next sensation Sommers experienced was a cold smooth surface pressing against his face. He opened his eyes. He was face down on the black polished slate of the stair landing—his arms, spread-eagle, his legs, awkwardly sprawled down the stairs. He raised himself to his knees and reached out to the iron stile supporting the railing, pulling himself up laboriously to a standing position. He looked down at the third floor corridor where the two people had stopped to talk a moment ago. They were gone. The walls were not painted in a light beige. They were wall-papered with a busy pattern of light green fern leaves.

Sommers struggled to make some sense of the phenomena. He had heard of people having flash-back experiences during which they might imagine they were living a past moment or period in their life, long gone. But this was a flash from the future. A disturbing view into an unknown cosmos. He thought it must be related to his state of mind following his unusual dream. Perhaps his subconscious had not quite finished dealing with the subject of his dream state and was still trying to tell him something. Whatever it was, he thought, he could very well do without it. He shook his head forcing himself to regain his bearings.

My God, he thought, the President is about to arrive and here I am having dizzy spells and, indeed, succumbing, without any warning, in a dead faint.

He wondered how long he had been out. He looked at his watch. It was 9:33, only three minutes since he had left his men—no significant lapse of time whatever. He couldn't have been out more than seconds. Whatever his state, he must get back to Helena.

This incident, he told himself, had to be some residual vestige of his unsettling dream. In the process of his awakening earlier, he had, after all, exhibited peculiar behavior, throwing cold water all over his head, soaking his nightshirt. Perhaps some other-world author of his dream was upset that he had emerged from his night journey before his odyssey had been played out and was even now hovering over him beyond some invisible veil, rearranging form and substance—suspending time itself until whatever scenario the dream author had penned had run its course.

Sommers shook off his strange notions and hurried on up the fourth floor stairs, eager to join Helena. He would not mention this episode to her; it would only cause her undue concern. He must focus on his responsibilities. He would need all his resources to face the coming afternoon—which could portend unpredictable events.

As he crossed the threshold into the Rock Building, Sommers looked down the fourth floor hall.

The door to room 490 was slightly ajar.

"Helena, dear," Sommers spoke as he pushed the door open and stepped through. "You must be famished, my love."

His eyes swept the room. Helena was not to be seen—nor was anything else familiar to him. Furthermore, the room was cold, freezing cold. He stood rooted in the doorway not believing what he saw. The bed had been dismantled. In fact, it was a totally different bed from the one in which he and Helena had slept. A large brass bedstead leaned against the wall. It was a wall covered with bluish wallpaper embossed with pale pink roses arranged in tiny bouquets. The paper in some sections was slightly water-stained, and in one corner near the ceiling, a section had separated from the wall hanging down into the room like a wilted leaf. A box spring and mattress leaned ungraciously against the wall next to the doorway from the hall. There were no white wicker chairs, only an oak Lincoln rocker with a cane seat and back and a sturdy oak chair with a high back and spool, spindle legs. A Victorian-style bureau and dresser, painted white, completed the room's sparse furnishings.

Sommers's immediate reaction was that he had entered the wrong room. He quickly stepped back into the corridor and reached for the door handle to pull the door closed. As he did so, his gaze shifted to the windows facing the lake side. Was that snow he was looking at across the lake coating the tops of the rock ledges and pillars of the labyrinth?

There had been no snow whatever that morning even though it was a sharp November day. His mind rebelled against his senses. What was happening to him? Was this still some remnant of his dream? As if to close out such inexplicable and unacceptable phenomena, he swung the door shut with a bang that reverberated down the corridor, shaking the corridor walls and echoing again and again in his ears like the sound wave of a tuning fork.

He looked at the room number on the door, 490. No mistake about that. It was their room. Helena must be there, had to be there. God, he thought, will this dream not end?

Shakily, he turned the knob once again, uncertain of what would meet his eyes as he swung the door wide open in a defiant-like gesture.

"Ah, Joseph, I'm glad you're back. I must say I've developed an appetite in your absence."

Helena's musical voice rained on Sommers like a sudden spring shower. His eyes quickly encompassed the room he had peered into just seconds before. There was the bed, in slight disarray from earlier use, although Helena had drawn up the covers as in some modest attempt to camouflage the dishevelment of sleep and lovemaking. The wicker chairs were in their appropriate places, as were bureau and dresser, covered with Helena's cosmetics and unguents common to the toilette of a lady of the early 1900's.

"Helena, is it you?" Sommers heard himself saying stupidly, still in a state of shock at what he had perceived just seconds earlier.

"Darling, of course it's me. Whom, might I ask, did you expect to find behind this door, Lillian Russell?"

Sommers breathed in deeply and tried to smile, taking Helena in his arms in a spontaneous hug. "Helena, I love you so much, I should be at a complete loss as however to recover my senses if I should ever lose you."

"Joseph, darling—why, you are shaking, my dearest. Are you quite all right? You seem quite in a quandary. Why in heaven's name would you think such thoughts?" She looked at him, puzzled by his mood.

"I should be at such a loss if you were to leave me—a prospect far more likely, I fear, than vice-versa." Helena studied her husband's face. She was perplexed by the tone of such conversation and at his unsteadiness upon entering the room, although he seemed to have recovered himself. Joseph, she thought, seemed prone to premonitions of late. She must deliver him from such a dark mood.

"Joseph, come now. Let's repair to the dining room. Otherwise we shall miss our breakfast. You don't want to greet the

President with your stomach growling. He might mistake you for a grizzly bear and shoot you."

Helena took Joseph's hands and backed out of the door pulling him gently through into the hall.

As he closed the door, Sommers wondered if he were to immediately reopen it whether or not it would disclose the same vacant characteristics of the unoccupied room that had greeted him just moments earlier. And would Helena suddenly disappear from his grasp? As if anticipating such a horror, he tightened his grip on Helena's hands as they proceeded down the corridor.

"Goodness," Helena exclaimed, "if you squeeze my hand any harder, Joseph, I should think it will end up looking like it got stuck in a meat grinder."

Chapter Fourteen

Breakfast at Mohonk offered delectable choices of absurdly large helpings of eggs, bacon, ham, pancakes, waffles, toasted breads, pastry, fruit juices, fruits, milk and steaming cups of coffee and tea.

All during the meal, sumptuously served to the delight of Helena, Sommers had nursed thoughts of the two episodes of disjointed time he had just experienced.

He felt perfectly well physically. In fact, for some moments now, he had experienced a growing exhilaration, a euphoria. It was almost as if he had quaffed some magic elixir that enabled him to apportion his thoughts in clear order, to establish a mind set in lock-step with the projected schedule which this significant day, Saturday, November 12, 1904, would require of him.

He also felt an enhanced sensory perception to such a degree he had never before experienced. The flowers in the tiny bouquet gracing their table in the dining hall—yellow daisy mums, white carnations and tiny red rose buds enfolded with green ferns and baby's breath—took on a chromatic brilliance in the morning sunlight that Sommers thought could not possibly be duplicated by the efforts of the most distinguished artists of the known world. The beauty of those tiny petals and delicately structured leaves, he was convinced, displayed the very essence of the perfection and intricacy of nature.

Good Lord, he thought, upon what strange wonderings was his mind embarking? This was not like him at all. A practical and, certainly, pragmatic man, Sommers felt as if he had just joined the ranks of poets and philosophers as he contemplated the awesome complexity of life beyond the narrow sphere of his daily experiences, mundanely encountered up till now.

His gaze shifted to Helena. She was smiling wistfully at him from across the table, her eyes silently questioning his quite sudden repose. He released an audible sigh which triggered a raising of Helena's eyebrows in a generally puzzled expression. She seemed about to speak but paused, as if she wasn't quite certain as to an appropriate beginning.

"Joseph," she said, finally, as she raised a lush red rosebud to her lips, the color of which, Sommers noted, blended perfectly with the velour-like petals, "you seem quite blissful somehow, as if you have touched upon some great secret meaning of life hidden from the rest of us mere mortals."

"Ah," Sommers smiled, "I was just contemplating, Helena, as a matter of fact, how perfect this exact moment in time seems for you and me."

Remarkably, Sommers's discomfort at the acutely unnerving interludes he had experienced earlier seemed to have vanished. He was overwhelmed by a feeling that his own small destiny, whatever proportions it might assume, would make absolutely perfect sense in the grand and infinite plan of the cosmos. Could it be that the strange splinter of another time which had penetrated the flat dimension of his own world so briefly, and yet so profoundly, that morning carried with it perceptions far beyond the spectrum of his present senses?

He could not, of course, articulate intellectually these feelings to Helena. He did not fancy himself a poet or a philosopher, nor did he, in the least, consider himself a scholar. But, most certainly, he was a man in touch with the symmetry of his surroundings, a physical man, in balance with the contradictions of life, and so he was prone, in his own fashion, to place a positive cast on happenings and events that he could not, perhaps, explain to anyone else.

Although guarded in his display of such feelings with his colleagues and peers in normal, daily intercourse, this tended, in the alternate, to effusiveness in expressions of his affections for Helena.

"You're very beautiful, my love," Sommers continued, "particularly in the morning sunlight of the Smiley family's magnificent dining hall. However, if I tarry here longer I shall have no recourse but to abandon my decorum and sweep you into my arms, oblivious to those around us who know little of the passion your beauty arouses in me." Sommers arose and took Helena by the hand. "That is, however, an occasion we shall have to suspend, regretfully, until the President of these United States of America is firmly and securely ensconced in the tower suite of this story book Mountain House."

He guided Helena through the dining hall to the entrance, waving at his two agents, who were also finishing their meal. Jerry Kenner rose and moved to the dining hall exit to intercept Sommers.

"Good morning, Mrs. Sommers." Kenner bowed slightly in acknowledgment of Helena as they reached the entrance.

"Good morning, indeed, to you, Mr. Kenner. A lovely day to welcome the President, is it not?"

"Indeed," replied Kenner. "The only slightly disagreeable aspect being that long ride to New Paltz on a spiny horse's back."

Jerry Kenner did not enjoy riding horseback anymore. He had had his fill of it with the Rough Riders of '98. Particularly after the distressing and embarrassing wound he had suffered to his buttocks caused, not by a Spanish bullet under gun fire, but by a nearly disastrous fall on top of a thorny cactus that severely punctured his behind and his pride and promptly sidelined him from further glorious combat with his Chief, Colonel Roosevelt.

"Darling," Helena said, "I shall leave you to your duties. Some of the ladies have organized a walk up along the carriage road beyond the gardens. After such a repast as a Mohonk breakfast, I dare say I shall need a long mountain walk if I am to survive the challenges of lunch and dinner tonight."

Sommers kissed Helena softly on the forehead. "Three to four hours on horseback this afternoon should ready me for the threat of a harvest dinner tonight. We should be back by 5:00 PM if the President keeps his arrival speech at New Paltz within modest bounds."

Helena laughed and, with a flourish of voluminous skirts and petticoats, whisked off down the corridor. Sommers turned to Kenner.

"Jerry, you'll be happy to learn that I am assigning you to Albert Smiley's carriage that will, of course, carry the President and his wife. You shall ride shotgun with the coachman, a cold and dusty ride perhaps but one with a cushion rather than hard leather to comfort your backsides."

"Thank you, Chief. I trust I shall not be displacing Meyers or Sachs. I should rather endure a hard seat than hard feelings from my colleagues." Kenner was referring to agents John Meyers and Vincent Sachs, whose assignments were to accompany the President from Oyster Bay to New Paltz.

"Not at all, Jerry." Sommers's face took on a slightly grim appearance. "I shall ride at the tail, coming forward from time to time to observe any untoward activity that might not be visible to you or the other agents from your vantage points."

"Excuse me, Chief, do you expect some sort of foul play? I've known you long enough to detect an extra alertness in your manner and I can hear the alarm bells ringing right now."

Jerry Kenner knew Sommers well enough. He had seen the same alert signal in Sommers's visage the morning of Sept. 3, 1902, in Pittsfield, Massachusetts. Later on that day, the President's landau came in to collision with an electric railway car. The President was thrown to the ground, resulting in a fairly severe injury to his left leg. William Craig, the Secret Service agent riding with the President, was cast out to his death under the wheels of the trolley.

There had been endless speculation as to the cause of the accident. Was it really an accident or might it have been a bollixed assassination attempt? In the end, the incident was considered to have been nothing more than a tragic encounter, precipitated by excited fans of the President riding the trolley car and urging the trolley car driver to an excessive speed to keep up with the President's carriage. This had caused the trolley to reel sideways at a point where the trolley car tracks veered closely to the carriage road way, resulting in the trolley striking the carriage, killing the horse, sending William Craig under the trolley wheels and the other occupants sprawling onto the road.

"No, Jerry, I have no reason for extra caution." Sommers felt uncomfortable in not revealing to Kenner the incident with Mrs. Sidon, but he had absolutely nothing to go on to support the woman's allegations.

Until there was some evidence of the perfidy she described,

he would keep his peace. The five men assigned to protect the President had enough to do, Sommers ruminated, just to maintain a perimeter of protection around Roosevelt. Constantly hovering in the background, they would seek to remain as anonymous as possible, anticipating the President's frequent spontaneous actions and movements which, too often, were displayed without prior warning.

The President was accustomed to, but not easily acceptive of, armed guards telegraphing his vulnerability by their mere presence, and he exhibited a degree of testiness if Sommers or his men demonstrated too overly a degree of caution regarding his safety and well being.

Theodore Roosevelt was a man who liked to ride free of the restraints imposed upon important public officials, much as he in his youth rode wilderness miles on horseback in the face of prairie winds coursing across the western plains that he loved so dearly.

"The carriage road from New Paltz to the Mountain House, as you know, Jerry, tracks through heavily wooded sections that could camouflage a militia of dissidents or, for that matter, a cordon of well-meaning sightseers seeking an advantageous location to view the Presidential party up close. Remember Pittsfield? Horses can be intimidated by unexpected and sudden surprises, like a group of well-wishers appearing unannounced from around the bend in the road. I should not like to see the President's carriage and eight or ten surreys with bolting horses marking out new and untried carriage routes through the woods and forest of the Mohonk Resort."

Chapter Fifteen

"Jerry, I should think it's time we made our way to the stables to see to the deployment of the carriages. It's nearly 11:00 and we should be leaving within the hour." Sommers led the way from the dining room, down the stairs to the ground floor and out to the drive on the west side of the Mountain house, which led down to the huge barn and stables.

The out-buildings sat less than a hundred yards below the crest of the carriage drive—great yellow buildings housing farm animals of every description.

The sounds of horses snorting and whinnying as they were led from their stalls to be harnessed to their appointed carriages were both plaintive and defiant. The horses inherently sensed their burdensome missions they were called upon to perform each day. However, after a few ceremonial protestations and stamping of hoofs, they would compliantly accept the reins and orders of the drivers as they trotted down the carriage way to New Paltz and back. Their daily routine changed little in the course of the seasons except for the vehicles and passengers they were called upon to haul.

A spanking new four-seater rock-a-way trap was being hauled from the carriage barn as Sommers and Kenner approached the paddock. This was the Smiley coach. The shiny, black cab was equipped with beveled plate glass windows all around to ward off the dust and grime of gravel drives. In the front, square brass candle lamps were mounted on either side of the well-appointed cab, that while providing rather feeble illumination on the road ahead, at least warned of the presence of the carriage to others as the vehicle, in twilight or dark of night, careened down narrow country lanes. Passengers entered through a rear door and sat opposite one another, sideways to the forward movement of the carriage. A gentle touch was provided by slender cut glass vases with fresh flowers affixed to either side of the front windows.

At least eight to ten surreys with quivering gold fringes attached to the canvas tops, each fitted with seats to accommodate four to ten passengers, were being lined up on the stone terrace in front of the carriage barn. Grooms and stable hands busily harnessed teams of mules and horses to these vehicles. Sommers smiled as he viewed with Kenner the harnessing of the teams.

"There's likely to be a lot of dust eaten today by the friends of the President. I'd hate to be in the last surrey in this train."

Kenner chuckled. "Thank the good Lord you got me in the Smiley carriage, even if I do have to sit on top with the driver."

"Don't worry, Jerry, you'll have company up there. At least one of the Roosevelt boys will have to ride up there with you. There's not enough room in the cab for both of them, what with Albert Smiley and the President and his wife riding inside. Archie and Quentin, if I know them, will never choose to ride inside anyway. There'll be a contest to see who gets to ride up front with the driver. Which ever one wins that slot will, no doubt, pester the driver to let him take the reins. You'll have your hands full, cushioned seat or not, Jerry."

Half a dozen buckboard run-abouts were now being wheeled from the carriage barn. A number of two-seater buggies and six baggage wagons completed the entourage.

All together, twenty-eight carriages of assorted sizes and descriptions made up the long train now being festooned with red, white and blue bunting, fitting decorations to declare their mission of transporting to Mohonk the newly reelected 26th President of the United States.

"Time to mount up, Jerry." A stable hand appeared from stalls holding the reins of a beautifully groomed chestnut mare, the mount Sommers had requested upon his arrival after his first-hand perusal of the riding stock. The mare, high spirited and impatient to take to the trail, stomped the cement pavement lightly with her forelegs and shook her wheat-colored mane. She swished her tail and weaved her head back and forth, gnashing her teeth in a fruitless effort to dislodge the silver bit thrust irrevocably in her gaping jaws.

All but a few of the carriages had by now merged into the long line of departure stretching more than two hundred feet down the carriage way from the stables toward the gardens and winding around to the portico of the Mountain House at the beginning of Lakeshore Road.

Jerry Kenner had taken his place next to the driver on the Smiley coach, which had already debarked to the east entrance to pick up Albert Smiley. Major Hertzog had commandeered a four-seater buck board in which he and General Sidon would follow directly behind the Smiley carriage.

A grizzled, raw-boned man dressed in rough tweeds and jodhpurs swung up into a saddle astride a large, gray appaloosa. He shouted commands to carriage drivers as he made his way to the head of the procession. Smiley's trail boss, he urged the drivers to keep their distances, maintain a good pace, and to be careful braking on the steep grades on the way down.

As Sommers rode around to the east entrance to the front of the train, Daniel and Albert Smiley, accompanied by General Sidon, strode around the broad expanse of the office porch of the Mountain House and down the steps under the portico's enormous stone arches.

Daniel Smiley's favorite mount, Sunshine, a handsome Chestnut stallion, had been brought around by one of the grooms. Daniel, immaculately dressed in tan jodhpurs, shiny boots and a forest green tweed riding jacket, mounted Sunshine like a cavalry General.

He cast an appreciative eye over the long assembly of carriages, buck boards, surreys and other assorted traps. Horses and mules, hitched in their shiny, oiled harnesses, collars and traces with brass and silver buckles, stomped restless hoofs. Apparently pleased with what he saw as he surveyed the length of the carriage train, Daniel smiled broadly, stroked his goatee and waved to his trail boss.

Albert Smiley acknowledged Jerry Kenner sitting next to

his driver and took his seat in the Smiley family coach. General Sidon joined Major Hertzog in the buck board and Daniel Smiley quickly urged his mount to the head of the train to join his trail boss. The long procession slowly began its passage across the Lakeshore bridge, hoofs clumping, and carriage wheels rumbling over the thick, heavy planks, producing clattering echoes which reverberated from the stone monoliths and the rock faces of the labyrinth.

As the last buckboard runabout skidded across the bridge, wheels rasping against stone pebbles and rough boards, Sommers took up his position. The train picked up speed and disappeared into the woods heading toward the Spring House.

Sommers trotted Sally effortlessly at the end of the train observing both sides of the wooded carriageway as it circled the rugged cliffs of Sky Top looming high above on the approach to the spring. Off the trail to the left, the gazebo sheltering the spring like an ancient woods temple came slowly into sight. Sparkling, cold water flowed in a continuous stream from a pipe into a small pond, normally a welcome trysting place for thirsty horses and riders, but not today.

The caravan moved on without pause down the steepening grade, past cascades of conglomerate stone boulders at the base of the slopes below Sky Top. The scarred face of the huge overhanging escarpment high above was barely visible through the thickets of hard woods, hemlocks and pines that pushed profusely from the forest floor, their straggly branches striving to ascend the cliffs and ledges much as a climber would search for finger and toe holes in the cracks and crevices of the sheer heights.

Far below in the Walkill Valley, Sommers could see the church spires and the building outlines of New Paltz. White farm houses and red barns punctuated the flat farm lots which reached to the banks of the Walkill river.

The long procession wound its way down toward the valley floor. It stretched across the now shorn hay fields and connected to the well traveled New Paltz Wawarsing Turnpike leading into New Paltz. The carriage way then crossed the narrow iron bridge spanning the Walkill river and met the rail line at the New Paltz Depot, not more than a hundred yards from the river bank at the edge of the village.

Sommers galloped up the length of the train to the head of the first carriages as they began to cross the bridge over the

Walkill river. He could see crowds of waiting admirers and curious bystanders lined up along the front of the station depot. He estimated their number at about three to four hundred.

The local constabulary, a half dozen mounted uniformed officers drawn from the town and county ranks, were patrolling along the railroad tracks and beside the station platform trying to keep the crowd within the bounds of bright yellow barriers that had been set up in a line parallel to the track.

A speaker's platform, about three feet in height and some twenty in width and depth, had been erected along side the station house, and a pathway had been delineated with more yellow barriers from the platform right to the edge of the track where officials were obviously planning to have the train stop and disembark the Presidential party.

Sommers had been through this disembarking procedure with the President in many rural stops and many cities. Some had been grotesquely ill-arranged and had resulted in all but stampeding mobs as people thrust forward and broke through barriers of police cordons to get a glimpse or shake the hand of T.R. himself—maneuvers the President seemed always too eager to encourage. Those were the times Sommers and his men dreaded more than any other. Among emerging throngs, the President was most vulnerable to an assassin's bullet.

Today, Sommers was impressed with the efficiency of the locals in organizing the arrival. True, there were probably no more than four-hundred people in the station area, but that was enough of a number to cause serious problems in crowd control if no disciplines were in effect.

Sommers rode up to the group of mounted officers, saluting a police Captain who had just finished issuing some instructions to his men.

"Good work, Captain," Sommers addressed the man with a smile and a wave of his hand toward the platform, the railings of which had been draped in traditional red, white and blue bunting. A large American flag hung from behind the platform. What appeared to be the mayor and Chief Jordan were upon the platform with several other distinguished looking political types, all with tall silk top hats and wearing black chesterfield frock coats, some with striped trousers, rather rumpled looking.

"You seem to have the situation well in hand," Sommers addressed the Captain. "I have seldom seen such efficiency demonstrated in large cities where the President has called, let alone villages the size of New Paltz. You are to be congratulated, sir."

The Captain wheeled his mount about and came along side Sommers. "Thank you, Mr. Sommers. We aim to make your job as easy as we might. We would not cherish an incident in our village during the President's visit that should provide us with a reputation entertained by the city of Buffalo."

The Captain was, of course, referring to McKinley's assassination in Buffalo three years previously where, due to a lack of proper security afforded the President, the approach of an anarchist and a fatal shot was affected as easily as an autograph and a handshake.

"Indeed, Captain, we should likely not be here this day welcoming President Roosevelt had there been more caution exercised in the care and safe keeping of Mr. McKinley."

Again, Sommers thought uneasily of Mrs. Sidon's ominous projections. He wondered what the Captain's reaction would be if he knew of his strange midnight meeting with Mrs. Sidon.

Sommers turned Sally toward Smiley's carriage, which had reached the fringes of the crowd at the south end of the station. He tried to shake off his forebodings. He would deal with substance and facts, not speculations. For this moment, he had to be concerned with getting the President safely to Mohonk. He would allow nothing else to contaminate his thoughts or his actions. He had dispatched to a less conscious corner of his mind the disquieting time fractures he had experienced earlier on the Mountain House stairs as well as the dislocation effect when he had opened the bedroom door and discovered an empty room.

Dream fragments, he repeated to himself—ephemeral gymnastics of the cortex. What do we really know of the mind? Sommers asked himself. Too many wrong turns along the path of reason, and the mind becomes whatever it wills itself to be—like a factory forge out of control, spewing out its own creations, following no sensible pattern or design, stamping out useless parts—none of which would have any utility. The asylums were filled with people with minds like factory forges.

Sommers wrenched his attention away from the subject. For the moment he was relieved that the trip down the mountain had gone well, secure in the thought that he had performed such duties dozens of time since he had first begun his service with the President, and nothing yet had ever gone wrong.

Well, not quite so, he corrected himself. The Pittsfield incident had been a worrier, and then, of course, there was that wild evening when a crazy farmer appeared at Sagamore Hill and tried to shoot the President for not entertaining the proposition that Roosevelt's comely daughter, Alice, should marry him. The man was wrestled to the ground by one of Sommers's men, but he had gotten very close to Roosevelt, who had appeared on his piazza at the sound of a disturbance. A fully loaded .32 caliber pearl-handle revolver had been found later in the farmer's carriage.

Sommers reached the Smiley carriage as Albert Smiley alighted. Kenner jumped down from the driver's seat and assumed a watchful stance to one side as he looked over the milling crowds. General Sidon walked over to the rear of the train platform. Major Hertzog was conversing with some gentlemen near the speaker's platform. Daniel Smiley consulted with his trail boss as the carriage train was being turned and arranged to pick up their passengers for the trip back to Mohonk.

Lining the village street adjacent to the railroad station were eight more carriages and buckboards from local New Paltz liveries, on hand to supplement the Mountain House transport in case extra guests beyond the prearranged numbers carefully tabulated by Major Hertzog were to appear.

The mayor of New Paltz rushed over from the speaker's platform to welcome the Smiley brothers just as a banshee-like whistle pierced the air from the southerly direction of the railroad track where it snaked its way along the bank of the Walkill river into the village.

The whistle blast continued its insistent announcement as the President's train hove into sight just south of the bridge crossing. The huge black locomotive, leading a half dozen pullman cars, belched white smoke in thick intermittent puffs. Steam hissed and escaped from the ponderous cylinders as the huge rod arms cranked the drive wheels which, as brakes were applied, screeched loudly in seeming protest at having to cut short their headlong flight along the shiny steel rails.

As clouds of steam poured out from around the engine's wheels and the train slowed with remarkable precision in approaching its designated stop, Sommers reviewed the crowd pressing against the barriers.

Chapter Sixteen

His eye had caught General Sidon moving through the crowd to several men standing apart in the rear of the main body near the station house. Major Hertzog was not with him.

As the General approached the men, one of them, well dressed, sharp featured but generally swarthy in appearance, separated himself cautiously, looked all around as if wary of being observed, and handed the General a small packet for which Sidon exchanged a packet of his own, something of the size that might have held a half dozen cigars. That done, both men looked carefully around them in such a way as to assure themselves that none had observed their hasty exchange. Sidon looked briefly in Sommers's direction.

Did the General note his observation of him? Mrs. Sidon's words echoed like pistol shots, 'conspiracy,' her husband's 'comings and goings at all hours of the night.' Sommers felt strangely exposed, as if the General was telepathically picking up every shred of his thoughts. Was he being over sensitive to Sidon's sidelong glance? What in God's name was exchanged between the two men? Sommers certainly couldn't confront the General on suspicion alone. Furthermore, the act could be perfectly innocent. Maybe they were trading brands of cigars. General Sidon was an inveterate cigar smoker and the swarthy stranger, indeed, had a cigar in his mouth at that very instant.

However, Sommers had no time to pursue any tack at the moment, suspicious activity or not. The train had lumbered to a reluctant halt, wheels emitting a final groan of steel on steel, hissing steam dying down to breathy sighs. And should any doubt such manifestations of the train's final halt, a brass bell mounted on top of the iron boiler began to clank merrily, urged on by a tugging line manipulated by the handle of an unseen engineer.

Already, Sommers could see passengers through the train windows lining up in the corridors eagerly moving toward the vestibules at the head of the cars where several conductors and train crewmen had jumped off and were placing wooden landing platforms with steps to assist the passengers in alighting.

The only move Sommers could make was to quickly advise Kenner to instruct the two agents who had accompanied the President from Oyster Bay to stay in especially close to him and his family, risking the President's ire at their proximity, but hopefully warning off any sudden attack coming from God knows what corner.

Sommers wheeled Sally in the narrow corridor between the train and the crowd and trotted up to Kenner who was already at his station at the vestibule of the Presidential car. Special Agents Vincent Sachs and John Meyers, who had appeared in the vestibule, were just stepping off as Sommers approached and reined in Sally. Lean and angular, clean shaven except for sporting conservative side burns, the two men would have been indistinguishable from the average business man on the street in the bustling metropolis of Washington D.C. except for one distinctive characteristic both shared.

If one were to observe carefully the facial features, particularly their eyes over an extended moment or two, one could not help but note a penetrating gaze that would appear to pick up every fly speck within the periphery of their vision.

A great swelling cheer arose from the crowd as the President appeared in the car's vestibule. T.R. doffed his silk hat, squinted in the bright sun and waved both arms to the crowd, his face wreathed in a broad smile that showed nearly as much ivory as a bull elephant. Mrs. Roosevelt joined him at his side and the two Roosevelt boys, Quentin and Archie, age eight and ten respectively, mischievously poked around the sides of their parents, also waving wildly at the welcome. The three agents were on the arrival platform just a few paces in front of the

President, who had not yet stepped down. The President was enjoying the crowd's cheering welcome and apparently decided he would relish it a bit longer before disembarking.

Sommers leaned over in his saddle and shouted to Kenner, "Have the men stay in close to the President, Jerry. Keep a sharp eye. There's something I don't like, but I don't know what it is. Be alert." With that, Sommers backed Sally away from the corridor still kept open by several mounted officers of the New Paltz Constabulary and searched the crowd for signs of General Sidon and the strangers.

The mayor of New Paltz and two very political appearing, well-dressed gentlemen had by now approached the vestibule as the President shouted a vociferous "Bully" and stepped down to greet them.

In the rear of the crowd across from the station house on bleachers erected for the occasion, there had been gathered a motley but energetic band of town and high school musicians dressed in what could most generously be described as 'mixed uniforms.' The band was led by an intrepid but unusually short conductor in a starched white uniform—jacket and sleeves laced with gold brocade. Gold epaulets danced and jiggled on the little man's shoulders as he rose on tiptoe with arms waving, baton stabbing the air in mad little circles in an almost cartoon rendition of John Philip Sousa.

The strains of Sousa's *Stars and Stripes Forever*, jarringly off key but stentoriously insistent, poured across the heads of the crowds, catching the Roosevelt ear as he beamed at the bobbing heads and faces of the surging crowd.

The President waived an appreciative hand at the band and began frenetically to shake every hand thrust upon him or toward him. Teeth flashing and gnashing, pince-nez tottering uncertainly on the bridge of his nose—head shaking, shoulders and arms pumping, palms of hands occasionally lofted skyward in spirited accompaniment of some verbal expression of delight, the President moved through the crowds.

As many times as Sommers had observed the phenomena of a T.R. arrival either at train stations, formal dinners or political gatherings, he had never become desensitized to the almost magical accompaniment which T.R.'s appearance engendered in the welcoming street crowds or adulating audiences of campaign rallies. Theodore Roosevelt's entrance was always an electrifying event. Even now as he stood with the crowds, relishing his moment of arrival in the relatively small and politically insignificant enclave of New Paltz, the President's familiar grin continued to flash from ear to ear, rows of gleaming teeth clenching and unclenching, mouthing syllables of appreciation unheard by Sommers from his position in the rear ranks of the teeming populace.

The increasing din, hundreds of voices of various timbre and pitch, finally blended into one great, congregate roar. Accompanied by the rousing, if somewhat dissonant Sousa march, it was an acoustical tidal wave that drowned out even the last piercing aspirations of steam released from the locomotive's boiler as the engineer shut down the remaining control levers that had powered the black behemoth to its New Paltz destination.

It wasn't just the Roosevelt smile, itself overpowering in its great sweep, T.R. exuded a body language that suggested massive stored up energy in his gyrating arms, shoulders and torso. Body muscles twitched, contracted and expanded, giving harmonious vent to the President's words that tumbled out in veritable torrents of high-pitched Harvard accents.

Roosevelt's eloquent pronouncements cascaded over audiences, drowning them in a plethora of visions that gave color and shape to America's destiny and the individual roles of her citizens in the world's most powerful nation and greatest democracy. It was a theme articulated and gesticulated at every whistle stop, every assembly and on every occasion that presented to T.R. an audience ranging from one person to thousands.

The President moved slowly forward through the tightly packed throng, never allowing himself to be corralled or deterred as he swung from hand to welcoming hand, propelled by the synergism of the crowd itself. As Sommers watched from his mount, the President's hand-shaking path, inexorably moving him toward the speakers platform, reminded him of a square dancer linking hands with one partner after another in an 'alaman-like' maneuver.

Roosevelt was never awkward as he worked the crowds. He seemed to know just how long to hold and shake this hand or that one, ever reaching ahead, his squinting but piercing gaze always fixed on the next objective. The President could cut through seemingly impenetrable human bounds like a destroyer slicing through heavy seas, its bow sometimes submerged by drenching swells but always bursting through, topping the waves in one victorious succession after another.

Sommers's men observed the scene from a discreet distance but in very alert condition behind the President as he and Mrs. Roosevelt, followed closely by the two lesser members of the 'White House Gang,' Archie and Quentin, finally reached the bunting-covered speaker's platform.

The President assisted Mrs. Roosevelt up the three steps to the platform, followed by the two boys who leaped up the rough stairs like two hungry beavers in search of a clump of aspens. T.R. himself scrambled up onto the platform as if he were once more charging up San Juan Hill under a rain of Spanish bullets. Once on the platform, Mrs. Roosevelt and the two boys were ushered to seats just behind the flag-draped rostrum. Albert and Daniel Smiley, as the distinguished proprietors of the Mountain House and leading community business leaders, had already mounted the platform to greet the President and his family.

The mayor of New Paltz held his arms up as high as he could reach in a gesture designed to quell the noisy crowd. At the same time, the intrepid band conductor slashed downward with his baton extinguishing all of what remained of Sousa's great patriotic march except for a few brassy rasps from several inattentive cornets.

The mayor, in a squeaky, whisky tenor, spoke a few appropriate ceremonial words marking the visit of the distinguished President of the United States to the Highland Valley town of New Paltz, an honor the mayor never expected to have in his life time and one that would, no doubt, ever be surpassed in his remaining life time. He turned to T.R. with a magnanimous gesture.

The 26th President of the United States left the Smiley Brothers and the knot of local politicians and briskly strode to the rostrum to receive, once more, the wild overtures of a partisan multitude who themselves knew that they would probably never witness again the largess of a United States President in their little Hudson Valley town.

A large group of school children had been ceremoniously ensconced near the front edge of the gaily decorated platform just prior to the President's arrival. Each child waved a tiny American flag as high as he or she could reach.

A contingent of about a dozen young lady students from the New Paltz Normal School stood admiringly next to the children. One very pretty girl blushingly reached up from her position just in front of the rostrum to hand to the President a bouquet of roses which seemed to dance at arm's length towards the President. The President reached forward to take the flowers to the delight of the presentor and her student friends. With eyes shining and faces beaming and smiling, squeals and sighs involuntarily escaped from the small group like the high dissonant notes of squeaky violins tuning up for a concert.

President Roosevelt, his face partially ruddy from the mid afternoon sun in the western sky and even more so from some inner fire sparked by the tumultuous ovation, looked across the sea of faces.

He adjusted his pince-nez and raised his arms like a preacher embracing his flock of evangelicals, all of whom waited expectantly for a message of prophecy that would frame their destiny from that moment on. T.R. did not disappoint them,

"Mr. Mayor, distinguished leaders and guests, citizens of New Paltz in the Hudson Valley of this great state of New York. I am glad indeed to have this chance to visit this wonderful and beautiful community nestled on the banks of the great Hudson River and overlooked by the magnificent Shawangunk Mountains.

"As described by one of your most distinguished neighbors, the eminent naturalist, and world renown, John Burroughs, it is indeed nature's very paradise."

As the President completed his introductory paragraph, he stepped back to gauge its effect, beaming forth a great toothy grin that would have shamed the efforts of an African hippo to match it. The assembled clans caught the cue as if a stage manager had announced over a bull horn, "Okay, let's hear it now for the President."

The roar that erupted would have very likely lifted the tiny roof from the quaint New Paltz station house if it had not been securely fastened. Sommers, watching from the rear side corner of the crowd could feel his ear drums tingle from the impact. Drums rolled and trumpets from the little band blasted in acquiescence to the wide approval of Roosevelt's preamble.

Sommers could feel Sally paw the earth, the mare's shoulders and neck twitching in a sudden restlessness, her blonde mane rippling, eyes bulging as she raised her head and snorted at what might have well have been interpreted, in horse language, as utter disdain of the proceedings.

Roosevelt stepped forward again, raising his arms to quiet the adoring crowd. Looking down at the children and young ladies directly below him he continued.

"I am mighty glad, my fellow citizens, that you do so well with the growing of crops and all of that in this great farming community. But I am also mighty glad and even more pleased that you are doing so well with children. And to you children and young people, I have this to say—and that applies just as well to the grown-up people too.

"I believe in play and I believe in work. Play hard while you play and when you work, don't play at all. We need strong bodies. More than that, we need strong minds, and finally we need what counts far more than body, more than mind—character, into which many elements enter—morality, decency, clean living—the faculty of treating and speaking fairly of those round about us, the qualities that make a decent husband and a good father and a good neighbor, that makes a man a good citizen of the State, careful to wrong no one.

"Men and women of this great Empire State of New York, I believe in you. I believe in your future, because I think that the average citizenship of this state has in it just exactly the qualities of which I have spoken. I believe in the future of this Nation, because I think that the average citizenship of this Nation also is based on those qualities—the quality of decency, the quality of courage and the saving grace of common sense.

"And so, I greet you today. I am glad to be here in your beautiful community to visit this glorious countryside of Mohonk, which I last visited in 1892.

"I wish you well, and I firmly believe that our mighty future will make our past, great though our past is, seem small by comparison.

"Good-bye and good luck."

The President managed to inject such an air of solemnity as he finished, with arms raised and looking heavenward very like a preacher extolling his congregation to invoke with him the blessings of the Almighty, that Sommers, from his observation post, thought for a moment that he was going to offer up a benediction of sorts. Instead, T.R., a master of the dramatic pause, clenched his upraised fists, thrust his arms high in the air and broke the reverent moment with a rapacious "Bully!"

This favorite expression, shouted at the top of his lungs, was accompanied by a great consuming and consummate grin baring every gleaming tooth in his mouth.

The crowd loved the gesture and shattered what was left of the relatively calm New Paltz afternoon with a vocal explosion that blasted high into the sky, washing over a flock of crows that had been passing overhead at just that moment, causing them to wheel and recoil in raucous disharmony, as if a regiment of shotgun-wielding hunters had lashed them with a volley of double O buckshot.

Dozens of straw party hats brought for the occasion went soaring into the air as the nondescript little band of earnest but off-key musicians struck up a galvanizing *Hot Time in the Old Town Tonight*, T.R.'s favorite campaign song.

Roosevelt waved again to the partisan swarm from which hundreds of tiny American flags had now magically blossomed above a sea of cheering faces. He then turned to his family and the small group of dignitaries at the rear of the platform.

Albert and Daniel Smiley moved forward to take proper care of their important wards, ushering the Roosevelts off the platform and through the milling crowds who were something more than reluctant to give leave to the 26th President of the United States after their brief moment of glory in his proximity.

Prior to the arrival of the Presidential train, Daniel Smiley's 'trail boss' had organized the carriages in a remarkable turnaround, snaking the vehicles like a giant centipede all the way from the station house back and along Huguenot Drive, which branched off the main road leading into New Paltz. From such a disposition, drivers and cabs could easily move into place, embarking their assigned passengers in an orderly and disciplined fashion for the trek back to Mohonk.

The President and his family were taken in hand by the Smileys along a corridor cleared through the crowd by the New Paltz constabulary, T.R. waving and smiling incorrigibly.

The Smiley carriage with Agent Kenner aboard had been drawn up in the lead followed by the seemingly endless queue of buggies, surreys, assorted traps and buckboards. Major Hertzog and several military aides rushed about assembling the party faithful into lines of embarkation.

Daniel and Albert Smiley assisted the President and his wife up into the cab while Archie, after a word and a quick wink from Albert Smiley, scooted up with a helping hand from Agent Kenner to take his place on the driver's bench between the coachman and Kenner. The younger Quentin, desolate and near tears, was relegated to the cab to join his mother and father and Albert Smiley while an ecstatic Archie, who had just passed his tenth birthday, fancied himself as Ben Hur about to drive his chariot around the sand track of the Circus Maximus.

The friends and members of the Presidential party were assisted into the standing carriages by Daniel Smiley and his trail boss while Major Hertzog saw to the orderly flow of the long line of privileged patrons. Each carriage, one after another, under careful observation by Sommers and his agents, moved up in stately procession despite the crowds pressing close for a gander at the Washington swells that had suddenly poured into their little back water community.

All of the traps from the local livery stables that had appeared on the scene hoping to importune the Mountain House powers to be for any guest overflows were pressed into service. Major Hertzog's carefully advanced logistics had been dealt a nasty blow with the unannounced arrival of between twenty and thirty additional Presidential friends and party faithful. These carriages were quickly filled and the column led by the Smiley carriage with the President aboard headed out of the station to the New Paltz Wawarsing Turnpike heading west.

From the time the President left the train, to the loading up of the carriages, Sommers had been watching closely the movements and antics of the crowds from his vantage on Sally. General Sidon had reappeared in the brief interlude as the President, after disembarking from the train, made his way through the crowds to the speaker's platform. As observant as he had been, Sommers had missed Sidon's reentrance. During Roosevelt's speech, the General, along with Major Hertzog, had taken a position to the side of the platform. Upon the close of the ceremony and the loading up of the carriages, Sidon and the Major had climbed aboard a carriage with two other men who Sommers recognized as members of a select military affairs committee the President had recently appointed to evaluate the conditions and state of the country's armaments. There was no sign of the swarthy stranger Sidon had encountered earlier.

Triggered by Mrs. Sidon revelations, Sommers's imagination had the General and the members of the select committee, along with one or two other dark characters, sitting around a table smoking cigars while they examined a deadly device designed to blow up T.R. at some appropriate time of their choosing. Nonsense, he almost said out loud. Nobody needs a bomb to kill the President. Why go to such a bother? T.R. could be eliminated by a rifle shot from anywhere on anyone of a dozen hikes he takes every month at Rock Creek Park in Washington. Lord knows how a dozen agents, let alone a meager three or four men, could ever stop such an ambush. And now, Sommers thought, here we are at Mohonk with woods and forest that could hide an army of assassins, anyone of which could, from a secluded cover, pump a dozen bullets into an unsuspecting target. If there was a conspiracy afloat to kill the President, Sommers knew he could only hope to block such an attempt if he discovered the rudiments of the attack in advance. Forget any other defense, there was none.

Chapter Seventeen

Sommers herded Sally on ahead along the stage road beside the long column of Mohonk-bound carriages rolling toward the sun as it now tracked across the Shawangunks, directly west toward the Mountain House nestled behind the gargantuan escarpments that loomed up over the Walkill Valley. The carriage train turned off the turnpike about one mile after crossing the Walkill River and entered the carriage-way at the southeast border of the Mohonk property. From the lead Smiley carriage, with its precious human manifest, to the final buckboard, the wheeled column stretched for more than half a mile.

For the return passage up the mountain side, a somewhat longer but more gentle, less steep route had been chosen. The countryside along the turnpike was mostly open farmland with good visibility on all sides, but as the colorful parade passed the junction known as White Oak Bend, a thickly treed section rose up from the pastoral carpet.

Hasbrook Woods, as that part of the forest was known as by the locals, was a high seawave of late autumn foliage, seemingly impenetrable except for the tunnel-like opening where the road thrust boldly through on its way up toward the base of the Sky Top cliffs.

Sommers spurred Sally up ahead midway of the column and

trotted along side as the carriages entered the woods. The bright sunlight was suddenly eclipsed by the forest canopy of giant virgin hemlocks and mixed hardwoods that had slowly invaded the territory of the evergreens. The sounds of creaking carriage chassis, wheels scratching on the gravel road surfaces, horses and mules snorting and wheezing under their burdens, were oddly muted in the cushioning absorbency of the undergrowth.

At the end of another half mile north and uphill, the carriages turned onto Forest Drive, which, after a wide sweeping turn, followed the almost level contour at the base of Sky Top southwesterly for about three quarters of a mile to the Mohonk Spring and the junction of Lakeshore Road where Agent Yost had been posted by Sommers to intercept the Presidential entourage.

The staccato shouts and whistles of more than three dozen drovers, urging their charges along the steepening trail, intermingled with the sharp cracks of whips to the faltering flanks of the teams. The alien sounds drifted through the woodlands in a weird chorus that, at a distance, might have suggested a small army of gnomes and elves chasing one another in a mad scrambling game of hide and seek.

For all his vague apprehension at the prospect of the trip back to the Mountain House, Sommers was relieved as they passed along Forest Drive coming toward the Mohonk Spring. He could see the lead carriages just passing the fanciful gazebo perched over the little spring-fed pond as they turned up onto Lakeshore Road on the last leg to the Mountain House.

Agent Yost, as instructed, was on post at the spring mounted on a beautiful strawberry roan which was standing remarkably motionless as the carriages passed his station in grand review. Both agent and horse could have passed at that precise moment as models for a Frederick Remington sculpture. Sommers signaled Yost to join him as the last carriages climbed the slight grade up to the south end of the lake.

Horses were sweating now despite the November cold. Traces and harnesses were bathed in lather. Steam rose from the shoulders and flanks of the teams that had plodded up the slowly steeping grade below the Sky Top cliffs.

Without urging from their drivers, horses and mules perked up, stepping out briskly as the carriages began their final encirclement of the lake and rumbled across the timber bridge toward the east entrance of the Mountain House.

Sommers guided Sally to the head of the column, which had just reached the east portico. Daniel Smiley had dismounted and was just approaching the Smiley family carriage from which Agent Kenner was attempting to assist young Archie Roosevelt down from his privileged perch. The coach driver was holding tight reins to prevent horse and carriage from a headline bolt towards the barns, a priority on the horses' agenda that far out-weighed the immediate objective of safely disembarking the President of the United States and his family.

Sommers dismounted and handed Sally's reins to a waiting groom, who had already taken in hand Daniel Smiley's horse, Sunshine. Young Archie, disdaining Agent Kenner's helping hands, took a great leap from the top of the coach, demonstrating the same dauntless abandon of his father, T.R., who, in younger days, might have in a like manner bolted across a chasm in the Dakota Badlands on the trail of a rustler or horse thief. But for Sommers's quick reaction and outstretched arms arresting the ten-year-old's forward pitch, young Archie would have gone sprawling across the gravel drive, necessitating, no doubt, new knee patches on his britches and a dose of iodine on scraped knees.

At the same time as Daniel Smiley reached for the carriage door, which opened from the rear, it burst open and out popped Quentin like a cork from a seltzer bottle. Daniel Smiley, his face awash in a broad grin, caught the young boy under the arms as he literally flew through space and gently deposited him on the grassy shoulder.

Mrs. Roosevelt was the next to alight. A woman of great charm and ready wit, with a smile and a nod towards Sommers and Daniel Smiley, she tossed some appropriate words towards Archie and Quentin. "You boys remember, now, this is not the White House where everyone is used to your pranks. Try not to look like you were raised in an Indian village and ride wild buffaloes to school everyday."

Mrs. Roosevelt turned back toward the carriage just as T.R. forced his boxy frame through the cab door. He signaled for Sommers's attention and waved the agent to one side out of earshot of family members and a number of Roosevelt family friends who had dismounted from their carriages and had gathered around Mrs. Roosevelt and Daniel Smiley.

Albert Smiley stepped out following the President and exchanged pleasantries with a now growing number of guests as the empty carriages, having dislodged their occupants, were wheeled away toward the Mohonk barns.

"Sommers," the President began in a confidential tone, "I am glad to see you. You people have done a fine job in herding this crowd up here from New Paltz. I dare say, I for one would prefer to punch cows along the old Chisholm Trail before I would care to organize a trek of politicians and party faithful to Mohonk."

"Thank you, Mr. President."

Roosevelt's face had suddenly lost its perpetual smile. Now there was consternation as he continued. "Sommers, I don't have time now to explain. I want you to come to my suite at"—he drew a shiny gold watch from his vest—"precisely 6:00 PM. I have something I must discuss with you."

Without waiting for an answer, T.R. turned away from him and walked back to Mrs. Roosevelt and the now quite large gathering on the steps of the Mountain House porch, leaving Sommers to ponder the cryptic instruction he had received from his chief.

Normally, he would not have had a second thought regarding such a command from the President. Indeed, there had been, in times past, rather unusual telephone calls from the President, some at outrageous hours of the night, requesting Sommers's attention to such diverse items as a new saddle for Archie's pony or the best horseback route from Oyster Bay to Sayville, Long Island. Given the scarcity of telephones as yet in 1904, the White House, nonetheless, had several. Sommers's Washington apartment was so equipped as was Sagamore Hill. The President utilized the latest technology at the drop of a hat. But this sudden exhortation from T.R. seemed to carry with it a particular urgency. Sommers had difficulty repressing the direct connection between Mrs. Sidon's conspiracy theory and the President's low-key but compelling summons.

He checked his own watch—5:10. Hmm, he thought, barely enough time to round up his own men for a quick word and to recheck the assignments for the evening, to say nothing of locating Helena and freshening up for dinner.

By now, the last of the guests had been unloaded, and the remnants of the long procession of weary horses and creaking carriages were ambling down the drive around the lower end of the Mountain House, which housed the huge kitchens busily engaged in preparing the bounteous Presidential victory dinner.

Meanwhile, a late tea was being hastily served at special tables set up where every space allowed within the Mountain House lobby, reception and foyer areas. Throngs of grateful guests were overflowing the office parlor and registration areas enjoying the pick-me-up preliminary to dinner, which was not scheduled to begin until 8:00 PM. The welcome respite allowed for numerous young men and women of the Mohonk staff, who were fluttering about like barnswallows, to deliver room assignment cards and keys to the registered guests and assist in the registration of those of impromptu status.

Major Hertzog hovered around the edges like a dedicated concierge answering questions regarding baggage handling, locations of baths and water closets and other—what he considered trivial—items, the resolution of which, nonetheless, the guests held as essential to their welfare, peace of mind and very survival within the cavernous reaches of the Mountain House.

Albert and Daniel Smiley escorted the Roosevelt family into the Mountain House lobby and headed for the elevator. The Smiley brothers would personally accompany the President to his fifth floor tower suite in the most recently completed Stone Building where private tea awaited the Roosevelt family. The President, who always preferred first floor quarters in hotels due to the possibility of fires and the need for a quick and safe egress, was, nonetheless, persuaded by the Smiley brothers that the new Stone Buildings at Mohonk, completed in 1902, had been built to be virtually fire proof.

Sommers waved Kenner to his assignment of seeing to T.R.'s safe settling in his rooms, which meant Kenner running up five flights of stairs to meet the elevator at the fifth floor connecting to the Presidential Suite and the southwest tower. He addressed the other three agents and handed out a short list to each which indicated their assignments and schedules for the next three days.

"You men will note," Sommers explained," there are to be four six hours shifts, two men to each shift, around the clock. But during daylight hours there will be some overlapping in relation to various activities in which the President may wish to indulge. That will mean that there may be periods when all of us will be on board for a specific function such as tonight's dinner. You will also note that at tonight's dinner, we will be scattered randomly around the hall at tables which, because of their locations, are strategic for observation and implementation of aggressive security measures should such, for any reason, be required. Any questions?"

The three men exchanged glances and returned their attention to Sommers.

"Good. Now let me caution you to be particularly alert tonight and for the next two days. Observe these people here tonight. I want an immediate alert to any individual that suggests any air of suspicion or untoward behavior around the President, even if it is a set of crossed eyes."

A light chuckle erupted from Agent Sachs. Agent Meyers, a more serious type, questioned, "Chief, do you know something we don't that maybe we should? You're reading us the text book."

Meyers did not mean to sound insubordinate. He respected Sommers immensely. They had all been together for at least three years, ever since the McKinley assassination. But something in Sommers's stringent rendition of fundamental security measures usually practiced without special emphasis, led to a suspicion that Sommers was holding something back. For Sommers's part, he was slightly annoyed at Meyers's response, principally because Meyers had immediately sensed the increased tension in him, which was, of course, what he had been trained to do. Psychological overtones, inconsistent behavior, shades of emotional dissonance, these were clues to a man's actions, overt or inert. Actually, Sommers was more annoyed at himself for allowing his screen of professional aplomb to be penetrated.

Meyers, of course, was correct. Sommers had not realized his growing uncertainties were so evident. He certainly wasn't going to tell them about Mrs. Sidon's trepidations, not until he knew there was a sound basis for her fears. He had nothing to go on regarding the General and the peculiar exchange of packages at New Paltz with the dark-looking stranger. As for the President asking to meet him, that could be nothing more than a special request the President might have regarding a good spot to look for eagles within the vast acreage of Mohonk. No, he would sidestep Meyers.

"You're right, Meyers." Sommers responded with what he hoped to be a disarming smile. "No special reasons—just that with new territory we need to evaluate security as we go. Mohonk has its own requirements. It's not quite like a Republican campaign rally or State dinner or, for that matter, a hike in Rock Creek Park.

"Just be alert men, and let me know, as I said, if you see anything out of balance that you think I should know about." Sommers smiled again as he finished and slapped Meyers lightly on the back in a camaraderie fashion.

"Now, you men know your duties. I'll be checking with each of you through the evening and the night. Get your rest when you're off duty. You never know when the President might want us to accompany him on a midnight canoe trip up the lake. He may wake up and think he's back hunting grizzlies in the north woods."

Sommers joked affectionately about the President's prowess and outdoorsmanship. They all respected T.R.'s manliness and marveled at the tales he would sometimes spin about his experiences in the Dakotas—cow punching and eating buffalo steaks off the tailgate of a chuckwagon.

The men smiled in accompaniment with Sommers's partiality towards the President's foibles and dispersed up the steps of the porch toward the entrance to the Mountain House office parlor and registration area. Sommers watched them go.

What comes next? he thought. He would know soon what the President had in mind. It was 5:30. He would have to locate Helena. She was probably in their room. There was no time for freshening up until after his rendezvous with the President.

He turned and traced the path of his men along the Mountain House porch, but instead of entering the reception area, he entered the lobby and started up the central stairs to the fourth floor.

The halls had darkened in not unsurprising proportion to the descent of the late afternoon sun, which now hovered in the west over the distant Catskills, a molten disk that slowly knifed into the mountains, giving up its volcanic iridescence reluctantly until all that was left was an after-glow of amber, rose and deepening purple hues which garnished fleeting cloud islands in diminishing tones of pink and gray.

Sommers reached the fourth floor corridor and turned into

the wing leading into the Rock Building. Only he and his agents, along with several administrative members of the President's staff, occupied the Rock Building and only the fourth floor at that, since it was approximate to the President's quarters in the fifth floor tower suite. The President's guests and friends of the Smiley family who had been invited to the Presidential gala were all assigned to rooms in the Central and two Stone Buildings, from the ground level through the fourth floor. For security reasons, only the President and his family occupied rooms on the fifth floor. The sixth floor had likewise been closed off to guests as had all of the Grove building guest rooms.

Indeed, the Presidential gala would be the last guest event of the season. Although the Mountain House was equipped with central steam heating, there was little prospect of substantial occupancy during the late fall and winter months, since travel was restrictive during the severe weather routinely encountered in the upstate regions beyond New York City. Except for an occasional winter season when the 'Great House' might be opened especially for Smiley family Christmas and holiday festivities with ice skating on the lake and sleigh rides through snow-coated woods, the Smileys closed the Mountain House on or about the end of October and migrated to the warm and semitropical climes of California, where they had established a colony of family and friends in Redlands and the surrounding San Bernadino Valley.

Sommers finally stood before room 490. The events of the afternoon had nearly purged his mind of his morning experience and his abrupt thrust into a seemingly future time. Now the memory of that moment erupted sharply in his mind, forcing an involuntary shudder as he raised his hand to announce his presence. Would he once again open the door into an alien room and find only the signs of some future life reflected in disparate furniture cast askew? Would there be no sign at all of Helena?

He knocked on the door, somewhat more insistently than he had meant. At the same time, he turned the knob and pushed open the door in an aggressive move that brought a startled response from its occupant.

Chapter Eighteen

"Joseph, darling." Helena turned from her position seated on the wicker stool in front of the dresser. "From such a boisterous entrance, I should think that you had suspicions that I was entertaining a gentleman friend in your absence."

Helena rose to greet a very relieved Joseph Sommers, who smiled sheepishly as he embraced her.

"I'm sorry, Helena, must call housekeeping and get that door latch fixed. It is entirely too loose to deter a man bent on ravishing his lovely wife, particularly one who has not enjoyed the delights of love since before breakfast."

Sommers nibbled on Helena's left ear and gently lifted the palms of his hands to the soft undercurves of her breasts. She murmured incoherently and nestled against his chest, her hands reaching up to stroke his hair and curve around his neck urging his head down to her upturned face and lips. He kissed her very gently, his passion growing as he breathed in the beguiling scent of her perfume, a faint mixture of wild flowers and a wisp of Arabian musk. He eased from the embrace and took her face in his hands.

"My darling Helena, a few hours separated from you and I doubt if a sultan's harem could provide more than a warm-up for your delicious offerings."

"Joseph!" she cried in mock alarm, then moved seductively to arm's length. The flimsy black negligee she wore fell away from her shoulders and drifted like a cloud to the floor, revealing a delicate black lacy undergarment that did nothing to diguise her Rubenesque cleavage. "Do you think that such a sultan would dispense of his other wives if he could have me?"

Helena shimmied provocatively in front of Sommers, mimicking a belly dancer, arms waving sensually over her head, hips swivelling and pelvis thrusting enticingly towards his midsection.

"Helena, I believe that if the President of the United States could see you right now, he would gladly give up the White House for one night of abandon in your arms." He stepped forward and embraced her again very gently. "You are a lovely vamp. However, I must take my pleasure with this warm body of yours at a later time. The President wants to see me at 6:00 PM." Sommers looked briefly at his watch. "Hm, 5:50, I must go. You know how T.R. is when it comes to appointments."

He felt a tightening in his stomach as he anticipated his audience with his chief. At least he hadn't suffered a relapse with room 490, even though he had startled Helena, himself too for that matter, with his unexpected burst through the door. His strange dream and its residual effects, he decided, were nothing more than what they were—little mind crazies, intemporal as shifting desert sands. He did not think it likely that he would experience such episodes again. He certainly needed, more than ever, to concentrate on ferreting out whatever substance there might be to Mrs. Sidon's premonitions.

"I shant be long, I'm certain," Sommers said as he moved to the door. "The president has his family with him, and I doubt he will tarry with whatever instructions he has for me. I'll dress upon return. We have until eight for dinner." He paused, his hand on the doorknob. "Good-bye again, sweet."

His rationalization notwithstanding, he felt a sudden flicker of apprehension as he faced Helena. Was it simply T.R.'s coincidental summons coupled with Mrs. Sidon's dire warnings—or was it something else?

Chapter Nineteen

The fifth floor tower rooms which served as the Presidential Suite could be quickly reached from room 490, up one flight of stairs almost opposite the Sommers's room, a left turn, down a short length of corridor up three steps to the Stone Building and another hard left leading to the corridor of the fortress-like tower at the southwest corner of the building. The rooms were ideally located for a Presidential sojourn, perhaps even a siege. Since they were at the apex of a right angle formed by the two corridors, an agent posted at that corner could easily give full visual attention to the main corridor without being distracted by any activity on his right in the shorter hallway leading from the Rock Building.

Agent Kenner was in his assigned post by the door of room 571.

"Jerry, I take it the Roosevelts are safely tucked away?"

"Yes, sir," replied Kenner, "although corralling those two youngins is a little like trying to stuff a mountain lion down a rabbit hole. Pretty quiet in there now, though."

Sommers checked his watch. It was just 6:00 PM.

"I guess Mrs. Roosevelt is used to it by now. She's had a lot of practice with Theodore Jr. and Kermit, to say nothing of Alice and Ethel. Keep a sharp eye, Jerry. I'd best go in and see what the President has on his mind."

Sommers knocked quietly on the door of 571. From within came a booming high pitch command, clearly the President's voice.

"If Agent Kenner has no objection, identify yourself and come aboard." Having served for a time as Assistant Secretary of the Navy, the President often delighted in using nautical terms almost as much as he enjoyed employing the vernacular of the wild west.

Kenner initiated the standard routine, which called for the agent on duty to announce in a loud voice the name of the visitor before the door would be opened from within, either by the President's personal secretary or by another staff person. It was a rule that the President would never open a closed door which did not provide some vision by way of a window or port.

The door was opened by the President's secretary, William Loeb, Jr., who welcomed Sommers and stepped out into the corridor, having been temporarily relieved in observance with the President's wish to discuss directly with Sommers some subject of confidentiality.

"Come in, Joseph, come in," the President sang out. "What do you think of this?" The President waved his arm about the large circular sitting room, comfortably appointed with two rather overstuffed sofas and matching chairs and a massive mahogany banquet table to one side that could easily accommodate ten people. A crackling fire had been set in the ornate neoclassic styled fireplace fitted, as other Mohonk fireplaces, with miniature Romanesque columns supporting two separate mantels, one above the other, backed by beveled plate-glass mirrors and set off by several antique oriental vases filled with fresh flowers.

The curved west tower wall of the suite was set with three large, double hung, single-pane windows and a glass door leading to a balcony. These provided an irresistible view of the Rondout Valley and the Catskill Mountains. The placement of the windows gave the appearance, from the perspective of one entering the room, of living landscapes in a distinguished Victorian art gallery.

Sommers, in a sweeping glance, observed the room and its contents, noting the door to an adjoining room and the location of the bathroom and closet near the main door from the corridor. The murmur of young voices indicated the presence of Mrs. Roosevelt and the two boys in the adjoining room.

"Very proper quarters for a President it would seem, sir," he observed. Inwardly he thought it was well secured as long as the President drew the curtains in the early evening, eliminating the off-chance possibility that a marksman's bullet fired from a balcony set forward from the western face of the adjoining building, uncomfortably in line with the projecting tower suite, would find its target. He must remember to inform his men to check the windows in late afternoon and to inform maid service to draw the curtains in the absence of Presidential propriety.

"Sit down, Sommers, I've got something here to show you." The President wasn't wasting any words. Sommers would rather have remained standing since the President showed no sign of halting the restless pacing he had begun almost immediately upon Sommers's entrance.

"Take a look at this and tell me what you think." The President drew from his coat pocket a crumpled bit of paper and thrust it into Sommers's hand. Sommers smoothed the paper against his palm. It was a note with words cut from a newspaper pasted somewhat haphazardly upon what appeared to be a page from a child's copy book. The crude words spelled: ALL RULERS SHOULD BE EXTERMINATED!

"Do those words sound familiar to you, Sommers?" T.R. barked out.

"A slogan of the Anarchists, I believe, sir. How did you come by this, Mr. President?" Sommers studied the note as he rose abruptly, his action, in effect, arresting the President in his pacing.

"The words are from a fanatic, wouldn't you say, Sommers?" Roosevelt continued, disallowing any comment from Sommers, "a fanatical anarchist who would dare to approach the President of the United States close enough to thrust this confounded scrap of venial uttering into his coat pocket."

Sommers had seen Roosevelt's anger a number of times, never aimed at him but at selected political opponents and often the business men who headed the big trusts. 'Robber Barons, loggerheads and mugwamps,' Roosevelt called them. Men who threatened T.R.'s ideas of reforms but up till now, never his person. The anger the President displayed at this moment differed from the anger he usually reserved for 'dolts and idiots' of opposite persuasion. This was the anger of a prize fighter who had just discovered his opponent had secreted brass knuckles in his gloves.

Roosevelt's face, contorted by his fury, calmed momentarily and his high-pitched voice dropped several decibels as he said, "Sommers, this happened in the crowd at New Paltz as I was moving along shaking hands. You're not to blame; you've warned me time and time again about the dangers of Presidential hob-nobbing with the populace. Still, that's what a President or any public official, high or low, may find it to be his duty from time to time. Myself, I don't give a rap about being shot, but to threaten the person of the President of the United States, the leader of the world's greatest democracy and free world, is not to be tolerated. This is an attack against the highest estate of the people of this nation and, as such, an attack upon each and every law abiding citizen who strives to do his duty, provide for his family and create a great country with privileges and justice for all classes of people, be they rich, poor or totally indigent."

Roosevelt was getting into stride, Sommers thought. This was turning into a major oratory. He had to carefully draw the President back to the main issue: the fact that a fanatic had gotten close enough to the President to, yes, shoot him, if that had been his objective. Sommers and his men would have been powerless to prevent him. "Sommers," the President usually addressed Sommers by his last name when he wanted to emphasize line of duty talk as opposed to pleasantries of the day conversation. "Sommers, do you remember what that crazy anarchist, Leon Czolgosz said when he confessed to shooting McKinley?" Without waiting for Sommers's reply, Roosevelt continued his verbal rampage. "He said he was only following Emma Goldman's doctrine that all rulers should be exterminated." The President buried a fist in the palm of his hand.

"I declare, Sommers, that woman and all her anarchist followers should have been rounded up years ago. Their unceasing mischief and fulmination against world order and the moral authority of government by the people have a cast a shadow of terrorism over all the decent and responsible leaders of government everywhere. Who ever wrote that note and stuck it in my pocket deserves to be thrown into a jail cell, if not summarily lined up against a wall and shot in the same manner that these anarchists propose to do away with governments and their leaders.

"Do you know, Sommers, these anarchists are known to meet regularly in London in the Soho district. Following President McKinley's assassination, the London police raided one of their dens of iniquity and found a list of world leaders targeted for elimination. McKinley's name was on that very list, and it would appear from this dastardly note that my name is now taking McKinley's place."

Roosevelt had been pacing furiously as he spoke without any apparent intention of soliciting Sommers's response, even though his declamations were framed as questions. Sommers, of course, realized this and patiently waited for the rip tide of Roosevelt's anger to ebb long enough for him to interject his own reflection on the matter of the note. The chance came as Roosevelt paused, the 'tide' seeping back into the ocean swell for a moment. Sommers took the opportunity.

"Mr. President, this note, more than likely, does not reflect, I believe, a serious premeditation against you. Most assassins or murderers are not likely to wave red flags of warning before striking."

"Dash it, Sommers, don't you think I realize that? It's not the attempt or the prospect of the attempt on my life that angers me. It's the insult and the assault on this office, the highest elected position in a free government by the people, that makes my buttons pop."

If you knew of the ramblings of one Mrs. Marcus Sidon, wife of your armaments expert, Sommers thought, you'd pop more than a few buttons. Sommers was not prepared to divulge that information, not yet. He still had nothing whatever to go on. What was the connection between the note and the Sidon conspiracy?—if there was indeed such a conspiracy. Sommers didn't think there was any, but it muddied the waters. It reminded him of his experiences patrolling on Broadway in New York in the 90's. It was like looking over your shoulder to ward off the approach of a runaway horse while straight ahead a robber with a pistol drawn comes tearing out of the National City Bank.

"Mr. President," he jumped in, "I shall alert the men to this development. As you may surmise, we've already screened all the Mountain House employees with the helpful cooperation of the Smiley family. The guest list has passed muster with Major Hertzog and your able secretary, Mr. Loeb. If there are any strangers or unknowns hovering around, we'll smoke them out."

It sounded brave and ostensibly reasonable, but Sommers, and for that matter the President as well, knew that they were reduced to small boys whistling as they passed through a grave yard in the dark when it came to shadow-boxing with unknown assailants having the single minded purpose of eliminating the President.

The President eased into a chair opposite Sommers and motioned Sommers to sit once again. "Joseph, you know you don't get to be President by lecturing to a local chapter of a Women's Christian Temperance Union on the evils of drink. The road to the Presidency may appear to be a popularity contest—kissing babies and smiling at swooning females and promising prosperity for American business with full dinner pails for the working men of this great country, but along the way a man makes himself a passel of enemies. That is typical of any man who dares to strike out in new directions, explore new frontiers. I've been that kind of pioneer all my life. I've ridden saddle-weary miles through the Badlands of the Dakotas, led men to heroic achievements during war beyond whatever they thought they could ever attain on their own. Brave men have become heroes at my urging and brave men have died under my command. I have never shirked my duty no matter where it has led me. And I shall not be moved now by some shadowy threat from some cowardly minion that sneaks through the underbrush like some hyena waiting for an opportunity to attack some helpless prey. We're not helpless, Joseph. We'll beat these blackguards at their own game because we are in the right, and the forces of right shall prevail. Bully they will."

Sommers marveled at how T.R. could turn a conversation regarding a security problem into a full blown declaration regarding the rights of the common man, the common good and the inevitable supreme role T.R. himself believed he had to play in the destiny of America. It was very close to a religious experience to hear the President carry on in such circumstances. Sommers felt like a man walking down the sawdust trail of a summertime church camp meeting. Roosevelt always inspired in him a zeal to exert untapped energies to assure that no harm should come to this man of the people who, for his rather ordinary stature, stood head and shoulder above those of the highest ranks of men that surrounded him.

The President adjusted his pince-nez and bounced out of

his chair, hand aimed at Sommers. Sommers rose awkwardly, caught unaware at the President's sudden upward thrust, an action not dissimilar from a ruffled grouse breaking away from a thick cover, exploding into the air and jolting the wits out of anyone who might have come too close to the bird's habitat.

"Joseph," said the President, "my complete confidence and trust rest with you. I shall put this matter aside now that I know I have the right person in place to deal with such perfidious mad men who would dare disrupt our country's march toward lasting peace and prosperity."

Sommers turned to the President's outstretched hand and winced as he felt the iron grip of T.R., vise-like, his arm pumping up and down like a well handle. T.R. broke the connection abruptly. He walked slowly toward the center window in the west wall.

"There is one other matter of considerable importance that will occupy my calendar here at Mohonk, Joseph." He turned to Sommers, his face was solemn. "Such a matter must not be compromised or placed in any kind of jeopardy, and the nature of such business must be kept top secret."

"Yes sir, of course, sir," Sommers uttered, wondering what new adventure the President had in mind.

"No doubt you have observed the Japanese gentlemen and his wife in the company of my secretary, Mr. Loeb," Roosevelt began.

"Yes, sir, a distinguished couple."

T.R. continued. "Baron Takahira is a representative of the Prime Minister of Japan and is here in mutual accordance between the Minister and myself to informally discuss the status of the war between Japan and Russia which has been going on unceasingly now for more than nine months, resulting in bloody casualties and mutual destruction for both nations." Roosevelt hardly paused. "It is not in the interest of America that these two countries should grind each other down in such a fashion that one or the other should emerge victorious, thus upsetting the balance of power in the Pacific. Further stability and peace in Asia requires that the Russians and Japanese cease pursuing their territorial prerogatives. An overwhelming victory on either side would result in a deep threat to the territorial integrity of China, to the Open Door Policy, and, in general, to other American interests in the Far East.

"The Japanese envoy and his charming wife are here, as far as the general public is concerned, as guests of the Smiley family. Not for a moment are they to be thought of as under the sanctions of the U.S. Government. They will not be seated at the head table this evening. As you must know from your table assignments, they will be in your company at your table, Joseph."

Once again the President, thought Sommers, reveals his remarkable attention to details, stage-managing the operation of the evening program so as to insure that all of his particular interests and objectives are realized.

"Baron Takahira, Senator Lodge and myself will be discussing later the implications of this dreadful war with an eye toward implementing more formal negotiations in the near future. We need to bring this bloody and useless conflict to an end before half the nations of Europe begin to assess their stakes in the proceedings and complicate the entire business by sticking their noses into the beehive.

"No word of our talks must escape these grounds. The American press and the international press will play this episode up to a fare-thee-well if they get wind of it. The Czar and the Kaiser, to say nothing of the French and certain English do-gooders, might well characterize such discussions as my trespassing in their backyard or taking sides. After all, we don't take lightly to Europeans trampling roughshod over the Monroe Doctrine. As for taking the side of Japan against Russia, which is entirely false but certainly what the press would construe if some muck-raker digs up that I've been talking to the emperor's envoy, well, you can imagine the effects of that bomb shell exploding all over the front pages of the *New York Times.* No, both sides must be brought to the table in due time and a just and equitable settlement determined for the sake of both countries and hope for peace in the Pacific hemisphere. If I can be of some assistance in ending this remorseful slaughter—and that's what it is, Joseph, make no bones about that—then it shall be my duty to do so. Meanwhile, we must see to America's best interest for the immediate days ahead and for the future.

"Japan is going to be a giant of a nation one day if she continues her present pace. We must bring her into the family of nations and guard against unbridled expansionism if we are not to fight a disastrous war in the future with this remarkable country.

"Japan's interests, indeed, parallel our own more than we might realize today. We must never allow those interests to become divergent or we will find ourselves sending our brave young soldiers into the rising sun to be cut down like stalks of rice. We would, of course, be victorious in a war with Japan, but our losses would be such that I doubt if there would be one family out of ten that would not be grievously deprived of a son, a brother or a father.

"I firmly believe, Joseph, the destiny of the United States and the world family of nations today is to keep the peace by assuming a ready position of armed strength to, indeed, be prepared to accept the challenge of going to war if we must go to war to quell any tyranny in any form or substance it assumes. That is the key to lasting peace.

"We may well be called upon before many years have past—let there be no mistake about it—to apply such aggressive but righteous force of arms upon the European continent. "We came very near to such conflict in our own hemisphere during the Venezuelan affair in 1902 when Germany and England decided to collect their long overdue debts at gunpoint. This nation, and quite possibly the European powers as well as our South American neighbors, were saved the calamity of what might have been a bloody international war by successful arbitration of the dispute at the Hague Tribunal. It was seen as an action that I strongly endorsed, but I was prepared to enforce a settlement in other terms if adjudication had not been successful.

"Indeed, the Smiley brothers and their families have invited me here to Mohonk to enlist my support in their quest to join all nations together in common agreement for international arbitration—a glorious idea but not pragmatic in these days of unstable regimes and downright outlaw governments. The nations of this world in which we live, Joseph, are not yet disposed to do away with their armies and meekly surrender what they conceive as their national prerogatives in the name of conciliation and compromise. That would be like a cattle rancher confronting a gang of rustlers stealing a herd of his prize heifers and suggesting that they all throw down their Colt .45's and retire to the Dead Wood Saloon for a round of whisky and negotiations.

"Well, I should have a bit more to say about all of this at dinner this evening." The President moved toward Sommers, his face considerably more relaxed than when Sommers first encountered his umbrage stirred up by the surreptitious note. "So, Joseph, there you have it. I doubt if my cabinet members are, at this point, better informed than you are in the pressing affairs of state as of this date. But then, none of them are responsible for my protection."

Roosevelt gave Sommers a broad smile that seemed to miraculously brighten the entire suite as if someone had turned on extra lights. T.R. once again pumped Sommers's hand in a final, friendly vigorous shake that signaled the interview was at an end.

The President reached for his watch. "My goodness, Joseph, I've kept you a full forty minutes. You must return to your duties and your charming wife who I have not yet had time to greet. Please give her my regards and petition her forgiveness on my behalf for keeping you from your preparations for tonight's dinner. I'll look forward to seeing her later."

"Thank you, sir. I'm sure Mrs. Sommers will look forward to greeting you as well. I shall see to my men and check the final arrangements for dinner."

"Bully, Joseph, I can see you've got the saddle up and the cinch tight." He paused. "Hark now, to my instructions—not a word about this Japanese business, not even to Helena."

"Yes, sir, you have my word on it."

"Very well then, off with you, Joseph, and send that secretary of mine in if you would. I've just got time for a couple of letters before the Smiley brothers appear and traipse off with this family of mine to the dining hall."

Sommers opened the heavy oak door and stepped into the corridor. William Loeb, Jr., who had been waiting patiently in the hall for the President's call reentered the suite, and the massive door closed with a soft thud. Kenner had been joined by Agent Yost, who had come on duty while Sommers was talking to the President.

"Now, men," Sommers said, "only one of you need remain here after the President and his family goes to dinner. That will be you, Yost. Sachs and Meyers will be reporting shortly and accompany the President with the Smileys down to the dining hall. You join them Kenner. You will be relieved, Yost, when Jerry here takes over this station following dinner. They'll save a dinner for you down in the kitchen, but get back up here as soon as you finish your dinner. I don't need to tell you to maintain a high alert tonight and don't ask me why this night should be any different than any other."

The agents nodded, and Sommers turned toward the passage leading off to the Rock Building, anxious to get back to Helena and to freshen up before the gala celebration.

As he approached room 490, Sommers felt a flutter in his chest, a slight palpitation—a totally unconscious reflex indicating that his nervous system still had not yet caught up with his rational mind regarding the brief time warp he had seemingly experienced earlier in the day.

Nonsense, he reassured himself. He was simply experiencing a delayed physiological reaction that would soon pass as he once again entered room 490 and greeted Helena, who by this time would be well along in her dress and toilette for the evening celebration. Nonetheless, he paused before the door, his mind alert and unaccepting that there should be anything amiss upon his entering.

Unbelievable, he thought, how the senses dictated to the mind, often controlling and counteracting to its perceptions, unwilling to accept a subordinate role in the measure of events and participate willingly in the prescription for rational action. It was something like placing a foot in the cold water of a spring-fed lake with the intent of submerging one's body for a refreshing swim. The senses always screamed and warned against entering such frigid currents, no matter how many times the mind had previously forced the body below the inhospitable surface, always to find upon immersion that the senses accepted their new environment and adapted quickly to the cold temperatures, relishing a new and unexpected comfort. But the cycle was repetitive, body and senses consistent in refusal to accept, without trial, what the mind prescribed. Still, all and all, Sommers concluded, the dichotomy of mind and body was a miraculous factor that worked to ensure survival.

Sommers knocked softly on the door, at the same time turning the knob to enter, this time less intrusively than his earlier arrival.

Chapter Twenty

Helena was standing before the bureau mirror, radiant in a rust-colored velvet and satin gown cut low and off the shoulders. A gold chain with a brilliant emerald pendant hovered over her bosom at that mystical and sensuous point of cleavage which suggested, in the gracious uplift of her breasts, exotic pleasures to come for that one man of special designation she had chosen to receive her ardor. Matching emerald pendant earrings, like green icicles, flickered in the soft glow of the dresser lights. Cloud-white taffeta gloves, elbow length, and brushed gold evening slippers completed her dress. As she turned from the mirror, Helena smiled and curtsied.

"Will I do, my darling Joseph?"

Sommers could not restrain a gasp. Helena, he thought, was surely the most beautiful woman in Washington. In Helena's case, his senses and his mind merged in total agreement of her charms.

"I doubt, Helena, that this distinguished assemblage of party faithful will ever note the President's presence in your company. It's a wise thing that you and I are not occupying seats at the head table. As it is you will eclipse every woman in attendance, poor things. I should think that they could turn off at least half of the dining hall lights once you make your entrance. You are incandescent."

Helena laughed. "There you go again, my Joseph—you are a great flatterer, but I love it." She snuggled close to Sommers and gave him a light, velvet kiss.

"Mustn't smear my lip rouge, dear. I shall give the President a special smile. I wish him to secretly covet me and quietly suffer knowing that I am yours alone."

Sommers smiled. "Such merciless treatment. Poor Mr. President. To think he will be forever denied the excitement of your embrace."

Sommers looked around the room as he held Helena. Initially mesmerized by Helena's visage upon entering, he suddenly realized that he had not passed through any curtain to another time. It seemed truly over. The door to 490, henceforth, would not lead to other worlds, and the corridors of the Mountain House were finally freed from the shades of strangely garbed guests of future years.

"Joseph, dearest, have you departed from me?" Helena looked up puzzled by Sommers's brief silence and pensive mood.

"My love," Sommers said as he stepped back from Helena, slightly, "I confess to an advanced state of Nirvana induced by this image before me that is quite overpowering for a mere mortal. However, I feel myself coming back to the world of the flesh accompanied by a surge of lust that I doubt I can resist without help from heaven." He tightened his hold around Helena's waist. Helena stroked Sommers's cheek with her right hand and drew back slightly.

"Joseph, you will have heaven on your head, indeed, as well as the President, if you do not ready yourself for tonight's festivities. You really must get dressed. It's nearly 7:15."

"Right, my love, prepare my threads and stay out of range lest you trigger the unpredictable forces of raw nature."

Sommers disappeared into the bath while Helena laid out Sommers's dress clothes—white tie and tails. The evening celebration would entail an etiquette very like an official State dinner, only instead of foreign diplomats to be recognized, it was the President himself that would be the subject of honor and adoration.

As Sommers dressed, his mind was busily reviewing a series of steps that would ensue upon the initiation of the evening's events. First, everyone was expected to be seated no later than 8:15 PM, even though the dinner hour had been announced for eight. There were always a few stragglers in any group of 200 or so people. The President and his family, escorted by the Smiley brothers and their wives, would make their entrance exactly at 8:15 PM.

The Smiley family, being Quakers, disallowed music in worship services but often encouraged modest musical programs at Mohonk, particularly during the international conferences held at the Mountain House. For tonight, a concession had been made to hire a string quartet to supply dinner music. As a special tribute to T.R., the quartet was instructed to play *There'll be a Hot Time in the Old Town Tonight* upon the President's entrance. It was a Presidential favorite, stemming from the days of the Rough Riders when the Colonel led the First volunteer cavalry on its victorious escapade through Cuban cane fields and jungles and up the slopes of San Juan Ridge.

At 7:45, Mr. and Mrs. Joseph Sommers stepped out into the fourth floor corridor of the Rock Building and commenced their passage down the long shrouded corridors of the Mountain House, joining on the way a growing phalange of brilliantly dressed guests, all having as their destination the beautiful, bountiful tables d'hôte of the Mohonk dinning hall.

Chapter Twenty-one

The entrance to the dining hall was artfully draped in swirls of red, white and blue bunting gathered on each side of the portal with swatches of stars on fields of blue, held in place by golden eagles. At the very top of the archway, the Presidential seal was affixed, and underneath, a wide white banner, ablaze with the words 'Welcome T.R.' stretched across the opening. Although no one, not even members of the press, called the President 'T.R.' to his face, practically everyone employed the initials at one time or another when referring to him. The President was aware of this liberty assumed by the public, both friends and strangers alike, and, privately, he was pleased because it lessened the distance between himself and the man on the street.

Upon entering the dining hall, there could be seen rows of American flags hanging from the highest two-story sections of the paneled ceilings, giving the appearance of a high-powered campaign rally about to embrace crowds of partisan Republican faithful with an unending volley of speeches extolling the virtues of every subject dear to the American voter—from apple pie to motherhood. About half way up the soaring fireplace that reached up to the rafters was another gleaming banner which stated, 'Congratulations, President Roosevelt, 26th President of the United States.' Beneath the banner, on a raised platform forward from the fireplace, a string quartet was playing incidental music from Mendelssohn's *Mid-Summer Night's Dream*. To the right of the entrance there was a long head table, on another raised platform, centered and facing the length of the hall to the west looking toward the Catskill Mountain ranges.

Daniel Smiley and Mrs. Effie Smiley were stationed at the entrance to greet guests. It had been decided that Albert and Mrs. Eliza Smiley would escort the President and his family from the Presidential Suite to the dining hall. Sommers and Helena took their place in the line that had formed at the entrance as Daniel and Effie Smiley cheerfully greeted each guest.

Sommers looked into the small parlor on the right where a few hours ago in the heart of the night he had listened to Mrs. Sidon pour out her frightful ruminations regarding the plot to assassinate the President. The room was empty now except for an attractive middle-aged lady with gossamer hair who was busily examining a small, cloisonné vase filled with straw flowers, sitting delicately on the fireplace mantel. At that moment a distinguished gentleman entered the parlor from an interior door to the left of the fireplace. Sommers recognized him as the British diplomat, Cecil Spring-Rice, who was also a close personal friend of the President.

The table charts Sommers had been given by Major Hertzog indicated that Spring-Rice would be seated at the head table along with the Smiley families, T.R.'s long time mentor and confidante, Senator Henry Cabot Lodge, and the minister who would deliver the invocation.

The hall was filling up quite rapidly, Sommers observed as he and Helena finally reached Daniel and Effie Smiley. However, the corridor behind was jammed all the way to the Grove parlor with fashionable couples—their conversational murmurs punctuated with occasional exclamations of delight as they excitedly speculated on the evening's activities and happily reviewed the chain of events that had propelled them to this special ceremony of dining with the President of the United States.

A warm greeting was extended by the Smileys and a particularly gracious acknowledgment by Mrs. Smiley of Helena's elegant gown. "My dear, you are beautiful. Mr. Sommers, you must be quite proud of your lovely wife."

"Thank you, ma'am, indeed I am. I consider myself the envy of all men," Sommers responded with a proud grin.

"Well said, my boy." Daniel Smiley shook Sommers's hand almost as vigorously as had the President a short time earlier. Smiley's years of working on the many trails and roads of the Mountain House had hardened his muscles while the bracing mountain weather and raw seasons of winter had bred in him a robust nature and vigor reflected in his leathery complexion and twinkling eyes.

Sommers and Helena were gathered in hand by a pretty young hostess in a starched white pinafore who floated across the floor like a summer moth. She led them to their assigned places at a large round table sparkling with crystal goblets that reflected shards of yellow light from a candle center piece surrounded by colored autumn leaves and sprouts of pine needles. It was a fitting touch which extended the beauty of the fast fading autumn.

There were three other couples already seated. Sommers knew the table assignments since he had consulted with Major Hertzog on the disposition of his agents who enjoyed strategic but well separated locations. He had seen to it that he had been assigned to General Sidon's table in view of Mrs. Sidon's revelations. As they reached the table, the General rose, as did the two other men—one, the diminutive Japanese diplomat that Roosevelt had mentioned would be in attendance—the other, a stocky, smiling State Department official whom Sommers did not recognize. Sommers assumed his most professional front, hoping that the General would not see in his eyes the flicker of suspicion that he felt was as obvious as a nervous tick. Mrs. Sidon gave Sommers a wary look.

"Good evening, Sommers, Mrs. Sommers," the General said with a gracious smile.

Strange, Sommers thought, Sidon was certainly calm, cool and cordial—not a hint of scheming in his almost syrupy welcome. Was this the man who threatened the office and person of the President, leader of the world's greatest democracy and likely the most powerful nation in the world since the days of the Roman Caesars?

"General, I see you weathered the trip back up the mountain very well."

Sommers felt an almost irresistible impulse to ask Sidon the identity of the dark stranger he had met at the New Paltz station. Instead, he acknowledged Mrs. Sidon with a polite nod as the General responded.

"A real challenge you have, Sommers, trying to safeguard the President in a crowd like that. I shouldn't like to trade places with you."

"Well, General, your work with armaments isn't exactly like brewing a cup of tea, is it?" Sommers really wanted to ask Sidon how small a bomb could be made. Say, small enough to fit the package Sidon had exchanged with the stranger? Helena broke in.

"General, why don't you introduce us to these nice people so you poor men can sit down and relax."

"Why, of course, Mrs. Sommers, please forgive me." The General gestured to his left toward the Japanese diplomat.

"May I present Baron Takahira and his wife, Hitomi, visiting from Japan as guests of the Smiley family. And this is Richard and Maryann Sturgis of the State Deptartment, Far Eastern affairs."

The Baron and Madame Takahira smiled and bowed demurely. The Sturgises beamed happily at the new arrivals. How-do-you-do's swirled back and forth and the men reclaimed their seats as the last of the guests filtered past Daniel and Effie Smiley and were escorted to their tables.

The music abruptly changed cadence to a brisk Sousa march, *American Patrol*, as Daniel and Mrs. Smiley led a small parade of distinguished guests to the head table. The assembled company clapped and rose, signaling acknowledgment of the main event, the President's imminent appearance.

The members of the cortege took their appointed places, and everyone turned to look expectantly toward the dining hall entrance where there appeared, as if on cue, Agents Kenner, Sachs and Meyers, followed slightly behind by Albert and Eliza Smiley. The agents halted and stepped back away from the passage way. Mr. and Mrs. Smiley had stopped momentarily and were engaged in speaking to someone directly behind them. The Smileys then turned and briskly marched to the center and up the risers to the head table. As they took their places and turned toward the entrance, they joined in applause as did the head table guests.

The musicians abruptly broke off the Sousa march and segued into a chorus of *It'll be a Hot Time in the Old Town Tonight.*

As the opening notes rose to the ceiling of the great hall, President and Mrs. Roosevelt appeared in the entrance way,

T.R. grinning from ear to ear with both arms up-raised. Mrs. Roosevelt, smiling and demure, basked softly and assuredly in the limelight of her husband. The two Roosevelt boys, their jackets festooned with 'T.R. FOR PRESIDENT' buttons, clutched the hands of their mother, excited by this infectious tribute to their father. They happily waved a hand at their father's prompting.

The family group moved slowly to the center, Roosevelt looking all the world like a circus ringmaster preparing to announce a stupendous act. His enjoyment of the ceremony knew no bounds. He had just won an election in his own right in a landslide despite concerted opposition by his enemies to sweep him out of office—never mind the might of the political bosses, the trusts, the power brokers who swore to defeat him. He had criss-crossed the nation to wherever railroad tracks led and to places they didn't. He had traveled into dusty western towns, along the grimy industrial corridors and coal towns of the East.

Wherever the working man took his lunch pail, Roosevelt had been there, appealing to the farmers, the miners, the steelworkers, the office workers and the stevedores of the cities and ports of America. He had ridden atop the crest of a great tide of labor and working class citizens that drowned the tycoons and indulgent rich who sought to control him. His victory gave voice and fulfillment to the words he so often pounded out on the campaign trail: "This country will not be a permanently good place for any of us to live unless we make it a reasonably good place for all of us to live."

The First Family mounted the risers to the head table, the President shaking hands with all the other guests—men and women he knew on a day-to-day basis but, in the protocol of political ceremony, greeting them all as if he had just been newly introduced to them. After the President and Mrs. Roosevelt finally progressed to their chairs at the center of the table, Archie and Quentin were steered to their seats each on either side of their father and their mother—a position that would allow slight mischief, if any.

Albert Smiley raised up his hand in a gesture that clearly requested a cessation to the thunderous applause. The assembly grudgingly acquiesced as Smiley addressed them,

"Mr. President and Mrs. Roosevelt, Master Archie and Master Quentin," Smiley winked at the two boys, "distinguished leaders and friends, good evening all. On behalf of our President and his family and my family as well, may I welcome you to the Mohonk Mountain House and wish for you a bountiful visit with us as we celebrate the election victory of the 26th President of the United States of America."

Smiley turned and ushered the President forward. Once again the hall resounded with the delirious response of the partisan multitude, hands clapping and now even feet stamping in what could only have been described as sheer, unbridled delight at having been invited to taste the fruits at the President's banquet of victory.

Roosevelt, at least a half head short of Albert Smiley, nevertheless loomed ever larger than life as he stepped forward, awash in the rolling waves of applause. Arms up-raised, eyes twinkling, his teeth luminous rows of whitish square ivory, the President's face was fixed in a grin so broad that it seemed his own ears were in danger of being swallowed up should his hemispheric smile extend any further east or west.

His bright high-pitched voice rent the air over and around the diners, finding its mark like a pitch fork thrown into a pile of hay.

"Good friends," he began, "we are indebted this wonderful harvest evening to these remarkable Smiley brothers and their full hearted wives and families for this gracious invitation to celebrate the beginning of a new chapter in the life of this great country of America."

Once again the hall let loose in a roaring tide of applause. The President raised an arm to soften the response.

"Since with your devoted and dedicated support, I won the election, I need not launch this evening into the normal polemics expected of politicians running for office, but instead my words will be those of gratitude and thanksgiving for extending to me your trust and forbearance for four more years of peace and prosperity and a chance to build this nation of ours into a citadel of democracy and justice—an America the beautiful that will continue to flower and set an example for the nations of the world in this great 20th century that lies ahead."

More applause—deafening this time.

"Now I believe it would be best if you all gave the utmost attention to this festive feast the Mountain House chefs are about to set before us before digesting anymore of what I might dish up for you. I should not wish to be guilty of destroying your appetite for the delights of the table with my rhetoric about what I believe is good for you and our great country."

A surge of spontaneous laughter and more applause swirled from the assembly. People exchanged glances across the table as if to say, 'That's our Teddy.' The President gestured toward Albert Smiley, who once again took to the floor holding up both hands in a motion to quell the chorus of admirers.

"Ladies and gentlemen, may we bow our heads as we ask our beloved friend, The Right Reverend Philip Stafford Moxom, to offer the invocation."

Heads lowered reverently as the patriarchal clergyman made his way to Smiley's side at the center of the head table.

In a ponderous, even sonorous voice, the Reverend began his prayer, beseeching the blessings of the Almighty upon the occasion of the 26th President's victorious election.

He presented for the Almighty a petition of special blessings on all present, the Congress of the United States, the Judges of the Supreme Court, the Army, the Navy, the poor and suffering of the nation's cities, teachers and educators of the great universities and colleges, farmers and workers in the fields and the factories, the nations and governments of the world and all world leaders. Lastly, he uttered an exhortation for peace among men, the end of war and strife and the elimination of disease and suffering among those less prosperous than ourselves. It was a work of art, a pastoral prayer par excellence, one that the Reverend, no doubt, had worked on with verve and singular semantic skill for days on end. But after eight minutes of invoking the Almighty without a pause, there began a restless shuffling of feet among the still standing guests that one could only interpret as boorish impatience. Even T.R. began to shift his weight from foot to foot, and Archie and Quentin, without the strong restraining parental hands upon their shoulders, would have been indistinguishable from two jack rabbits playing a game of hop scotch.

With a final uplift of his stolid face towards the heavens and a bold forward thrust of his jaw, for what could only be categorized as a dramatic gesture executed for those unrepentant heads, yet unbowed, and for whose eyes were unclosed, the good Reverend raised his palms in terminal supplication, his voice slowing and lowering to a deep base, very nearly like a phonograph winding down.

"And we therefore do beseech Thee, oh, Lord, to hear our prayers in the name of the Father, the Son and the Holy Ghost, Amen."

There was a pronounced scraping of restless feet and a brisk rustling of silk and taffeta gowns as the diners responded to Albert Smiley's call for everyone to be seated following Reverend Moxom's interminable invocation. Albert Smiley thought it judicious, after the lengthy but certainly thorough blessing, to note briefly to his guests that following dinner and a brief address by the President, there would be a short evening concert by the Hudson Valley String Quartet, which, he noted appreciatively, had rendered such a rousing musical accompaniment to the President's entrance. Another round of applause issued from the now comfortably seated diners.

Albert Smiley's gracious and beneficent smile, as he took his place at the head table next to the Roosevelts, seemed to signal expectant waiters and waitresses, who now burst forth upon the assemblage like a covey of prairie quail.

At the Sommers's table, Joseph and Helena exchanged glances. "I can certainly see why the Quaker worship services are conducted in silence," said Sommers. "Seems like a good idea after listening to sawdust trail preachers like the good Reverend there."

"Joseph," Helena gently rebuked her husband, although she secretly agreed with him. "Your irreverence is exceeded only by your good looks—lucky for you."

Baron Takahira smiled. "In America, Christians seem to have many different houses in which, strangely, they all appear to worship the same God. You have Quakers like the Smiley family, Methodists and Presbyterians and Baptists and Episcopalians, to say nothing of Catholics. It is indeed a rather puzzling and somewhat exhausting phenomenon for us in Japan to understand."

Richard Sturgis, the State Department official, looked like he was about to respond to the Baron's comment but seemed to decide against it. Religion was not in his purview; he had no instructions from his superiors regarding that kind of conversational topic. His duty at Mohonk was to escort the Takahiras and avoid controversial subjects or issues. However, his sense of humor broke loose from the diplomatic strictures binding him.

"Well, you see, Baron, we Americans don't like to take chances when it comes to piling up enough credits to get us into Heaven rather than Hell. It's like baseball—"

"Baseball?" Takahira asked, then his wife touched his arm and whispered into his ear. "Ah, yes, the sport. I visited one of your coliseums and studied the game. Mildly confusing."

"Well, yes." Sturgis smiled. "Like baseball players, we Americans like to touch all the bases, you know—collect all the runs we've got coming to us before the end of the ninth." Sturgis chuckled. "If we can't make it with one religion, we can always find another to try." The Baron smiled at Sturgis's ebullience and borderline sacrilege.

Helena decided to engage the Baron. "Mr. Sturgis's levity, notwithstanding, I fear you are quite right, Baron. We Christians have difficulty agreeing on a lot of things—such as whether we should kneel, sit down or stand up when we worship. We have an especially difficult time agreeing on the concept of Heaven and Hell, particularly as to who may, upon the basis of our earthly life, be eligible for Heaven. No doubt, those of us who are in the habit of consigning to the fires of Hell our fellow so-called believers who may not agree with our dogma may be surprised to find them as our neighbors in Heaven."

Baron Takahira laughed. "Very well put, Mrs. Sommers. It would seem that in the final analysis that all paths that lead to God are good. That is the way we Japanese believe. This is confusing to your missionaries that come to our land and seek to have us cast aside our Gods and beliefs and substitute your God in their place. We say to them, we like your God, we like your Jesus, but why must we discard our Gods to accept yours? Are the Heavens so finite that all of our Gods cannot live together in mutual respect and in peace as the people upon the earth strive to do?"

Madame Takahira smiled in obvious concert. Although she appeared to understand her husband's dissertation on Eastern and Western religious differences, Sommers had the feeling her English was somewhat limited to 'Good morning,' 'Good evening,' 'How do you do?' and 'Thank you.' This was born out almost immediately as Helena addressed her.

"Madame Takahira, have you been in the United States very long?"

Hitomi Takahira held her hands up to her face, smiled beautifully and giggled ever so slightly as she looked to the Baron for obvious guidance.

The Baron answered for her. "Hitomi has only 'skoshi'—little English. We are here only for a visit as guests of the Smiley family for a fortnight. I had the pleasure of visiting your beautiful country several times before, but this is Hitomi's first visit. We are hoping to return again soon, thank you."

General Sidon, who appeared rather detached until that moment, remarked, "Your English is quite impeccable, Baron. I, for one, am sad to say my Japanese is absolutely nil."

"Ah yes," the Baron replied, "many Japanese in early schooling and university years now study English as a second language. You see, we much admire the United States. Ever since your Admiral Perry sailed into Tokyo Bay, we have looked even more into the rising sun, indeed—toward America for insight and inspiration. We find knowledge in copying your ways. We have, I fear, become, in your American words, a nation of copy cats."

General Sidon chuckled at the Baron's disarming wit. Even Mrs. Sidon, who up to that moment had been totally noncommunicative except for a sidelong glance or two at Sommers, smiled despite, at least to Sommers, some visible show of apprehension regarding the evening's events. Sommers could only wonder what was going through her mind as a tray of appetizers appeared at the table.

Chapter Twenty-two

The last bars of the *Star Spangled Banner*, in particular, the phrase, 'Land of the Free,' were catapulted toward the rafters. The lift-off was assisted by a statuesque diva who possessed something of the proportions of Roosevelt's favorite battleship, the U.S.S. Dewey. The diva, at a table near the Sommers's, wouldn't let go of the word, free, until nearly everyone else had dropped out for lack of breath. The string quartet, intimidated by this formidable vocal force, chose not to do battle but meekly acquiesced in the endurance contest, moving on to the 'Home of the Brave' only after taking their cue from the obdurant soprano.

During the singing, Sommers had watched the President, who was not particularly noted for his musical cadences except perhaps at the times when he had led his regiment of Rough Riders in a display of dismounted drill on a military parade ground. The President, despite the exhaustive energy he had displayed in his short but rousing after-dinner speech, nevertheless sang with spirit and gusto—his piercing tenor producing powerful decibels, posing very nearly a threat to the eardrums of his closest relatives, Mrs. Roosevelt and the two boys.

The hall swelled with applause as the quartet finished. Roosevelt thrust up his hands, fists clenched and beamed a final smile at the assembly. Sommers could not hear it but had little difficulty lip-reading Roosevelt's exclamation: "Delightful. Bully, Bully . . ." his most famous words all but smothered in the blanket of jubilation expressed by the happy party faithful sharing in the victory spoils.

A short pause, and the quartet swung, as much as a string quartet could be imagined to swing, into a hardy reprise of *Hot Time in the Old Town Tonight*. The President turned and shook hands once again with those at the head table as an entourage formed around him and Mrs. Roosevelt, who maintained a sturdy grip on her two offsprings, both of whom were generating the motions of young bear cubs looking for a tree to climb.

The group slowly moved to the hall's exit where Kenner, Sachs and Meyers, not unlike the red coated sentinels who guarded Buckingham Palace, had resumed their staunch postures following dinner. Guests thronging around the Presidential group walked them through the exit. The agents picked up the step just behind the President as they proceeded down the long hall of the Grove building toward the main parlor, where the evening musicale was to be performed.

At Sommers's table, Baron Takahira spoke first. "Ah so, your President is—how do you Americans say?—a 'spell binder.' He has the art of moving people, making them believe in him and in themselves to do great things. A wise politician, he seeks not to displease those who may disagree with him. An artful balance, indeed. He is much admired in my country."

"Still, the President has his detractors, all the same," General Sidon remarked. "There are those who always seek to do such a man harm, eh, Sommers?"

Very crafty, Sommers thought. Here's General Sidon, who, according to his wife is blatantly preparing to eliminate the President of the United States, suggesting that there are evil forces always lurking in the perimeter of the President's daily life, plotting his down fall.

Clever, nothing like a veiled suggestion of acrimony by the villain himself to cool down his own trail. He must not underestimate Sidon. Sommers decided to parry what he judged to be Sidon's obvious taunt.

"President Roosevelt has never been accused of backing away from a position that might offend those who disagree with him."

Sommers stared directly at Sidon as he spoke. Their eyes locked. Would Sidon blink first and what would it mean? Did

Sidon suspect Sommers had information? There was no sign in Sidon's visage that gave Sommers the slightest indication that the man harbored a devious thought of any kind. Indeed, he looked even friendly. That was it, of course, Sommers thought. He knew Sidon did not like him, was jealous of his close relationship with the President. His seemingly friendly guise was a ruse. Would it be proved so? Sommers didn't know what to believe. He needed more information.

Sidon broke off the eye contact, and turned to his wife as he stood up. "Alicia, we must take our leave." As Mrs. Sidon arose, the other men at the table followed suit.

"As late as it's getting to be," the General stated, "I have some work to do. The President is awaiting a report from me in connection with the arming of two new battleships he expects to wheedle out of Congress."

Mrs. Sidon cast a quick glance at Sommers, catching his eye for a brief second. Her look was unmistakable. It said, 'I must talk further with you.'

"My distinct pleasure, Baron and Madame Takahira, Mr. and Mrs. Sturgis, Mrs. Sommers," Sidon continued, "and I suppose where the President is, I'll see you, Sommers, as well." The barest hint of sarcasm was not lost on Sommers.

"Indeed," Sommers replied. He was thinking—could something significant be going on in munitions development? How really close is Sidon to the President on such matters? After all, Roosevelt did bring him into the White House for his expertise on munitions. Could Sidon be turning over government secrets to a hostile government? What in God's name was in the box he handed to the stranger in New Paltz? Why did he choose to make such a transfer in such a busy exposed location? Perhaps it really was an innocent exchange of gifts. If there was a risk of being observed in such a way as for the event to be interpreted as suspect, such an exchange could have been made almost anywhere else.

No use—there were no answers, not yet anyway. Sommers would have to rely on Mrs. Sidon for more information, that is if she had any—and if this whole conspiracy was not just wild circumspection on her part.

"My darling Joseph, you look positively vacant." Helena stood up, leaned close and knocked playfully on Sommers's forehead. "Anyone at home up there?"

Baron and Madame Takahira emitted soft giggles at Helena's attempt to refocus her husband's attention.

As the Sidons finally turned to leave, Sommers's left hand was hanging by his side. He had placed his right arm around Helena's waist and had turned toward her and the others as the Sidons brushed by him. That is, Mrs. Sidon brushed by—very close, close enough to Sommers to gently place a small note in the palm of his left hand. Sommers was startled by the move and quickly closed his hand around the bit of paper, hoping his sudden surprise was not visible to the General who had chosen, just at that moment, to turn and telegraph a parting smile. Actually, Sommers had never moved but if anyone had been carefully watching his eyes he would have noticed a sharp, barely perceptible flicker. He thrust his left hand unhurriedly into his coat pocket depositing the note safely in the dark folds of the cloth sanctuary.

The Sidons by now were at the exit. Mrs. Sidon gave a backward look at Sommers. Her face was blank but for a slight wisp of a smile that quickly faded as she turned to accompany her husband from the hall. The Baron's wife and Mrs. Sturgis stood and joined the others in preparation for leaving.

"Well," Sommers said, "I suppose we must all repair to the main parlor if we are to enjoy the musicale. Baron, Madame Takahira, Mr. & Mrs. Sturgis. Darling," Sommers turned to Helena, "shall we?"

He offered his arm and with a quiet urgency ushered Helena rather hurriedly toward the hall exit. Helena immediately sensed the abruptness of Sommers's exit and gave an equivocal smile.

"Joseph, are we preparing ourselves for competition in the potato sack races for the next 4th of July? If we are, we're bound to win with such an early start."

"I'm sorry, darling," Sommers responded, slowing his pace slightly. "It's just that I need to check on my men. Actually, the President is going to meet with Baron Takahira and Senator Lodge shortly. There are some things I must do prior to that. Suppose you join some of your friends in the main parlor and I'll get back to you as soon as I've tended to my duties."

They approached the main parlor just beyond the central staircase. Sommers kissed Helena lightly on the cheek and, with a brisk step, headed toward the elevator. He had to read Mrs. Sidon's note but needed a private corner to digest whatever message it contained. At the same time, he felt a compulsive urge to immediately check the disposition of his men who should have, by this time, reestablished their stations outside the Presidential Suite preparatory to the confidential meeting of the President with the Japanese envoy.

The elevator operator was the single occupant as Sommers stepped into the oak-paneled cubicle and conveyed his request for a fifth floor destination. He reached into his pocket, observing the operator as if he might have been a secret agent ready to snatch the note from his hand.

The operator smiled innocuously and started the car upward by pulling on a thick cable which ran through the car from ceiling to floor where it disappeared just right of the elevator door. The car, activated by its water-powered hydraulic system, moved magically upward with soft bumping noises as it ascended in its tracks built along the walls of the elevator shaft. The movement was relatively smooth and surprisingly rapid. The remarkable machinery that lifted the car to the heights of the Mountain House needed only a strong tug on the cable to start and a likewise tug to stop upon arrival on the designated floor. It was, however, not without a high degree of skill and some little experience that the average Mountain House operator managed to maneuver the elevator base in ascension or descension to match the exact level of the floor called for. Such operator skills were usually defined by how often and how insistent the operator might be required to instruct his passengers to 'step up, please,' or 'step down, please.'

Sommers stepped back in the elevator to distance himself from the operator and glanced at the note as the little car squeaked and creaked upward. The note read simply, *the parlor balcony, second floor, 2:00 AM.*, nothing else.

The message, so brief and unrevealing in its content, sparked Sommers to wonder if Mrs. Sidon was simply enraptured at the thought of staging clandestine middle of the night meetings. What if Sidon were to follow his wife at such an hour, and where the hell should Sidon be at that hour when every one else would be in bed, either in his own or, perhaps, by discreet prior arrangements, someone else's.

Mrs. Sidon's conspiracy theory needed the light of day and hard, substantive facts to be taken any more seriously, Sommers concluded as the elevator was skillfully arrested at the fifth floor with a sharp tug by the smiling operator. His face clearly demonstrated the pride of performance.

"How is that, sir?" he beamed at Sommers. "Not a wooden nickel's difference."

Sommers was expected to acknowledge the nearly perfect matching of floor levels as the operator flung open the elevator doors to the fifth floor corridor.

"Good work, son. You are indeed an operator's operator. I shall speak to the management on your behalf." Sommers tossed the words over his shoulder as he stepped out into the dimly lighted hall.

Since the President's quarters, suite 571, was in the most recently finished Stone Building where it attached to the older Rock Building, a fair distance from the elevator, Sommers had to pass along a lengthy, very shadowy corridor with two ninety-degree turns before reaching the Presidential Suite.

The corridor was morgue-like. No sounds or voices filtered from behind the massive mahogany doors lining the hallways. But if one would allow his imagination to roam, one might almost feel the presence of past guests in the darkened chambers—muted voices mingling with the soft rustling sounds of dressing and fitting as ladies and gentlement prepared for dinner or other pastimes.

One might easily imagine doors opening and closing as guests passed to and fro, enjoying the visits of friends coming and going on rounds of merriment ranging from exploring the scores of trails that criss-crossed the mountain resort to spending quiet afternoons on the croquet and tennis courts, or in the ceaseless striking and chasing of little white balls on green lawns.

The sudden sound somewhere behind him was unexpected and quite deafening, given the supposed vacancy of the fifth floor. It caught Sommers totally unaware and his right hand reached automatically for the pistol grip on his .32 Colt revolver, safely nestled in a special holster he had specially made to wear close to the left side of his chest.

Chapter Twenty-three

It was a door banging closed, there could be no doubt of that—behind and around the corner he had just now turned, beyond the iron staircases he was now passing. Sommers turned back and cautiously peered down the passage way leading to the elevator. The recessed doors on both sides of the hall were darkened, brooding, almost threatening, as if waiting to embrace and smother anyone who dared to approach and cross their thresholds.

Sommers stopped short of pulling his gun from his holster. After all, it could be a maid or serviceman on some kind of chore. Which door was it? He looked at the thresholds as he slowly proceeded down the hall. No lights showed from under the doors. No sounds came through the heavy portals. Hold on, was that a flicker of light under the door on the right?

He moved quickly to the suspect door. The room number was 556, third on the right side. A soft thud like someone lowering a heavy object to the floor penetrated the door. At the same time, a dim but visible sliver of yellow appeared below the edge of the door. Something moved suddenly across the ray of light blocking it for an instant. Sommers withdrew his gun. Maid or no maid, no one was supposed to be on the fifth floor; he had given strict and clear instructions to the front desk on that subject.

His revolver at the ready in his right hand, Sommers knocked firmly on the upper door panel. The light disappeared instantly. A faint, rustling sound from within suggested body movement of some sort—furtive motion and then silence. Damn, he thought, I knew I should have picked up a master key.

"Who's in there? Open up now!"

His abrupt shout was met by silence except for a creaking sound like a door or window being opened from within the room. A balcony door, that was it. Whoever was in that room did not intend to be caught there. Whoever it was must have exited by the balcony door and was probably now leaping from balcony to balcony on the fifth floor level to elude him.

Sommers turned back to the iron stairs. He moved quickly to a large window beyond the stairs where the corridor turned down toward the Presidential Suite.

Too late he realized his mistake. As he reached the window he caught sight of a figure on the last balcony breaking through the balcony door into the room which would be closest to the elevator. He quickly retraced his steps back to the main corridor. He could just see, at the end of the hall, the stairway doors to the lower floors closing.

Sommers bolted down the corridor, cursing at himself for the precious seconds lost. He burst through the door and down the top most flight of stairs leading up from the Central building staircase, but he sensed immediately that his mission was futile.

The fourth floor landing was empty, nor could any sound of heavy footsteps be heard on the central stairs further down.

Several guests, who had apparently chosen not to attend the musicale, came sauntering along the fourth floor corridor and, from the look on their surprised faces as Sommers tumbled down the stairs like a Tasmanian Devil, whoever had preceded him had also eluded them. Nevertheless he gasped out, "Did you see a man coming down the stairs a moment ago?"

A tall, elderly gentleman, bald but for a few white streaks delicately plastered on his shiny pate, answered, "My dear boy, what ever is going on?"

Sommers repeated his question. "Just now, did you see a man running down these stairs? Did you see which way he might have gone from here?"

"I'm very sorry, old chap," the tall gentleman, obviously of English extraction, answered Sommers with a wry grin. "My eyesight isn't what it used to be, but I can assure you, dear fellow, that no one has come by us, save yourself. I say, do you have some kind of hide and go seek game in the offing? Good spot for it, I must say, this place, with all its nooks and crannies."

The man chuckled and his friends smiled in concert. All spoke up in an overlay of denial as Sommers once again asked if they had seen anyone or anything out of the ordinary.

Sommers grunted a thanks of sorts as he quickly moved to check out a water closet across the hall to the left of the stairs. There was a bathtub and two stalls and no one was occupying either one. A closed window looked out over a steeply pitched roof covering a third floor balcony. Nobody could have negotiated that route. Sommers slammed the door shut and continued down the stairs, taking several steps in one bound, trying to reason as to which direction the man might have fled.

Upon reaching the first floor foyer in the main parlor, Sommers realized he was on a cold trail. Even if the man had proceeded him, he could have easily slipped into the back of the darkened parlor while the musicale was still in progress. Or for that matter, he might have disappeared down the corridor into any one of a dozen of rooms that might have sheltered a co-conspirator.

Wait a minute. Sommers frowned fiercely. How stupid could he be? He remembered the little balcony at the front of the fourth floor foyer. Although he wasn't familiar with it, he thought it must surely overhang the main parlor roof. That had to be it. How could he have overlooked such an obvious escape route? The man could easily have shot down the stairs and out on to the balcony directly in line with the stairs. He could not have been seen because the central stairs would block visibility from anyone approaching from either corridor. Nor could he have been heard due to the plush stairway and hall carpeting which would have muffled even the most desperate of running feet. Sommers pounded up the steps back to the fourth floor, panting for breath as he broke out once again on the fourth floor landing. He threw himself against the unlatched door to the little balcony. The balcony was only about 3 feet deep and 14 feetwide. Sure enough, he looked down at the sloping wood-shingle roof only several feet below the balcony edge. The roof sloped gently all the way down to the second floor over the main parlor porch. It also afforded access to the several individual gables of presently unoccupied guest rooms in the wing built over the main parlor. Whoever the man was, he didn't have to be much of an athlete to scurry over the little balcony rail onto the parlor roof, down and around and up through one of the gable windows of the parlor guest rooms, waiting until his tracker had lost the scent.

Not hoping at this point to catch up to his adversary, but at least to prove his theory, Sommers jumped lightly over the balcony railing to the roughly shingled roof, knocking loose several splintered edges as he landed. He scrambled down the gentle slope and eased up and around to the gable closest to the balcony, a distance of only 15 or 20 feet. He was not at all surprised to find a splintered window sash, which had been broken and harshly thrust upwards to allow entrance. A quick look inside by the pale light of the moon revealed a brass bed and a mattress leaning against the wall as well as assorted bedroom furniture. The door opposite was opened to the hall.

Sommers grabbed the frame and hoisted his body through, certain that whoever had preceded him through the window had kept right on going through the door into the hall and out to the third floor foyer. From there, Sommers concluded sensibly, the man could have easily merged his identity with any number of the 250 or so odd guests who were currently enjoying the Mohonk hospitality, oblivious to the dark machinations that were beginning to swirl through the corridors and secret places of the Mountain House.

Feeling like he had botched things properly, Sommers decided he had better get a master key and check room 556. But first he needed to alert Kenner and Yost to the sudden turn that poised, on the face of it, a material threat to Presidential security. Whatever the underlying circumstances of the incident, it was going to require some definitive attention and, more than likely, a revamping of security measures.

Sommers raced back up to the fifth floor slowing down past room 556 on his way to the Presidential Suite. Only Yost stood guard outside the door to room 571.

"Where's Kenner?" Sommers shouted in some alarm.

Yost, visibly unnerved by something more than Sommers's abrupt and brisk salutation, replied, "We saw you down by the corridor looking through the window, Chief. You looked alarmed and when you didn't come back, Kenner thought he should go after you in case you needed backup." Just as Yost finished, from down the corridor, Kenner appeared, trotting like a faithful bird-dog trying to catch up to his master.

"What the hell is going on? Chief?" Kenner gasped out.

"I wish I knew," Sommers countered. "Listen the two of you. Somebody's been in room 556. When I challenged him, he took off through the outside balcony. I caught sight of him through the window at the end of the corridor there but he foxed me."

Sommers pointed down the hall to the large window which overlooked the outside of the Stone Building.

"He crossed the balcony to the next room and broke through and back out to the hall again. By the time I got back around to the elevator he had too much of a start on me. He slipped down the stair to the fourth floor foyer and from the foyer balcony, dropped onto the roof of the main parlor. From there he made his way across the parlor roof and climbed up through the gable window of a third floor room in the parlor wing. From that point, he reached the third floor foyer and disappeared. God only knows where."

"Not surprising," said Kenner. "I must have been about the same distance behind you as you were behind him. I never caught up to you."

"Whoever this man is, he knows this place. Whatever he's up to, he doesn't intend to get caught." Sommers spoke slowly as he continued. "First thing we have to do is to get into room 556 and see if he left anything that can help us. Kenner, you go and fetch a master key from the front desk. Tell them you just want to do a routine check of the fifth floor rooms, nothing else, understand?"

"Yes, sir."

"I'll be here with Yost." Sommers looked hard at Yost. "Yost is the President inside?"

"Yes, sir," replied Yost. "Senator Lodge and Baron Takahira will be joining him shortly, according to Mr. Loeb."

"Very well," said Sommers. "You stick here until relieved. Mum's the word, understand? I don't want any news of this to get to the President. Not yet anyway. We have to find out what we are dealing with. If the President comes out as if he has plans to go somewhere, you tell him out of earshot of anyone else that I asked that he not leave his quarters till he talks to me—that I'm checking on a possible breach of security, that's all. No details—do you have that, Yost?"

"Yes, sir," Yost answered, his voice strained slightly, his forehead showing a thin film of perspiration as the seriousness of the situation began to sink in.

Yost had not yet experienced any really threatening conditions in his duties during the few years he had been assigned to Presidential security. Was this now changing? It was certainly what he had been trained to expect. Reality, though, was different from hypothesis. At that moment, Yost felt vulnerable and very mortal. At the same time, he was surprisingly invigorated at the prospect of an unknown danger he might have to face. How would he respond in a clutch? Would he give a proper account of himself? Would he, indeed, give his life to protect the President, if needed be? On a primordial level, Yost was scared, although more frightened of the uncertainty of his performance than he was fearful of injury or even death.

Sommers sensed Yost's trepidations. He could read his men accurately. After all, without admitting it, he suffered from the same self-doubts. No one could predict how anyone would respond in life-threatening conditions. You maintained a certain discipline within yourself and tried to develop a context within which subjectivity was eliminated and actions transpired reflexively without conscious analysis of one's own individual role.

"Are you all right Yost?"

"I'm fine, sir," Yost replied. "Whatever is happening or about to happen, it breaks the monotony."

Sommers smiled. "It does indeed, Yost. I don't think any one of us is going to be bored this night."

Kenner appeared down the hall rounding the corner. Sommers held up his hand to hold him. "Remember, Yost, nothing of this to the President— we'll get back to you after we check out 556."

Sommers turned and faced off down the corridor where Kenner waited, master key on a large wooden panel clutched firmly in his right hand. As they rounded the corner and started down the main hallway, the elevator, unseen gears and wheels rolling and meshing, softly hushed by the walls and the shaft, approached the fifth floor. The gate was rudely opened by the operator and Baron Takahira and Senator Henry Cabot Lodge stepped out into the hall. Sommers motioned Kenner ahead toward the elevator.

"Ah so." Baron Takahira bowed and smiled, his eyes narrow slits in an otherwise wide open and beaming countenance. "We meet again, Mister Sommers."

Sommers found himself with an almost irresistible urge to respond to the Baron's contagious bow with a bow of his own but instead nodded his head in greeting.

"Baron, Senator Lodge, this is Agent Kenner. I trust you will not object to an escort to the President's quarters?"

Sommers smiled graciously, figuring that room 556 could await inspection for a few more minutes until the Baron was safely committed to the secure quarters of the President.

"I must say, Sommersan, I am impressed with the diligence and concern you show a humble servant of the Empire. I should hope upon the eagerly anticipated visit of yourself one day to our small country that I may return your courtesies and afford you the same generous protection and safe keeping you have provided this unworthy self."

The Baron smiled and bowed very low, and Sommers, once again, nearly bowed in return. Asian manners, he thought, were very disarming. Did they truly reflect inward intentions or were they a shield, a cover masking duplicitous objectives? Had there been a touch of sarcasm injected by the Baron in the word protection? Did Sommers's action seem a patronizing gesture to a proud Japanese nobleman?

Sommers hadn't had any experience with the Japanese psyche, nor had he ever confronted a man like the Baron prior to this evening. The President seemed to have a much better understanding of the Japanese mind and manners, Sommers thought. He'd better not draw any conclusions, puzzling as Baron Takahira's comments seemed to him. Sommers would leave that matter where it belonged—with the President and the State Department.

They reached the President's suite and Yost stepped back from the door. Sommers knocked and verbally announced their presence. The President's secretary responded and the door opened to admit the Baron and the Senator. It then closed with a distinct thump. The sound of the President's voice welcoming Baron Takahira was abruptly muffled by the thick portal.

"Remember, Yost, no forays until I talk to the President," Sommers said as he turned to lead off down the corridor. "Kenner and I will be inspecting room 556 just down the hall. If anything of particular moment occurs, you have your whistle."

Sommers had issued his men whistles for emergency use after the example of London Police who carried no side arms, only whistles to give an alarm.

As Sommers and Kenner reached room 556, all was silent within and no light appeared below the door. Sommers drew his gun.

"Open it up, Jerry. Let's see what we've got."

Kenner inserted the key into the nearly new, beautifully machined latch. Since the Stone Building was less than two years old, the hardware and finishings of the individual rooms were showroom status. The key turned and the heavy oak door swung inward, smoothly and without a sound. As the men stepped into the room, the door behind them began to swing closed—as if being gently pushed by unseen hands. Sommers and Kenner both jumped as the door slammed shut. The noise resounded down the corridor and filled the room like a muffled explosion.

"That's what I heard," Sommers said as he turned toward the door and reopened it. "The door must have been hung that way so as to close automatically for security reasons. That means whoever was in here must have been just behind me in the hall as I walked toward the President's quarters. He entered the room and the door slammed shut after him. He must have been carrying something and the door closed before he had a chance to catch it."

"Well then, he had to have a key, Chief."

"Not necessarily, Jerry—he could have picked the lock sometime earlier, perhaps while we were all at dinner. You see these two buttons on the face of the latch? Push one and the outside door knob will only turn and unlock with a key. Push the other and the latch can be opened from outside without a key. Probably makes it easier for housekeeping services when cleaning up between guests. Whoever was in here must have left it unlocked so he could easily reenter at his leisure. He must have known the fifth floor was closed off to guests so there would be no traffic up here except for the President, his family and us. He's been right under our feet, Jerry. He gauged it the safest place. A lot of nerve, wouldn't you say?" Kenner nodded. Sommers shut the door, walked over to the balcony door and continued his hypothesis. "Just why he wanted this room—that is what we have to find out, Jerry."

"Well, Chief, it's close to the President."

"Uncomfortably close, but somehow, I'm inclined to think that there is a more immediate reason rather than as a base for an attack on T.R. I think it may have something to do with what he was carrying.

"Just before I announced myself outside the door, I heard a thump—as if something heavy was dropped on the floor. In the quick glimpse I caught of him as he broke through from the last balcony into the room down the hall, he looked as though he was cradling something in his arms. Let's take a good look here."

Sommers pulled on a brass chain attached to a floor lamp with a large rose-colored shade and gold fringe. The room lit up, not brightly, but enough to provide a closer scrutiny. A mattress covered by a dust cloth and a bedstead leaned against the right-hand wall. A fireplace occupied the left-hand wall. To the left of the fireplace were two doors, one leading to a wash stand, the other to a walk-in closet. To the right of the entrance was a door leading to a bath which was fitted with a large porcelain cast iron tub and toilet. The wall opposite the entrance opened to a balcony. The door was ajar. The floor was covered with a reddish brown carpet with clumps of tiny flowers sprinkled like confetti from border to border. A quick examination of the side rooms revealed nothing of interest.

Sommers peered closely at the carpet. He knelt down and touched an area near the leaning bedstead. There was a spot more brownish than the color of the carpet.

"Mud, Jerry—the carpet is still wet. Whatever sat here or was put down here had to be muddy and wet." Sommers thought about the thump he had heard as he stood outside the door.

"Help me move the mattress and the bedstead, Jerry," Sommers said as he pulled on the dust cloth to expose the furniture. Both men grunted as they maneuvered the heavy oak headboard away from the wall. The movement revealed nothing.

"Well, whatever was here went with whoever it was," Sommers remarked wryly as he walked again over to the balcony door. "An easy escape, Jerry." he pointed out to Kenner how the cement balcony floor extended without a break beyond the adjoining room. An iron railing low enough to be easily vaulted provided the only demarcation to the two side-by-side rooms.

"In and out, and in again. Whoever it was, Jerry, with me pounding on the door like a silly housemaid, he knew he needed to get out of here fast. He took quite a chance not knowing for sure if I was outside in the hall."

Sommers ruefully recalled his chase around to the window in the corridor to catch sight of his adversary.

"If only I had stayed where I was, right outside the door, we'd have had him, Jerry."

"Maybe not, Chief," Kenner observed. "He might have gone over the balcony rail and shimmied down the corner pole to the next balcony."

"Well, if he had, good friend. he would have had to leave whatever he was carrying behind and he just wasn't prepared to do that." Sommers gave Kenner a piercing look. "No, we're dealing here with a mind that functions expertly under extreme pressure. The man fled to the balcony and simply waited for my move. When he saw me at the window in the hall, he knew that was his one chance and he didn't hesitate. By the time I recovered my senses, it was too late." Sommers clenched his right hand into a tight fist and pounded his left palm in a determined gesture.

"We've got to find him, Jerry, and we have to know what made that spot on the carpet."

Sommers began to sift through various strategies, convinced he was now dealing with a major crisis. First, he needed to ensure security in the immediate area of the President's quarters. That meant a search of the fifth and sixth floors. Next, he must alert the President to the incident and the inherent threat it implied. Wait a moment, he thought to himself, you know very well what the President's reaction to that would be. What should he say to the President? "Stay in your quarters, Mr. President. I believe there is someone around here, hell-bent to do you in."

He knew that kind of advice would be met with a scornful admonition from the President to get busy and find the perpetrator. The President would not change his program or agenda because of some foggy hypothesis of Sommers's that a mysterious intruder was on the loose. He must have more information. His only real chance for preventing an attack on the President, if that was the objective of the intruder, would rest on discovery of the culprit or culprits before an attempt could be carried out.

He looked at his watch. It was just past 11:00. The musicale would be over. Helena would be wondering what happened to him.

"Come, Jerry. Let's have a look at the rest of these rooms. What we have to do right now is to make sure that the fifth and sixth floors are secured."

The two men searched each room on each floor meticulously, discovering nothing more than the signs of a recent visit of clandestine lovers. The sixth floor room in question still had a bed positioned for use with the covers left in disarray and ashes in the fireplace, suggesting a romantic interlude on a snappy fall evening after the close of the October season.

Sommers turned to Kenner as they came down from the sixth floor search and joined Yost outside the President's suite.

"It's almost 11:30, Jerry. At 12:00, you take a post down by the elevator on this floor where you can watch the stairs at both ends of the hall.

"I'm afraid we're in for extra hours tonight, gentlemen. Yost, you'll be relieved by Sachs at 12:00. When you're relieved, I want you up on the sixth floor to patrol the corridors. If the elevator brings anyone up past Kenner on the fifth, arrest him—no questions asked, understood?"

"Yessir," Yost nodded.

"Handcuff him to a steam radiator in the hall foyer and get Kenner. He'll know where to find me. At 2:00 AM, Meyers will be relieving Sachs, Jerry. If I'm not around, you fill in Sachs and Meyers on what's going on and instruct Sachs to take Yost's place on the sixth floor. He's to stay up there until 6:00, when he's to meet you and Meyers at the President's quarters for his morning hike through the labyrinth. Yost, you get some rest from 2:00 to 4:00 and then get back up here to join Meyers at the President's suite. You stay on board with the President's family after Kenner, Sachs and Meyers depart with the President and his party for the labyrinth." Yost nodded again, his pulse racing despite a strong mental effort to curb his rising excitement.

"Jerry, as Senior Agent, you're in charge if I'm not around.

I intend to do some investigating on my own. I'll get back to check on things here sometime in between. Come breakfast, after the President has returned from his hike, we'll evaluate the situation. I'll speak to Major Hertzog to try to organize some plainclothes officers from the County Sheriff's office to fill out our numbers until we can find out what kind of cards our unknown intruders intend to play."

Sommers paused and subconsciously fingered the edges of his holster—the steel and pearl handle of his revolver, warm from his body heat, felt reassuring. However, at the moment, he was possessed by a growing compulsion to head down each corridor from the first floor and up, knocking on every door to query the occupants as to whether or not they might be harboring the mysterious fifth floor fugitive. Even that would be a long shot, he knew. There were hundreds of places a man could hide in the rambling Mountain House and still escape detection despite a posse of armed men dogging his footsteps.

No, he had to pursue the Sidon theory. It could lead to the intruder, or intruders, God forbid, more directly than his own flailing antics searching empty rooms and subterranean cellars, never mind the infinite possibilities in the woods and environs of the Mountain House.

For now, he surmised that the intruder was not likely to make any more overt moves, at least not for the time being. In all probability, he would stay in hiding for a while since he had already triggered an alarm. An element of surprise had been compromised. Now would follow a time of watching and waiting. The men were on full alert. They, at least, enjoyed the advantage of an early warning.

Chapter Twenty-four

He needed to get back to Helena. She would be worried since he hadn't appeared at the musicale. Of course, this wasn't the first time, or the second or third time, for that matter, that his schedule had been interrupted with no prior notice to Helena that he might be late or otherwise occupied. Such a vocation as he practiced, with its implicit dangers and much time assigned to investigative pursuits, did not lend itself to the comfort and security of a loving spouse, let alone the always present jeopardy of falling into an 'affair' with an attractive, but possibly duplicitous woman engaged in some ominous intrigue in the 'corridors' of political power.

It was a good thing Helena had such faith in him. She was absolutely trusting. It never occurred to her that her Joseph could ever entertain the prospect of an illicent love during the disparate moments he was not with her, which were many.

Sommers took comfort in the knowledge that her faith was not lost on him. It was impossible for him to perceive of how any man enjoying the sweet affections of a woman such as Helena could hope to mix in the fleeting passions of a chance encounter without a grave disassembly of his psyche.

With a final nod to Kenner and Yost and an admonition to keep alert, their long day notwithstanding, Sommers proceeded on to the entrance to the Rock Building at the fifth floor level and down to the fourth floor to room 490.

He knocked before entering. There was no answer.

Although he did not expect a repeat experience of the morning, the episode sprang fresh to his mind again, nevertheless. He could feel the pores of his body responding at the thought of opening the door and, once again, finding an empty room with Helena gone.

He frowned and reached for his key. He pushed open the door, calling to Helena as he entered.

"Helena?"

The room was empty—but not shorn of its furniture. The bed was neatly turned down. Helena's cosmetics were spread in a casual display across the dresser. The faint scent of her new perfume, so recently anointed, invaded Sommers's nostrils as he stepped into the room, his heart thumping in reflexive anticipation of some unexpected calamity.

Then he saw the note on the top of the bureau next to the door.

Darling, he read, *Richard and Miriam Sturgis have asked us to join them in their room, 353, after the musicale. If your duties will allow you a respite, please join us. (after which you may have your way with me, if your energies will permit such endeavors)*

Your shameless paramour,
Helena

There was a post script: *Please destroy this note upon assimilation, for I do not believe I should care to have my lustful yearnings for you come to the attention of others, lest they dare to entertain such vain hopes that I might heed petitions from one or another of them to exercise such rights and privileges as are yours alone.*

Sommers smiled as he finished reading. Despite the present crisis, the advent of a few amorous moments in Helena's warm embrace was more than tempting; it was overpowering. However, that sensation of delight was suddenly displaced by a feeling of sharp inquitetude.

He read the note again—room 353. For some reason, that number stirred uneasy feelings in him. Why?

His skin began to feel prickly as he repeated the three numbers aloud. He began to find it difficult to draw a deep breath.

An alarming and growing discomfort beset him. He could not suppress an involuntary shudder which racked his body. His chest muscles began to twitch uncontrollably. He could feel his brow dampening and at the same time, an uncomfortable chill extended throughout his body. What was happening to him? Was he having a heart attack? There was no pain, just an unalterable coldness that gripped him as if he had been immersed in icy water.

He attempted to override the shuddering, which had, quite without notice, overtaken his body. With a massive heave of his shoulders and arms, he moved to the door, intent that he must, without delay, take himself to room 353. Helena was there, but something or someone beyond Helena's presence seemed to be 'speaking' to him about that room. From some unacknowledged recess of his psyche, he felt a strange and frightening attachment to room 353.

As he opened the door into the hall, a succession of amorphous images and sensations instantly engulfed him like a fiery shower from a holiday sparkler. He could see a smoldering fireplace, and next to it, a beautiful woman in a black velvet dress who looked disturbingly like Helena. He could hear the sound of water running, and a woman's soft, earthy sighs and moans. He was inundated by the scent of a strange and unfamiliar perfume. His throat felt suddenly parched and then burning from the dregs of a fiery liquid—whiskey—strong, with the scent of oranges. His body shivered from an unquenchable cold. What in hell was all of this?

He stepped out into the hall. The images swirled around him as if in a giant, slow-moving centrifuge. He forced himself along the corridor toward the juncture of the Rock Building with the Stone Building and the iron staircase leading down to the third floor.

Room 353 was just two rooms along the corridor, southerly from the central staircase and foyer. Sommers, however, was approaching the room from the opposite end, down from the iron staircase.

The full extent of the preternatural forces that were about to engulf him began as an unexpected and inexplicable dimming of the corridor lighting upon his descent.

As he reached the last step on the stairs, he found himself plunged abruptly into an infinity of darkness, the tiny ceiling fixtures having dissolved into pin-pricks of light, like distant stars in an otherwise black firmament. The floor beneath his feet seemed to drop away like the bottom of an elevator, leaving him suspended midway in a tunnel-like shaft, at the end of which there appeared a flickering light, similar to a brakeman's lantern on a train. The light receded, nearly, but not quite disappearing down unseen tracks that stretched on into some limitless pitchblende of night. A terrible loneliness—a despairing grief, a sense of deep, personal loss, as in total and final separation from a loved one, swept over Sommers. From some, deep, far-off valley-like space, a great, mournful sigh, as if from a chorus of lost souls, rose up out of the ether and then died away again to a whisper.

He moved in a trance, his vision totally obscured, his feet guided by some inertial force over which he had no control. He was both conscious and unconscious—conscious of his body slowly moving, as if under some inebriate command, through unbounded space toward the tiny light that hovered yet ahead of him down the long, black tunnel—but unconscious to the extent that his deductive processes were completely on hold. He was devoid of cerebral function. His mind and body, at differing levels, sensed acutely the unsettling phenomena, but the cortical juncture of reason and response were all but suspended. He moved like a swimmer in a heavy surf, forcing his limbs through the swarming subsurface current.

The tiny light grew brighter. One conscious thought emerged now from some spongy crevice of his mind. He must reach room 353. He must find Helena. He must remove her from the mysterious shrouds that seemed to encompass that particular room.

The light became a glimmer under a door. The uncommon darkness which had enwrapped Sommers in its smothering canopy as he had stepped off the stairs onto the third floor had now dissipated. He found himself standing before the door to room 353, the brass numerals brightly polished, innocuous in their innocence. The corridor, which only moments before had been a forbidding crypt-like passage of unbearable loneliness in which unspeakable and unknown horrors seemed to hover in clouds of black sediment had, once again, emerged to become itself, a typical Mountain House corridor, couched, albeit in its normal Victorian gloom. The charming but quite dim ceiling lights once more cast their yellowish pales against the ochreous walls in a languid attempt to cheer up dark corners and parlor crannies.

Sommers, remarkably, retained nothing of his short but esoteric journey from room 490 to room 353, at least on a conscious level. To be sure, he felt an uncomfortable foreboding as he now stood before the door, but he could not attach reason to his uneasiness. His conscious memory as regards his peculiar perceptions and the physiological sensations he had experienced upon reading the note from Helena still prevailed, although muted now that he had actually arrived at room 353. However, the rest of his experience in passing through the halls to room 353 remained nothing more in his now awakened mind than a tug from some deep corner of his subconscious that he had some remote connection with the third floor room where Helena was, at the moment, enjoying an innocent after dinner drink with friends.

He stretched and heaved his shoulders, took a deep breath and knocked on the door.

Chapter Twenty-five

The door to room 353 was thrown open to the accompaniment of happy voices.

"Joseph, my dear—" Helena's voice rose above the cacophony.

"Mr. Sommers." Miriam Sturgis welcomed him with a broad smile as she drew the heavy door wide into the room. "Do come in out of that drafty hall."

Sommers crossed the threshold and moved immediately to Helena, who had risen to meet him. He took her roughly, almost crushing her in his arms,

"Helena, are you all right?" His breath was short, almost gasping.

"Why, Joseph, of course I'm all right—how in Heaven's name should I be otherwise?" Helena smiled, puzzled at his mood and brusque entrance.

A man's voice broke into the unsettling atmosphere Sommers's arrival had engendered among the room's occupants,

"Mr. Sommers, I certainly am glad you've been able to join us. Please, allow me to offer you a cognac. I'm sure this has been a long and arduous day for you."

Richard Sturgis handed Sommers a brandy glass filled with a burnished, golden liquid that swirled tantalizingly from rim to rim. Sommers took the glass and swallowed a heady swig, not bothering to sniff the aroma of the twenty-five-year-old highly-distilled wine. The brandy burned Sommers's throat as it absorbed the volcanic-like flow. The alcohol seeped rapidly through his arteries until he could feel his arms and hands tingle and the back of his neck flush from the fiery potion.

Sommers could hear voices all around him—even the sound of his own voice in response, but part of him had, somehow, become totally disconnected from the convivial scene.

On one level, at one moment, he was conscious of his integration within the normal social context of friends engaged in small talk, enjoying drinks around a cozy fire, while another part of him, at that very same moment, was reduced to a detached and separate entity with the uncanny ability to observe everything independently but without participation.

That part of him beheld a smoldering log fire in the fireplace in the center left wall of the room just opposite a shiny, brass bedstead with a cream coverlet and matching wool blanket at the foot. Very queer, he thought. Moments ago, upon his first entering the room there had been, indeed, a bed, but it had been a bed with a rather ornately carved headboard.

The rest of the little group, at that very moment sitting in random armchairs in front of the fireplace, were absorbed in an animated discussion of the day's events—the carriage ride from New Paltz, the President's jocular presence at dinner and the prospect of enjoying, on the morrow, more of the Mountain House hospitality and delights including some hiking on the scenic trails and overlooks such as Eagle Cliff and Sky Top.

In the midst of the conversational hubbub, in which Sommers's conscious self was peripherally involved at best, his alter-ego discerned an extraordinary phenomenon. Standing in front of the fireplace, as if she had just risen and left the circle of small talk, was Helena—except that Helena was still sitting on Sommers's left.

Sommers, startled by such an anomaly, stared at this Helena, who stood smiling, but mute, her gaze focused on him and him alone. He could not remove his eyes from this hauntingly beautiful woman who, in every aspect, seemed to be his beloved Helena. There were differences, though. This Helena was equally as lovely as the Helena sitting at his left, still caught up in polite conversation with Miriam and Richard Sturgis, but her hair was much shorter and lighter in color—almost strawberry blonde. Her curls bounced around her shoulders as she moved her hands upward to fluff out the tresses. She was wearing a black, velvet, low-cut gown with wide, bouffant shoulders and a daring display of bosom.

As Sommers watched, she threw her head back in a soundless laugh. Her hazel eyes sparkled with gold flecks, mirroring the firelight. She raised to her lips a tumbler filled with what appeared to be an orange liquid and drank deeply.

Then, in an instant, she was gone and Sommers's disjointed self merged to become one again with his conscious being as peals of laughter crashed around him.

Richard Sturgis was giving a rendition of the little band leader at New Paltz as he had whipped up the motley assemblage of local musicians.

"And then, when the mayor of New Paltz raised his hands to quiet the crowd and introduce the President—" Sturgis could hardly contain himself, his deprecating glee at the expense of the little man who fancied himself as the poor man's John Philip Sousa, all but convulsing him into a helpless mass of quivering jelly, his knees nudging precariously the tea table which held the drinks—Miriam Sturgis clutched at her brandy glass as it minced toward the edge of the little table, a near casualty of her husband's frivolity as he continued his story, " the bandleader slashed down with his baton as if he were delivering a coup-de-grace to St. George's dragon. You should have seen the fire-eating look he gave the trumpet section when they missed the cue and sort of wheezed away like a couple of teapots taken off the boil."

Great guffs of belly sounds issued from Sturgis's gaping mouth. He slapped his knee and shook his head from side to side as he regaled the group with the final administrations of the ill-fated New Paltz band and its indomitable leader.

Both Helena and Miriam Sturgis were nearly out of control themselves. Their girlish tittering at the outset of Richard Sturgis's performance had rapidly given way to outbursts of earthy laughter that undermined their feminine mystique and poise, almost to the extent that they might have, in a less delicate setting, been characterized as raw cowmaids listening to the hired hand tell an off-color joke.

As for Sommers, he felt oddly removed from the raucous humor generated by Sturgis's recounting of the events at New

Paltz during the President's arrival. He could not extinguish the image of the 'other' Helena. He was content, for the moment, to tolerate his hosts' expansive display of merriment while he quietly ruminated over the astonishing apparition he had witnessed within a room that was numbered 353, but which had been unreservedly unlike the room he had entered moments earlier, a room in which he now reposed, once again, with the Helena whom he knew so well, the woman who was the most precious love of his life.

Sturgis remained undaunted. He was now doing a parody of the President's short speech, depicting T.R. receiving the bouquet of flowers from the young women of the New Paltz Normal School, complete with toothy grin, exaggerated bowing and wide arm gestures to the crowd of admiring ladies.

"Thank you, my dears," Sturgis carried on in Roosevelt's manner. "You are all, indeed, a delight to these sore eyes which are the victims of sooty trains, the unfortunate wont of those who must needs travel the rails of this great country to bring a message of hope to the downtrodden and a challenge to the people to make our country the very best for all of us, regardless of our stations in life."

Another great guffaw burst from Sturgis as he hastened to point out, "That part of Roosevelt's speech was obviously not intended for the ears of any beyond the front ranks of those charming and quite pretty young ladies. I swear, I thought, for a moment, that they would all swoon at the President's attention, indeed, one might say, 'flirtation.' They swayed and rocked about and tittered to the point where I believe they were just about to collapse like a row of dominos. Do you agree, Joseph?"

Sturgis hardly hesitated in his rollicking reenactment as Sommers, distracted with his own muddling thoughts and disorientation, found himself responding in the affirmative.

"Yes, I must say from my vantage point, although I could not hear the President's words, he certainly seemed to be enjoying himself."

Sommers felt a vague, wrestling sensation within himself. On a conscious and verbal level, he felt inextricably linked with these three people enjoying their brandies and engaged in such conversational trivia, but deep inside, the amorphous image of the 'other' Helena, standing by the fireplace moments before and now gone, lingered like the fragrance of a bouquet of fresh flowers one might pass in a parlor or alcove of the Mountain House. Try as he might, he could not equate the strange hallucinations with any sensible pattern of reason within his present reality.

Sommers shrugged, as was his general habit in dealing with the inexplicable. He convinced himself that the strange events of the day following the seemingly portentous dream of the previous night were responsible for his mind wanderings. He must force his attention back to the moment and the very real threat that presented itself with the sudden appearance of the unknown intruder in the midst of Presidential goings-on. Implausible hallucinations, troubling as they might be, could not be allowed to interfere with his actions of the next few hours. Somehow, there would come meaning to such happenings, he was certain. In the meantime, he had stringent duties to see to.

He addressed the very visible and the very real Helena who was just sipping the last drops of her brandy as the laughter finally faded, "My dearest, sad to say, but we must, or at least I must bid adieu to our friends here. To extend the limits of a time-worn phrase, 'Duty calls.'"

"Oh, yes, of course, Joseph," came Helena's almost too eager response.

"As a matter of fact, I find there are one or two items of which I must inform you. It has been a long day and we've had little chance to exchange much more than glances over breakfast and dinner, have we?"

Helena looked at Joseph like a little pixie, a decidedly impish smile translating her normally demure features into an enchanting expression that telegraphed a secret striving to break its bounds.

"Indeed, Joseph," Miriam Sturgis was bubbling over. "You must see this young lady to her rooms and within the confines of your assignment to duty, allow her to share with you some bit of news she has already shared with me." She ushered Joseph and Helena to the door. "And, now, the two of you—off you go." She opened the door and literally shooed them out into the corridor, bustling and tittering for all the world, Sommers thought, like a Dickensian midwife. Richard Sturgis tossed off a goodnight wish and a final evocation as only he of such broad girth might muster.

"If anyone gets hungry during the night, folks, I've managed to secret a cache of survival rations with the help of a friend of some influence with the Mohonk chef. Just knock twice and stand clear." Sturgis let fly one last gleeful burst as final goodnights accompanied the closing of the door to room 353.

Chapter Twenty-six

"Now, then, my sweet love," Sommers said as he gently placed an arm around Helena's waist and guided her toward the stairs at the end of the long third floor corridor, bereft now of the dark shadows and menacing currents that had swirled around him as he had made his way earlier down to room 353, "just what is this bit of news of which you are dying to divest yourself?"

"Oh, Joseph, it can wait until we reach our room." Helena toyed with him mischievously, dangling just out of reach the announcement that tickled the tip of her tongue to deliver.

Instead, her face grew serious. She changed the subject as they reached the iron stairs ascending to the fourth floor.

"Joseph, when you came to the Sturgis's room, you looked ever so distraught—very much beside yourself. I noticed you staring rather fixedly at the fireplace. Is everything all right? Are you having any problems with the security for the President? I suppose I should rightfully say, are you able to tell me of any such difficulties, if they do, indeed, exist?"

Something of his murky flight down the corridor to room 353 stirred in Sommers again. The frightful hallucinatory journey had faded from his conscious memory, but an air of discomfort still lingered, particularly as he recalled the image of the 'other' Helena, a woman of such ephemeral beauty, so like, and yet, so unlike the woman who now walked by his side as they negotiated the last few steps to 490. He could not, surely, tell Helena of his viewing of the woman by the fireplace. Even she would think him quite daft, fairly well fit to be cashiered from the Service and to be squirreled away to spend the rest of his days in an asylum.

No, nothing of that sort could be shared with Helena. Whatever the cause for such aberrations, Sommers had to believe they must have their roots in the chimerical nightmare of the previous evening and that they would soon pass.

"My darling," Helena whispered softly in Sommers's ear. "Are we to stand here in front of this door until some magic 'sesame' is to be uttered for us to enter?"

Sommers broke from his reverie with a laugh. "Sorry, darling, I suppose I was thinking of how the President was getting on with his Japanese friend, just now. And, in response to your query as to security this evening, the answer is no, there are no special problems," he lied. "Everything is under control. The men are alert and the President and his family are in as safe a bower this evening as if tucked into their beds in the White House."

He unlocked the door and lovingly swept Helena into the room and into his arms.

"So, now, you bewitching little minx—what is this so-called bit of news that you've been absolutely expiring to tell me. Another moment or two, and I should be able to read it all in those give-away eyes of yours. You never could successfully hide a secret of either little or great import."

Helena stepped in close to him, soft murmuring sounds coming from her throat as she smiled, eyes shining and laughing. She reached up with her two hands and drew his face down gently until her lips reached his. With a soft, wet brush of her mouth on his and a darting tongue-tip, she kissed him, her lips like the wings of a butterfly flitting across his cheeks, his nose, upward to his eyes and then across from left to right, blowing softly into the sensitive folds of his ears. Then came a whisper from parted lips.

"My darling, Joseph, if it's a girl, would you agree to calling her Josephine? Naturally, if it's a boy he shall be Joseph, Jr."

Sommers, as stunned as any man alive would have been in receiving such a pronouncement in such a tantalizing fashion, placed his hands on Helena's bare shoulders, warm and slightly moist from her inner excitement,

"Are you telling me I am to be a father?" His voice almost squeaked in its rise to a very surprised falsetto.

Helena giggled and nodded her head. "Don't you think it's about time, my darling? You're middle-aged, you know."

Sommers could not contain himself. He let go of Helena's shoulders and took her in an embrace that lifted her off her feet, turning her in a complete circle like a child hugging and swinging a rag doll.

"Joseph Sommers—a father, can it be true?"

"Easy, my sweet—we must give some heed to the little one's well-being. I should not think dancing lessons were quite in order at this early date."

"Oh, my God, Helena—you're right. I'm so sorry. Are you all right?" Sommers abruptly halted his gyrations and led Helena to the edge of the bed. Helena again giggled, teasing him in his obvious ignorance of even the basic procedures to be encountered in dealing with pregnancy.

"I am quite fine, thank you, my husband, and I shall be so, I am certain, for eight months or more, I should think. Childbearing in my family has a history of very monotonous and routine success with no complications further than that of arriving at acceptable decisions on proper names for the off-spring."

Sommers, never having experienced the elation of an announcement of a birth which would establish his progeny for future generations, grinned in such an expansive manner that Helena laughed and said, "Joseph, darling, if the President were here to compete in measure with that great grin of yours, I fear he would place a very poor second."

"Helena, is it really true? I am to become a father?"

"Of course, dearest, unless you believe such a fiction that would have this tiny life within me authored by someone other than you."

Helena was enjoying the tease. Sommers, who was not prone to subordination by any man, not even Presidents, was totally in subjection to this piquant, mischievous woman sitting next to him, nurturing his seed and relishing so immensely the small boy wonder of this paradigm of masculinity who had been reduced to the self-conscious smirks and vocal shuffles of a schoolboy caught in some awkward act.

"Helena, I can't believe—I mean, when—Oh, Lord—do you—what do we do now?—that is to say—what about—the doctor, does he—do you think it's—" Sommers was gasping in delight and perplexity. "Helena, will it be a boy or a girl? Can they tell about those things? How do you feel, my love?"

"Oh, my irrepressible darling." Helena was laughing so hard, she could hardly speak. "Really, Joseph—slow down. It did not occur to me that my news would subject you to such a paroxysm. I think you need time to acclimate. Perhaps we should indulge in the activity that occasioned my present condition. It might soothe your jangled psyche."

Helena reached up with her right hand to his face and leaned toward him, her lips parted, searching for his. She whispered softly as they closed, "I do believe the love act would have a salutary effect upon my own well-being as well as upon our yet unnamed."

They fell back gently on the bed as their arms and hands found familiar places. Their bodies melded—clothes, as in a choreographed ritual, falling from shoulders and limbs. There was no desperate clutching as in some encounters of irresistible passion occasioned by inconvenient settings or unfortunate time limitations. Theirs was a smooth, undulating symphony of sound and motion as excitement grew and the crescendos of their individual climaxes ascended, timed by the unspoken perceptions of body and mind tuned completely to one another's needs and pleasures.

Afterward, as they lay entwined under the soft Mohonk blanket, each caressing now quiet and unanxious muscles, damp from exertions, Sommers reexperienced a mode of utter peace and tranquillity, similar to that which flooded his consciousness that very morning at breakfast following his earlier horrendous time differential.

The dread and foreboding he had endured in connection with room number 353—the hallucinations, including the apparition of the 'other' Helena—seemed now to be nothing more than the fragments of a vague and dusty memory.

For whatever telestic forces deep in the cosmos which bound together life and death were responsible for the shifting dimensions in time Sommers had experienced, he had no explanations. The events, however, taken together, seemed to him at that moment as he lie with his arms around Helena, to blend into some whole and seamless fabric of truth—truth that was beyond his ken, perhaps—but inherent with meaning that one day would be made clear. If it purposed the intentions of the Divine to embrace him with such mysteries, then so be it. He would not subject his finite mind to further ruminations. There were now other priorities which demanded his faculties and his energies—incidents of intrigue that while presently indiscernible would, in time, succumb to deductive reasoning and investigation, areas for which he was trained to prosecute.

He reached for his watch, which had ended up on the floor by his side of the bed. Helena, having drifted off in a light sleep in the afterglow of their love-making, lifted her head from his shoulder. She purred sleepily, reluctant to release her hold.

Sommers looked at his watch. "Helena, darling, we must have drifted off. It's almost 1:00."

The image of Mrs. Sidon, like a magic lantern slide, flashed into his mind. He would have to see to his men and then, as Mrs. Sidon had proscribed, find his way to the main parlor balcony off the second floor for their 2:00 AM meeting.

The events of the evening came back slowly into focus—the intruder on the fifth floor, the search by Kenner and himself, the meeting of the President with the Japanese envoy.

Helena squirmed over to his side and placed a hand on his shoulder. For a moment, he had forgotten the earth-shaking news—he was going to be a father! Good Lord, he thought, everything was happening at once.

He leaned over to Helena. "Darling, Helena—mother of my brood—I love you."

"And I love you, my very dearest Joseph, father of my child."

They kissed, gently, not without passion but with a fresh sensation born of the miracle of life that now bound them together in an *au courant* and deeper union, his seed implanted in her womb joining them once and for all in an invocation of new life to come.

"My sweet," Sommers whispered, "reluctant as I am to leave your warm pulsating body and other attendant charms—if I do not check my men very soon, they will surely conclude that the President and I have dashed off on a midnight bear hunt."

Helena sat up, her voice still husky with desire. "Joseph, do, please come back soon—you leave here a woman who has not yet reached a level of satiation that would ensure restful sleep." She let fall the blanket from her shoulders to her waist and smiled seductively as she reached for him with her arms.

Sommers was just drawing on a turtle neck sweater he favored as appropriate field wear for active duty with a very active outdoor President. He sat on the edge of the bed and drew Helena into his arms, his manhood once again aroused.

"My darling, Helena, I will be shot for dereliction of duty if I stay another moment with you. I promise I shall return no later than dawn's early light, as the song goes."

As he held Helena very close, he was suddenly overcome by a great sadness—the same desperate sensation of yearning for something or someone lost that he had experienced earlier in the evening on his way to room 353. The feeling was so powerful, he felt close to tears. His body shuddered involuntarily as it had before and he could feel that same coldness welling up in his chest.

Helena could feel his body shake and his arms tremble as they tightened around her.

"My darling, do you feel all right? Are you catching a chill? If you have to go out, please be sure to take your mackinaw."

Sommers recovered himself as best he could, not wishing Helena to see his unsettling mood swing. He released his embrace, kissed her gently on the lips and forehead, squeezed her two hands in his and rose from the bed.

"I'll be all right, my love—just thinking, I guess, about Mrs. Sidon's strange tale—a bit unnerved." He looked intently at Helena who had drawn the cream-colored blanket around her shoulders and had arisen to join him as he moved to the door, preparing to leave.

"Remember, Helena, no matter what happens, my very dearest, I shall love you forever and a day."

"And I, you, Joseph." Helena's face lost, for a moment, its wistful smile. "My, you've become so somber of a sudden." She tried not to show the tinge of uneasiness his words evoked in her. "I believe your best course right now is to go and do your duty and come back to me as quickly as you can. I shall make it my mission to calm whatever jaded nerves I discover in you upon your return."

She smiled and pressed close to him, bestowing a last kiss as he opened the door and stepped through. Slowly, she closed the door to room 490. Sommers turned to watch her face narrowing in the closing fissure. Smilingly, she gave him a wink as she said softly, "I love you—come back to me."

As the door shut, the latch engaged. The sharp click of metal against metal, the muted thump of wood hitting wood echoed resoundingly in the empty corridor. To Sommers, the sounds carried an odd air of finality, as if a chapter in his life had been concluded.

He stood for a moment before the door. He had a macabre notion that if he were to open the door again, as in the early morning of that day, the room would be emptied and Helena gone. There would be no sign of their existence together, no vestige of the tender moments of love they had spent together there.

Then, just as rapidly as had come over him the fearfulness and dread as to whether or not Helena still stood behind the door to room 490, calm betook him. The desperate urge to fling open the door to prove Helena's presence left him. Of course she was there—cradling in her womb the tiny new life ignited by his seed.

He breathed deeply—God, how long had he been standing there in the hall in such non-productive speculation? He moved on down the corridor toward the stairs to the fifth floor trying to decide whether he would prefer a 'Joseph, Jr.' or a 'Josephine.'

He had about eight months to decide—he thought.

Chapter Twenty-seven

As he passed along the bleak hallway, Sommers tried to retain a light mood, buoyed by the knowledge that in less than a year he would be a father, if all went well.

But now that he had left Helena's presence and the comfort and affection derived from her singular devotion, it was difficult to position his feelings to accommodate the conflicting events of the last few hours. The constant, nearly sepulchral gloom of the Mountain House corridors at night certainly did not help to dispel in him serious notions of some form of encircling calamity regarding Presidential security.

He knew one thing, however. The business of the fifth floor 'intruder' combined with Mrs. Sidon's conspiracy theory required his immediate perseverance. Was there a tie-in between the intruder and General Sidon? He had no answers. Would he have them in time to prevent whatever action against the President might be planned? Only his projected meeting with Mrs. Sidon in an hour or so would lend any hope toward answering that one.

Sommers climbed the stairs at the end of the fourth floor of the Rock Building where it connected to the Stone Building. He checked his watch as he reached the fifth floor and crossed the threshold into the Stone Building corridor from where he could see Agent Sachs on duty at the entrance to the Presidential Suite. It was just 1:10. He still had time left before his rendezvous with Mrs. Sidon. He wondered whether she would, indeed, put in an appearance.

Sachs was looking slightly apprehensive. Kenner and Yost had no doubt passed on to him the news of the intruder.

"Anything of import happening here, Sachs?"

"Everything is calm, sir. Baron Takahari left a short time ago. Senator Lodge is still with the President. From the volume of the President's voice during the part of the meeting that took place after I came on, though I couldn't make out the words through the door, I'd say the President is either very happy or very angry."

Sommers grinned. "Yes, I know what you mean, Sachs. The President tends to audible excitement in either extreme. Did Kenner fill you in on what happened up here earlier?"

"Yessir—anything new, sir?"

"Not that we know about yet, Sachs, and in view of that, I'm afraid you and Meyers won't have much time for a further break, pending the situation here and the President's early arousal and trek through the labyrinth in the morning.

"He's scheduled to leave the Mountain House around 6:00 AM. I want you and Meyers to join Kenner and accompany the President and his party. In the meantime, after Meyers relieves you at 2:00, I want you up on the sixth floor to relieve Yost. Stay up there and patrol the corridors until just before 6:00, when you're to report back here to join Meyers and Kenner with the President for his hike. I'll have Yost stand by here with Mrs. Roosevelt and the boys.

"You know what to do if you find anyone up on the sixth floor. I don't care if it's one of the Smiley brothers, I want him arrested. We'll ask questions later. Absolutely no one is to be on either the fifth or the sixth floor without my direct knowledge and authority. Is that understood, Sachs?"

"Yessir, understood, Chief."

"Very well." Sommers turned to proceed down the corridor to Kenner's station by the elevator. "Keep alert, Sachs. I know it's going to be a long night, but I wouldn't want the President to find you 'sawing wood' even if you could sleep standing up. Pass the word on to Meyers."

"Right, Chief, you can count on us." Sachs's voice had

dropped to a loud whisper, as if he was in fear that an unknown prowler already lurked behind a nearby corner.

Sommers went on down the long hall. As he reached the corner by the iron staircase, he glanced out the large window at the end from which he had earlier viewed the escape of the intruder across the balconies outside the fifth floor rooms. He again berated himself for his stupidity in allowing the man to evade him. He could only wonder where the man might be at that moment—just about anywhere, he guessed, but he couldn't shake off a hunch that wherever he was, it was not far—and it was not in the woods or grounds that he believed that he might discover him. He had a presentment that the man was in the Mountain House and not very far away from him, right at that particular moment. It was not a comfortable feeling.

With something of a shrug, Sommers resignedly turned to the right past the stairwell and carried on down to Kenner who was standing quietly by the elevator.

"Jerry, anything unusual here?"

"No, Chief." Kenner gestured toward the elevator. "Nobody up, nobody down. The Baron left about fifteen minutes ago—seemed quite happy," he added. Kenner's unsolicited perception on the success or failure of the President's meeting, drawn from his simple observation of the participants, would go nowhere, of course, but it was probably more accurate than the reports of a good many of the journalists and reporters who constantly followed the President, often exaggerating events and statements in order to beef up or add sensation to their copy.

"I'll just hop up and have a word with Yost, Jerry. You hold the fort here. If nothing turns up before morning, I've a mind to shadow you on your hike through the labyrinth, maybe smoke out our man, or men, as the case may be—so don't be alarmed if you don't see me before you start out. I'll be close by.

"Remember, Jerry, anyone else who comes up on that elevator is not likely to have a ticket for a late tea with the President."

"Right, Chief."

The elevator was normally in service twenty-four hours. Sommers saw no reason for closing it down just because it might provide an avenue to reach the President's suite. He knew Kenner would take a bullet before he would allow any unauthorized person to get off on the fifth floor. He doubted that anyone would take that approach to reach the President, but you never could know. A brazen frontal attack might succeed if the assassin or assassins cared nothing for their own lives in the attempt.

It was an unlikely hypothesis, in any case, Sommers believed, what with the possibility of alternate means of reaching the President's quarters by the stairways and even from the rooftops and balconies.

Again, he felt the urgency of unmasking the conspirators and their plans prior to an attempt on the President. Mrs. Sidon, if she were telling the truth, just might provide that key.

Sommers backtracked to the iron stairway and made his way up to the sixth floor. The corridor lights barely afforded minimum illumination. He could see that the light bulbs in two of the ceiling fixtures were out. Was that by someone's design—or had they merely burned out? He hadn't noticed that earlier when he and Kenner had explored the sixth floor. Maybe it was just coincidence. He didn't really see how a few lesser lights would be much help to the intruder, in any case.

There was something else, though. The corridor seemed a lot colder now.

Yost, standing down near the elevator and the sixth floor foyer, had observed Sommers and walked briskly up the murky hall to meet him.

"All in order up here, Yost?"

"Yessir, except for a cold wind blowing down the corridor from an open window when I got up here."

"Open window?" Sommers's stomach recoiled. "Where?"

"Just there." Yost pointed to the large, double-hung window, now closed, that occupied the wall at the south end of the long hallway where it turned left and paralleled the iron stairs Sommers had just come up.

Sommers moved quickly to the window, Yost following at a dog trot. As he reached the window and peered out, Sommers's stomach did another pratfall. He could see across to the little balcony of the room immediately adjoining in the right-angle corner the Stone Building made as it turned from the end of the corridor and continued southward. The tower balcony of the Presidential Suite, one flight below, which projected out from the face of the building where it ended on the far south corner, was clearly visible. But that's not what triggered Sommers's adrenaline.

The edge of the balcony floor of the room adjacent to the corner window was at the same floor level and only two feet away from the window, an easy step across, not even a jump, from the wide stone ledge of the open window. Despite the dim November moonlight, it was easy to see that the balcony door into the room beyond, though closed, had a broken pane of glass.

Chapter Twenty-eight

In a sotto voice, Sommers said, "Yost, run down to Kenner on the fifth floor. He's near the elevator. Get him up here with the master key he's holding and move like a pair of wolves were at your behind. Go."

Yost hurtled silently down the massive iron stairs to the fifth floor in a few jumps, his feet barely touching down. Agile man, thought Sommers in a vague spare compartment of his brain that was all but consumed by speculation as to who and why such unknown person or persons had gone through the corridor window, breaking through into the adjoining room. Furthermore, who might still be in there even now.

Sommers walked softly around to the corner of the hall and the entrance to the room. It was on the right, the number, 663. He leaned close to the door. There would be no knocking or loud instructions from him to open up this time. If someone was in there, he would get an unannounced visit.

There was no sound from the room or give-away light under the door. Sommers moved back to the head of the stairs as Yost and Kenner came bouncing up like a pair of jack rabbits. Sommers motioned to silence them and held out his hand for the key. "Easy, men," he whispered. "We don't want to announce our arrival. Whoever may be in there hasn't baked a cake for us."

Sommers quickly briefed Kenner. "Whoever it is, Jerry, must have gotten up here after we left, sometime after 11:30, but before Yost was relieved and came up here at 12:00. He couldn't know Yost would be up here. That's probably why he didn't get a chance to close the window."

Unholstering his Colt, Sommers motioned Kenner to do likewise.

"Jerry, you take the left side. I'll take the right and try to open the door. Once the key goes in, there won't be much time —we may invite some shooting, but we'll have to chance it. Whoever is on the other side, that is, if anyone is in there, may try to bluff it out if they hear a key in the lock rather than a shoulder against the door.

"Yost, you cover the corridor window looking out to the balcony. Open the window as quietly as you can and be prepared to stop anyone coming out the door to the balcony. No shooting unless shot at, understand?" Yost nodded and trotted back to the hall corner, gently lifting the window sash as Kenner and Sommers took their positions in front of the door to 663.

"Ready, Jerry?" Sommers whispered. Kenner raised his revolver to signal he was. "Let's hope no one has set the dead bolt from inside," Sommers whispered once more as he inserted the key into the lock. His hand moved with the firm precision of a surgeon placing a scalpel into the soft warm flesh of a patient's abdomen while preparing to undertake the lance-like movement that would expose vital organs to observation. If there was any sound to the action, Kenner could not hear it.

Sommers glanced up at him. He was ready to turn the key in the tumbler. Fortunately, the Stone Building rooms didn't require a turn of the door knob to open—just the swift twist of the key would release the latch, provided that no one from inside had secured the dead bolt. Kenner once again nodded his readiness and Sommers turned the key swiftly, counting on the abrupt and unexpected opening of the door to off-set the noise.

As the key turned in the lock, Sommers could feel the door give. He shoved hard against the lower panel of the door with his foot in a joint action, which flung the door wide into the room. Both men thrust their revolvers into the darkened room.

There was no one—just the soft wan light of the moon which gave revenant dimension to the assorted bedroom furniture, typical of the Stone Building rooms.

Sommers quickly flicked the wall light switch by the door, bathing the room instantly in pale yellow light from the ornate brass ceiling fixture with its delicate flower-like glass shades.

Shattered glass from the broken window in the balcony door littered the carpet, mute evidence of an earlier forced entry from the balcony.

Sommers motioned Kenner to the clothes closet, covering him as he jerked open the door. The wooden skeletons of a dozen or so empty hangers, neatly arranged on a long pole innocently awaited their next array of guest garments. The closet would have been ruled out quickly as a refuge, Sommers thought, as, no doubt, the bath would have been—a brightly-tiled enclave of white porcelain fixtures that stared back blankly at Kenner and Sommers as Sommers thrust open the door and switched on the light.

"Well, Jerry," Sommers spoke for the first time, "that leaves the bed. I don't suspect we'll flush out any miscreants from under there, but you never can tell what you might find under a rock when you turn it over."

With that, Sommers grabbed the bare mattress, the bed linen having been removed earlier by housekeeping. He lifted up a side and let it fall over the other side of the bedframe and spring, exposing the floor area underneath.

Both men reacted with a loud, indeterminate sort of grunt as their eyes picked up the object in the area now revealed by the removal of the mattress.

It was a wheat-colored burlap bag that appeared to hold some kind of a box. Sommers kneeled down and pulled the bag out from under the bedspring by a pair of attached drawstrings, leaving a trail of brownish smudge across the carpet. A dark brown stain had permeated the bottom of the jute-like fabric.

"Mud, Jerry, just like what we found in room 556. Whatever is in this," he loosened the drawstrings as he spoke, "has been stashed somewhere outside and someone obviously has wanted it inside." Sommers withdrew a wooden packing case about one foot in length and, roughly, six inches square. On two sides of the box had been stenciled 'U.S. Army Ordnance Depot, Sandy Hook, NJ-SECRET.'

Sommers and Kenner exchanged glances. "Good God, Chief, what have we got here?"

"I don't know, Jerry. Maybe we should find out before whoever left it here comes back to lay claim on it."

Sommers leaned down and turned the box over. "It's damn heavy, whatever it is." His fingers found what appeared to be the top, which was slightly loose. An inscription was printed in bold black letters on the lid:

WARNING: HIGHLY EXPLOSIVE DEVICES
DO NOT SUBJECT TO AGITATION OR HIGH TEMPERATURES
HANDLE WITH CARE

There was a metal hasp that flipped onto a metal catch fitted to take a small padlock. There was no lock, however. Sommers released the hasp and lifted the hinged lid, revealing neat rows of metal cylinders, each about six inches long and, in diameter, about the size of a fat Havana cigar. It appeared that several cylinders were missing. Sommers instantly recalled the episode at the New Paltz station when General Sidon exchanged packages with the swarthy stranger. So, that's what it was, he thought. Whatever these objects were, Sidon must have passed some of them to the man in exchange. In exchange for what? Money? What else? A product sample traded for a deposit.

Sommers's palms were sweating as he gently removed one of the cartridge-like cylinders.

Whatever the devices were and whatever their designated purpose, he had to examine them. He gently grasped the cylinder he had removed, noting a smoothly-machined, tight fitting cap on one end. It appeared to be threaded and would unscrew with the application of some force. Sure, enough, the cap, after a bit of effort loosened and was easily removed.

Inside, Sommers could see there was another cylindrical device which fitted into slots in the outer container. Sommers correctly deduced that it was meant to slide out. He tipped the container slightly and the object slid forward and out into his waiting hand. The instrument, of polished brass, was slightly pointed on one end and flared out at the other end. It was quite heavy, for its size, and was, in general, very much the shape of a cigar.

Sommers handled it gingerly, noting some letters and numbers stamped on the side.

U.S.A. P.D.S.Q.M46

Not being an armaments expert, Sommers couldn't be sure, but he surmised the device might be some kind of detonator for an artillery shell. It all seemed to come together. He was more than sure now that several of the objects must have been in the package Sidon gave to the man at the New Paltz station.

He was not yet ready to inform Kenner or the rest of his men of what he already knew about the General, but the finding of the explosive devices, whatever their ultimate purpose, certainly seemed to implicate Sidon. This he would report directly to the President. However, there were measures to be taken first.

The question was, though, at the moment, should they remove the case with its supposed detonators, highly dangerous if they were to be somehow exploded within the confines of the Mountain House? Were they the makings of some crude bomb designed to blow up the President's quarters? Sommers didn't think so. The mechanics of such an exploit would be complicated. He concluded the devices were to be traded off—exchanged, as Sidon had already done so with the 'samples' at the train station.

Risky or not, Sommers made his decision.

"Jerry, we must put all of this back as if we've never been in this room. If we're to ferret out the people responsible for this, we need to lie in wait for them, not arouse any suspicion as to what we know—which is still little enough, at this point."

Sommers quickly replaced the cylinder in the case and closed and fastened the lid. He then took the still damp and somewhat muddy burlap bag and placed the case inside, pulling the drawstrings closed. He pushed the case under the bed so as to cover the slight smudge trail the burlap bag had made as it had been drawn from under the bed earlier.

"There, Jerry, now help me get this mattress back on the bed. We've got to remove ourselves before someone gets on to us." The two men adjusted the mattress and the bed silently. Sommers surveyed the room as he moved to the door and reached for the light switch. "Come along, Jerry, let's decide our next move."

Chapter Twenty-nine

The two men exited the room and Sommers motioned Kenner back around the corner to the window at the end of the hall where Yost was still stationed. Yost was barely able to cap his urge to ask what they had found in room 663, but he knew from past procedures not to query Sommers directly. He did not enjoy the same access to Sommers that Jerry Kenner did. However, Sommers informed Yost as to the cache of secret explosives, feeling that he must ensure the linkage of his men in understanding as much as possible in preparation for whatever action might be called for in the next few hours.

"Obviously," Sommers instructed them, "we have some kind of plot underway that would seem to place the President in jeopardy. I believe our best hope of discerning who and what is involved rests in collaring whoever is responsible for juggling that case of explosives from one end of the Mountain House to the other. The man I chased earlier took the case with him out of room 556, no matter how heavy it was. Shortly after eluding me, he cached it somewhere, maybe in the sunken terrace area just off the porch of the office building. Then, he must have sensed we would search the fifth and sixth floors pretty thoroughly to be sure no other unauthorized people were around. After Jerry and I left the sixth floor, shortly after 11:30, he must have waited and then sneaked his way, sometime just before 12:00, back into the Rock Building. Since the Rock Building doesn't have a sixth floor, he went up the Rock Building stairs to the fifth floor corridor where it joins the Stone Building."

"But, if that's the case," Yost responded, "he would have had to come by me by the President's quarters to get to the Stone Building stairway and on up to the sixth floor."

"Not so, Yost," Sommers said, his face a picture of chagrin. He didn't have to pass you. Just where the Rock Building joins the Stone Building at the fifth floor level, there's another stairway up to the sixth floor directly. You wouldn't have seen him, Yost, because there's a partition that blocks that stairway from your line of sight looking down to the end of the corridor from the President's rooms. I should have realized that and had that stairway access blocked off. That's my mistake and a serious one, too, it looks like.

"However, maybe we can turn my misjudgment into an advantage. The boldness of whoever we're dealing with might just be his—or *their*—undoing—and I don't hesitate to stress the word, *their*. It took a lot of daring for whoever has authored this scheme to pick the sixth floor as a hiding place after we chased Mr. X off the fifth. But whoever is calling the shots figured we had searched the sixth floor and wouldn't be coming back. If it hadn't been for that open window, Yost, that our friend didn't get the chance to close because you happened on the scene, we might never have discovered anything. That was his mistake—that makes us even on errors but we're still way behind on hits and runs.

"Gentlemen, our man just may have set his own trap. That's provided he doesn't discover we've found his box of firecrackers." Sommers's mind slipped out of gear for a moment.

He had just thought of Mrs. Sidon and their meeting. He looked hurriedly at his watch—God—1:50. He would miss her if he didn't move.

"Jerry, go down and brief Sachs. Tell him to hold fast until Meyers relieves him. Afterward, Jerry, take a post back along the fifth floor corridor of the Rock Building where you can watch the stairs coming up and the end of the corridor where it connects with the Stone Building. Yost, you go back to the sixth floor, down by the elevator and watch the corridors and stairs until Sachs relieves you. You're to report back to the President's quarters at 6:00 to relieve Meyers, who, along with Kenner here and Sachs, will fall in with the President for his hike through the labyrinth. You'll look out for Mrs. Roosevelt and the two boys. Jerry, you've got the inside track. If somebody comes up here in the next few hours, whoever it is, he'll have to come by you to get to up to the sixth floor.

"What about the roof, Chief?" Kenner gestured toward the iron stairway that continued up one last flight from the sixth floor to open directly onto the roof.

"I'm discounting the roof for the moment, Jerry. The door up there is locked. I checked it myself and it's the only access from the roof directly to and from the sixth floor. It's true that somebody might get up to the roof by some other way, but he'd have to climb up over the edge of one of the balconies and those roof tiles are not only slippery, they're brittle and loosely laid up. In the darkness it's not a risk I would think anyone would want to take. Whoever might be crazy enough to try it would still have to climb down to reach the President's balcony on the fifth floor level—too risky and too noisy. No, I think our friend or friends may lie low for the while. Whatever they have in mind, they have no reason to think we've discovered their trysting place, unless we throw some kind of alarm, which we are most definitely not going to do." Sommers finished his instructions and briefing and lifted his shoulders in a motion given to reducing the tension he was beginning to feel in the small of his back.

"We'll keep to the schedule we've established," Sommers said. "Understood, men?" Kenner and Yost nodded affirmatively.

"Very well. Now I have some arrangements to make." Sommers's manner was suddenly recondite. Both Kenner and Yost wondered what he had in mind, but neither of them were inclined to question their chief. He would inform them in his good time, they knew from past experience, if he so deigned.

"You men know your stations. I don't need to remind you what our charge is. Good luck and stay awake. It's a long night ahead, I'm afraid. We'll get this straightened out soon enough. I know I can count on you." Sommers smiled encouragingly. He wished that he felt just half as confident as tried to pretend he was to his men.

He left Kenner and Yost and moved down the corridor to

the central stairs beyond the elevator. He decided not to take the elevator. He could be in the main foyer and reception area in the parlor wing before the elevator even reached the sixth floor. Also, he couldn't afford to get marooned between floors if the elevator decided to play tricks and wedge itself halfway down the shaft.

There was no sign of life in the central hall and stairway as he made his way down. As he passed the third floor foyer, he could easily see the dark, recessed door to room 353. Although the corridor and lighting underwent no sea change as he had experienced earlier in his hallucinogenic journey to that abstruse room, nonetheless, as he paused on the third floor landing, his stomach rose and fell as if it were a butter churn being stirred up by an impatient farm maiden.

He turned away from the object of his discomfort and completed his descent to the second floor.

The balcony serving the main parlor was accessible by a double door leading off the second floor foyer, almost directly across from the central stairway. Both doors were closed.

Sommers looked down each of the second floor halls as they merged on the foyer. They were deserted. Everyone appeared to be asleep behind the row upon row of closed doors of the graveyard-silent passageways.

He wondered if Mrs. Sidon was already waiting for him behind the balcony doors. He turned the doorknob of the right-hand door, which opened onto the foyer and tentatively stepped inside onto the rear riser of the balcony floor, which stepped down in several descending rows toward the balcony front railing overlooking the immense chamber.

There were no lights on the balcony level. Only a shimmer of orange from several lamps still left burning in the main parlor reflected dimly off the parlor ceiling. The deep chocolate brown of the mahogany-paneled walls and ceilings of the balcony swallowed up the feeble light, allowing little or no visual penetration of the umbrageous balcony corners and consequent disclosure of whatever objects, human or otherwise, might be hidden there. It was, thought Sommers, a very spooky place for a meeting. Furthermore, he could not discern the presence of any living person as he squinted against the dark, trying to make out Mrs. Sidon's figure. She was not there. Should he wait? He moved back toward the door to the foyer, which had silently swung shut behind him.

The voice that came from the obscurity of the shadows at that moment—raspy, low, barely a whisper—settled against Sommers's spine like an icy sliver.

Chapter Thirty

"Mr. Sommers, over here." Mrs. Marcus Sidon, who had been shrinking against the rear wall, broke from the volume of dark and moved toward Sommers.

No matter Sommers's preparedness in expecting Mrs. Sidon's presence, he was truly startled at her appearance. At first, an almost formless shape, she assumed a more corporeal outline as she hastened to Sommers's side. She was wearing a long diaphanous robe of a purplish hue, which gave her a spectral quality. The garment appeared to be an outer cloak designed to lend the wearer stylish, if only slight, protection against some of weather's harsher elements. She was fully dressed, Sommers could see, in the same gown she had worn to dinner earlier.

Sommers smiled and spoke in a whisper. "Mrs. Sidon. I confess you startled me—"

Mrs. Sidon allowed him no further expression. "Mr. Sommers, what I have to tell you will startle you, indeed." She hurried on with her news. "Please, listen carefully; we have little time to engage in trivia."

She drew him by the elbow back into the shadows of the balcony wall. Her voice was urgent. "Mr. Sommers, I have come into possession of further information. But, however damaging it is in itself, I fear it still does not proscribe the full extent of the conspiracy against the President."

"Carry on, Mrs. Sidon—to what do you refer?"

"First, sir, I have here a note—a code of sorts, I believe, for I can make no earthly sense of it. Perhaps to you, with your training and experience, it will unfold its mystery." Mrs. Sidon handed a scrap of note paper to Sommers on which had been written a series of numbers and letters in a seemingly meaningless sequence:

3—6—20—L—EN—D5SB—MTF—SHPG—J—15

Sommers scanned the code—he had not the foggiest idea of what the assembly of symbols could possibly mean. His training, contrary to Mrs. Sidon's expectations, did not include cryptography. The sight of the coded message, however, triggered a fresh apprehension.

It was not because of its mystery, but its tangibility—hard evidence of some enigmatic endeavor which the code's author deemed should remain unfathomable to the uninitiated. But, did it have anything to do with a conspiracy to destroy a President? For all Sommers could deduce, it might be nothing more than a series of secret chess moves or a harmless abbreviated memo, a reminder to complete some task. Of course, to apply the most sinister interpretation, it could also indicate the time and place of an attack on the President. For that matter, did Sidon compose it—or was he merely the intended recipient?

"Mrs. Sidon, how did you come into possession of this?" Sommers held up the paper in the very dim light, as if expecting the symbols to translate themselves, magically, into some sort of intelligent message.

"I copied it from a note I found under the inner sole of one of my husband's boots this afternoon while he was away from the room. I should never have discovered it but for having found earlier, you will recall, the note I told you of last evening revealing the conspiracy against the President. It would seem my husband favors his boots for hiding places.

"I have been possessed by a quite restless urge to try to uncover something more of substance to undergird my suspicions regarding the General's complicity."

Sommers, once again, studied the jumble of letters and numbers. "By itself, it is impossible for me to suggest what this might mean, at least at this moment. Is there anything else of which you can think which might illuminate this?"

"There may well be, Mr. Sommers, or at least there might

be something that could lead to further discovery." Mrs. Sidon looked anxiously over her shoulder as she said 'discovery' almost as if she expected someone might burst through the balcony doors and 'discover' the two of them in their covert conversation.

She leaned even closer to Sommers and lowered her voice, which, up to that point, had been not more than a whisper at best. "I overheard my husband in the adjoining room talking to a stranger just before dinner this evening."

"Adjoining room, Mrs. Sidon?"

"Yes. You see, my husband snores insufferably. We have slept in separate rooms for sometime now, otherwise I should not bear the ordeal of sleepless nights—one following the other without respite." Mrs. Sidon cast a modest, self-effacing glance downward as she reflected on this personal aspect of her life with the General.

"My husband was preparing for dinner in his room. I heard the outer door open and close and the voices of several men, the General conferring with whom, I do not know." She paused, appearing to stand upon another threshold of self-effacement. "I confess, once again, to an act of intrusiveness in that I listened closely from behind the door connecting our rooms."

"Yes, Mrs. Sidon, please go on." Sommers's voice was as close to trembling as the Chief of the White House Security Detail would allow himself. He took a deep breath as Mrs. Sidon continued.

"I overheard discussion of a meeting to be held in his room, number 256, at 3:00 this very morning. I could not distinguish another word, for there were very few spoken either before that declaration or thereafter. The men departed forthwith and the General's door to the corridor closed." Mrs. Sidon shook visibly as she took a shallow breath and continued. "I tell you, Mr. Sommers, I had not half a moment to compose myself as the General almost immediately came through the door to my room without first knocking. My guilty senses perceived the look he gave me as suspicious. But he merely announced that it was drawing time for dinner and that we should hasten our toilette lest we be late and arrive following the President's entrance."

Sommers looked at his watch. It was 2:30. "Very well, indeed, Mrs. Sidon. You've done admirably. Now, we have only a few minutes to devise some means of eavesdropping at that meeting. It could provide us with some details of whatever in this mad plan is to follow." Sommers felt a quiet desperation as he probed his mind to think of some way of following up Mrs. Sidon's revelation.

"I cannot impose upon your sanctuary, of course, by secreting myself in your quarters. The General, if he were to discover such business, would seek explanations for which we would, to say the least, be totally indisposed to deal."

"Wait, Mr. Sommers, I believe I have come upon a possibility for such an eavesdropping."

"Oh," Sommers exclaimed expectantly. "What possibility might that be?"

Mrs. Sidon continued, her whispers clothed now in quiet but growing excitement, "There is a passageway from the corridor, disclosed by a small door, that would appear to run behind a wall next to the General's room, 256. If you were to secret yourself in that shaft, you might well hear more distinctly any words spoken in the room itself."

Sommers marveled at Mrs. Sidon's coolness and courage, in disclosure of her own husband's traitorous behavior. She seemed unapparent, or unconcerned for the incredibly compromising position in which she was placing herself, in view of her relationship to the General. Surely, he thought, she must be speaking the truth.

"Capital, Mrs. Sidon. Let's find this access door." Sommers looked again at his watch. "We have a little more than twenty minutes before the General's meeting."

The two moved to the balcony doors. Sommers peered out through the small crack between the two doors.

"No one. Now listen, Mrs. Sidon. I'll exit and locate the door which must lie just around the corner of the corridor from here."

"Yes, yes," came Mrs. Sidon's excited reply.

"You stay here for a few moments while I take a look into the shaft to see if it's large enough to allow an entrance. It may be necessary for you to shut the door after I'm in place.

"Afterward, proceed to your room and resolve not to take any part in whatever follows. It's time for you to divest yourself of any further involvement. What follows may turn out to be very dangerous for you if the General suspects in any way that you've compromised him. By the by, how will you explain to your husband your absence for these past minutes if he should discover you missing from your room or just returning?"

"I've thought of that, Mr. Sommers," she said with something of a conspiratorial smile.

Sommers could swear that, despite the dreadful overtones of the events of the last few hours and her indomitable persistence in the face of menacing consequences, she was secretly enjoying her role in bringing down her husband. She must have had a very troubled and unhappy marriage, he thought. How sad. He thought of his own life with Helena and of how perfect their relationship was, so full of affection and caring. Mrs. Sidon's voice cut into his thoughts.

"You see, Mr. Sommers, I've disabled the toilet in my room by clogging it with tissue—at least that is what I should tell my husband. Under such circumstances, it would, of course, be necessary to use the public W.C. off the hall foyer, would it not? I am not accustomed, you might surmise, to using the General's private W.C." A faint smile lingered on her face.

"You are a devilish clever woman, Mrs. Sidon and one to be much admired. This country will undeniably be in your debt if we are successful in scotching your husband's plot, whatever direction it is bound to take in the offing." Sommers took Mrs. Sidon's hands and held them to his face, implanting a gentle kiss on them. He didn't think Helena would object in view of the circumstances. "You are a very brave woman. And, now—I must go. Please, dear lady, heed my instructions. I promise you no harm will come to the President. You have done your part."

Sommers broke quickly away and stepped out into the dim corridor. He wished, ardently, that he could believe his own words that T.R. would suffer no ill in the hours to come.

The second floor corridors, in both directions from the central staircase, were empty. Sommers once again checked his watch—almost 2:45. Not much time left. It was only a matter of several steps to the corner on the left and the elevator where, just beyond, the Sidons' rooms, 254 and 256 fronted.

The access door to the shaft or chase area was a few feet on the other side of room 256. The door was of paneled oak construction, stained very dark brown, similar to the main room doors. Approximately three by four feet in size, it appeared large enough for a man to enter, as well it should, since it was an access to the plumbing and electrical workings which required attention from time to time. Sommers wondered as he walked by casually if the chase area beyond the door opened to a height great enough for a man to stand up without crouching. He noticed a small latch at the top of the door which indicated the door, when opened, was hinged to drop down into the corridor. After he entered and pulled the door shut behind him, would the latch, which obviously was designed to lock from the outside, permit opening from within? No matter, his course was set. If he had to, he believed he could jimmy the door open from the inside with the small pocket knife he carried with him.

He thought momentarily that, as an alternate to entering the chamber immediately, he might wait in the corridor foyer until the announced meeting time, hoping to catch a glimpse of a conspirator or conspirators upon their entry to room 256. No, he dismissed it as quickly as it came to mind. Too risky—there wasn't a good place to stand, completely unobserved in the foyer. What might such already suspicious suspects think of him outside the Sidons' rooms at 3:00 AM if he were to be seen? Also, the possibility of his entering the shaft after the meeting had started was replete with problems—noise, for one thing, as he settled himself in unknown surroundings. Then, too, he might miss important details if the meeting turned out to be a short one and he hadn't gotten in place in time.

While he had been deliberating, he had walked almost to the end of the corridor. Minutes were slipping by. He must tuck himself away quickly, lest he be observed.

He turned and made his way back to the access door just as Mrs. Sidon came around the corner on her return to her room. Sommers smiled and stopped by the door, flipping the latch and lowering the door, indicating to Mrs. Sidon to close the door as he entered. The entire action took only a few seconds. The door closed as Sommers, on his knees, crawled deeper into the dark recess of the shaft, having noted in the brief duration of the light from the hall that the little room was about eight feet in height.

Relieved, he stood up and gave a cursory glance around him in the limited light leaking in from around the edges of the door which did not, fortunately, fit snugly in its frame.

He observed a conglomeration of plumbing—water supply,

drains, insulated steam heating pipes softly hissing and electrical cables, all hugging a good portion of the structural wall separating him from room 256. It was a tight squeeze, but he had room to turn, the wall opposite being about four feet away. The entire length of the shaft from the corridor opening seemed to run to the outside wall, which he estimated at about fourteen feet. The bit of light from the ill-fitting access door helped to cut the blackness of the space to afford, at least, a dim view of his quarters. He was particularly interested in the construction of the partition wall separating the shaft from room 256.

His side of the wall was unfinished. The framing consisted of full-cut 2 x 4 wooden studs, 16 inches on center, covered from the room side by horizontal strips of lathing and plastered over to provide a finished surface. The thick, gray tongue-like edges of plaster, which had oozed through the gaps in the narrow wooden strips of lathing during application had hardened to the consistency of cement.

Although several nails could be seen protruding from the wall, no doubt the result of random picture hanging from inside of room 256, Sommers could see no holes into the room that might provide an observation port and disclosure of the room's occupants. He could hear no noise from within. The only sound, at the moment, was the whisper-like hissing of one of the steam pipes in the shaft and a faint, intermittent rustling, similar to that a chipmunk might make scurrying around in dry leaves. It was sure and certain evidence of mice which probably ranged, at will, up and down the insides of the Mountain House, cavorting in a silent, parallel world of their own amidst the well-fed Smiley family guests, occasionally intersecting with their human hosts in the matter of sharing the ample provisions of food from the larders of the Mohonk kitchens.

Sommers could just detect the face of his watch from the tiny rays of light shining through the door from the corridor. The minute hand rested on 11. Five minutes to go, if the meeting was to commence on time. Settling himself on the floor, which resulted in the displacement of several years' accumulation of dust and a near sneeze as he breathed in the acrid particles, he leaned his face against the rough wall between two studs. He was surprised to hear what sounded like two voices, both men's. Had they been in the room all the while or did they just enter? He had not heard a door open or close to the corridor.

As he dissected this finding, he did hear a door open and close. Could that be a third man entering? The murmur of several voices, indistinguishable except for an occasional cough or clearing of throat, began to frustrate him. He had to hear what was occurring. He would miss everything unless he arrived at a quick and satisfactory solution to tapping into the conversation, now growing more animated but no more intelligible.

Hold on—what if he were to chisel a tiny hole through the plaster, small enough not to be heard in the doing, but, hopefully, large enough to transmit sound from within. It was dangerous, but he had no choice. It was the only way.

He withdrew a small folding knife from a hidden pocket attached to his leather shoulder holster. The blade, about three inches in length, was not exactly a lethal weapon but Sommers had found it useful, particularly in his earlier career as a New York City policeman, in picking obstinate locks, as had been sometimes required in his detective duties.

The tip of the blade was well-pointed, allowing him to manipulate it somewhat like a small drill. He picked an area near the front access door, approximately three feet up from the floor, which he thought might not be so obvious from the room side of the wall. Slowly, he began to twist the blade in a circular motion, the dry, hard plaster between two lathing strips responding to the cutting edge and falling out in small chips and powdery fragments. He worked slowly and silently until he felt a slight give of the blade tip which had finally broken through into the room, creating a tiny hole through which a pin-point ray of light immediately pierced the darkness of the chase area.

As he withdrew the knife and leaned his ear toward the minuscule opening, he was surprised at the dramatic attenuation of the voices. Although he was not able to make out complete phrases, he was able to distinguish some words spoken by a man with a foreign accent which he could not identify.

"Labyrinth" was mentioned twice, followed by the number "6" and further vocal murmurs that Sommers was at a loss to interpret. He just caught the syllable —ax— but lost the rest of the word. This would not do. He must widen the opening and try to assimilate enough parts to make sense of the whole.

He carefully applied his knife, once again, to the minute

opening, slowly turning the blade, scraping bits and pieces, trying not to let any particles fall through on the room side.

He was just about to finish. The hole was larger and more sound was coming through. He caught the word "Roosevelt," followed by some guttural sounds and the word "bridge" when it happened.

His knife had loosened a too large chunk of plaster which cracked under the stress of the crude drilling process. Too late to prevent it, Sommers could hear the chunk fall into the room hitting an uncarpeted section of the floor with a soft but audible 'thunk.' Faint though it actually was, to the horrified Sommers, it sounded like a brick falling. He sat for a second staring at the much too large opening.

There was an immediate reaction in the room. Voices overlaid—Sidon's, in particular—in a chorus of protestations—"What in Hell"—"Who the devil"—"Look there"—"Next door"

Now angry shouts merged with the movements of chairs, heavy steps and the dousing of room lights as a door to the corridor opened and threatening voices spilled out into the tomb-like silence of the hall.

Chapter Thirty-one

Sommers's first reaction was to draw his Colt from its holster and flatten himself against the wall—at the same time, shrinking back away from the corridor access door as far as he could retreat. His back brushed against the exterior wall a good fourteen feet from the door. He could see through the thin crack surrounding the door opening indistinguishable shapes passing back and forth, breaking the transmission of light. Several voices, guttural and hushed, seemed to be debating a further move, although Sommers could not discriminate individual words. Apparently, whoever had poured out into the hall in such alarm could not now decide on a judicious course of action in confronting the unknown person concealed in the space between the two rooms.

Sommers felt something of the same apprehension. He assumed his potential assailants were armed but, more than likely, not anxious to precipitate an action with unpredictable circumstances, to say nothing of creating a disturbance that would betray their presence. How do you explain shooting into a wall space at 3:15 AM with a significant number of Mountain House guests sleeping soundly nearby?

For his part, Sommers did not relish having to shoot his way out of a darkened tunnel without having more information as to whom would constitute his target.

A perfect stalemate, so it would seem, but only for brief seconds. A decision had been made on the other side of the door. Whoever was there had decided to unlatch the door. Sommers could hear the fumbling of the latch as fingers worked to free the bolt.

The door dropped abruptly into the corridor, allowing a shaft of light to flood the cavity. For a moment, no one appeared in the doorway. Sommers felt trapped as the light from the hallway, dim that it was, caught him full in the face. To Sommers, it felt as bright as the noonday sun.

For a fraction of a second, the head and shoulders of two men suddenly filled the small access door opening. The men moved aside again quickly, aware that they presented an excellent target to the man in the shaft. Sommers then heard a command barked out—not a loud summons but an ominously sounding one. It was a voice clothed in some kind of accent unfamiliar to Sommers. German?—Russian?—Turkish? It could even have been Japanese. There were only four words spoken: "You—come out now."

Sommers stared at the open door. The men must have been standing just on either side of the opening, completely out of Sommers's line of sight. Sommers did not answer. If he had to, he would await his pursuers from where he crouched in the half-shadows, half-light of the utility shaft.

The voice repeated itself: "You—come out. We have you." The command was louder, now, insistent, threatening. Sommers could not hope to avoid the challenge. The men were simply not going to go away and it did not appear that anyone would be coming down the second floor hall to his rescue, not at that hour of the morning. Briefly, and only briefly, Sommers thought of screaming at the top of his lungs to attract assistance, but he ruled that scenario out. An innocent party might be hurt in the offing—worse, the men would disappear and he would be back where he started in trying to identify the conspirators. Worse even yet, now that they were alerted to his knowledge of them, insubstantial as his information was up to that point, they would be truly spooked and might withdraw altogether. On top of that, General Sidon would easily surmise that his wife had put Sommers on to him, placing her in great jeopardy.

No, now that a confrontation seemed inevitable, Sommers knew he had no choice but to see it through. No matter he was cooped up in the shaft, the odds were still about even.

Sommers resigned himself to exchanging shots with the conspirators if that was the only way to go. He would await their move. He moved as far back against the outside wall of the shaft as he could. There was still enough darkness in that more distant corner to confuse any shooter firing from the doorway. In addition, the shooter would be exposing himself in the brief seconds he would take to aim and shoot. No, the odds were fairly equal. Sommers was convinced he would take at least one of the men, if not both, in the encounter. He aimed his Colt squarely at the door opening and pulled back the hammer of the revolver. The silver barrel gleamed in the light spilling in from the corridor.

There was no hiding anymore. Leaning tightly against the wall of the shaft, Sommers braced his right shoulder and arm to steady his aim. He believed the men would attempt some kind of move at any moment, though he was unsure of the form such action might take.

He was totally unprepared for what did happen next.

Chapter Thirty-two

The section of the wall Sommers had been leaning against as he aimed his gun gave way behind his shoulder. Thrown off balance, his right arm flew up reflexively, the barrel of the pistol hitting something very hard over head as he fell sideways through an opening to his immediate right. The Colt dropped from his fingers as it struck a beam while he struggled to recover from the sidelong pitch, almost a catapult, into another shaft.

As he fell through the opening, his body fought to recognize the unexpected void and adjust to its unknown dimensions. It couldn't have taken more than a second or two in real time. It felt to Sommers that he would never hit bottom, although he had dropped only three to four feet to a platform. The sickening sound of his revolver falling through what appeared to be some kind of scaffold, bouncing off several obstructive braces as it fell on and on to lower depths, merged with the voices of men who had gingerly stepped into the chase area in their pursuit.

Sommers quickly realized, as he regained his feet, that he had pushed through a hidden access door from the utility shaft into an auxiliary stairway which, he determined by feeling with his hands, led upward and downward. A voice just above him coming from the second floor chase barked, "He's gone—wait, there's a door at the end."

Sommers could hear steps approaching the area he had just pitched through. Slowly, carefully, heavy footsteps shuffled across the dusty floor boards, nearing his miraculous and unexpected escape hatchway.

Sommers's right hand hurt from the collision with the beam—his gun was gone. His right shoulder ached from the painful impact of his fall, but he was not seriously injured. He couldn't be sure he was any better off for his remarkable dodge. There was no way of retrieving his gun, not in the pitch blackness of the lower stairs, even if he had time, which of course he did not have. His pursuers were only a breath away. Sommers could swear he smelled garlic as he climbed up past the second floor level, having quickly decided his best course of action was to move up the rough steps to whatever level they might take him. Apparently, the hidden door to his 'secret' stairway had slammed shut after his inglorious break-through, slowing down for precious seconds the men who sought him out.

Although there was no light on the stairway, Sommers could feel his way upward without difficulty. Where did the stairs lead? No matter, he had no choice, now. The voices sounded from directly below him. The men must have found the way into the parallel shaft. He guessed he had about a flight and a half lead on them. His only advantage was the caution his stalkers were exercising in their ascent to avoid a possible ambush. They could not know he was now unarmed save for his little pocket knife, the careless operation of which had consigned him to his present predicament.

If the stairs led all the way to the roof, which he assumed, he might be able to elude or ambush his adversaries. There were a lot of places one could hide on the roof—behind fanciful, decorative stone battlements or a score or more of huge stone chimneys. Also, different roof elevations, both flat and pitched surfaces, might offer refuge.

Sommers had gained on his opponents. They were still coming, but cautiously. They were in no mood to catch a bullet from an unseen gun. Feeling cold air from somewhere above, Sommers calculated he had reached the sixth floor level. Surely, there must be a door on each level, giving access to the utility shaft off the stairs. He made a stab at feeling for one in the blackness of the sixth floor landing, but he could not detect any framework or casing that might indicate an opening, and the rapidly approaching steps from below eliminated any slight margin of time that remained for any further exploration.

He could feel cold air coming from above. The roof had to be just above. There surely must be a trapdoor. There didn't appear to be enough head room for a doorway passage onto the roof.

Sure enough, as he scrambled up the last flight, he reached up and felt a cold metallic surface. He pushed on it. It gave slightly but resisted opening. There had to be an inside latch. He ran his fingers around the four sides of the trapdoor. On the front side, where the stairs met the frame surrounding the door, he discovered a latch with a small ring. He pulled the ring with his left hand and pushed hard upward with his right. The trapdoor swung upward easily and flopped over heavily onto the flat roof.

Sommers clambered up and over onto the roof as voices, like the guttural growls of a wolfpack on the trail of a wounded caribou, filtered up the open stairwell. The men were still about two floors below but closing fast. Quickly, Sommers threw the trapdoor closed and circumscribed the Mountain House rooftops with his eyes, frenziedly weighing his chances for overcoming his unknown pursuers in a direct confrontation.

This presented undesirable odds of at least two, no doubt, armed men against his own, unarmed self. Might it not be more discreet, he thought, in the alternate, to slip into a hiding place somewhere on that vast rooftop forest of massive chimneys and crenelations from whence he would enjoy added seconds, if not minutes, to develop a strategy that would allow for improving the odds?

From where he stood on the flat-roofed section of the Mountain House, he noted six towering stone chimneys, each at least six feet wide and about twelve feet high, ranging up like fortifications on either side of the ridge line of a vaulted, copper roof on the adjacent connecting building.

A catwalk, approximately three feet wide, had been built on top of the ridge line of the gabled roof. In the indeterminate light of the pale moon, the copper roof plates reflected a greenish patina, the result of weathering since the completion of the building four years previously.

Remarkable, Sommers thought, how the mind could independently, if not entirely calmly, perceive of its surroundings, though so distinctly threatened by sudden emergent hostile forces of such a nature, that, once enjoined, could easily result in destruction of the total organism.

On one level of consciousness, Sommers's mind was absorbing the architectural marvels revealed in the rambling structure of the connecting Mountain House roofs.

The monumental chimneys, parapets, turrets, tower gazebos, crenelations and gothic adornments wandered before his eyes in the fragile moonlight like a strange medieval landscape.

On a more pertinent level, he was mulling over at the same time, in something less than split seconds, the comparative survival rates offered by confrontation with his pursuers and/or avoidance, if such could be achieved.

The concept of confrontation was momentarily discarded as the heavy footfalls of his stalkers, rounding the last landing and heading up the final flight to the roof, echoed through the closed trapdoor.

Sommers dashed to the catwalk and, in several long strides, reached a large chimney to his left rising from behind a parapet separating the two Stone Buildings. The chimney, which must have enclosed multiple fireplace flues, could easily have hidden a small squad of Roosevelt's 'Rough Riders.'

Once sequestered behind the chimney's bulk, Sommers experienced an immediate, if somewhat relative, degree of comfort. He knew instantly that he had made the right decision as he carefully peered back from around the edge of the chimney and watched as the trapdoor was elevated ever so slightly. The 'hunters' still anticipated their quarry was armed and were not eager to reverse their roles.

Sommers watched as, after a moment or two, the trapdoor was thrown violently open by an arm, which quickly removed itself from any possible line of fire. Seconds passed—no one emerged. Obviously, he reasoned, whoever had pounded up those darkened stairs in rabid pursuit was having second thoughts about exposing himself to a bullet fired by a now hidden antagonist.

Could it be that the hunters would give up the chase—fearful of the new equation that pitted them against unpredictable odds?

No, there was movement. They were going to call his bluff. Perhaps they had reasoned that Sommers, not having confronted them directly at the trapdoor, was unarmed after all. They were going to chance it.

A head appeared over the rim of the square opening. It was too dark for Sommers to make out any features. The head was followed by a pair of shoulders and a convulsive body movement that thrust the man over the edge of the trapdoor in a crouching stance that immediately reduced itself to a flattened position on the roof surface. Sommers could see moonlight reflected off the shiny steel barrel of a pistol held in the man's right hand.

The man's face was slightly upturned. He was scrutinizing the scene before him—the same rooftop view Sommers had observed fleeting moments ago. The man seemed to be expecting alien fire. Sommers rubbed his right hand in self-reproach over dropping his revolver in the shaft. His hand still hurt from the sudden collision with the overhead beam. He could still hear it as the gun tumbled downward through the wooden scaffold.

The man must know by now, Sommers thought, that he was unarmed and hiding somewhere in that vast rooftop forest of stone and shadow.

Slowly the hunter raised his head and shoulders. The movement was not answered by enemy fire which encouraged him to assume a kneeling position. He leaned back toward the opening. Another head raised itself above the edge. There were words exchanged, nothing of which Sommers could distinguish at his distance. The words were not English. He could discern that much.

The two men were growing braver. The first man stood abruptly and ran to his right across the roof to Sommers's left into the shadow of the stone parapet demarcating the roof edge overlooking the lake. The other man scrambled up over the edge of the trapdoor like a rifleman vaulting up over a trench with fixed bayonet. It wasn't a rifle with a steel bayonet he held in one hand, however, but it was close.

A long stiletto blade flashed in the moonlight as he ran, crouched over, toward the outside edge of the building's roof, opposite to his cohort, overlooking the Rondout Valley to Sommers's right.

It was immediately apparent to Sommers as to their next action. They were going to hunt him down like a wild boar. Only they would not shoot him when they discovered him. They would knife him—much quieter—no need to disturb the sleeping guests of the Mountain House.

If they followed the simple strategy Sommers deduced from their initial movements that they seemed to have decided upon, they would each follow as closely as possible the roof perimeters, moving slowly toward the stone chimneys that paraded along the gable edges of the adjoining roof where Sommers was now positioned behind the second in line of the chimneys, directly in the path of the man with the stiletto.

Sommers was sweating despite his lack of recent movement. He concluded he would either have to engage the stiletto man or chance a swift run back toward the trapdoor, hoping that the two men, as widespread as they would be in following the outside walls, would not be able to catch him before he dropped through the access door.

If he were to jump the stiletto man, the other would probably shoot, noise or no noise. They had to get rid of him now, regardless of the consequences of discovery or the necessity of shelving whatever conspiracy against the President they had planned.

Sommers could hear both men as they approached, widespread as they were. After crossing the flat-roof to the adjoining building where Sommers was hidden half-way down the avenue of chimneys, they were advancing along the lower edges of the gently sloping copper roof. The dull, drum-like sounds of their boots on the flanged roof sections as the sheet metal gave way slightly to the pressure, telegraphed their positions to Sommers.

He would have one chance as they moved in line toward him from opposite sides once the stiletto man reached a point about ten feet in front of him.

Chapter Thirty-three

Sommers enjoyed one advantage—surprise. They didn't know how close they were to him. From their maneuvering, it was clear they had no idea where he was. If he ran for the catwalk on the ridge and back to the other building and the trapdoor, he might get down before either one of them got off a shot. They would be too widely separated at the edges of the roof to team up on him.

The copper roof sections groaned under the incursive boots of the hunters. They were getting uncomfortably close. The stiletto man reached the chimney just ahead of Sommers's sanctuary. It was time for Sommers to move or enjoin him.

Having decided that discretion would be the better part of valor, Sommers leaped from behind the chimney so surprisingly that the stiletto man, who was by now only a few feet from him, let out a cry and very nearly lost his footing on the slippery copper roof.

Sommers reached the catwalk literally on the fly, hoping that the hunters were Turks. The Turkish military, at least, he knew to be notoriously poor marksmen.

He didn't notice the gun's report but the sharp snarl of a light caliber bullet whined past his left ear like a home-coming hornet. He dropped to his knees upon reaching the trapdoor and thrust his lower body into a twisting motion that brought his feet and legs over the edge of the opening. Two more quick flashes from the gable roof edge and soft pinging sounds indicated the arrival of more hornets. The bullets dug little furrows in the flat-graveled roof not six inches from the edge of the trapdoor as Sommers disappeared down the narrow, dark well.

A thin veil of moonlight spilled over the stairs as they led down, the faint rays of which after the first flight were absorbed in the spongy blackness as Sommers stumbled bottomward into the bowels of the lower floors. Spiraling blindly down from each floor landing, he wondered whether he might have gained time if he had tried to shut and lock the trapdoor. Probably not—in any case, it was academic at this point. He briefly weighed the idea of trying to find the exit from the shaft at the second floor level where he had originally fallen through. That idea was quickly abandoned as the heavy crunch of boots on the stairs above signaled the pell mell descent of the hunters. This time there was no longer any need for caution on their part since they now had adduced for themselves that their quarry was unarmed. There were no seconds to give up in a speculative search for a concealed utility door to the accompanying shaft.

Sommers continued his downward plunge, floor by floor, to some unknown terminus he hoped would provide an exit on the lowest level.

From somewhere below, a sliver of light appeared as he rounded what seemed to be a final landing. It had to indicate some kind of egress, he thought, hopefully, as he stumbled down the last flight.

At the bottom, his boots hit a hard surface—a cement or rock floor. Off the stairwell, directly in front of him, was an access doorway, the edges of which were outlined with light from the other side.

The door, fortunately, was unbolted, and Sommers burst through into a subterranean tunnel, sparsely lighted, leading off in opposite directions from the shaft from which he just emerged.

The walls of the tunnel were built of massive, cutstone blocks of the same kind of conglomerate stone used in the upper walls of the Stone Buildings. Pipes of all sizes stretched along the bottom of the far wall like endless umbilical cords, giving life and sustenance to the super-structure of the Mountain House which rose seven stories directly above. His pursuers could not be far behind him. Which direction should he take?

Notwithstanding his vulnerability at being unarmed, he was beginning to wonder whether he might devise some sort of ambush for his relentless foes. He had little time for a decision. The tunnel, in one direction, wended its way into deeper and decidedly darker regions, more than likely into the vast reaches of the dungeon-like cellars of the Stone Buildings. The light in that direction diminished alarmingly about twenty yards from where Sommers stood. The other direction was far better lighted. There was a partition and doorway about thirty yards farther down the tunnel. Affixed to the wall was a light that shone bright red. Sommers could just make out a sign on the door which stated: FIRE DOOR, KEEP CLOSED. He reasoned that that meant 'civilization' as opposed to the 'unexplored territory' that beckoned from the opposite direction.

All of this analysis took him less than seconds to conclude that his direction should be for the fire door and whatever lay beyond. He dashed along the tunnel as the boots of the hunters pummeled down the last few remaining steps to the tunnel egress.

The fire door was unlocked and Sommers broke through into a well-lighted but somewhat roughly finished tunnel extension that provided access to further utility and service areas established beyond the partition and the fire door separating the tunnel areas.

He had no time for sightseeing. As he burst through the fire door, he could hear the men behind him noisily exiting the door from the shaft.

Sommers realized that even if he wanted to keep on running, the men would be upon him in seconds. All of his past training, his experience to date, his very instinct for survival, all melded together to advise him as to an inevitable consensus. It was time for the hunted to become the hunter and there was no place that offered a better advantage than where he now stood.

Quickly, he stepped to one side of the fire door which he had slammed shut. Luckily, some rough pieces of lumber lay to one side of the tunnel corridor. He snatched a short but heavy member from the pile. Only one man could come through the door at one time. He could, with a single blow, at least even the odds.

He raised his arm, leveraging the heavy piece of wood to a point strategically high enough to administer a blow to whatever part of a man's anatomy appeared first through the door.

He waited, expecting momentarily, a frenzied, all-out breakthrough. There was nothing.

Strange, the last thing he had heard was the scraping of boots on the hard rock surface of the tunnel floor as the men had poured through the door from the shaft into the tunnel. The sounds coincided almost exactly with his own noisy escape through the fire door. Now, as he waited, resigned to an unavoidable confrontation, he could hear no continuation of a noisy pursuit. What was happening?

Could it be that the hunters had once again decreed caution, thinking that they had cornered their prey? Seconds passed—nothing.

Sommers, a moment ago resigned to a stand, come what may, had been quite collected, absolutely prepared to give no quarter. The affair would be ended and the consequences left no longer in doubt. Now, awaiting an attack which did not materialize, he grew uneasy.

More than a full minute had passed since he had slammed shut the fire door. He waited—his arm tiring from holding the heavy cudgel over the door.

Another minute passed, he was sure. He listened—no sounds whatever passed through the fire door or partition—no heavy breathing, no boots scraping on a hard surface—no footsteps—nothing.

Wait—there was something. A humming—a kind of low frequency buzzing, was it? No—more of a hum. Sommers leaned toward the door. It seemed to come from just beyond the door. He looked around him as if he might find on his side of the door a clue as to what could be causing such a sound. He noticed several large conduits overhead against the ceiling. Funny, he hadn't noticed them before—just the pipes along the floor of the tunnel.

One of the overhead pipes was affixed with a steel bracket painted white, on which was lettered in red the words: DANGER HIGH VOLTAGE.

Sommers could swear the humming sound had increased in volume since he had first detected it. He assuredly didn't notice it when he first came through the fire door. He lowered his makeshift weapon and listened again through the door. The humming was certainly loud enough but it seemed steady now. It wasn't getting any louder.

He couldn't make it out. The men had to be just on the other side of the door. Maybe they were waiting for him to make a move. Maybe they were lying in wait for him. What a queer standoff. It didn't make sense.

Sommers was sure at least five minutes had now passed. He had been too preoccupied to think to check his watch after first coming through the door. He was growing impatient. Waiting for something to happen was always more difficult than the happening itself.

Well, then, if the men were on the other side of the door waiting for him to make the next move, he would oblige them. He would enjoin them on their own turf. He, at least, had the element of surprise left. They could not really know if he was still standing on his side of the door. How did they know he hadn't disappeared down his side of the tunnel and gone on up to alert his men, possibly even at this minute organizing a search to root them out? His thoughts piled over on one another like football players scrambling for a loose ball. One thing was clear, he had to make a move. Despite the danger in a confrontation, he was concerned that the conspirators might decide, at this point, to give up the chase and lie low until a more convenient time. After all, it was doubtful, from their point of view, that Sommers knew anything more about them or their plans.

No—not logical, he concluded. They couldn't let him go. What little he might know was too much. They had to silence him, regardless of what such an action might do to their present plans. There was always another day, another place to continue their machinations.

Sommers was resolved to force the issue. Without the men on the other side of the door, he had nothing of substance, knew nothing more than he did before his meeting with Mrs. Sidon. Beside all of that, she was in frightful danger, exposed to her husband's obvious awareness, now, of her disclosure.

He reached for the door handle. The door swung inward, releasing a rush of very warm air from within. The humming sound was very loud now but there was no reaction otherwise from the other side. Sommers could hear no sign of life, not a sound save the incessant humming—no furtive movements, no scraping of boots on the hard floor. No bodies leaped from the shadows—nothing alive stirred on the other side of the fire door, which remained in a wide open position.

The humming from the other side was certainly insistent. There didn't seem to be any reason for waiting any longer. He again raised his makeshift armament and poised himself to break through.

Hidden in his position to one side of the door, he awaited in vain for some sign from within the tunnel which might betray the presence of the two men. There was nothing—just the unremitting humming. He decided he would have to see just what was on the other side of the door, even if it did mean exposing himself to bullets or knives.

In a cat-like maneuver, he dropped to his stomach in front of the open door, peered through and rolled sideways until he had cleared the opening and ended up out of the line of the door opening behind the partition on the right side of the door. His eyes picked up no crouching figures, no sight of revolvers or knives waving in the air. There was nothing that would give any indication of the conspirators who had pursued him up the rickety stairs to the roof and down again to the musty, dungeon-like surroundings of the Mountain House foundations and cellars.

Sommers's eyes, however, in that deft roll-over he had just executed, did pick up something else that he hadn't noticed before when he broke out of the stairway shaft into the tunnel.

To the left side of the passage was a floor to ceiling steel mesh enclosure, painted red, which encased a number of heavy steel cabinets with conduits, panels and switches galore.

He got to his feet and stepped cautiously through the door. There was no one in sight anywhere along the tunnel for as far as he could see. The tunnel, itself, seemed crammed with all sorts of plumbing and pipes, far more so than he remembered in his rapid dash through, minutes ago. He now noticed huge, strange looking valves and cylinders with what appeared to be control panels with dials and levers, all painted in red.

There was another white sign with a red border and red letters attached to an access door of the enclosure. It also stated: DANGER HIGH VOLTAGE NO ADMITTANCE. A heavy steel padlock was secured to a hasp and next to it a white card was fastened to the steel mesh door. It appeared to be an inspection report. On it were a list of nearly illegible signatures followed by dates, which, by comparison, were unmistakably clear.

Sommers stared at the last date on the chart. It read: February 15,1993. The signature beside the date was Kevin Moore. No, that should be 1903—not 1993—a careless zero that ended up looking like a 9. He looked at the date just prior. The month indicated was January 10,1993— the signature, again, was that of a K. Moore. There was a rather crumpled sheet under the top one. Sommers looked unbelievingly at the list. Every month was accounted for from January through December for the previous year.

That year was clearly visible on all the sign-offs. It was 1992.

Chapter Thirty-four

It couldn't be happening again—this was 1904, not 1993. Helena was upstairs, sleeping peacefully in room 490. He had four men on duty in the upper chambers of the Mountain House. The President and his family were safe behind the doors of 571 and the adjoining suite. Mrs. Sidon was, no doubt, sleeplessly awaiting his further discoveries of a mad scheme to destroy the President of the United States. There were conspirators, even now, running amok through the halls and, perhaps, the grounds of the Mountain House.

This was 1904,1904,1904—Sommers found himself shouting the numbers aloud as his eyes wandered over the unfamiliar installations and hardware packing the tunnel walls.

Yet what else could explain the mysterious disappearance of the conspirators?

He had to get out of the tunnel. He would find his way up to the lobby and the reception area where he would find the night clerk and a sleepy elevator operator in their accustomed positions. He would calmly instruct the elevator operator to take him to the fifth floor, where he would check on Meyers guarding the President's suite. Then he would go on up to the sixth floor and check out Sachs, who was watching the room where they had discovered the detonators. Next would be Kenner, whom he had left on the fifth floor of the Rock Building monitoring the stairwell from the Rock Building up to the sixth floor of the Stone Building.

Everyone would be in place as assigned, except for Yost, who would be off duty until 6:00. After checking on Kenner, he would pass on down to the fourth floor of the Rock Building to room 490 and look in on Helena before calling a hurried conclave to inform his men as to his findings, after which he would report to T.R., himself, of the bizarre conspiracy. Regardless of the hour, it was time to notify the President.

He would place General Sidon under arrest and arrange for the New Paltz and County Constabulary to block all roads out of Mohonk. He would request an armed contingent be sent to the Mountain House to conduct a thorough search of the grounds and the Mountain House for the conspirators, floor to floor, room to room, if necessary.

God, all hell would break loose. The President would be furious. He could see T.R. now, raging like a wounded polar bear chasing hapless Eskimo hunters over jagged slabs of ice.

After another quick, visual perusal of the tunnel corridor, Sommers backtracked to the egress of the utility shaft and stairwell.

The door was missing, not just missing—the wall was a continuous sequence of stone blocks. Where the door should have been, no unbroken line in the stonework showed to suggest a doorway had ever been there in a sometime distant past—or was it future from Sommers's point of view?

In growing confusion, Sommers clutched at his head and closed his eyes, thinking he might open them again and find himself in the familiar surroundings of the tunnel of the recent chase. Would the conspirators also reemerge from the mist of fractured time?

Oddly enough, he desperately hoped that they would. He felt far more capable of dealing with flesh and blood adversaries of 1904 than the discarnate settings of a future time.

He removed his hands and opened his eyes—the red steel mesh cage emblazoned with the words HIGH VOLTAGE still stood against the wall, overwhelmingly existent, embracing and securing within its metal frame the strange panels, switches and cabinets that generated the pervasive humming sound—a drone that seemed to absorb and incorporate within it all other lessor decibels in the tunnel milieu that might, if not for such ceaseless din, offer the normal night mosaic of sounds produced by crickets, mice and other scrawling creatures indigenous to the dark subterranean climes of the Mountain House.

In a lunge like a punched-out prize fighter verging on the edge of collapse, Sommers staggered through the partition doorway into the more finished area of the tunnel corridor.

He searched for another stairway leading up, passing service quarters on either side of the passageway—laundries, linen storage bins, a flower shop, a room entitled 'Fitness Center,' and more sidelong pipes, conduits, extensive plumbing and equipment with indicator dials and shut-off valves labeled 'Sprinkler.' Tiny cloud tricklets of steam, accompanied by whistle-like sighs wafted from joints of overhead pipes wrapped in coils of white plaster-like material.

Sommers finally came upon a doorway with glass panels, through which he could see a carpeted stair leading up. Relieved, he blindly coveted the hope that he would, upon ascending, find himself once again on the familiar 1904 ground floor of the Mountain House only steps away from the main foyer and parlor wing reception.

With a dry, raspy throat, the metabolic consequence of extreme stress, Sommers coughed his way up the narrow stairs and pushed open the door at the top. The scene was only vaguely reminiscent. To his left, off the main corridor he stepped out on, was another glass door, an entrance to a curio shop. Sommers peered in, totally uncognizant of the shop's confines, which displayed dry goods of descriptions completely foreign to him. To the right, he could see shelves heaped with sweaters and outerwear garments in bright colors. In the far reaches of the shop, he could see counters covered with jewelry, books, greeting cards, stuffed animals, trinkets, colorful demitasse cups, decorative shiny stones, embroidered towels, ladies' dresses and hats—all clearly discernible despite the diminution of a night light.

He turned to pursue a course down the corridor to the main foyer. To his left, he passed a parlor posted with a sign marked 'Winter Lounge.' It was a long room furnished with overstuffed chairs in colors and styles incongruous with 1904 fashions.

He reached the main central stairs in the lobby, to the right of which was a counter and apparent office area devoid of clerks, night or otherwise. There was no activity visible, save for the clacking of a peculiar machine, churning out reams of paper sheets printed with numbers and endless lines of figures, all of which just fell into a heap on the floor in the untended office.

Sommers turned toward the parlor wing and area he knew as the reception and business offices. The doors to the area were closed and blinds drawn from the inside.

He decided to put off an investigation of the parlor wing. He needed to check upstairs. Surely, by the time he reached the fifth floor, things would be back to normal and this horrendous nightmare of fluctuating times and shapes would dissolve as it had before and he would find his men on duty and Helena sleepily wondering what he was presently up to at such an ungodly hour.

He looked to the elevator, which seemed to have divided itself into two, both doors of which were closed. No operator was in sight and he saw nothing of the familiar paneled single elevator door through which he had customarily entered in previous hours.

He turned back toward the main staircase and bolted upward, trying to put everything out of his mind except the thought of his men on the upward floors and Helena awaiting his return.

At least the stairs and corridors seemed the same to him, although, if hard-pressed, he would have had difficulty describing in detail the pattern of the hall and stair carpets as well as the wallpaper designs of the hallways as they were in 1904. He did remember a fern-like leaf design on the third floor corridor walls near the iron staircases in the Stone Building, where he had endured his brief, earlier brush with the future world of 1993, following the morning staff meeting in the main parlor.

He decided to branch off the main staircase on the third floor to check that corridor. As he reached the staircases, the walls mocked his efforts at striving for familiarity. The broad expanses were bereft of wall covering, the surfaces glaring back at Sommers through a covering of light beige paint.

He dashed on upwards, his breathing labored from his ordeal, until he reached the fifth floor. Meyers should have been outside the President's suite at this time of the morning. He could easily see from the fifth floor stair landing to the end of the corridor to the Presidential Suite.

As he looked down the hall, he realized he hadn't prepared himself for the eventuality he now faced. The hall was empty. Meyers was nowhere to be seen. Sommers could feel the sweat trickling down between his shoulder blades.

It was true. Somehow, he was no longer in 1904.

"My God," he spoke out loud. It was both a plea and an oath at such an intervention that had imprisoned him without recourse in a virtual penitentiary of time and space, escape or parole from which seemed to be solely at the whimsy of whatever Spiritual Judiciary ruled temporal affairs. "Helena," he shouted as he raced along the corridor and turned at the end to the connecting hallway down to the Rock Building.

He gave no thought to Kenner, who should have been, but was not, at his station on the fifth floor of the Rock Building, his duty to monitor the stairs leading up to the sixth floor of the Stone Building and room 663 where the detonators had been stashed. If this was 1993, of course, there would be no detonators, no Kenner and, God forbid, no Helena!

Sommers reached room 490, his mind blocking out everything except what he prayed he would find as he opened the door—a sleepy Helena in bed with the glow of candlelight on her face, her hair all tousled, lying in dark wisps and strands across her pillow, the faint scent of her perfume transforming the room into a delicately fragrant garden of spring roses.

He placed his key, or tried to, in the lock. It did not seem to fit. Careful now, don't go to pieces, he urged himself. Try it again. No use—there was no way his 1904 key was going to fit a lock of 1993. Desperate now as the edge of realization cut like a saber into his crippled mind, he was about to thrust his shoulder at the door when he noticed it was already slightly ajar. He pushed on the door, which gave way reluctantly, the door jam worn and sticking from years of use.

It was the final shock. His eyes swept the room, his mind rejecting what he saw. The room was the same as he had found it earlier in the morning of that day—furniture disarrayed, mattress against the wall, wallpaper drooping from one upper corner—and no Helena.

Chapter Thirty-five

He closed the door absently and leaned against the wall, exhausted and drained, in utter despair. He could take no more. Slowly, his mode gave way to an almost catatonic stupor as his senses, overburdened, ached to shut down. He stood for long minutes, barely perceiving of his surroundings. Was time, any kind of time, still an operative dimension or was he in some state of suspended animation?

His mind mushily contemplated this new displacement. He had been translated ninety years into the future. His life in 1904 had dissolved once again into nothing more than a tissue of memories. Why? Would he return once more to the familiar fabric and structure of the world of 1904 or would he, this time, become a pawn, lost forever in a fickle shuffle of time engineered by some behind the scenes *Deux ex machina* engaged in a grotesque cosmic chess game?

He didn't even bother to look for Yost on the sixth floor. He knew he would not be there. He needed to get out of the building. Perhaps clear of the haunted hulk of the Mountain House, he might collect himself.

He walked slowly back down the hall of the Rock Building and crossed into the Stone Building. He would descend the iron stairs and exit into the winter night, or early morning, as the case might be, since he had no concept of the hour, day or month in which he was now entrapped. He knew only that it was winter in the year 1993.

As he passed down the stairs, he looked out on the lake from a hall window on the third floor. There had been a light snowfall on top of an existing crusty base of about one foot. Tree limbs and ground cover of laurel and rhododendron had been transformed into white lace under the wet flakes. He continued another two flights down to the first floor, where he decided he would continue out onto the main parlor verandah and thence down to the ground floor porch which wrapped around the office and reception area just below.

Sommers decided on such a circuitous route since he was apprehensive of meeting anyone who might belong in 1993. He wasn't at all sure of just how such a conversation would proceed. Although he was seriously disjointed from his abrupt transfer to an alien future year, he stubbornly tried to convince himself that his exile would be temporary, as, indeed, it had been earlier.

The cold winter air embraced him as he traversed the wide expanse of the parlor verandah. His face and hands bristled in the icy currents that rose from the lakeside to curl about the wooden rocking chairs that stood, lined up in a perfect row facing the balustrade, awaiting fresh guests to wile away somnial hours.

As he reached the little rustic stair at the end of the verandah that descended to the lower porch, he felt snow flakes brushing his somewhat feverish face. Light flurries still drifted down from the leaden night sky but the ashen clouds had begun to break their tight formation, allowing a cream-colored moon to assert an intermittent presence. A ghostly iridescence stealthily infiltrated the wooded, snow-blanched slopes across the lake from the Mountain House.

Sommers stepped off the porch under the east port-cochere and strode without particular purpose past the lakeside dock and up the slight slope beyond some outbuildings toward the trail to Sky Top. His mind now was quite empty. He no longer felt terror or desperation. He was gradually becoming inured to his unique position but it was not due to an exercise in logic or a mental process. The effect was more that of a man who had been drugged and was slowly surrendering his grip on wakefulness. Observing him, one might have described Sommers's state, at this point, as intoxicated. His cognitive processes had become nil—metaphysical musings no longer coursed about in his soggy consciousness. He was neither sad nor happy. In fact, as he meandered aimlessly up the trail toward Sky Top, he was barely aware that he was rapidly losing perception and balance.

The last thing his inconstant senses told him before he had lost consiousness was that the ground on which he had just fallen so heavily seemed soft and cushiony—indeed, even warm and welcoming. As his eyes closed, it was as if Joseph Sommers had returned to his mother's womb.

Chapter Thirty-six

Just how long he had lain on the cold, damp, leafy bower he found himself in as he awakened to the dusky swill of an overcast dawn, he had no idea. It had to have been several hours since he had left the Mountain House and started up the path to Sky Top. He remembered looking back at the lights and of how haunted everything had seemed in the polar moonlight. Then there was nothing.

Although he felt a bit stiff, he felt no numbing cold in his limbs. Indeed, his blood seemed to course through his veins like hot soup. His toes and fingers, which might well have been frost-bitten under the circumstances, were warm with no loss of movement or dexterity.

There was no snow—the air seemed almost balmy.

He had been lying in a nearly fetal position at the base of a ledge outcropping in a little hollow amidst clumps of laurel, virtually hidden from view from the Sky Top trail which followed the pinnacle-like formations above the labyrinth. As he sat up, Sommers began to recall with an icy knot in his chest the arcane events of the previous hours.

God, he thought, what am I doing up here? What year am I in now? He remembered his chilling chase with the two conspirators. Slowly, every incident of the pursuit became chisel-sharp, from his discovery in the utility shaft to the madcap climb to the Mountain House rooftops, down to the underground tunnel and foundations of the towering structure, followed hard on by his inexplicable, split-second banishment to the year of 1993.

Helena, where in God's name could she be? And the President? What now? he thought as he looked around him. How he had ended up in his present sanctuary, he had no memory, but in whatever year in which he was presently entombed, it was unarguably dawn. The sun, as it crept inexorably upward from the east, rising from behind Sky Top, cast a diffuse ambiance through the cloud canopy hovering over the lake and the Mountain House.

Damn, he thought disjointedly, the President will be preparing for his hike through the labyrinth. Although he still couldn't perceive as to what year he was presently gracing, he sat up and had a look at his watch. 5:30 AM—1993 or 1904?

Hold on—the ground was clear. There was no snow. Not a flake was in evidence. The lake surface, clearly visible from where Sommers was positioned, was not locked in ice. The dark waters rippled under a light surface breeze. Yet, last evening, he had stumbled out from the Mountain House onto a typical deep winter landscape. New flurries had dusted the mounds of drifted snow on and around the lake etching the surfaces whiter yet as he had passed the boat dock on his aimless saunter toward Sky Top trail.

That was it! He was back!

He did not know how, why, or wherever, but he knew he was back in 1904. It was November. There was no doubt in his mind about it. It was his world again—engaging, familiar in every aspect. He wanted to shout, to sing. He felt that if he stood up and raised his arms, he would find himself soaring upward to the tree tops.

And, as before when he had 'come back,' it seemed that his sensory perceptions had undergone fine tuning. His awareness of everything now surrounding him was taking on euphoric proportions. It was not incomparable to a young child's first discovery of the delights and sensations of a circus all wrapped up in rainbow colors, with its menagerie of wild animals, tumbling clowns, soaring acrobats and pulsing steam calliopes combined with the pungent aroma of sawdust, cigar smoke, sweating horses and sun-drenched canvas tents all topped off by the irresistible taste of cotton candy and cold lemonade. He drank it all in. The sudden exhilaration he felt was overwhelming.

The cool morning breeze wafted across Sommers's face like the touch of velvet fingers. The air that he now breathed was tinged with wispy scents of pine and hemlock, laced with the heavy, not at all unpleasant, earthy ambrosia of decaying vegetation, giving itself up in the never-ending cycle of life, death and renewal.

He felt infused with a vigor and mental acuity that dispelled any residual weariness he might have experienced after several hours of exposure between his collapse and his awakening.

And, Helena—she would be in their room, 490, awaiting his return for an early morning breakfast following his assignment.

The President—good God—he remembered the conspirators. He needed to gather his wits, evaluate what he now knew of the plot to assassinate T.R., and warn him. If his watch was correct he had only a half hour before the President would be launching his hike up to the labyrinth.

From high up, out from the crown of a giant white pine, a bluejay of remarkably graceful proportions floated soundlessly down through the tangles of interlocking tree limbs to a perch on a twisted branch jutting out awkwardly from an old chestnut oak, many of whose aged and brittle boughs had long-since been dismembered by a century of gales and storms. As Sommers moved his head, the bluejay, unmindful until that moment of an alien presence, flapped his wings in indignant protest and lifted off again, screaming a warning to all his woodland friends that their territory had been breached by an unwelcome visitor.

Sommers was about to raise himself from a Buddha-like sitting position he had unconsciously assumed during his momentary nirvana, when his eyes caught sight of a small gazebo directly ahead of him. It was anchored to a rocky promontory that gave way to a chasm over which a tiny cedar bridge had been constructed to reach another lofty stone pillar that angled up from deep within the labyrinth, thirty to forty feet below.

He observed, abstractly at first, the inscription on a wooden plaque that someone had tacked up on the edge of the little gazebo's peaked roof.

It read: EAGLES' NEST.

At first, it meant nothing to him. Most of the gazebos that dotted the landscape surrounding the Mountain House had names or inscriptions of one kind or another. But there was something about this one. Eagles' Nest—why should that name evoke any reaction? "Eagles' Nest," he repeated it to himself several times.

Wait—the note Mrs. Sidon had given him—the note she had copied from the one she had discovered in the General's boot. Of course, 'E-N.' The note could refer to Eagles' Nest.

Quickly, Sommers dug into his coat pocket for the scribbled script. It was rumpled but readable: 3—6—20—L—EN—D5SB—MTF—SHPG—J15.

3—6—20—L—Eagles' Nest—he substituted for the letters. Now what about the remainder? The initial 'L'. Of course, it was absurdly simple. The note wasn't in code at all. It was simply an abbreviated memo. The 'L' stood for labyrinth. Hadn't he overheard the word spoken in Sidon's room prior to his being discovered? 'Labyrinth—Eagles' Nest.' Now then, what about the numbers? 3—6—20. How about the time the meeting had been scheduled for? 3:00 AM, wasn't it? 6—Could that refer to Roosevelt's departure time—6:00 AM—the hour scheduled to begin the hike through the labyrinth?

Roosevelt was another word he had overheard through the wall in the chase. Whatever had been discussed in that secret meeting, Sommers doubted it had anything to do with organizing a poll to determine Roosevelt's popularity.

Sommers continued his deciphering. 20—could mean, surely it must mean—twenty minutes, just about the time it would take a hiking party to reach Eagles' Nest from the labyrinth entrance.

He had it now. Something was going to happen at Eagles' Nest. He was sure of it. And here he was, by the fates, at the exact place the conspirators had apparently chosen for an attack on the President. It had to be so. But how had he come to be here? What extraordinary forces had guided him along this path without his active will or knowledge to this designated point? What, for that matter, was the plan?

Would they shoot T.R.? Why pick this place? They could have shot the President just about anywhere—well, almost anywhere. No, there wasn't going to be a fusillade. There was only one other way Sommers could deduce in the killing of the President at this particular place, bridging the chasm below Eagles' Nest.

It would have to be a rock slide, or fall of some sort, from overhead. Sommers had familiarized himself with the area of the labyrinth, knowing of the President's expressed interest in exploring the rugged trail. The chasm was deep and narrow at the point of Eagles' Nest. Near where the little bridge passed over were several wedges of rock that might be loosened to drop, virtually silently, from the heights to crush anyone in the path below.

However, direction and some distraction would be needed from a fellow conspirator below within the Roosevelt party to ensure the President would not be aware of the action and to guarantee that T.R. would be far enough out in front of the others in the hiking party to catch the full force of the hurtling stones. Roosevelt, himself, Sommers thought, would contribute unwittingly to that objective with his obsession to command an unquestionable lead ahead of his hiking companions, including Secret Service agents.

But why, Sommers asked himself, a rockslide? There could only be one answer. It had to be made to look like an accident—a terrible, tragic accident, but nonetheless, an accident, a calamitous act that had to look like it evolved, naturally, from Roosevelt's dispensation toward risk-taking and his well-documented shunning of caution in the face of dangerous odds.

The conspirators had studied well the habits of their quarry. Whoever they were, the plotters seemed unanxious to drag the U.S. into the throes of self-flagellation which a successful assassination might inspire, particularly following on the heels of McKinley's assassination less than four short years before.

The authors of this fresh attempt to destroy a President, Sommers began to realize, did not, apparently, wish to see the reins of government slacken so as to precipitate a messy investigation that might have unpredictable and negative results for their interests. On the contrary, if the theory of an "accident," after a cursory investigation, was to be accepted, such would divert attention from the conspirators, allowing them to proceed with whatever further schemes they might have scripted. Such persons, particularly if they were anarchists, might have learned something from President McKinley's awkward, but effective, removal which, though successful, focused the world's attention and outrage directly upon their movement.

But what about the rest of Sidon's memo? Quickly, he spread the note once more across his palm. D5SB—SHPG—J15. Sommers recalled that the case of detonators was stenciled with the words, SANDY HOOK PROVING GROUNDS—SHPG? What else? The U.S. Military Arsenal, of course, at Sandy Hook, New Jersey. Now, then, D5SB? How about: Detonators—fifth floor, Stone Building?

Sidon had planned all along to stash the case of detonators on the fifth floor of the Mountain House, convenient and safe—only a few doors away from the President's suite.

Who would suspect? An unparalleled display of nerve, all right, but certainly bordering on the foolhardy, thought Sommers. There had to be a lot at stake to warrant such risks.

Well, then, what about MTF? Could it be 'more to follow'? Could be. And J15? Try a month and a day—January the 15th. It had to be. He had it all now. And now that he had it, what was he going to do about it?

Sommers had no time to speculate further on the vagaries of why or even who, at this point, were intent on despoiling the President's election victory by burying him under several tons of Shawangunk conglomerate. He had to formulate some plan of his own.

First, of course, he must immediately warn the President, evidence of malefaction in hand or not.

He was about to dislodge himself from his vantage point when, without warning, the sharp scream of the errant bluejay, winging silently over his head, pierced the morning silence. It was such a loud, strident and unexpected cry of bird rage that Sommers jumped despite himself. At the same time, he could clearly hear in the still of the mountain air another resounding cry coming from the porch of the Mountain House across the lake.

"Bully morning—bully, men!" Other good natured shouts and words merged and covered the President's ebullient greeting of the Mohonk dawn. Sommers stole a quick glance of his watch—6:05. The President's party was assembled and ready to strike out for the labyrinth.

Chapter Thirty-seven

THE BLUEJAY'S SCREECHING had become incessant. The bird was now wheeling and dipping directly over Eagles' Nest, scolding in a continuous stream of vituperative that Sommers was certain broke new frontiers for 'blue' language. Maybe that was why it was called a bluejay, he thought in a dry twist of wit that belied his rapidly growing apprehension.

Strange, why the bird should be wheeling overhead for so long. Something, it would seem, was disturbing the bluejay to the point of frenzy. As he watched, the bird executed a dive at some undergrowth just off the trail ahead of Sommers about twenty yards from Eagles' Nest. The thick tangle of underbrush, mostly low lying laurel and young but fully skirted hemlocks about four to five feet in height, created an almost impenetrable screen from where Sommers was positioned.

The bluejay made one final sweep over the thicket and dove off down the trail toward the direction from which the President's party was advancing in the early reaches of the labyrinth. It seemed the feathered creature was determined to mount an effort to reproach the newcomers for their untoward invasion of its territory.

Then, as Sommers rose cautiously to his feet to head down the trail to intercept the President, the thicket moved.

Quickly, Sommers crouched down as a shadowy outline, low to the ground, separated itself ever so slightly from the twisted tangle of laurel and hemlock. Was it a deer rustling itself from its sheltered bed?

The shape moved, sluggishly, head and shoulders raising up warily. Sommers could see it was not a deer. The head and shoulders attached to the torso of a man, darkly clothed, rose up above the thicket. His face was not clearly visible, but there was sufficient light now through the cloudy overcast for Sommers to recognize one of his two adversaries of short hours ago.

Body alarms jangled, heart pounded, blood coursed through arterial plumbing as Sommers focused on this new event. His face burned as if he were standing too close to an open fire, but his fingers were cold. He realized that some horrific scenario was about to unfold in front of him. There was no longer any question of racing down to warn the President. Whatever plot had been designed to do in the President appeared to be underway.

The man had not moved. He seemed to be watching and waiting. The voices from the labyrinth, muffled and hollow as the sounds echoed from the sheer rock faces, grew ever louder as the Presidential party slowly traversed the winding footpath leading directly to the deep chasm that underhung the little bridge at Eagles' Nest.

Armed or not, Sommers knew he had no choice but to try to capture the assailant. The odds were somewhat improved over last night. At least, he possessed the element of surprise, this time. But there had been two men chasing him last night. What about the second man? Where was he? Sommers, hidden in his leafy shelter, chanced a 360 degree sweep with his eyes. There was nothing to indicate any presence of another human being anywhere in sight above or below Sky Top trail.

If Meyers and Sachs had followed his instructions, as he was certain they had, they would be close on the President's heels along with Kenner. Could it be possible the second conspirator was also with the Presidential party? He knew General Sidon would be in the party. Would Sidon have had the gall to wheedle the second conspirator into the group, posing as one of the General's advisors? Who else would be along? Cecil Spring-Rice, of course, had been scheduled to accompany

Roosevelt. Having been a friend of the President for many years and enjoying the close proprietorship of T.R., Spring-Rice was above suspicion. Could it be that even now the President was conversing jubilantly in his unique vernacular of the outdoors with his own appointed assassin?

Sommers had no time to ponder that irony. The man in the thicket had untangled himself from the dense undergrowth and was slowly, in a hunched over position, making his way for the small bridge at Eagles' Nest. There was something in his right hand, Sommers observed from his cover, although he could not see the object clearly enough to identify it. Sommers, himself, upon recognizing the conspirator, had shrunk into a prone position, hugging the ground, hoping that a furtive look in his direction by the conspirator would reveal nothing more than the outline of a rotting tree trunk against a hillock.

The echoes of men's voices from the Roosevelt party reverberating from the depths of the labyrinth lent an erie quality to the scene. No words could be distinguished. Syllables would rise and fall, merging together in a sing-song fashion, probably not unlike, in eons past, a file of Indians on their way home after a successful hunt, trotting happily through the labyrinth in soft moccasins, cat-calling to one another, regaling each other with their exploits.

One thing was certain. The President and whoever made up his party were fast approaching the deep, narrow cleft below the bridge at Eagles' Nest. Sommers watched the conspirator's movements as he slipped beyond the protective cover of the undergrowth and boldly, but cautiously, moved ever closer to the gazebo and the bridge.

Sommers could now distinguish what the man had been dragging behind him. It was a long, thick iron bar. It appeared to be about six feet in length. The man reached another clump of laurel and thornberry bushes growing close to the cliff edge just short of where the bridge connected the cliff by Eagles' Nest with a rocky pinnacle jutting up abruptly across the narrow crevasse.

It became immediately evident to Sommers that his conjecture about a rock slide or stone fall was about to be rendered into reality. He watched in quiet horror as the conspirator elevated the iron bar to a vertical position. With both hands near the top, the man appeared to wedge it into some cleft and then began to work the bar tenuously to loosen a gigantic splinter of stone.

Sommers was out of the ditch and across the intervening ground separating him from the conspirator at a speed just a shade under that of a mongoose attacking a King Cobra.

The man was totally surprised. Sommers noted his thick eyebrows twitch erratically as his eyes literally popped wide open. The man gasped, his face contorted in a ridiculous expression of protest. Sommers lunged at the bar, grabbing it and thrusting it upward at the same time out of the hatchet-like crack in the top, flat edge of a large rock slab that had split away for about ten feet from the upper face of the main cliff. The slab, Sommers concluded even as he struggled with the conspirator, could easily have weighed several tons. Nothing in its path could have survived its mayhem.

The conspirator nearly lost his balance but did not loosen his grip on the bar as Sommers, exerting all his strength, tried to wrest it away. With an animal-like snarl, the man pushed the bar toward Sommers's face, catching him across the chest.

From this point, everything happened with the rapidity of a Kansas cyclone bursting over a field of parched corn. Overlapping voices from deep in the chasm hurtled upward. "Hey, get away from there!"—"What's going on up there?"—"Look out!"—"Get back!"—"Out of the way!"

Sommers could hear Kenner's voice over the din. "Chief—careful, stay back . . ."

Roosevelt's voice boomed upward. "You men, stand away there—"

The two men on the edge of the cliff, stick figures silhouetted in the growing light of the morning, poked and wrestled with the iron bar, each trying to smash an end over the head of the other.

From the corner of his eye, Sommers caught a glimpse of another figure on the trail. There was a pistol in the man's right hand.

In a last convulsive thrust, Sommers wrenched the bar from the grip of the conspirator and flung it heavily out over the chasm where he could hear it ring like a bell as it struck and bounced off the sides of the sheer precipice on its way to the bottom. At the same time, he shouted—screamed would be more descriptive—"Cover the President! Cover the President!"

Sommers twisted around toward the newcomer on the trail. The man was maneuvering for a shot over the edge of the cliff, not paying the slightest attention to Sommers's threat.

Just as he began a lunge toward the second man, Sommers felt a vulture-like grip on his shoulder, turning him back violently. The man who had held the bar faced Sommers. He was struggling to free a pistol from his inside coat pocket. As the revolver finally whipped out, the barrel in deadly aim at Sommers's throat, Sommers reacted like a gymnast on a balance beam. His right foot swept up in a swift arc, delivering a bone-cracking blow to the man's hand. The pistol flew up over the chasm edge in a perfect half-circle and darted downward as if a juggler stood poised below, waiting to catch the elusive weapon.

With an angry growl, the man lurched at Sommers, who had ended up perilously close to the cliff edge. Sommers tried to side-step him, but it was too late. The man tripped as he brushed by Sommers, hurtling toward the edge and the rocks forty feet below. He grabbed at Sommers's jacket in his maddening rush. Sommers tried to free himself, but the momentum of the other man was too forceful. They both teetered in a kind of absurd waltz, arms flailing and grasping at one another in a futile attempt to arrest their motion toward the oblivion of the chasm. Slowly, excruciatingly, their balance gone, the men veered beyond their delicate fulcrum and pitched over the side down into the deep reaches of the chasm floor.

The last thing Sommers heard was the sharp crack of a pistol shot from behind him. The last image he had before blackness mercifully enveloped him was of General Marcus Sidon reeling backward, falling to his knees and clawing at his chest. Sommers did not hear an answering shot fired from the bottom of the crevasse upward toward the cliff top.

Chapter Thirty-eight

The man's eyelids fluttered like tiny birds' wings seeking to test the rigors of first flight. Then, as the fluttering ceased, the lids opened, exposing the eyes to the sightedness of the man's surroundings.

His first visual consciousness was of light coming through a frame—several frames to his extreme right.

He was lying on his back. Whatever was beneath him was soft and yielding.

His mind now struggled to reach a level of consciousness that could translate the physical sensations his body felt as he slowly awakened.

He was warm. He seemed to be lying under a coverlet or blanket of some sort.

Of course, he was in bed.

He could see that he was in a room. To his immediate right, there was a wall with a window and a door. Daylight poured in through the slats in wooden shutters that covered both window and door, ribbons of light slicing through to fall in a ladder-like pattern across the carpeted floor, a melange of russet and golden flowers merging from a bluish-green background.

At the foot of the bed was a fireplace, the grate filled with the ashes of the previous evening's fire. Above the fireplace mantel was a large, beveled plate-glass mirror before which, on the mantel, sat a half empty bottle of Jack Daniel's Tennessee Mash. Next to it was an empty 6 ounce bottle of Tropicana orange juice.

A woman lying next to him stirred sleepily. "Jamie, are you awake?" The woman rolled over and snuggled close to him, casting her arm possesively over his chest.

Jamieson Stanner, now fully awake, bolted straight up in such a manner that Jennifer Dickson's arm was unceremoniously thrust away from him, eliciting a cry of alarm,

"Jamie, what is it?" Jennifer sat upright and leaned over, touching Jamie's arm. "Are you all right? God, I've never had that effect on you before in the early morning."

Jamie tried to speak. His lips moved, but only stuttering sounds issued from his throat, "Wha—huh—I—a—"

"Jamie, honey—it's okay. You must have had a nightmare. Did you have that dream about the attic again?"

Jamie looked at the woman beside him. He swallowed hard and began again, "Ja—Jen—Jennifer." He put his hands to his head, drew his fingers through his hair and shook his head vigorously. His eyes blinked reflexively, and he placed his fingers over his closed eyelids, rubbing them in an effort to calm the muscles, which were twitching almost uncontrollably.

Jennifer squirreled herself around in the bed until she was on her knees facing him.

She placed her own fingers on his as he massaged his eyes, trying to erase the host of images that still flickered and lingered on his retinas.

"Poor Jamie—it must have been a bad one this time, huh?" Jennifer had been with Jamie on other mornings when he had awakened after the recurring childhood dream he still experienced from time to time. But he had never shown such a delayed reaction in awakening as he was demonstrating now.

He seemed lost to her. Indeed, a part of him was. That part of him still seemed to be falling through endless black space. At least that was the memory that merged with his now conscious state in which he clearly recognized who he was, where he was, and that the woman he loved so desperately was kneeling in front of him with a puzzled smile, softly caressing his eyes and his face.

He reached up to take Jennifer's hands in his own, smiled wanly and pulled her close, clasping his arms around her and holding her face against his chest.

After a stumbling start, he finally found his voice, "Ja—Jen—I—we—I mean, I'm back, aren't I? I'm really back in our bed, room 353—I'm not dreaming?"

"Well, honey—of course, you're not dreaming. You're back—room 353. I didn't know you had gone anywhere," she said, trying to make a small joke. "Of course, if you had gone anywhere last night, I wouldn't have known it. I was absolutely zonked—you weren't, by any chance, chasing around the Mountain House corridors looking for the 'mystery woman,' were you?"

"Jennifer." He hardly heard Jennifer's tease. He was desperately sorting out his experiences of the last few hours. He inherently knew that what he had been through was not a dream, but how could it have been otherwise? He knew he had gone to bed with Jennifer last night after the meeting with the 'mystery woman' and a few belts of J.D. He had just awakened minutes ago in the same bed in the same room, and there was the half-empty liter of Jack Daniel's sitting on the mantel with the empty bottle of orange juice that Jennifer had used to cut her drink.

Yet, that did not explain it. It didn't explain anything at all. The world which he, as Jamieson Stanner, had entered just hours before—although 90 years removed from 1993—was a world as real to him as the world to which he had just now returned.

That he had intersected not only with an earlier time but with another life was undeniable. He had come back from a world of the century's turn in which he had, albeit for short hours, lived the life of a man by the name of Joseph Sommers. He had exercised the mind, experienced the perceptions and carried out the responsibilities of a man whose job it was to protect the 26th President of the United States, Theodore Roosevelt.

It had not been a world in which Jamieson Stanner had existed along side this other man. There simply had been no Jamieson Stanner.

The only question was—How? and Why? What mystical disciplines had decreed that Jamieson Stanner should have been thrust backward, behind the curtain of time, to an era in the history of the Mohonk Mountain House replete with such bizarre intrigues as an attempt on a President's life?

True, he was back, Jamieson Stanner, in the year 1993, but every detail, every twinge, mind thread, perception and feeling of a certain Joseph Sommers for an approximately twenty-four-hour period in November, 1904, was headline clear to him—from the time he awoke in room 490 with Helena at his side until the horrifying plunge into the deep chasm of the labyrinth off Sky Top trail.

"Jennifer," he began again, "I know now who the mystery woman is—or was."

"Ho, ho—so you were roaming the halls last night, after all." Jennifer took her pillow and playfully placed it over Jamie's head. He wrestled with the pillow and pushed Jennifer gently away.

"No—Jen—now listen to me. This is serious. I know you're going to have trouble believing what I have to tell you, but you've got to hear me out."

"Oh, Jamie, I don't want to hear about your old dream," she said petulantly. "I'd much rather make love. Let's fool around a little first. You can tell me about your dream at breakfast."

"Please, Jen, not now—"

He extracted himself from her embrace and moved to the end of the bed. He reached for his robe and stood up, walking to the balcony door. He opened the shutters, admitting the morning light as if, in its wash, his mind would be purged of the caliginous ruminations which so clouded his present sensibilities, disallowing rational analysis of his broad jump backwards into the world of 1904.

It was not a sunny morning. An overcast sky, bleary and milky, threatened new flurries and, perhaps, more serious accumulations as predicted the previous evening at dinner by Niko Shimomura.

He returned to Jennifer who was sitting cross-legged on the bed. "Jennifer," he said as he sat down again on the edge of the bed and took her hands in his, "what I have to tell you—it's not a dream—it really happened. I don't know how or why. I know, to you, or anybody else, for that matter, it has to be a dream. After all, we did go to bed here last night—we woke up here this morning.

"But I'm telling you—something happened in between—something very real. I don't have any explanation. Maybe there isn't any. I just don't know.

"I do know that, somehow, between the time you and I went to sleep and the time I awoke this morning, here, I woke up in another time of 90 years past—November 12, 1904, to be precise. I woke up in another man's life, in a room in this same Mountain House—room 490 in the Rock Building, the very room in which I first met the 'mystery woman.'

"Only that wasn't really her room. It was my room—our room in 1904. You were there, Jen, but it wasn't really you. She looked like you—even acted like you to some extent, but she wasn't you.

"She was my wife, Helena—that is, she was Joseph Sommers's wife. And I was Joseph Sommers. The 'mystery woman' was Mrs. Marcus Sidon, wife of General Marcus Sidon, consultant to President Theodore Roosevelt, just like Betty Harrigan told me last night and as I told you after my meeting with her. Only she wasn't Betty Harrigan at all. The 'mystery woman' was really Mrs. Sidon, except that when she and I met last night in the little parlor by the dining hall, I hadn't yet crossed over to become Joseph Sommers. I mean, I was still in 1993, but she was in 1904."

He stopped for a moment, as if he, himself, began to realize how preposterous the story was beginning to sound. He stood up and in a restless movement walked to the window and turned back to Jennifer.

"Jennifer, I know this isn't making any sense to you—but it's true—all of it. It all really happened."

Jennifer was suddenly serious. She began to sense Jamie totally believed whatever had happened, whatever he had experienced, was not a dream—no matter that, as far as she was concerned, there was absolutely no other explanation for what he was recounting.

She thought about his fall the previous afternoon. She rose and followed him to the window, throwing her terrycloth robe around her shoulders against the cold of the room, not yet warmed by the somewhat diffident wall radiator that was beginning to issue soft tapping sounds, indicating the invasion of new steam from the Mountain House boilers.

"Jamie, you had a bad dream. It couldn't be anything else." He moved stiffly away from her to the fireplace now cradling only cold, gray ashes—remnants of last evening's cozy flames.

She persisted. "Jamie, darling—no matter how real this all

was to you, believe me—you were here all night with me. I could feel you tossing and turning from time to time. You even snored some. Maybe that fall was more serious than you think. We better make sure—"

Jamie cut her off. "Jen, this had nothing to do with a knock on the head on an icy bridge at Eagles' Nest. I'm telling you that what I experienced was real." He paced to the bed and back. "Okay, my body was here last night—all night. I'll concede that. But I wasn't—I mean my mind, my being—my soul, if you will—I don't know, whatever you want to call it. I'm telling you that Jamie Stanner's body may have been here, but I woke up in room 490. It was early morning, November 12th, 1904. I woke up in that room with the consciousness of Jamie Stanner—but only for a few moments. I knew who I was and that I didn't belong there, at least not as Jamie Stanner. I thought I was dreaming. I even tried calling to you, Jennifer. You were lying next to me in bed—only it wasn't you at all. I found myself saying 'Helena.' I simply couldn't say your name, Jen. The next thing I knew, I was in the bathroom throwing water over my head, trying to wake myself up—only, you see, I was already awake, but I was Joseph Sommers. I looked in the mirror." Jamie turned and gazed into the mirror over the mantel and touched his face. "I couldn't recognize myself. I had sideburns. My hair was longer and dark brown, not blond. I remember saying some kind of prayer . . . 'Please, God, let me wake up.'

"The last thought I had as Jamie Stanner was of you. I wanted to get back to you in room 353, but I couldn't—because you weren't there, anyway. It wasn't 1993—it was 1904. It wasn't February—it was November."

He walked slowly to the chair by the fireplace and sat down on the edge. "Those were the final thoughts I had as Jamie Stanner. I felt myself falling—the room began to spin, fade out. I thought I was dying and then I thought—let this all be a dream. Let me wake up in 1993, in your arms in bed in room 353."

Jennifer slumped down in front of him on the floor, reaching for his hands and looked imploringly at him, as if to say, 'Oh, Jamie, my God, what's happening to you, my darling?' She was silent, though. He clasped her hands gently and continued.

"I must have lost consciousness at that point, because the next thing I knew, my head was in Helena's lap and she was stroking my forehead." He stared straight ahead, speaking softly, trance-like. "I was Joseph Sommers. I had no memory, not even the remotest thought of a man by the name of Jamieson Stanner. I only remembered a strange dream I, that is, Joseph Sommers had about being in a future time, coming here to Mohonk with you, but you weren't Jennifer—you were Helena, and, as with all actual dreams, the details and happenings of that dream faded very quickly."

Jamie paused and put his hand to his forehead. "From that point onward, nothing but the feelings, the thoughts, the responsibilities of Joseph Sommers occupied my mind—a period of about twenty-four hours, of which every detail is now as fresh in my mind, more so even, than what you and I did yesterday."

Jennifer was stunned but not yet willing to concede to Jamie's perception of his dream state. She was trying to think of how she might persuade him as to the total irrationality of his position. She felt apprehensive and perilously off-balance about what appeared to be an obsession of serious dimension. She decided to make a joke about it.

"Well, at least I looked like Helena. You see, you can't get away from me, even in your dreams."

"Jennifer." He rose abruptly and moved again to the fireplace. "I know you think I'm a candidate for a lobotomy, but let me tell you the whole story, everything—just like it actually happened. Then I'm going to search the archives here and anywhere—Washington as well, if I have to—to find out some corroboration of what I know and experienced—of what really happened on November 12th and 13th, 1904, here at Mohonk.

He moved to the bed and sat down on the edge. He spoke softly and focused intently on Jennifer as she came over to join him. She couldn't help notice a feverish caste in his eyes as she sat down next to him and reached for his hands.

"I believe it all began with this ring." Jamie raised his left hand and removed the signet ring gently, placing it in Jennifer's palm.

Chapter Thirty-nine

"Remember my fall on the bridge at Eagles' Nest? It's true I nearly went over, but thanks to your grabbing my leg, probably saving my life, I wasn't hurt.

"However, I sensed something very unnerving as I found myself staring down into that chasm. It was as if something or someone down there was beckoning to me, speaking to me. I couldn't know at the time what it was, but I found out later as Joseph Sommers. I didn't say anything to you about it at the time because it was such an ephemeral thing. It just didn't make any sense to me.

"And then the sleigh and jingle bells at Pine Bluff—you didn't see the sleigh or hear the bells?"

Jennifer, wide-eyed, nodded. "Oh, yes, Jamie, you thought I was deaf and blind, if I recall."

"But you really didn't see the sleigh, Jennifer. You didn't hear the bells, because there weren't any—not to you. Remember when you turned to look toward me—or through me, I should say. You didn't see me, because, to you, I wasn't there. Yes, I know I saw you. I couldn't understand why you didn't see me or the sleigh, but that had to be because I wasn't quite back altogether in 1904, or whatever wintertime it was when that sleigh actually came through, and I wasn't in 1993, either.

I was somehow straddling two different worlds, just as later, in the Rock Building before dinner, I wasn't completely through the"—he searched for a word—"call it the 'time curtain' for want of a better description.

"The mystery woman addressed me as 'Mr. Sommers,' both in room 490 and later at the midnight meeting in the little parlor. Remember how I mentioned she spoke 'toward me,' not at me, and how she paid no attention to what I was saying? I even moved around the parlor while she was talking. She never shifted her gaze from the spot opposite on the chaise lounge. That's because Jamie Stanner wasn't there. She couldn't hear me because I wasn't in her world—but someone else was.

"Someone else had been sitting on that chaise lounge right where I had been—someone from another time. Someone from Mrs. Sidon's time, 1904. Someone by the name of Joseph Sommers.

"Everything that happened in the Rock Building and later in the little parlor with the mystery woman, that is, Mrs. Sidon, actually did happen—only it happened in 1904, not 1993. And it happened to the real Joseph Sommers. He was the one that opened that door to room 490 to Mrs. Sidon, and he was the one who sat on the end of the chaise lounge that evening at midnight in 1904, listening to Mrs. Sidon pour out her wild tale of a conspiracy to assassinate President Theodore Roosevelt. I was witnessing a scene recorded some 90 years ago, stored in some kind of plasmatic memory chip of time, waiting to be played back if the right password or trigger could be found."

He took the ring again, but did not place it back on his finger. "From the time I put this ring on, Jen, things started to happen—although I had no idea what, until I woke up in room 490.

"This ring was the trigger that, somehow, catapulted me back to 1904. The initials, J.S. stand for Joseph Sommers. This very ring, I believe, was given to Joseph Sommers by his wife, Helena." He held the ring and pointed out to Jennifer the engraving on the inner band. "I would venture a guess that Helena Sommers gave this ring to her husband on New Year's Eve, 1900, just as you surmised in the Gazebo Shop where you found it, Jen."

Jennifer's face was blank of any expression. She was so

stunned by Jamie's dream tale, she seemed paralyzed. As he paused, however, she came back to life. As usual, she had a way of cutting to the core of an enigma.

"Jamie, are you saying you once lived the life of a certain Joseph Sommers and that by wearing this—his ring, you experienced reincarnation in reverse for twenty-four hours?"

Jamie stood up and placed the ring on the bedside table. "I don't know, Jen—I told you, I don't have any wrap-around explanation for any of this. I'm only telling you what I experienced, not why or how." He paced over to the fireplace, staring for a moment at the charcoal and ashes that had scattered from the firebox over the hearth due to a slight backdraft from the chimney flue. He walked back to Jennifer, who was still sitting silently and gravely on the bed. He sat down once again on the edge of the bed next to Jennifer and took both of her hands in his. By now, Jennifer had propped herself up against the headboard with the pillows.

"Jennifer, let me tell you what Joseph Sommers lived through during those hours of November 12th and 13th, 1904. I remember every detail of every hour and every minute from the time I became Joseph Sommers until I woke up with you this morning."

Chapter Forty

Jamie began with the staff meeting Sommers attended on the morning of November 12th, in preparation for the President's arrival in the afternoon. He left out the love-making with Helena, but even now, he could still recall every sensate moment of Helena in his arms, both at the beginning of his strange sojourn and later.

He recounted the astounding flash forward to 1993 Sommers experienced during his unexpected, momentary collapse on the Mountain House stairs.

"I realize now that was another point of intersection of our two lives, but Sommers had no inkling of the connection. To him, it was simply a continuing manifestation of some crazy dream he had had the night before, and he expected such a phenomenon to pass. It didn't, of course. It happened again, later—but I'm getting ahead of the story."

He went on to describe something of Sommers's job as Security Chief of the five-man Secret Service Detail assigned to protect the President.

"The Smileys had invited the President to Mohonk for a celebration to commemorate Roosevelt's election victory. The President was scheduled to arrive by train at New Paltz in mid-afternoon on November 12th. Sommers had the responsibility of escorting the carriage train dispatched from Mohonk to meet the President and bring him and his family, together with selected guests and friends, back safely to the Mountain House."

Jamie telescoped most of the rest of the events that followed, but elaborated somewhat more on Sommers's meeting with Roosevelt and his further meeting with Mrs. Sidon, along with the discovery of the intruder and the secret cache of detonators stolen from the U.S. Military Arsenal at Sandy Hook Proving Grounds, New Jersey. He described the wild chase with the conspirators on his heels up to the roof and down again to the Mountain House cellars after they discovered him eavesdropping on their secret meeting.

"When I passed through that door in the tunnel with these guys breathing up my—sorry, Sommers's backside, it looked like it was all over."

Jennifer was looking as if she was watching an old 'Alfred Hitchcock' movie. She was entranced by Jamie's account but seriously unnerved. She decided she should keep things light and forced herself to believe that a little time and TLC would help Jamie get things in focus and come to realize that his weird episode was nothing but a dream, real and vivid though it was to him at the given moment.

"Jamie, I think this would make a great movie, seriously. Maybe there's a writer in you that wants to get out. Maybe your imagination has been so saturated by all the time you've spent here over the years that it's trying to tell you something."

Jamie's face darkened. "Jennifer, you can treat this lightly if you like—I don't blame you. I know the whole thing sounds impossibly crazy to you, and it does to me as well. But I'm the one that went through this and I don't understand any of it. So how can I expect anyone else to buy it?" He frowned and said, "I think you should hear the rest of it before you write it all off as the ravings of a mutiple-personality."

Jennifer immediately regretted her words which, of course, masked her more material concerns about Jamie's state of mind and of what to do about it.

"Jamie, I'm sorry. Please go on. I do want to hear the rest. Forgive?" She smiled and placed a hand on Jamie's check. He smiled back, took her hand and kissed it gently.

"Forgiven." Without commenting further, he continued his story. "Well, it so happened that Sommers experienced another pitch forward into the future, into, if you will, Jamieson Stanner's world of 1993." Jamie went on to tell of how such a time warp had resulted in Sommers's eluding the pursuing conspirators, but had left him imprisoned in a world with unfamiliar boundaries, without his men, his Helena or his mission.

He described how Sommers had finally wandered out into the snows of February, 1993, how he had collapsed and awakened at dawn—in balmy weather—the weather of a November morning in 1904—and of how he had found himself lying in a protected hillside retreat opposite Eagles' Nest.

"Something brought me to that spot up on Sky Top—I had no knowledge of how I got there after I collapsed." By this time, Jamie found himself interchanging the personal pronoun, 'I' with the third person, 'he,' in reference to Sommers. He found it increasingly difficult to refer to Sommers as a detached personality.

Jennifer also noticed it. "Jamie, you're beginning to sound more like Joseph Sommers than Jamie Stanner." Her face showed tiny worry lines as she tried to cover up a frown bred by her growing discomfort.

"Yes, I think I know what you mean, Jen. But you have to remember, I was Joseph Sommers for twenty-four hours, not Jamie Stanner standing off to one side reporting and recording the events like a newscaster on the CNN Channel. "Anyway, I'm almost finished." Jamie's face took on a grim look as he chronicled the final moments of his odyssey and his ultimate encounter with the assassins.

Jennifer could swear she saw a pinpoint glow of red light in Jamie's pupils as he slowly, rather distantly, disclosed the last minutes of Sommers's travails on the edge of the chasm, grappling with the unknown assassin, followed by his agonizing plunge over the precipice.

Jennifer was frightened, not only by the graphic description of those last moments, but of the visage Jamie presented as he outlined, nearly step by step, the last few seconds before Sommers lurched over the edge of the cliff.

He looked tortured. His words drifted off as he reported the last thing he—Sommers, that is—saw: General Sidon dropping to his knees, clutching his chest.

He fell silent—staring several moments, not at Jennifer, but at something far beyond that only he could see. His face reflected a wrenching mixture of pain and anguish.

It was only for seconds but it greatly disturbed her.

"Jamie, Jamie—please, come back to me." She reached over to him, took his hands, pressing them to her lips, kissing them softly. "Jamie—I love you, Jamie—I do love you. Please, come back to me."

Jennifer could not stem the tears that began to flow down her cheeks touching Jamie's fingers as she held them close to her face and kissed them. The pinpoint spots of red in Jamie's pupils slowly dissolved and his face relaxed, the haunting, tortured look giving way to a peaceful expression, almost one of solemnity.

"Jennifer, forgive me—I guess I got a little carried away for a moment. It's just that this whole episode, particularly those last few moments of falling through space—and then my waking up here with you—well, I have to find some answers. I have to find out if there really was a Joseph Sommers. I have to know what really happened here at Mohonk on that weekend in November, 1904. "Maybe in the Mohonk archives, period newspapers—there has to be something that can shed some light on all of this."

For the first morning in a long time since Jennifer had been with Jamie, she discovered something on her mind besides making love. She didn't know what to think about Jamie's 'dream.' It was certainly unbelievable to her. She knew it could only be a dream, despite Jamie's attributing absolute reality to it. It was incontrovertible that Jamie believed everything had happened 90 years ago exactly the way he had described it.

She had to go along. She couldn't distract him. It was obsessional with him. She could only hope that the images, figures and events of this 'other' world he was so convinced were still enshrouded in the 'ether of time,' as he had said, would have no confirmation in the known world, at least as history reported it to be. Then, Jamie's dream world would fade, and he would return to be the Jamie she recognized and felt comfortable with.

She made a decision. "All right, Jamie, what can we do first—where do we look to find the truth?"

Jamie smiled, relieved that Jennifer was going to be cooperative. He cupped her face in his hands and kissed her eyes lightly, one by one. At that moment, he felt very much like Jamie Stanner and tottered on the edge of succumbing to her initial desire to 'fool around a little,' but something stronger over-rode his latent lust.

"First, my love, we get dressed in some warm duds. We're going to take a hike up to the labyrinth before breakfast. I have no idea what's drawing me there, but that's where I have to start."

Ordinarily, there would have been cries of protest from Jennifer, what with the weather as it was and on top of yesterday's trials and tribulations up on Sky Top Trail, but this time she was totally acquiescent. "Okay, Jamie—first stop, the labyrinth, before breakfast. But if I don't at least get a cup of hot coffee, you'll have to thaw me out in the microwave when we get back."

Chapter Forty-one

Jamie and Jennifer walked through the Lake lounge. It was nearing 8:00 AM. They had just finished their coffee, served before the dining hall opened for breakfast. They had decided they would skip the immense spread of the breakfast buffet and its devastating effects upon a sensible diet. Instead, upon their return, they would have a continental breakfast, which was scheduled to begin serving at 9:30 after the main dining hall had closed.

Jamie, although at a loss as to what discoveries he might hit upon in a casual stroll to the labyrinth, nevertheless felt an irresistible compulsion to visit the spot where he had, in the guise of Joseph Sommers, met some kind of unknown fate. He had to fill the gap between the time Sommers plunged over the cliff edge into blackness and his awakening that morning with Jennifer in room 353.

He took Jennifer by the hand as they stepped off the east porch and walked up toward the boat dock, leading to Lakeshore Road.

A few flurries had fallen during the night, lending a bleached-white shimmer to the weathered crust of the several existing inches of snow blanketing the grounds and the frozen lake.

"Jen, I know you're not happy about a hike in the labyrinth in this kind of weather, but I'm only interested in the area directly below Eagles' Nest. I think we can reach that spot from Lakeshore Road without traversing the whole trail from the beginning. It shouldn't be too tough going and you can always wait for me at the lakeside gazebo, there, if you feel nervous. At least, we'll be on the bottom. We won't have far to fall if we slip on some icy patch."

"Oh, Jamie—I'm more worried about this—mystery and—your state of mind." She wanted to say 'dream' but didn't want Jamie to think her mind was closed to his effort to uncover some evidence of Joseph Sommers's existence, although what he could possibly hope to discover in the labyrinth on a winter morning 90 years after the fact of some bizarre event that was supposed to have taken place there, totally escaped her.

"We'll be all right—we'll take it easy." She really didn't want to leave him alone in his present state, no matter her uneasiness. She reached up on her toes and gave him a very tender kiss, not passionate, but loving—warm and lingering. "I love you, Jamie Stanner—even if you do ramble on and tell strange stories and forget what time of day it is."

Jamie gave her a little return buzz on her forehead and said softly, "C'mon, let's go, before I end up ravishing you on the boat dock, snow or no snow."

Hand in hand, they tramped up toward the Mohonk Council House and branched off to the right down the slight slope leading to the wooden bridge nestling against the sheer stone face of the cliff that rose upward toward the beginning of the Sky Top trail.

Lakeshore Road, leading on from the bridge was, suprisingly, already well trodden by early morning hikers and cross-country skiers. Last night's light snowfall had, apparently, been sufficient to induce new excursions from those hardy guests who seemed reluctant to remove their skis for anything other than the most basic exercises of human needs. Even now, as early as it was, shouts of eager children gamboling on the trail ahead, with occasional remonstrations by not so indulgent parents, echoed from the rock faces of the looming hulks and overhanging pediments and ledges of the labyrinth along which Lakeshore Road marked its course.

They came finally to a high pyramid-like opening, giving into the interior of the stone pillars and jumbles. One sign pointed the way to the main crevasse, which snaked along a tortuous path through the heart of the monolithic masses. A second sign, white letters against a warning shade of red, announced the trail into the labyrinth, at that juncture, was closed due to icy conditions.

Jamie looked up beyond the signs toward two gigantic wedges of rock that leaned against one another, forming a kind of gateway into the interior of the labyrinth and the narrow crevasse that he was sure led directly under Eagles' Nest. The path, mostly a series of randomly strewn rocky steps, marked with arrows pointing the direction, led to a sturdy-looking ladder reaching up to a more level area. Having the protection of the overhanging stone juggernauts, the path was clear of snow and the wooden ladder had only a dusting.

"Let's start here, Jen—this doesn't look too bad and once we're up over that ladder, it can't be more than a few yards more to the crevasse."

Jennifer put on a brave face and took Jamie's outstretched hand. "Do you think, maybe, we should rope ourselves together like they do when they climb Mt. Everest? That way, if we fall, we'll at least be together at the bottom—and we can die in each other's arms." Jennifer's attempt at a joke made Jamie feel better. He laughed out loud and helped her up, scrambling over the rock steps to the base of the ladder.

"Well, Jen, that means you'll be on the bottom since I'm leading the way."

"Well, Jamie," she said with a mischievous grin, "isn't that the way you like it?"

"Now, behave yourself, you little vixen. This is serious business." Jamie smiled, despite the morass that blanketed his mind as he contemplated what might be revealed upon reaching the bottom of the crevasse where the fateful incident of yesteryears had, supposedly, taken place.

Both struggled silently and carefully over the slanting slabs and gradients of the labyrinth as they made their way toward the main crevasse.

"Look, Jen, there it is." Jamie pointed to a sloping rock face that gave way at its base to a dark, deep narrow slot between two high, almost vertical cliff faces. "We should be able to look up and see the bridge at Eagles' Nest from that opening."

Jennifer shuddered. "Gosh, what a creepy place. It doesn't look the sun ever gets down here." She wrapped her arms around

Jamie's waist. She couldn't decide whether she was more discomforted by the dank, shadowy reaches of the crevasse or by what Jamie might discover, within his own mind, once back at the very apex of his so-called journey to the past.

"Let's move along, Jen, we're almost there."

Jamie had not replaced the ring on his finger after removing it earlier. Once off, he did not think he would feel comfortable wearing it anymore. He had placed it back in the gift box the clerk in the Gazebo Shop had given them.

He wondered what he might be feeling if he were still wearing the ring. Would he be cast back, once again, to 1904? Would he meet himself as Joseph Sommers in that deep crevasse under Eagles' Nest? Or would he simply merge, as before, into the body and mind of Joseph Sommers, leaving no trace of his own existence as Jamieson Stanner?

Would Jennifer, for that matter, just as suddenly, dissolve into the elegant and sensuous Helena?

Disquieting thoughts, all—and another, even more chilling possibility, struck him as he groped his way through the constricted passage way. Did Sommers survive the fall?

Jamie had only Sommers's last memory of a terrifying descent into a black void from which he, Jamie, had awakened in room 353.

In looking around him at the jagged splinters of rocks scattered along the floor of the crevasse and measuring the distance with his eye from the edge of the cliff from which both men had hurtled, he could not imagine how any man could have survived such a fall.

"He must have been killed," he said, almost under his breath.

"What, Jamie? What did you say?" Jennifer's voice was tremorous. She was beginning to shiver in the dark cold of the deep stony cleft.

"I said, I don't see how Sommers could have survived this fall." Viewing the actual setting, sensing the reality of what must have occurred, caused a visible shudder to rack Jamie's shoulders.

"Let me take a little walk over to that—it looks like the remains of a bridge of sorts that must have crossed the chasm somewhere up above."

Jamie pointed toward a section of wooden slats attached to two timbers, obviously portions of an old catwalk or bridge that lay between several sharp-edged slabs which would have almost masked the debris from any sighting above. Also, because of its location at the very base of the overhanging parapet, little snow had covered the remains.

"C'mon, Jen—it's easy going here."

Together, they minced their way over the few shambles of remaining rocks in their path leading to the mostly rotted bridgework.

"Wonder how long that's been down here—looks as if it gave up the ghost a good while ago," Jamie said as he reached down to lift an edge of one of the supporting timbers. It came away quite easily. "Looks like the nails have all rusted out."

"Do you think anyone was on it when it fell?" Jennifer said curiously. She had visions of the old bridge collapsing, as in an 'Indiana Jones' movie with bodies pinwheeling down into the chasm.

"I doubt it, Jen, but I'm convinced anything can happen here after what I've been through."

Jamie was poking aimlessly around the debris with his feet while he was talking.

He didn't see it at first glance, but as his foot pushed aside a rotted piece of wood, it disturbed the decaying layer of leaves and vegetation which had sifted down over the years, filling countless cracks and small crevices in the floor of the crevasse until the material had composted itself into rich black earth.

There, just below the surface, his foot had dislodged a curious object. Jamie could only see about six inches or so of it. He leaned down on his knees and brushed away the dirt surrounding the uppermost visible part and reeled back in alarm as if a copperhead had slithered out of a hidden crack to sink his fangs into an unprotected ankle.

He couldn't be mistaken. What were the odds of finding such an object in such a place unless a certain, very specific action had occurred to place it there?

He resumed his position on his knees, ripping the rotted remnants of the old bridge out of the way so he could uncover the rest of the object.

"Jen, c'mere," he shouted over his shoulder. "I've found something." As it happened, Jennifer was nearly at his shoulder. She had approached closer when she saw Jamie drop to his knees after his first reaction of surprise.

"What is it, Jamie? What have you found? What could it possibly be?"

Jamie dug furiously, using a broken piece of the bridgework as a shovel to dig up whatever it was that had caught his attention. He reached down to grip the object and pull it free from the entanglement of the years which had seen it slowly buried beneath layer after layer of crumbling leaves and other organic matter that had sifted down to regenerate the earth in the never-ending process of renewal.

He finally loosened and pulled the object from its earthly rootings. Although rust had reduced its girth by probably more than half, there was no mistaking what it was and had been—an iron bar about six feet in length.

Chapter Forty-two

Consternation was barely word enough to describe the look on Jamie's face as he silently hefted the derelict iron bar and held it before Jennifer's eyes.

"This bar was waiting for me, Jen—If I had been magnetized, I doubt if I could have found it faster."

"Oh, Jamie, my God—this is eerie. Do you really believe this rusty piece of iron has anything to do with your dream?" Jennifer took the bar gingerly, nearly dropping it as Jamie loosened his hold.

"Jen, I'm not a metallurgist, but I think it's a safe bet that ninety years of oxidizing, rusting away down here would reduce an iron bar to this state." He took the bar and turned it point up. "Look, you can still see the chisel end. The assassin jammed this into the crack up there before I—before Sommers grabbed it away and tossed it down here."

"Jamie, this place is frightening. Can we go now? I can't stop shivering, and I'm not even cold."

Jamie smiled. "Okay—truth is, the place has me spooked too."

He looked around, high up to the cliff edge and down the steep rock face. He hadn't the slightest idea of what he was looking for but peered intently in the direction from which the two men would have plummeted downward.

In a niche near the top, about twenty feet below the precipice where the two men had engaged in their frenzied attempt to regain their balance before hurtling over, a crippled, stunted hemlock clutched at a rocky anchorage. It appeared to have sprouted from the stump of a much larger tree that had long since fallen after having achieved its destined height, dictated by the sparse nourishment of its rootings.

Jamie gestured toward the tree. "Amazing, isn't it, Jen, how these trees can root themselves into a crack and grow as if someone comes around and waters them every day. I suppose there's a life lesson in that for us, but I don't feel philosophical at the moment."

Jennifer brightened unexpectedly. "It could mean, my lover, if you persist and hang on long enough, you just might get your reward." She took Jamie's face in her hands and gently kissed him. "I wonder what it might have been like to kiss Joseph Sommers?"

Jamie smiled. He was having very mixed feelings. As he was looking at Jennifer's face, studying it—he could see Helena there, just as he remembered her standing in the candlelight of room 490 as he had said his last good-bye before his final rounds as Joseph Sommers.

"Let's get on with it, Jen. We have one clue"—he lifted the bar—"one very hard piece of evidence that connects me with this place—with Joseph Sommers." He hoisted the bar in his left hand. "Let's go and find out what the Mohonk Archives can tell us about 1904."

He took Jennifer by the hand and they nimbly picked their way across the slanting rock table leading out of the bottom of the crevasse, back to the rustic ladder and down to the yawning maw that opened out upon Lakeshore Road.

Chapter Forty-three

"That would be Jane Easton, sir," the clerk at the reception desk responded to Jamie's request as to who was in charge of the Mohonk Archives.

"Mrs. Easton is not usually in on Sunday mornings," the clerk continued, "but she lives on the grounds. Would you like to have her telephone number?"

"Yes, please." As he answered, Jamie was nearly jostled out of place by two twin boys, about eight years old, tugging impatiently on their mother's arms, imploring her, as only two hypertense youngsters could, to allow them to go sled riding on a designated slope near the Mohonk gardens. The long-suffering mother was trying to get information on child care procedures, obviously anxious to farm out her charges for a brief respite since a 'father' did not seem to be in evidence.

"Now, the two of you behave or you'll go right back to the room." The mother's voice merged with the whimpering adolescents until the three of them sounded like a mild eruption of Mt. St. Helens.

"Would you mind stepping over this way, ma'am? I'll have the child care supervisor meet with you in just a moment," came the harried voice of the Mohonk activities *Charge D'affairs.*

Jamie couldn't help thinking of his own first visit to the Mountain House. He had been about the same age as these vociferous twins busily setting about the matter of driving their mother into a nervous breakdown. Of course, he had had ghosts and haunting on his nine-year-old mind then, not sled-riding, and had only given thought as to how he could successfully elude his parents so that he could wander the creepy corridors and crannies of the Mountain House by himself. He had eschewed adult non-believers interfering with his fantasies of ephemeral shades floating in and around the shadowy lengths of unexplored halls and cellars of the vast mountain top mansion.

He was jolted back to the present by Jennifer. "Jamie, what do you think? Should we call her now and then have a little breakfast?"

"Why not? Maybe she can meet us later." He turned to the clerk. "By the way, miss, where are the archives?"

"They're located on the ground floor in a new fire-proof wing attached to the printshop in the house just opposite the old Power Plant across the Main Drive."

Jamie stepped over to the left of the lobby where the telephones were arranged in oak booths, the kind that were once to be found in drugstores of the forties.

He entered a booth having a house phone and dialed Mrs. Easton's number. After several rings, a pleasant, friendly but recorded voice answered. "Hello, this is Jane Easton. If you leave a message, your name, the time you are calling and a number where I can reach you, I'll return your call as soon as possible."

Jamie recited his room and name and his request to visit the archives that morning after breakfast, if possible. He hung up and looked at Jennifer. "Let's get some coffee, Jen. We'll have to wait until Jane Easton gets back to us."

Together, they walked down the corridor of the ground floor to the east dining room, where continental breakfast was being served.

Jamie was very quiet, preoccupied, as they munched on sweet rolls and sipped their coffee. "What are you thinking about, Jamie? You look like you're mulling over the Big Bang theory of the Universe."

He smiled and came back from somewhere light years away. "I was just wondering, Jen. If Sommers was killed in that fall over the cliff, it ought to be easy to check in some local newspaper of the period. That would have been something of a story, what with Roosevelt's involvement. And, General Sidon—he was shot. I saw that much." Again the Stanner-Sommers overlap demonstrated itself.

"This whole episode would have been a big story—and yet, there was no mention of it last night when Gary Hopkins reminisced about Roosevelt's visit here in 1904. Also, there's nothing I've ever seen about an assassination attempt here at Mohonk in any recounting of the Roosevelt years or in any of his biographies that I've read—to say nothing of his own autobiography."

"Then, maybe it didn't happen, Jamie, don't you see? All of this has to have been a bad dream—although I know it seemed real to you," Jennifer hastened to add, not wishing to jar Jamie's sensibilities with a too contradictory judgment on his 'other life' fixations.

Jamie smiled tentatively at Jennifer. "Believe me, Jennifer," he said as he rose from the table and took her by the hand, "I'd give a lot to believe all of this really was just a dream. C'mon. Let's go find Jane Easton."

They left the east dining room to walk to the lobby with Jamie reciting an outline of his 'research' objectives.

"First, I want to check the registry for Thursday, November 10, 1904. That's the day Sommers would have arrived with Helena and Agents Kenner and Yost. General Sidon and his wife and the rest of the advance party would have come up somewhat earlier since Sidon and his aide, Major Hertzog, were responsible for coordinating with the Smileys the logistics of the affair—you know, meals, programs, schedules, etc."

"What happens if you do find his name, Jamie?" Jennifer's voice was small, tremulous.

Jamie slowed his pace. They had just come to the ground floor parlor of the Grove building off which the stairway down to the fitness room and the basement utility areas was located.

"I don't know yet, Jen," he responded to Jennifer. "I suppose the next step will be to see if there's any record of the events of that weekend—you know, anything unusual, guests of note, that sort of thing. I know—that is, Sommers knew who was here, what went on. Is there a record of what happened—particularly at Eagles' Nest?

"I have a strong suspicion, don't ask me why—that we're not going to find out much about that. As I said, the history I'm aware of is silent on Roosevelt's visits to Mohonk, other than acknowledging that he did come here. Never mind any report of uncovering an assassination attempt or a conspiracy to pirate away U.S. Military secrets." Jamie frowned. "The truth is, I'm not at all sure how much corroboration of all of this I can absorb."

Jennifer squeezed his hand, also uneasy about how the effects of whatever they might be about to discover would hit Jamie.

They had reached the front lobby and Jamie stepped over to the desk to see if there was a reply from Jane Easton.

"Yes, Mr. Stanner, she told me to tell you she would be in the archives at 10:00 AM, if you'd like to join her there." The receptionist smiled brightly, as if she had just assisted in arranging successfully the reunion of two friends who had not seen each other for something more than twenty years.

"Thank you, miss. You're very helpful." Jamie flashed the very pretty girl a dazzling smile which further enhanced his prospects of future service, need such be required of the young receptionist. Jennifer could hardly help noticing Jamie was fast recovering his charm with the distaff side despite his mind-set to probe musty archives for clues to another man's past.

The walk to the archives required exiting the Mountain House from the west side and following the main drive back just past the Mohonk barns and stables to a yellow frame farmhouse-style building across from the old power house.

"That must be it, Jen." Jamie pointed to a square, concrete one-story addition to the rear of the house next to a basement office that advertised itself as a 'Print Shop.'

Jennifer shivered and clung close to him as they approached. "It's certainly gotten cold all of a sudden." She wasn't at all sure that some of the shiver wasn't due to the apprehensions she had for what Jamie might find in the archives.

It appeared that one had to enter the print shop in order to reach the archives. There was no sign of an outside separate entrance into the archives wing or even a sign announcing the trysting place of Mohonk's memorabilia.

"I guess we have to go through here to get to the archives office, Jen," Jamie said as he opened the door to the print shop. As they entered, their noses were immediately assailed by the acrid odor of ink, their ears assaulted by the clanking and whirring of printing presses.

The printer, with an apron that probably had never been pure white and was now a rainbow of inky blotches, pointed to a door at the side of the room between two belching machines spewing out sheets of neatly printed copy.

"Looking for the archives?" he shouted over the din. Jamie nodded. "Right there, folks. Jane Easton said she was expecting you—asked me to point the way."

Jamie and Jennifer waved a thank you and passed through a tiny vestibule to the archives where Jane Easton arose from a rather cluttered desk-like table to greet them.

"Good morning, Mrs. Easton, I presume?" Jamie smiled and accepted Jane Easton's proffered hand. "I'm Jamieson Stanner."

"Good morning to you, sir. I'm very happy to meet you," said Mrs. Easton as she took Jamie's hand and then turned to smile graciously at Jennifer.

Jamie turned to Jennifer. "This is my friend, Jennifer Dickson."

"Oh, yes and how lovely she is." Jane Easton shook hands with Jennifer. A woman of about seventy-odd years, Mrs. Easton was slight but sprite with friendly eyes. She was brimming with quiet energy.

"I'm really happy to meet you, Mrs. Easton," Jennifer countered.

"Oh, please—let's not be so formal. I'd feel much younger if you called me Jane."

"Well, then, of course, it's Jennifer and Jamie for us, Jane." Jamie felt an immediate warmth and connection with Jane Easton. For all of his inner qualms about what his search would reveal, in the presence of this gracious lady, he could not see how such findings would suggest negative implications.

"Very well, then, Jamie, Jennifer. Welcome to the renowned, if somewhat jumbled, Archives of the Mohonk Mountain House. As you might observe, from the stacks of boxes and materials here on the table, we are in a continual process of organizing and assembling thousands of items of memorabilia, including such things as early post cards and photos of the Mountain House, architectural plans, accounting records, minutes of the many conferences held here, guest letters and comments all the way back to the 1870's. We also have newspaper clippings and advertising over a period of 124 years since Albert and Alfred Smiley opened for business in 1870."

She pointed to a windowless room off the office area about the size of a two-car garage. "This room contains most of the collection. It's really nothing more than a fireproof vault with temperature and humidity controls to ensure the safe-keeping and guarantee the longevity of the records, we hope, for decades to come"

Here in thousands of minutiae and interrelated fragments of over one hundred years of history, Jane Easton pointed out, lay the life and breadth of an institution. But, most importantly, it was the only tangible record of thousands of lives, all with separate destinies, intersecting with one another, lives whose paths over the years had all merged at one time or another for brief moments within the confines of the Mountain House.

Here in these papers, documents, pictures and millions of words were the echoes of lives lingering yet in the ether of the ages. How much imagination would it take to envisage the drama of the moment as a great host of world figures gathered in the splendid Mountain House parlor with the Smiley families on the occasion of one of the historic conferences dealing with the subject of encouraging international arbitration among nations as a way of settling differences and disputes rather than by force of arms. Could one miss the pathos in reviewing any given page of the minutes of one of the conferences dealing with the welfare of the American Indians, for whom the Smiley brothers were so ardently the champions?

Merely by reading the lists of the attendees at such conferences, one could note the significant role the Mountain House played in the annals of American history and on the world scene in the late 19th and early 20th centuries.

Jane Easton reeled off name after name: "Rutherford B. Hayes, 19th President of the United States; General Oliver Otis Howard, founder of Howard University; Clinton B. Fisk, President of the United States Bd. of Commissioners for Indian Affairs; Lyman Abbot, minister, editor and author; General Hugh Lenox Scott, Superintendent of The Academy at West Point and Chief of Staff, U.S. Army; John Burroughs, world renowned naturalist and writer; David Josiah Brewer, Associate Justice, U.S. Supreme Court; Andrew Carnegie, founder of U.S. Steel Co.; John D. Rockefeller, scion of Standard Oil Co.; Chester Arthur, 21st President of the United States; Theodore Roosevelt, 26th President of the United States and William Howard Taft, 27th President of the United States.

"These were merely a smattering of the national and world leaders," Jane Easton hastened to instruct, "who visited Mohonk in years past. We've yet to compile an up-to-date list of important people who have toasted their toes at a Mountain House fireplace on a cold winter evening," she added whimsically. "Now, then, my speechmaking is finished. Let's get to you. Is there any particular area of interest you two would like to explore?"

Jane Easton's question infiltrated the reverie that had enveloped both Jamie and Jennifer as they had listened to her expound on Mohonk history and list the famous people who had visited the Mountain House. "Well, yes, actually there is, Jane." Jamie looked at Jennifer, as if to say, 'Ok, here goes—'

"I'm interested in Theodore Roosevelt's visit in 1904. I believe he arrived on a Saturday, November 12th. Do you have the register for that week? I'm doing a little story on Roosevelt's political strategies leading up to his reelection campaign in 1912," Jamie lied easily. He couldn't exactly recount to Jane Easton his misadventures of the past hours in the guise of one Joseph Sommers. They'd be putting him away in a hermetically sealed vault of his own for safe-keeping, only instead of humidity controls and storage shelves, this one would have padding along the walls.

"Oh, my, Jamie—" Jane Easton's face was a cross between a frown and a rueful smile. "I'm afraid you've touched on a period for which our records are incomplete. You see, we used to store all the records, registers, practically everything, in a cellar area of the Grove Building. It wasn't very adequate, I'm afraid, and subject to the elements even if it was indoors.

"It was quite damp," she continued, "and mildew caused a great deal of damage over the years. But the main problem was a mishap in the sprinkler system that served the storage area. Sad to say, one of the rooms was flooded when the sprinkler was set off by an accident. The registers and records for several years, beginning with 1903, through 1906, were hopelessly lost. Needless to say, it was then that a decision was made to build this new building. We were really fortunate in saving and preserving most of the collection, except for those years I mentioned."

Jamie didn't know whether to feel relieved or upset. A path of discovery was apparently closed to him. "You mean, there is absolutely no written evidence of Roosevelt's visit here in 1904 and the guest list for that week?"

Jane Easton smiled again, somewhat painfully. "Well, we do know he was here and the room he was assigned. We have had over the years a kind of oral history passed down. In fact, some of these oral traditions have been gathered together in a kind of a diary based on the best recollections of various people regarding certain times and events. I don't know if the information contained in it would be of much help to you in your research for Roosevelt's political strategies, but you're very welcome to peruse the material, if you like."

Jamie brightened considerably. It was at least a thread. "I certainly would like to have a look at it, if I may, Jane. You never know when you might strike the mother lode," he remarked—rather stupidly, he thought.

"Well, then, I have a copy here—just let me get it for you." She disappeared behind the shelves toward the back of the vault.

Jamie's and Jennifer's eyes met. Jennifer reached for Jamie's hand and, with a darting look at the shelves behind which Jane Easton had disappeared, she lifted her face toward Jamie and brushed his lips with a soft kiss. She gave him another quick buzz—"That one's for you, Joseph, if you're in there somewhere."

Jennifer decided she would not let this get too heavy. She was beginning to realize after all the time she had spent with Jamie over the past three years that she cared a lot more for him than she had been willing to admit, either to him or herself. This new feeling she was experiencing—was it because she sensed something different in him this weekend? Jamie had become quite suddenly more complicated since he had awakened that morning with his strange dream. Of course, she still believed it was nothing but a dream, despite the discovery of the iron bar. That had to have been a coincidence—a mysterious coincidence, to be sure, but just a coincidence, she was convinced.

Funny, she had always been able to control Jamie up until a few hours ago. Not that she was a controlling person, but she had always been the center with him. She knew she could always have her way with him. She knew she held an almost obsessive hold over him and it had given her some discomfort. She really did not wish to control him. She wished for more give and take. She almost wished that he controlled her. She was always able to persuade Jamie to move in any direction she wished. That, she sensed, was changing.

He was the one suddenly selecting directions. This dream

had so possessed him, she realized that she had become subordinate. Even in the short hours since their awakening that morning, it was fast becoming more difficult to garner his attention for herself by application of her highly honed sexuality, something Jamie had had absolutely no track record for resisting before. She was ambivalent about this change in him. She was unsettled by his persistence in exploring what was to her simply a very vivid dream, but she was, at the same time, oddly stimulated by his indifference to her attentions. She wanted to help him. She wanted to cooperate but she was no longer writing the script. She felt unnerved, off-balance. This was definitely a new side to Jamie—one that changed the formula of play between them. Jamie had awakened that morning with perceptions that frightened her but also fascinated her. There was no doubt that in her eyes he had taken on a new stature that enhanced him. She couldn't say why, really, except she knew inherently that she would never again be able to play power games with him at which she excelled.

Surely, this whole business would slowly fade away in his mind, as dreams did. She would just have to be patient and go along until that time, even if it meant tagging along after him, letting him work this thing out in his own time.

"Sorry it took so long." Jane Easton reappeared from the heart of the stacks, clutching a small spiral notebook. "I'm afraid there's not a great deal in here for 1904, but why don't you take it along with you."

"Oh, thanks, Jane. Jennifer and I are indebted to you for taking the time on a day when you're not normally on duty and for this we're grateful." Jamie held up the notebook. He was burning to open it right then and there but resisted the impulse. Something inside of him seemed to say, wait, you better be sitting down when you read this.

"If you'll just sign the register, Jamie, with your address and indicate in the column that you are borrowing the dairy and the date, then we'll know where to come after you, should you not return it." She gave a teasing smile and a wink and turned to Jennifer as Jamie sat down at the table to register his visit to the archives.

"Are you two enjoying the weekend? I'm afraid it's been a bit frosty for hiking."

"Oh, it's so beautiful up here, Jane. We had a great hike

yesterday, and last night—well, last night we certainly learned a lot about the early 1900's. It was a lovely evening. Everyone enjoyed it. I could really believe we were back in time. Jamie, I know, felt it too, didn't you, Jamie?" It was an oblique, half-hearted attempt, for Jamie's benefit, to persuade him that the effects of last evening could easily have led to the sort of dream he was insisting was real.

Jane smiled mysteriously. "Yes, and do you know, we had several curious reports from guests during the night of peculiar noises in the corridors—the sound of laughter, running footsteps, slamming of doors, men's voices arguing? When security was sent to investigate they found nothing, nobody." She laughed lightly. "I suppose some of the spirits of our previous guests of that period may have been having a party or celebration of their own. Of course, no one that I know of has ever seen a ghost at Mohonk, but who knows—these halls have seen a lot of history over 125 years."

Jamie thought that if he didn't get out of there and get a chance to sit down with the notebook that Jane Easton had just turned over to him, he would have a stroke, his heart was pounding so hard and fast in anticipation of what he might find.

"Again, thanks, Jane. We'll see this gets returned to you soon."

"Oh, my dear, keep it as long as you like. We have several more copies and I don't believe there is a burning interest at the moment among Mohonk adherents for such as may have taken place in the period of 1903 to 1906."

"Good-bye, Jane." Jamie shook Jane Easton's hand. Jennifer gave her a friendly hug and a kiss on the cheek as she said, "I hope we'll see you again, soon."

"Do come back, the two of you. As you can see, there's a lot of history here if you ever have the need to know such things as how many carriages and horses made the trip to the train at New Paltz to pick up guests before automobiles came into fashion."

There were several more overlapping good-byes and Jamie and Jennifer found themselves dodging around printing presses as they retraced their steps through the print shop to the exit.

As they passed through into the sharp edge of outside air, Jamie stopped dead. He had been glancing at the notebook.

"Jen, listen to this." He quoted from a page midway in the

little book: "'On Sunday morning, November 13th, General Marcus Sidon, U.S. Army, consultant to President Theodore Roosevelt on armaments, who had accompanied the Presidential party on the trek through the labyrinth that morning, suffered a fatal heart attack at a point somewhere below the popular observation place known as Eagles' Nest! General Sidon was attended by Dr. Elias Coover, a physician and close friend of the President.'"

Chapter Forty-Four

The Delta Shuttle, on its final approach to Washington National Airport, banked directly over the heart of the city. The lights of downtown Washington, molten crystals against the black velvet of the early March evening, were displayed in a paroxysm of geometric patterns, the edges of which were defined by lacy ribbons of street lamps.

The jet slowly descended, circling the east side of the Capital, its luminescent dome lighted by artfully placed spotlights. The building gave the appearance of holding majestic court, emplaced as it was at the head of the deep avenue of the Mall and its lagoon stretching to the threshold of the Lincoln Memorial.

Jamie Stanner, in his window seat just ahead of the starboard wing, had an unobstructed view of the city. He thought of William Manchester's book, *Death of a President*, as he watched. The dustcover of Manchester's book portrayed a view of Airforce One coming in over the Capital on its final approach to nearby Andrews Airforce Base, carrying the slain President John F. Kennedy to his last landing on that fateful night of November 23, 1963.

The conspiracy surrounding President Kennedy's assassination had never been satisfactorily resolved in the more than thirty years since the event. Jamie wondered if the attempt to assassinate T.R. on November 13,1904, which, as Joseph Sommers, he had so vividly witnessed within that strange sliver of disjointed time, would be explained or resolved by what he might find in the National Archives. Or, like Kennedy's assassination, would such an attempt on the life of the 26th President forever remain a mystery?

The Mohonk notebook of recollections was certainly sparse on the whole account with only the mention of General Sidon's so-called heart attack. There had not been another word on the whole affair, other than a report that President Roosevelt abruptly departed Mohonk early Monday morning on November 14th.

Well, he would know soon enough. There were the daily records of the White House Secret Service Detail to review—also, period newspapers, President Roosevelt's correspondence, his daily agenda—anything that might reveal the mystery of those impenetrable events surrounding the weekend following the President's election victory.

Jennifer had been upset when he had insisted on leaving Mohonk early after obtaining from Jane Easton the dairy on Mohonk traditions.

"Jamie," she had said, "the man died of a heart attack—it's a coincidence, that's all. The record says a heart attack, not a bullet, caused your General Sidon to collapse. Whatever you experienced, you have to accept it as a dream."

They had had something of an argument over it all. Jennifer, of course, had absolutely no doubt that Jamie's experience had been nothing but a dream—a dream which, she admitted, could have been something of a precognition in reverse, but, nevertheless, still a dream.

"What about the iron bar, Jen? Was that a dream?" he had argued. He had kept the bar and had taken it home to Connecticut with him.

"No, Jamie—but, after all, that old bridge we found in the labyrinth had been dismantled by someone. Maybe the workers just accidentally dropped the bar and didn't bother to look for it."

Jamie had had to admit the logic of Jennifer's reasoning but he couldn't accept it.

"Jennifer," he had persisted, "I know whatever happened was real—don't ask me—you know I can't explain it or prove any of it. But I can't accept what I lived through as being the result of too much rare roast beef or chocolate mousse before going to bed that evening." He had made up his mind. "I'm going to Washington, Jen. The records of the Secret Service should, once and for all, show whether there was a real Joseph Sommers or not, and also—where he lived, if he did live, and just where he was on November 12th and 13th. That's where I intend to start. Where it will lead to from there—I don't know. Maybe God knows—I don't."

Jennifer had recognized that it was useless to try to dissuade him and, in the end, agreed that he should go. She thought it would clear things up and prove to him better than she could that his dream was just that and that he would finally clear his own mind of his obsession.

On the Monday of his return to Connecticut, Jamie had done some quick research in the Stamford Library on the origins of the branch of the Secret Service which was organized to protect the President.

The branch had casual beginnings in 1894 as a step-child of the Secret Service, U.S. Treasury Department which, itself, had been created earlier to combat counterfeiting of United States currency. President Grover Cleveland, who occupied the White House at that time, was assigned just two men with specific duties to provide for his protection.

From such humble beginnings, the agency had grown to its 1993 elite complement of scores of agents—a gargantuan body compared with the size of the contingent which, despite the assassination of President McKinley, had grown to only a total of five men by 1904 during Theodore Roosevelt's tenure as President.

The comings and the goings, the adventures and misadventures, the successes and failures, everything would be there in the records, thought Jamie. All he need do is review the microfilms of the daily reports of the Secret Service special agents during November, 1904. A prior phone call to the National archives office had assured him there were such records on file.

The wheels of the 727 hitting the runway jolted Jamie back to the exigencies of the present. The precipitant roar of the jet's engines in reverse thrust and the accompanying inertial push of his body against the restraining seat-belt signaled him that he was now within stretch distance of his objective and only hours away from discovery.

Discovery of what? he thought. That there was once a living, breathing Joseph Sommers? That he was killed in an extraordinary incident trying to protect the President of the United States from assassination? Was he really ready for whatever disclosures he might find hidden in obscure reports of obscure Secret Service agents in what now would be considered the obscure year of 1904?

He knew he would not sleep much that night. He hadn't, for that matter, slept much for the last three nights since he and Jennifer had returned from Mohonk. It was Wednesday evening, March 2nd and he knew he had to pursue his course before he could hope to have any peace of mind—before he could adjudge his own sanity, or lack of it.

The rental car was waiting—a yellow Ford Escort. Jamie liked highly visible cars for city driving. His usual choice when renting was a compact. He worked too hard for his money to waste it on show and politely refused the attractive clerk who had offered him an upgrade to a Buick Riviera for only $10 more per day.

He had decided to stay at the downtown Washington-Sheraton rather than drive out that evening to the suburb of Suitland where the National Records Center was located. He didn't feel like a motel room off the beltway even though it might be a more sensible location in view of the next morning's commuter traffic. Most of the traffic would be incoming to the city center, anyway, rather than outgoing.

A comfortable bed, preceded by a Jack Daniel's—maybe a double—a filet mignon, medium rare, with a half bottle of St. Emillion, would do nicely, after a call to Jennifer. She would be relieved to know he had survived one more airline flight without more serious incident than that the young and very pregnant woman who had been seated across the aisle from him had looked as though she might have need of his services as a midwife half-way through the flight. She had been fine all the way, however. Jamie suspected, as he had watched her disembark and happily waddle off down the terminal corridor, that she just might make the baggage area before she collapsed and was forced to deposit her newborn neatly in her luggage trolley.

Chapter Forty-Five

He needn't have bothered with a wake-up call. He had slept restlessly, fragments of Mohonk passing in and out of his night visions. At one point, he found himself chasing around the lake, the two assassins Sommers had confronted. At the end of the lake, the two men had stopped as he caught up. They bowed politely and suggested, to keep things even, that they chase him around the rest of the way. At least, he knew that was a dream—crazy, he thought.

It was just 7:00 AM. He was wide awake. The Records Center at Suitland would open its doors at 8:00, although, as the archivist had advised him the day before in his telephone call, you could only call for the research material you requested at certain hours—the earliest being 9:15 AM, the next at 11:15. This procedure was necessary, he was told, to avoid having gridlock generated by archive clerks wheeling around the stacks like rush hour traffic on the Washington Beltway. He had been allowed to make his request over the phone for the materials he wanted to be ready upon his arrival at 9:00 AM, Thursday, March 3rd.

After a quick orange juice, coffee, and dry toast, in deference to the heavy Mohonk fare of the previous weekend, he joined the stream of traffic threading into Pennsylvania Avenue heading east past the White House and Capital to pick up the route to Suitland, about twelve miles outbound from downtown Washington.

He arrived at 8:50 after a couple of false turns as a result of his misreading the hurried directions to the Records Center given over the phone. As he drove into one of the parking areas fronting the center's main entrance after a half-mile long approach drive, he marveled at the size of the facility. The building was a relatively new, one story structure.

However, it spread out over the landscape, beyond the initial front lawns, like a sea of brick and cement, lapping up every square foot of available space between itself and the perimeter roads and streets of an adjoining residential community—a neighborhood obviously suffering asphyxiation from the unchecked governmental sprawl. Jamie guessed that the huge complex could easily accommodate under its roof, in one seating for dinner, all of metropolitan Washington and still have room left over, within its vast network of walls, for a joint session of Congress.

He was surprised that he had been able to find a parking space so near the main entrance. He supposed most of the researchers slept late and would show up for the 11:15 records call.

Once inside, he received detailed instructions regarding the use of the archives. He was informed that lockers were provided along the corridors for the storage of personal property, which was not allowed in the research rooms. Overcoats, hats, copying equipment, briefcases, purses or containers of any type, notebooks, folders, legal pads—even fountain pens had to be stashed in corridor lockers. Paper for notes and pencils would be supplied by clerks inside the research rooms and thoroughly inspected upon one's leaving the sacrosanct quarters.

Copies of documents or printouts from micro-film could be obtained through purchase of a debit card to be utilized with the copiers installed with the micro-film projectors inside the research rooms. Jamie did his best to observe the procedures, but once inside the restricted area, after filling up a locker with practically all but one layer of clothing left on his body, a surly female clerk noticed an innocuous and blank index card in his shirt pocket. He was informed that he would have to leave the card at the security desk.

"But, why?" he said. "There's nothing on it. Look for yourself."

The response was short and pointed. "Those are the rules, sir. There are no exceptions. How do we know that card does not have some incendiary chemical on it that could cause a fire if slipped into some archives document? You can have the card back when you're ready to leave, sir."

Jamie turned over the card. He guessed it made sense. Too bad that airport security wasn't that tight. All they did was check everyone with metal detectors and x-rays. He thought they'd have a hell of a long time loading up a flight at Kennedy if this archives clerk was doing the security check. But then, nobody would be carrying any guns or bombs on board, either.

"Mr. Stanner," the clerk had already moved on to other more important considerations, "your reference service slip has been processed and the materials you requested have been assembled. You will find them on the cart there by the work table to your right. Please see to it that the materials are placed back in their appropriate containers when you are finished. If you wish to make copies, you may purchase a debit card at the copy desk and utilize any micro-film viewer not in use."

She pointed to an assembly line of viewers stretching along the outside wall of the research room. Only three or four viewers were presently being operated by various researchers, winding back and forth rolls of micro-film—the ratchety sounds of the reels, whirring and clunking to occasional halts, being the only sounds in the long bowling alley-size room.

"Thank you, miss," Jamie directed toward the security clerk, but was interrupted before he could get out another word.

"And please observe the 'no talking' rule, Mr. Stanner."

"Yes, of course, miss." He wondered if the clerk objected to polite conventions such as in offering thanks, or whether she was merely programmed with instructions that took her a given segment of time to deliver and had no tolerance built into her 'chip' to accept extraneous comments.

He shrugged and moved to the work table, peering at the records-loaded trolley that had been wheeled up next to the table. He had requested for review all the records of the daily reports of Secret Service agents assigned to the President for the periods from 1901—1904. He had had no idea of the vast amount of paperwork involved in such reports over a four year period. The trolley carried neat little micro-film containers, approximately two-inch by two-inch cubes, piled nearly two feet high. They were divided into days and months and reports by individual agents. That translated to five agents times 48 months, or 240 individual micro-film containers.

Formidable, he thought—he could now see why, as he had been told, the Secret Service no longer required daily written reports from each agent. No wonder the National Archives people seemed to be constantly on the lookout to annex more land and buildings for future government paper chasing.

Well, he thought, for the time being, he would confine his attention to the three days of November, 1904, covering Roosevelt's visit to Mohonk and the five agents' reports for that period. One of them, he thought nervously, should be the daily ledger of one Joseph Sommers for November 12, 13 and 14th.

His right hand shook visibly as he removed from the stack five separate micro-film containers, being careful not to disassemble the entire stack of 240 containers—not an easy task since the particular micro-films for November 1904 were near the bottom of the pile. The entire superstructure wavered and stood on the verge of an embarrassing collapse before he could stabilize the shaky mass.

The square boxes were all marked, U.S. Dept. of Treasury, SS Daily Reports, November, 1904. The individual agents were not named on the outside identifying labels of the containers.

He picked one box at random and removed the film, neatly encased in another metal cylindrical container. The label on the cylinder also repeated the ID as on the box with no mention of the individual agent. He wondered if he would have to inspect all five containers before reaching the one with Sommers' reports—if there were a Sommers.

He approached the clerk in charge of printing and purchased a debit card for printing copies. He then gathered all five containers and proceeded to a viewer, his heart pumping like a reciprocating steam engine. God, he had to calm down.

Another clerk, an attractive African-American young lady, more laid back than the security desk check-in clerk, could see he was not familiar with the equipment and assisted him in placing the micro-film reel on the machine.

"Just pick the lens you wish to use by rotating the lens holder and push the forward button to start and reverse to go back."

"Thank you, miss," came Jamie's grateful response.

"You're very welcome, sir. If you wish to make copies,

just insert your debit card and push the print button, okay? Just raise your hand if you have a problem."

Hmm, Jamie thought, parenthetically, keep up that friendly, helpful manner, young lady, and you'll give a new meaning to 'Government service.'

He pushed the light switch on the viewing screen. The beginning of the film repeated the title, date and some unfathomable letters and code markings. Then came an official heading on a Treasury Department form. At the top center was printed DAILY REPORT OF AGENT. To the right and just below was printed in old English Script: *United States Secret Service.* Typed in below that was: *Washington, DC District.* To the direct top left was an official stamped seal which stated:

Office of the Chief
Nov. 1, 1904
S.S.Division

On the left margin, just below the stamped seal was the name in capital letters:

JOHN E. WILKIE
Chief, U.S. Secret Service
Treasury Dept.

Then began a salutation:

Sir:

I have the honor to submit the following, my report as— (there was a blank after 'as') *Operative for this District for Tuesday, the first day of November, 1904, written at Washington, DC and completed at 11 o'clock on the second day of November, 1904.*

In Washington, DC.

On special detail with the President at the White House:

(There followed a list of the agents on duty on that day.)

The anticipation had been so great that, to Jamie, seeing the name in print was something of a relief. He released a gasp audible enough to turn the heads of several researchers bent over their files and viewing screens.

There it was: Operative Sommers—no initial signifying a first name, just 'Sommers,' followed by four other names: Spl. Opr. Kenner, Spl. Opr. Yost, Spl. Opr. Sachs and Spl. Opr. Meyers.

They were all there, as if lined up for roll call.

Jamie was overwhelmed. He had the childish urge to jump up and shout to everyone in the room, "I was right—I was there! I was Joseph Sommers. Do you know what that means, everybody?"

Instead, he read the rest of the report Sommers had submitted. It consisted of a very routine and very brief accounting of going on and off duty at certain hours, coupled with a list of reimbursable expenses, including subsistence allowances of $3.00 daily and salary of $5.00 daily. Finally, the report, on the second page was signed in full:

Respectfully submitted,
Joseph Sommers

So, there was a Joseph Sommers— as well as all four other agents. Nevermind the iron bar in the labyrinth—would Jennifer also call this 'precognition in reverse'?

Now for the record through November 13,1904. Just what would the daily reports reveal of the morning of the day Sommers plunged into the labyrinth along with one of the assassins? And General Marcus Sidon's so-called heart attack—surely there would be a notice of that event. Finally, what about the other assassin who fired the shot that dropped Sidon in his tracks?

Jamie's hands shook as if he had Parkinson's disease. Slowly, he turned the reel ahead, skipping over the days just prior to the President's election victory on November 8th. The reports indicated all five men had accompanied Roosevelt to Oyster Bay, Long Island, on the weekend beginning November 5th and served on duty at the President's home at Sagamore Hill through the election on the 8th.

The report of November 10th described the departure from Sagamore Hill of Sommers, Kenner and Yost, and their arrival at Mohonk. However, it included a mention of Sommers's detour to Tarrytown, New York, to pick up his wife, Helena, who accompanied him to Mohonk.

Jamie dialed the micro-film on to the report for November 11th, which detailed briefly the events in preparation for T.R.'s arrival on Saturday, November 12th. The tension he felt was becoming unbearable. He could feel his pulse beating in both ears. He had to calm down, get a grip on himself. He thought he might be on the threshold of a stroke.

He took a deep breath and punched the forward button. The micro-film speeded up unexpectantly and when he slowed the forward rate with the reverse switch, the micro-film was clear—nothing, a blank screen.

"Wait a minute," he whispered to himself. "What happened to November 12th and 13th?" He went back to the November 11th report, and this time, he slowly inched the film ahead. Blank screen came up again after the report of the 11th.

There was no doubt about it. There was no report for November 12th and there was none for the 13th. In fact, as Jamie moved the film ahead, faster this time, the screen remained absolutely blank.

There were no more reports from Secret Service Operative Joseph Sommers. Jamie allowed the micro-film to wind itself out. The end of the film flapped noisily on the take up reel and the clerk, hearing the commotion, came over to ask him if everything was all right.

What she saw was a face nearly drained of all color, Jamie's eyes staring sightlessly at the blank viewing screen. What she heard was a voice, almost a monotone, saying over and over again, "It's true—he was killed. He was killed." Jamie looked up at the clerk, who was displaying an obvious concern at his strange and unexpected outburst.

"It's true, you know. Joseph Sommers was killed on November 13, 1904."

Chapter Forty-six

"Sir?" The clerk, in her experience working in the archives, was often privy to the sometimes rambunctious exclamations of researchers hardly able to contain themselves upon discovery of, what was to them, startling bits of hitherto unpublicized or unknown historicity that, once brought forth from moldering records, might change the face and the progress of modern day civilization. She had become quite blasé to such outbursts.

But now, facing Jamieson Stanner's vacuous expression and repetitive pronouncement of the untimely fate of one Joseph Sommers, she wondered if she should call security to restrain, or, more to the point, EMS to prescribe treatment and assist in the removal of this man in a nearly catatonic state, staring at the blank viewing screen, mumbling incoherently to himself about a man falling to his death from a cliff.

"The blackout—that was the terminal point." Stanner was transfixed. His focus was totally inward. He was barely aware of the clerk who, while not wishing to disturb the sanctity of the research hall, nevertheless raised her voice as she moved in closer.

"Mr. Stanner, are you all right?" She got through, finally.

"Wha—ah—oh, sorry, miss." He was back. "I guess I was distracted—no, really, miss, I'm perfectly all right—just found some corroborative evidence that—" He felt foolish suddenly. He didn't really wish to share what he had discovered. In his initial shock, he had already revealed a demeanor that, if extended by explaining what he had been looking for, would certainly qualify him as a classic case study of *dementia prae cox* and earn him an open-ended stay as a mental patient at the nearby National Health Institutes.

"It's okay, miss—some information I found—a little unnerving—sort of confirms a theory of mine. I suppose you often get these kind of responses from people as they wheel through the dusty past." Jamie tried to smile reassuringly.

The clerk was relieved. It was not that she was really persuaded that Jamie had mentally derailed, but research rooms were like libraries. Unmitigated outcries were not to be encouraged or tolerated and, aside from assisting clients and researchers in their missions of discovery, the clerks were also commissioners of decorum. Sentry-like, they were expected to maintain quietude. "Yes, well—we do on occasion have to admonish over-eager scholars anxious to share their discoveries, particularly when we have a lot of people working in here."

"I promise to behave, miss." Jamie placed a finger to his lips. "Mum's the word."

The clerk smiled and returned to her station. Jamie had recovered himself to some degree, although adrenaline still surged through his system. The muscles in his thighs and legs quivered in synaptic response.

He knew his next step. He would turn to the series of daily reports, starting with Kenner. He would then check the personnel service files for the period to ascertain Sommers's Tarrytown address.

He located Kenner's daily reports and quickly affixed the reel of micro-film, advancing the film without hesitating to the daily report for November 13, 1904. The report was actually written on November 15th. It appeared to cover the period of two days—the 13th and 14th, but included no details whatever as to the events in the labyrinth, except for the cryptic comment: *General Marcus Sidon suffered a fatal heart attack while accompanying the President on a morning hike.* There was no mention of the labyrinth, Sommers's fall or the assassin's demise—and not a word about the assassination attempt or shots fired.

Jamie felt a flush on his face. His hands were sweaty. What is this? he thought to himself, a cover-up? Why? How? And Sommers . . . what in hell happened to him? He's alive and well on the 11th and on the 12th and 13th, he utterly disappears—as if he never existed! Then, too, the assassins—they had also disappeared—no mention, no record, no nothing. Jamie was at the proverbial stone wall.

All right, he thought, Sachs and Meyers were with Kenner in the labyrinth. He would review their daily reports—then follow up with Yost.

It was the same—no mention by Sachs or Meyers as to the labyrinth. There was not even a report of General Sidon's 'heart attack' in either report. There were just monotonous details on routine matters—arrival at Mohonk, hours of duty, reimbursements due, subsistence payments. Yost's report was almost a carbon copy. There was nothing in it regarding Sommers nor the episode in the Mountain House relating to the intruder and the cache of detonators found on the sixth floor.

All of the agents' reports, however, recorded one significant event in unanimity, brief as the details were. They all stated that the President and his immediate party departed Mohonk on November 14th, Monday morning to catch a special train that had been dispatched to New Paltz for return to Washington, DC.

Jamie assessed what he had so far. First, the names of the agents—there was no mistake there. All were on record, including Sommers, in black and white officialdom of the U.S. Treasury Department, Secret Service. Next, the dates—November 10th, Agents Sommers, Kenner and Yost arrived at Mohonk—November 12th, the Presidential party arrived at Mohonk. And on Sunday, November 13th, nothing on the labyrinth but a brief announcement of General Marcus Sidon's death by a heart attack while on a hike with the President.

Strangely absent, however, were any details of confirmation of Sidon's death such as mentioned in the Mohonk diary of recollections. Who was Dr. Elias Coover, the physician who attended Sidon and who was supposed to have signed the death certificate?

Maybe he was wrong, after all, thought Jamie. Maybe Sidon did drop from heart failure. Perhaps the shot he had heard as Sommers was just a coincidence in timing. Yeah, and just maybe the Smiley brothers were Pentacostal snake handlers! No. Jamie couldn't buy it. As Sommers, he had seen Sidon drop—from the impact of an outside force, a bullet slamming home. Jamie had seen enough men drop from bullets in Vietnam not to recognize what had smashed into Sidon's chest.

So what did he have? Simple—or was it so simple? A cover-up—apparently engineered by President Theodore Roosevelt, himself. Who else could have instrumented such an audacious action. Reasons? T.R. had to have them and whatever they were, they were strong enough to ensure the silence of at least four Secret Service agents and Roosevelt's close friend, Cecil Spring-Rice, to say nothing of gaining the unlawful complicity of a physician, Dr. Elias Coover, to issue a fraudulent death certificate. And, Sommers, what of him? He couldn't just disappear—he had been too visible as a Secret Service Operative.

Jamie was just beginning to realize the awesome dimensions of the cover-up. He had to track down Sommers. The reasons for the cover-up had to rest with Jospeph Sommers's abrupt disappearance from the face of the globe.

Chapter Forty-seven

Jamie reassembled the containers of micro-film covering the agents reports and carried them back to the stack of other films on the storage trolley next to the work table to which he had been assigned.

There was one more micro-film he needed to examine—the personnel file listing special operatives with their home addresses for the year 1904. He thought it would be a short list since there had only been five agents assigned to T.R. at that time. That list, however, had been incorporated into a much longer compilation starting with President Cleveland in 1894 and on to 1898 when John E. Wilkie became head of the Secret Service. The list continued through December, 1912, and covered the period when Theodore Roosevelt was shot on October 14, 1912 in Milwaukee, Wisconsin, during the course of his campaign as Progressive Party candidate for President. Also included in the list were District of Columbia policemen responsible for guarding the entrances to the White House and other District policemen who might be called for special duty when Roosevelt visited public places in and around Washington. For long years the list had been classified and had not been made available to the public until it was considered that the safety and security of the agents were no longer a question, all principals having been deceased by 1993.

There was only one name on the list that interested Jamieson Stanner, and that was Joseph Sommers, late of Tarrytown, New York.

A further plan was now taking shape in Jamie's mind. He would locate Sommers's home address in Tarrytown and schedule a visit. Perhaps there were family members, descendants still living there who could provide information on the real Joseph Sommers. After all, Helena, as Jamie so vividly and poignantly recalled, did announce to Sommers on the evening of November 12, 1904 that she was expecting a child. If still alive, the son or daughter, as the case might be, of Joseph and Helena Sommers would be eighty-eight in 1993. Lots of people lived to that age these days, Jamie thought. He or she might not be in Tarrytown. Likely, there would have been a marriage, perhaps, but, surely there would be a record somewhere of Joseph Sommers's progeny and, for that matter, there should be some trace of Helena despite Sommers's misfortune at Mohonk.

Jamie was beginning to feel more confident, though not necessarily more comfortable, that he was on a track. If he could just get that Tarrytown address, he would have a truly tangible lead to follow.

But, before Tarrytown, he would go to Aberdeen, to the U.S. Ordnance Department Proving Grounds and Museum. Perhaps he could find some lead or evidence regarding the cache of detonators secreted at Mohonk and General Sidon's possible connection. There had to still exist some continuity between whatever munitions development had occurred at the previous military proving grounds at Sandy Hook, New Jersey, in the early 1900's, particularly 1904, and the later transfer of such operations to Aberdeen, Maryland, some years later.

Jamie located the micro-film covering personnel files from 1894 through 1912 and moved back to the viewer. He smiled calmly at the clerk who smiled back, relieved, obviously, to note that he was functioning like a rational human being once again.

It took him only a few moments to activate the viewer. He pushed the advance button, wondering how long it would take him to search through the hundreds of names that flashed by, the take-up reel of the viewer whining like an electric shaver getting up to speed. He pushed the stop button arbitrarily and the film buzzed to an instant halt.

He was getting good at this, he thought. He was in 1903. He didn't need to reach 1904, since Sommers had been employed as an agent from 1901 on. Personnel were repeat listed each year, apparently, for as long as they stayed on the Government payroll.

The names were listed alphabetically, surnames first. The micro-film had stopped at the M's so Jamie advanced the film to the S's.

There it was, bold and clear: Sommers, Joseph. 1135 Franklin Blvd, Washington, DC. Also: 33 Irving Street, Tarrytown, New York.

One more item to check, Jamie decided. Was Sommers listed on the personnel file beyond November, 1904? He advanced the film to 1904. Sommers's name was still carried through December. He quickly advanced the film to January, 1905.

He shouldn't have been surprised. It was consistent with the rest of the record that had been expunged of any reference to Sommers later than November 11th, 1904.

Chapter Forty-eight

The Baltimore-Washington Parkway, also known as U.S. 295, merged, as it entered South Baltimore, with U.S. 95, euphemistically named the John F. Kennedy Memorial Highway.

The U.S. Proving Grounds and Ordnance Museum at Aberdeen, about forty miles northeast of Baltimore, could easily be reached just off U.S. 95 at exit 85. Jamie had blocked out the route after returning to the Washington-Sheraton following his discoveries the day before at the National Archives.

He had decided to drive on to Aberdeen the next morning after a phone call to the Ordnance Museum. The curator, a Dr. Kenneth Waters, would only be available on Thursday, the 28th, due to an extended trip to the southwest from which he would not be returning until mid-April. Jamie could not imagine having to wait two more weeks before investigating the Marcus Sidon connection. Just what linkage had the General enjoyed with the U.S. Ordnance Depot at Sandy Hook, New Jersey, in 1904? Was he the one who had spirited the case of detonators out of the munitions stores of the Proving Grounds? And, if so, what key position did the General have in U.S. Ordnance development?

What was his connection with the conspirators, or should that read 'assassins'? thought Jamie, as he approached the Harbor-Point District of Baltimore and the southernmost port area of the city.

Baltimore had certainly changed since the mid 1960's when Jamie had periodically traveled through the city on his way home on holiday breaks from college in Tennessee to his then home in upstate New York. He watched the downtown skyline emerge as he drove—sharp, knife edges of buildings thrusting skyward in the morning sunshine. The harbor seemed wall to wall with merchant ships of every size and shape from dozens of foreign countries. Freighters and tankers lay at random anchorages or nestled against loading piers, while the skeleton limbs of overhead cranes unloading cargo weaved and bobbed like so many real-life counterpart cranes feeding in the rushes of salt bays and marshes.

The harbor scene passed beyond Jamie's peripheral vision as he accelerated in the sparse early morning traffic on Rt. 95 heading north toward Philadelphia and New York.

Aberdeen was just minutes away now as he finally turned off 95 and drove toward the business district, picking up the road signs directing visitors to the Proving Grounds along a rather stately boulevard leading to the formal gate-like entrance to the museum grounds.

As he passed through the now unmanned gateway entrance, Jamie could see beyond on his right, an open space of several acres on which reposed, tread to tread, scores of tanks and forbidding-looking military vehicles.

Substitute African sand for the February snow of the Maryland winter landscape and one could almost imagine famed British General Bernard Montgomery squaring off against Hitler's 'Desert Fox,' Erwin Rommel, at the onset of a blazing WW II tank battle.

Near the museum building, situated between the two ghost tank armies, there was even a scarred and blackened German V-2 rocket lying on its side, its mission now mute testimony to the unbridled ravages of WW II and the technical genius of that age gone devastatingly awry.

Jamie parked his car in a lot adjacent to the museum entrance, about twenty yards in front of approximately thirty tons of a German Panzer, its long 88 millimeter gun barrel leveled alarmingly in line with the rear trunk of the little Ford Escort. In other circumstances, particularly in company with Jennifer,

Jamie might have shot off a line or two regarding the vulnerability of his rear end facing down such a probing cannon. But today, on the threshold of possibly new revelations, he could think of little else other than how fast he could locate Dr. Waters to turn over a few more dusty pages of history covering a November weekend in 1904.

Chapter Forty-nine

The Museum foyer, except for its highly polished black and gray granite walls, was unpretentious—not unlike a typical theater lobby, wide and shallow, almost antiseptically barren. Since there was no admission charge, Jamie passed directly into the main hall.

As he stepped into the exhibit area, he was confronted by an almost building-wide display board—a sort of 'program guide' on which was printed, in white script on, aptly enough, a blood-red background, a synopsis of the history of the U.S. Ordnance Corps with representative pictures of arms and armaments illustrating the development of weapons from revolutionary cannons to guided missiles. Graphic photo samples were offered of every conceivable type of destructive device imaginable emanating from the mind of man.

Jamie continued on into the main hall—a large open area, reaching up to a cathedral ceiling two-and-a-half stories high, the front portion of which sported a mezzanine level. On that level, in floor-to-ceiling glass cases, there were entombed machine guns of every vintage, caliber and design that had ever been fired in the heat of battle, all with a single express purpose—the efficient elimination as quickly as possible of an advancing enemy.

On the main floor, an evil-looking guided missile, gleaming

white, perhaps twenty feet in length and having a girth of about two feet, fitted with dual sets of red-tipped fins or vanes and a very lethal looking warhead, was aimed directly at the lobby and front entrance, as if to ward off invading aliens, if circumstances were ever to warrant such action.

On the right-hand side of the hall, Jamie observed a staff car which had been assigned to General 'Black Jack' Pershing in World War I. Ironically, the shiny, black, 12-cylinder sedan with leather seats and spare tires mounted on the 'mud guards,' later called by the more sophisticated term of 'fenders,' was only utilized once by the General. That occasion, at the war's end, was a parade in which the vehicle proudly carried the victorious Chief of the U.S. Expeditionary Forces in France through the heart of Paris.

As on the mezzanine level, there were glass cases everywhere, with all manner of small arms suspended from hidden wires, displayed with the same particular artistic delicacy a curator might apply in arranging a collection of Caldor mobiles at the Museum of Modern Art in New York

On the left of the hall was a gift shop, which Jamie suspected breathed distinctively economic breath into the museum's daily life through the sale of countless souvenirs—tiny replicas of guns, model airplanes and tank kits, and scores of books detailing the world's armaments over a period stemming from the age of medieval catapults to present-day intercontinental ballistic missiles.

A revolutionary cannon of the type found on the U.S.S. Constitution stood anachronistically just outside the gift shop, aimed, Jamie couldn't help but think as a kind of inside joke, at the hapless guided missile, which gave no heed or notice of its figurative vulnerability.

It was time to check in with Dr. Waters. Jamie sought the assistance of an Army T-5 grade enlisted man who directed him just off the cavernous exhibit hall to an office with a sign marked 'Curator.' A light knock on the door was met by a hearty, almost booming voice with a tinge of Kentucky or Tennessee—maybe Texas—accent, Jamie couldn't tell which.

"Come in." The door opened as Jamie was about to grab the knob. "Come in, sir—come in. How are you?"

"I'm fine, thank you. Dr. Waters, I gather?"

"Yes sir, that's me."

"How do you do, sir? I'm Jamieson Stanner." There was a momentary blank expression on Dr. Waters's still smiling face. "We talked yesterday about some research I'm doing regarding the development of detonators?" Jamie continued.

"Oh, yes, of course, come in, come in, Mr. Stanner. I recall you wanted to know something about the development or the status of the development of detonators for high explosive shells at the turn of the century?"

"Yes, that's right—particularly, say the years, 1903-1904, during the Russo-Japanese War. Actually, I'm doing a piece on international espionage, citing various historical episodes when U.S. military secrets or devices found their way into the hands of foreign agents." Jamie lied fluently to Dr. Waters. It wouldn't do very well to inform the good doctor that he was looking for evidence to corroborate his time warp experience in 1904 when Joseph Sommers discovered the cache of detonators at Mohonk, 'requisitioned' by means and persons unknown from the munitions stores of the then U.S. Military Proving Grounds at Sandy Hook, New Jersey.

"There was a lot of development going on in those years regarding detonators and high explosive shells," Dr. Waters replied. "Up to that time, it was a tricky business handling high explosive shells and getting them to explode when you wanted them to—on the enemy, that is, and not in your own gun turret or breech block. It wouldn't be much of an exaggeration to say that, prior to the Russo-Japanese War, one side firing heavy caliber shells suffered almost as many casualties in the firing as the enemy they were shooting at. A safe and accurate detonating device was needed to make sure the enemy got wiped out faster than your own gun crews.

"The Japanese," continued Dr. Waters, "invented a new type of detonator, which they first used in the war against Russia in 1903 to 05. They beat the hell out of the Russian Navy at the battle of Tsushima as a result."

"Really? How was that?"

Waters moved across the room to a huge bookcase and a long row of reference manuals. He pulled out one entitled *Japanese Explosive Ordnance* and leafed through to about midway, pointing out to Jamie a technical schematic of a high explosive shell and detonator.

"The Japanese had invented a detonator with a new fuse

device timed to set off high explosive shells just outside the hull of a ship or over a ship's deck. This caused an enormous concussion that blasted huge holes through the armor plate, flinging shrapnel from the hull as well as from the shell over, God help, anyone in their path."

Curator Waters was just warming up. "Japanese guns decimated most of the Russian Navy, destroying all the Ruskies' aiming and directional devices and killing off the pour souls trying to shoot back.

"The Japanese also used a new filler in their explosive charges—picric acid; that made the explosives more stable or less prone to premature firing. This made the shells safer, more accurate. All in all, the Russians were at the mercy of the Japs. By the time the war ended in 1905, most of the Russian Navy was at the bottom of the Sea of Japan off the Tsushima Straits."

Jamie listened to Waters's succinct report with a consuming interest. "These new detonators, Dr. Waters, were really important then in measuring the outcome of the war itself?"

"Absolutely—everybody in the world wanted to get their hands on them." Waters moved to another reference shelf on the other side of the office and selected a thin volume from another long row of similar-looking volumes with the ease and expertise bred from years of chronicling every pertinent moment in the world's history of ordnance development. He drew out a neatly bound black book, which gave the appearance that it had just come from the bookbinders and had yet to be cracked open for the first time.

"Of course," Waters went on to say, "the U.S. was pretty much on to what the Japanese were developing at that time. We had our own program. We just didn't have a war to try out our product on. We were developing an advanced version of the Jap detonator with a really exquisite timing device, or fuse, if you will."

Waters flipped through the little black manual with the eye of an eagle searching for prey, placed his thumb on a particular page, and handed the book back to Jamie.

"This book is the report of the Chief of Ordnance, U.S. Army, for the year ending, June 30, 1905, Volume IX, written by Brigadier General William Crozier, Chief of Ordnance, Sandy Hook Proving Grounds, New Jersey. Take a look there at the bottom of page 60 under 'Fuse and Primer Department.'"

Jamie grasped the volume and read out loud where Waters had indicated.

"'An object sought in the investigation has been a time-detonating fuse that would enable the maximum effect of shrapnel fire to be developed at all ranges in all calibers of field, siege and seacoast projectiles with the service high explosive.

"'Experiments with detonating fuses have been conducted during the year, resulting in the approval for manufacture of three forms of these fuses for major, medium and minor caliber projectiles, respectively.'"

Jamie, as he finished reading, could feel cold sweat dripping down his backbone. His face felt like it was burning up.

"Tell me, Dr. Waters, what would have been the typical size of such a detonator as this report refers to?"

Waters scratched his chin. "Darned if I didn't forget to shave this morning. Always starts to itch by noon. Size? Well, they varied. Depending on the use and shell size, they generally would be somewhere between an inch to an inch and a half wide and about three to six inches in length."

"Would you say, Dr. Waters, you might fit several in a container about half the size of a cigar box?"

"Don't see why not. C'mon, I'll show you the real thing. There's a display on the mezzanine level of some detonators of that period, if you'd like to take a look."

Jamie swallowed hard—his heart beat like a metronome timed to Chopin's Minute Waltz. "Well, yes—I would like to see one, if it isn't too much trouble."

"Not at all—just as long as you send me a copy of whatever it is you're writing about. Sounds like it might make a good story."

If only you knew, Jamie thought as he smiled at Waters and followed him out of the office to the front of the exhibit hall and up the stairs to the mezzanine level.

The display of detonators was just beyond a glass case holding a model of an ancient medieval catapult. We've come a long way, Jamie thought. He moved over several feet to the front of the exhibit of the detonators. There were, perhaps, a dozen evil looking instruments answering to the basic description of detonators as Dr. Waters had conveyed to Jamie.

Jamie's eyes ranged over the still shiny brass hardware. There it was, in the middle of the second row—the exact replica of the detonators found in room 663 of the Mohonk Mountain House by a certain Joseph Sommers and Agent Jerry Kenner of the U.S. Secret Service.

Jamie estimated the size of the deadly device at about 1 1/ 4 by 6 inches. The markings were clear: U.S.A. P.D. S.Q. M46. Jamie was feeling shaky. This was no coincidence. The iron bar might be dismissed—not this, let alone the confirmation of the names of the agents at the National Archives.

"Those markings, Dr. Waters, on that detonator—the one marked M46. I assume the U.S.A. stands for United States Army. What about the other letters?"

Waters never hesitated. "P.D. means Point Detonator. S.Q. means Super Quick. The M46 would stand for the model number and series. That type detonator was designed for the nose cone of a shell, activated by point of impact as opposed to a detonator in the base of a shell set off by a primer."

There was just one other question Jamie had for Waters. "I guess these little toys were highly classified in 1904?"

"Oh, yeah. There were all kind of secret agents and spies running around in those days. Every country had an ax to grind. Theodore Roosevelt was concerned we might have a war with Japan at some point because of the noises they were making about the Pacific and their 'territorial prerogatives.' He even had Secretary of War, Elihu Root, draw up war plans for such an eventuality.

"Do you know, we also had plans to go to war against Germany, Mexico, China, Russia—even Canada and Great Britain? They're still on file, declassified now, of course—all color coded. Black for Germany, Orange for Japan, purple for Russia, and so on. A Marine Corp. Lieutenant Colonel by the name of Pete Ellis drafted the Japanese plan. Brilliant guy—only thing was he had a taste for the bottle. Drunk most of the time. Better stoned than he was sober though, they say. Disappeared in Kobe, Japan, one day in 1904. Never heard from again."

Jamie did not interrupt Waters's monologue, but as he paused, he jumped in. "Could anybody have walked out of Sandy Hook, say in November, 1904, with a case of those detonators under his arm?" Jamie pointed to the M46. He could still feel the cold brass of the detonator in the palm of his hand—correction, the palm of Joseph Sommers's hand as he had slipped it out of its cylindrical protective case.

"Not likely," Waters answered him, "unless he was a General, in charge of something or other. Yeah, a General officer might have gotten access. They didn't watch Generals too closely in those days. I'm not sure they even watch them too closely today."

So, that was it, thought Jamie. General Marcus Sidon, Munitions Consultant to President Theodore Roosevelt, walked into the Sandy Hook Arsenal one day, probably early in November, 1904, more than likely had lunch with General William Crozier, Chief of Ordnance, and then checked out a case of M46 detonators just like a traveling salesman packing up a suitcase of neckties, heading for the open road. Nobody would have reported a theft. Nobody would have reason to.

Jamie didn't feel he needed to check into the inventory and records of the Sandy Hook Arsenal to prove that point. He already knew where the detonators went and now he pretty much knew how they got there. There was little else Dr. Waters could add to clarify matters any further.

"Well, Dr. Waters, you've certainly been helpful." Jamie thrust his right hand toward Waters, who returned the shake. "I wonder, sir, if I might have copies of that file on Japanese Explosive Ordnance and, also, if possible, a copy of page 60 of General Crozier's year-end report for 1905?"

"Sure, why not? Your tax dollars should buy you something besides a look at tanks and machine guns." Waters led the way back down to his office. "By the way, regarding those detonators at Sandy Hook. You think somebody walked off with a case of them?"

"Could be. Maybe some General wasn't content with his monthly subsistence check, or—had a girlfriend who liked diamonds. Who knows? Just a theory." Jamie had said more than he had expected to. He had as much information as he felt he needed. He didn't want to expound on any more theories—certainly not the one involving Joseph Sommers. He was not about to speculate with Waters on the remote circumstances of a plot to steal U.S. military secrets in a long forgotten period of ninety some years ago, to say nothing of a conspiracy to assassinate the 26th President of the United States.

Waters finished the printing of the documents Jamie had requested and handed them to him. "There you are, Mr. Stanner. Hope that'll be some help to you in your story. Just let us know if you need any further information. Be glad to assist. Come back and see us again."

"I'm indebted to you, Dr. Waters. Thanks very much. I'll be sure to send you a copy of the article once it's finished." Jamie was restless. He shook hands again with Waters and moved quickly out to the exhibit hall. The museum had become very oppressive. He felt like every gun in the place was aimed at him, ready to fire if he didn't get out.

As he moved through the exit into the lobby, the T-5 was welcoming a boy scout troop—thirty or so youngsters with shiny, bright, scrub-clean faces—all eager to examine the varied instruments of death within, many of which, Jamie speculated, might well have cut down in murderous war-time fire all sorts of family members and friends of the innocent youths in present or previous generations.

Jamie shook his head and breathed in deeply the crisp, early March air as he stepped through the heavy glass entry door from the museum lobby onto the front sidewalk leading to the parking area. As he approached the little Ford Escort, parked so defiantly and yet, so vulnerably, just twenty yards ahead and in perfect alignment with the long, threatening barrel of the 88 millimeter gun thrusting from the turret of the German Panzer, he wondered that if the gun were actually to be fired in that position whether there would be enough left of the car to make a set of dog tags.

Driving out of the parking area, Jamie couldn't help but observe that the Museum appeared as though it was about to be completely overrun by the hostile-looking hordes of tank armies surrounding the mausoleum-like structure.

With a last glance over his shoulder at the renowned United States Ordnance Museum of Aberdeen, Maryland, Jamieson Stanner contemplated his next stop—Tarrytown, New York, 33 Irving Street, to be exact. The last known residence of one Joseph Sommers.

Chapter Fifty

It was 11:00 am by the time Jamie pulled out from the Aberdeen museum parking lot. He had a quick lunch, called Jennifer and left her a message. She was probably in the field appraising some million dollar home in Weston or Darien.

Although it was at least a three hour drive just to New York, he had an overwhelming compulsion to continue on to Tarrytown before returning to Connecticut. He didn't relish the idea of driving back to Stamford and returning to Tarrytown later. He was closing in, he felt. Joseph Sommers could not elude him much longer. He had to find some answers in Tarrytown. He didn't want to think about the kind of answers he might find or how they might affect him for the rest of his life—that would come later, after he tracked down the real Joseph Sommers.

He thought about the library in New Paltz. It had been closed when he and Jennifer had left Mohonk on Sunday afternoon. Before Tarrytown and whatever discoveries he might uncover in Sommers's hometown, he really ought to check out the New Paltz area newspapers in print during November 1904. Would he have time? With luck, he should be able to make New Paltz by 4:00. The library would probably be open till 5:00. He would chance it. Surely, the local papers would have covered the election and Roosevelt's visit to Mohonk. What else might the small-town paper or papers of New Paltz have to say about the events at Mohonk that the Mohonk notes omitted?

Traffic was remarkably light on the Delaware and Jersey Turnpikes until he approached the crossover of the Garden State Parkway below Elizabeth, New Jersey. There the Turnpike turned into a parking lot as what had been light traffic converged on some distant highway mishap. He decided to hit the Garden State, which was still unhurried in the northerly direction. Connecting with the New York Thruway off the Garden State a few miles below Newburgh, New York, he continued on to New Paltz, leap-frogging any vehicle not in league with his something-better-than-70-miles-an-hour speed, giving little heed to the frequent warning signs of radar surveillance. He continued unmolested on into New Paltz, turning left off the exit ramp onto Main Street as he glanced at his watch. It was exactly 4:05 PM.

The New Paltz Library, formally the Elting Memorial Library, started off its 20th-century life within the pre-Revolutionary walls of a French Huguenot stone cottage constructed in 1750. The cottage stood in the very heart of the village of New Paltz among a veritable parade of handsome well-crafted field stone homes built by the original Huguenot settlers of the area. The small building bordered what had once been an important toll road and which was now, in 1993, known, unglamorously, as 'Main street.' Over the years, the library had outgrown its modest 18th-century farmhouse confines and, through the generosity of a local patron, William Elting, had assumed new and impressive proportions which lent much-needed expanded quarters but did nothing to diminish the picturesque charm of the hoary, rough-cut original stone structure.

Jamie parked at an empty meter on Main Street just short of the library entrance, noting with detached amusement that the meter was of an ancient type that still accepted a dime for a single hour of parking.

Entering the library foyer, a small hall that had been pressed into service with a single check-out desk, strategically placed as if to guard the main entrance and exit, Jamie observed to his left, several steps below, a low-ceilinged room cluttered with shelves of books and materials characteristic of miscellaneous library functions. Occupying the back wall of the room was an inglenook fireplace in which there hung a huge, black, cast-iron pot—a just slightly smaller cousin to the version employed by cannibals in darkest Africa to boil erstwhile missionaries as depicted in 1930's Tarzan-type movies. The pot was now filled to overflowing with books of all descriptions. Apparently, shelf space at the Elting Library was still at a premium.

It was not at all difficult to imagine darkly-dressed early 18th century French Huguenots in stiff white collars sitting around the blazing fireplace, smoking their long-stemmed clay pipes and roasting their toes before the glowing coals.

"The reference room with the historical collection is just on down through the fiction section at the very end of the building beyond the children's wing," the librarian, a motherly, grayish-haired, sparish woman replied to Jamie's request for directions to the newspaper archives.

"The newspaper published in New Paltz in 1904 was the *New Paltz Independent*," the librarian continued. "Most of the editions of the *Independent* have been micro-filmed. You should be able to find the 1904 copies for November 11th and the 18th." She smiled and offered Stanner her hand. "Mrs. Bersholt is on duty as reference librarian. She can fix you up with the micro-film." Jamie smiled in return, mumbled a thank you and set off down the new wing toward the reference room.

The door to the room housing the historical collection was at the end of the children's section. As Jamie entered, he was accosted by a smiling, plump, middle-aged woman who, he thought, must have been lying in wait for him, so starved she seemed for human contact and conversation. Apparently, there had not been many visitors this day to the Elting Historical Collection.

Jamie immediately found himself the recipient of a capsule orientation on the collection's principal items by the loquacious Mrs. Bersholt, which included a lecture on a modest exhibition of sundry artifacts such as old belt buckles, coins and civil war uniform buttons dug up by a local farmer with a metal detector.

During a respite in the Bersholt recitative, Jamie managed to inform the good lady, without visible sign of the impatience he felt, that he wished to examine the micro-film of editions of the *New Paltz Independent* for November, 1904.

"Oh, why, of course. Why in the world didn't you say so?" Before Jamie could phrase a half-way appropriate reply to such a rhetorical question, Mrs. Bersholt was on the move.

She seemed completely undismayed at being unceremoniously shunted from her well-rehearsed indoctrination speech. "Let's see, now, 1904—here we are." Not unlike an opera singer advancing to the forestage to deliver an aria, she moved fluidly to a wall file where she unerringly plucked without hesitation from several dozen micro-film containers one bearing the label, *New Paltz Independent*, Jan-Dec, 1904.

"Would you like me to place it on the viewer for you, Mr. Stanner?"

Jamie nodded affirmatively. He was restless and impatient and did not wish to repeat another episode of winding and reeling, as at the National Archives, if he could help it.

"Just roll the film forward, like so, to November," the ubiquitous Mrs. Bersholt droned, "and adjust the focus with this knob on the lens here." She swiftly executed her own instructions, winding the film until the November 3rd edition appeared. "The *New Paltz Independent* was a weekly so there were, of course, four publications in November."

"Thank you so very much, Mrs. Bersholt. I believe I can master it from here on."

Jamie telegraphed the librarian an unmistakable look which he hoped would leave no doubt as to his wish to proceed apace through the possibly rocky shoals of micro-film viewing without benefit of further navigational assistance from the head of the historical collection.

Mrs. Bersholt seemed anything but nonplused by Jamie's brusqueness. "Certainly, Mr. Stanner." she smiled broadly. With an almost musical lilt, she said, "I shall be available if you have need of further assistance—just up on the mezzanine level."

With an almost audible sigh of relief, Jamie turned his attention to the viewing screen in front of him. The front page of the *New Paltz Independent*, November 3,1904, a bit tattered and torn around the edges, but still readable, stared brightly back at him.

Strangely, there were mostly ads, columns of advice and short stories occupying page one. There was no local news or national news whatever. There would be nothing in the November 3rd edition, in any case, since that edition was published prior to election and the arrival of Sommers at Mohonk.

Jamie quickly wound the reel of film to November 11th.

He did not expect to see any particular announcements of events at Mohonk in the November 11th edition since that was prior to the President's arrival, but election results would surely have been reported.

True enough, the November 11th paper reported Roosevelt's election victory, but, oddly enough, on the second page—the first page, once again, being devoted to advertisements and pithy short stories, such as 'The Desertion of Daffodil,' by a Ruth Santbelle and 'Miss Mitchell's Sacrifice,' by a Keith Gordon.

On the second page, there was a two-column block with the lead:

SUNSHINE AND VICTORY

Republican Success Everywhere

"The Largest vote ever polled for a Republican President and Congress, a Republican Governor and Legislature and all Republican county offices."

Beneath was a rendering of a rooster with the caption, "Our Bird vigorous and so is the Grand Old Party in the Nation. Roosevelt has solid North, solid West, Maryland, West Virginia and probably Missouri. Electoral Votes: Roosevelt: 343 Parker: 141."

The *New Paltz Independent* certainly acknowledged Roosevelt's victory even if the publisher did relegate the news to the second page.

Jamie rolled the film forward to the November 18th edition. This would be the one that might reveal some inkling of the incidents of the November 11th weekend.

Again, the front page was smattered with large ads occupying the full two columns to the left: "Miss Carol's Fine Millinery"—"Van Wyck and Collins Steam, Marble and Granite Works."

The middle columns were taken up by a serial story entitled, 'The Price of a Threat' by an Alec Bruce, describing the perils of a female equestrian in a wild west show. The right-hand column displayed an article on 'Farm and Garden' detailing the measures for combating wheat rust and outlining procedures for feeding bees.

God, how provincial, Jamie thought. It was pretty obvious

that the locals of those days were not much moved by events that took place much beyond the radius of a day's horseback ride from New Paltz.

A slight flick of the film roller brought page two into view. The center column was devoted to Roosevelt's arrival at New Paltz on his way to Mohonk on November 12th and included excerpts from his speech. It was also announced that Judge Parker, the Democratic candidate and Roosevelt's opponent in the just-concluded election was planning to move from the New Paltz area, his native home, to New York City to practice law.

The three columns from the left to center were dedicated to local and vicinity news.

There were, however, several news items that would have found more significant space in present-day tabloids, thought Jamie.

The engine of an Erie freight train derailed after striking a deer on the West Shore Line. Luckily, no one was injured, except the deer, the remains of which were trundled off by Farmer Leroy Cartwright who operates a nearby rendering facility.

The column also announced the second fatal accident on the new West Shore Railroad bridge at Wilbur, New York. Richard E. Conklin fell from the bridge to the ground. There were no witnesses so no cause could be ascertained. A twenty-seven pound wildcat had been shot at Mt. Nebo, and a landslide was reported near the north end of the West Point tunnel on the West Shore Railroad, barely missing an express passenger train which had passed moments earlier.

There was nothing more about Mohonk—no mention whatever of General Sidon's death. Nothing of the events of the weekend, beyond the President's arrival at New Paltz, had filtered down from the Mountain House.

Unbelievable, thought Jamie—a complete cover-up, or so it appeared. Strange, what to make of it all? He decided to move on to the November 25th edition. If there was nothing in that paper, he knew he would find no information in later editions.

Slowly, he rolled the film forward until the front page of the *New Paltz Independent* for November 25th scrolled into place on the screen. As before, on page one, there appeared nothing but quaintly-worded ads proclaiming the virtues of house furnishings, millinery, kitchen stoves and other sundry items which might appeal to the farm families of the Ulster County area.

Almost at the point of giving up the search, Jamie advanced the micro-film to the second page. At the top of the center column, the lead virtually leaped off the page.

TRAGEDY AT MOHONK

The article went on to describe the demise by a heart attack of General Marcus Sidon, aide and consultant to President Roosevelt. It reported the President's abrupt departure on Monday, November 14th, for Washington. That was all. A week late, Jamie thought, but, at least, there it was—confirmation of the Mohonk notes.

As he ruminated on this discovery, Jamie's eyes shifted to the bottom of the column where another lead was displayed: VAGRANTS IN DRUNKEN BRAWL. This piece described how two unidentified men, on a cliffside about two miles from the Mountain House, had apparently become involved in an altercation which resulted in the deaths of both of them—one, the victim of a gunshot wound to the neck, the other, from a fatal fall over the precipice to the rocky out-croppings below. The discovery of a pistol on the cliff edge convinced the authorities the men had done each other in. Since there had been no witnesses, the investigation had been closed.

That was it, decided Jamie. There was little else to be discerned by going on through later editions of the paper. The authors of what Jamie believed to be a massive cover-up would have left no further trails. The realization that President Roosevelt had to have been instrumental in such an endeavor, to say nothing of the Secret Service agents on the scene, left Jamie with a numbing disbelief that anything so horrendous as an assassination attempt on the President of the United States could be so successfully obliterated for nearly one hundred years of history. Was he, Jamieson Stanner, the only living person privy to such an horrific event? For that matter, did such an event actually take place? Or had he been truly, after all, merely the mean victim of hallucinations and the mind spirals attendant upon a seeming concussion, as the Mohonk doctor had warned?

Jamie stared at the viewing screen, the time-worn pages of the *New Paltz Independent* staring back at him, silent, barren of the facts he had hoped to establish to clear his mind and restore his rationality. All he had was a deepening mystery confounded by his findings at the National Archives and the U.S. Ordnance Museum at Aberdeen, Maryland.

He had to move on. It was time to go to Tarrytown. No matter the unanswered questions of his arcane journey back to 1904—dream, nightmare or hallucinatory pilgrimage it might have been—there was one basic fact pivotal to everything else. Joseph Sommers was real. He had been a living, breathing man and he had been with the President on Saturday, November 12, 1904, at the Mohonk Mountain House in New Paltz, New York. Jamie would follow the trail to Tarrytown.

Chapter Fifty-one

The afternoon was fast graying as Stanner pulled on to the New York Thruway entrance at the eastern end of the village of New Paltz. It had taken him just about forty minutes to discover that the *New Paltz Independent* was practically mute as to the happenings at Mohonk on that November Sunday in 1904 when the 26th President of the United States was supposedly threatened with annihilation. However, he did have confirmation of General Sidon's death by heart attack, although lead poisoning would have been a more accurate diagnosis, he thought.

Jamie retraced his route back down the Thruway to Peekskill and the Hudson crossing. Although daylight was fast fading, his compulsion to get to Tarrytown to locate Sommers's one-time homestead allowed no unrelated objectives or disjointed thoughts to elbow their way into his mind. It was just a little after 4:45 PM. If he didn't get pulled over for speeding, he should be able to reach Tarrytown in about one hour, given no other traffic problems. He could feel his pulse beating through his fingers, tightened as they were in a death-like grip on the steering wheel of the Escort. He loosened one hand and then the other, stretching and flexing each finger in turn to relieve the inner tensions which were inexorably taking possession of his body.

As he drove through the flatlands and the scrubby elevations of Harriman State Park, he reviewed what he had discovered since he and Jennifer had left Jane Easton and the Mohonk Archives.

True, he had established there had been a Joseph Sommers and a General Marcus Sidon. But, maybe the real Sidon had died of a heart attack. Certainly, the secret service agents had been real. The National Archives had provided that proof. There were, however, a lot of blanks yet to be filled in.

In particular, how did he fit into all of this? Was all of this part of some psychic phenomena layered into the ether permeating all existence throughout all of time since the Big Bang birth of the Universe? Would all we have to do to tune in on the past, or the future too, for that matter, consist of finding the *Enter* key on some miraculous Enigma computer that would put our finite minds in touch with all the mysteries of the cosmos? Or was all of it nothing more than the result of a blow on the head, a concussion that set the mind reeling into mad flights of fancy?

Could all of what he had experienced as Joseph Sommers during that incogitable time rift of twenty-four hours from November 12th to the 13th in 1904 be nothing more, after all, than a kind of cortical short circuit that provided him a tantalizing glimpse of things past but refused him further linkage to a rational explanation?

What really happened at Mohonk?

Jamie felt depressed. He hated not having answers. Life for him, up till this past weekend at Mohonk, had certainly held its uncertainties, particularly when it came to speculating about a future with Jennifer. But now life had suddenly become a three-dimensional chess game.

Well, he, at least, knew what move he had to make next. There was only one other move and that spelled Tarrytown and the one-time Sommers homestead. It was all he had to go on, vague as the prospects might seem for answers.

He reached the riverside community of Peekskill and crossed the Hudson on the Tappan Zee Bridge, turning off on Route U.S. 9 going north. It was 5:40 as Stanner pulled into a parking space opposite a drugstore in downtown Tarrytown. He needed a street map. He had no idea where Irving Street was, only that it must have been named after Washington Irving of "Sleepy Hollow" fame. It seemed strangely fitting that his search might end in the legendary village of Tarrytown, the one-time home of one of America's greatest writers of historical fiction and fantasy.

Irving street, he was not surprised to discover, was in one of the older sections of Tarrytown not far from the lovely old Dutch Reformed Church with its ancient cemetery that rolled away uphill behind the church in a gently ascending slope toward a wooded crest.

As he turned into Irving Street, Jamie felt as if he were entering the 19th century all over again. The street was lined on both sides by tall, graceful elm trees. How they escaped the Dutch elm blight of some years past which destroyed practically all of New England's elms was hard to believe. These trees appeared to be very healthy with full canopies, their fluted branches high over the street merging from both sides to form an unbroken arch along the avenue.

The houses, set back from the street in majestic repose, were archetypes of the finest Victorian homes Jamie had ever seen. Even in the gray winter light of a late March afternoon, the homes appeared bright and sparkling, their decorative lacework trim in crisp, contrasting but complimentary colors to the more somber Victorian shades of their clapboards in blue, green, brown, dusty rose and ochre. Still, there were a few houses in white and bright yellow which, like rays of an emergent sun, served to highlight and disperse the lengthening afternoon shadows.

All of the homes were architectural confections characterized by turrets, octagonal towers, overhanging balconies and gazebo-styled porches, some large enough to serve as bandstands for Sunday afternoon concerts.

Irving was a fairly long street. No. 33, being an odd number, was on the left, counting from the corner. The numbers increased by 2 digits for each address: 3, 5, 7, 9. Jamie counted them off until he picked up No. 33. The number was clearly visible just below the leaded, frosted glass windows of a large double-entry door painted in a deep burgundy tone. The polished brass door hardware indicated someone took loving care of the property.

As he looked at the house, Jamie was nudged by a most peculiar feeling of having come home, although the house did not raise the slightest flicker of conscious memory that, as 'Joseph Sommers,' it would seem he should experience. But then, his memory of Sommers was confined to the events at Mohonk for brief hours up until the incident on the cliff above the labyrinth. There were no residual remembrances of Sommers's life prior to Mohonk and none following. Yet he could not shake the strange feeling of identity that 33 Irving Street seemed to hold for him. He could feel the house drawing him toward it—embracing him, absorbing him, indeed, claiming him.

The house was a magnificent gingerbread concoction, painted in light blue with burgundy trim. The entire front was encompassed by a wide covered porch, more in the style of a grand verandah. The left corner of the building was anchored by a three-story hexagonal tower rising through the porch, crowned by a steeply-pitched cap that would not have been out of place perched atop a small church. To the right side of the porch, beyond the entry door, was a beautiful, formal-styled gazebo with Greek columns and a lovely balustrade with delicately-turned spindles.

Jamie parked the car directly in front. As he stepped out, he noted the bluestone sidewalks typical of the late 19th century, prior to the days of ready-mix cement. His throat felt parched as he walked up to the front porch. His heart pounded so loudly that he thought that anyone inside would surely hear him, obviating the need to ring the doorbell.

Actually, there was no doorbell. Instead, mounted to one side of the door, was a wide key-like metal handle embossed with a floral design with the word TURN in elaborate Victorian script.

Abiding by the directions, Jamie turned the key to the right and was rewarded, from somewhere close inside, with a ratchety bell-like sound that ceased when he stopped turning the key. It was certainly loud enough, he thought, to alert any occupants to the prospect of a visitor, so he waited. A minute passed and he was about to activate the ringer with another swift turn when, slowly, the left half of the double door opened inward to reveal a diminutive, elderly lady squinting through eyeglasses that were close replicas to Benjamin Franklin's well-known spectacles. It seemed, these days, that even genuine grannies wore the popular granny-style, glasses that sometimes perched on the noses of gorgeous super models.

The rather perky-looking woman of some eighty-odd years who faced Jamie wore a long-sleeved, dark green dress with a pattern of tiny, pink and white flowers, fitted with a high, lacy white collar fastened in front with a stunning gold and emerald brooch. Jamie noted, not without something of a more than mild shock, that the brooch was amazingly similar to the one Helena Sommers had worn in a pendant setting, as he recalled, on the evening of the Presidents dinner, November 12, 1904. Was it possible then, that this woman could, indeed, be the daughter of Joseph and Helena Sommers?

Jamie smiled and offered a "Good afternoon, ma'am."

The little lady answered Stanner's smile with one of her own and returned the offer.

"Good afternoon to you, sir."

"My name is Jamieson Stanner, ah, Mrs. . . ?" He felt suddenly awkward. He didn't know quite how to address the woman. Was she married? a widow? He decided on the direct approach.

"Ms.—Miss Sommers?"

"Josephine Sommers, young man, but Miss Sommers will do quite nicely." She smiled again.

Josephine Sommers, my God, could it be true? Was this the living daughter of Helena and Joseph Sommers standing before him? What would Jennifer think of that? She was certainly a beautiful woman, thought Jamie, despite her age and the numerous lines around her eyes. Remnants of dimples in her cheeks which, over the years, had lengthened, now bracketed her mouth within a very engaging and happy face. He could see the resemblance to Helena as she smiled—remarkable, he thought. God, what have I stumbled into here? He felt a swift surge of exhilaration tempered with apprehension as to what now might follow.

"Yes, well, Miss Sommers," Jamie started up again in a bumbling fashion. After all, how do you entertain a conversation with the elderly daughter of a man—her very father—whose life you lived for 24 hours some 90 years previously?

Jamie decided to be somewhat oblique. "Miss Sommers, I have some information regarding your father—err, Joseph Sommers was your father, was he not?"

"Why, yes, my father's name was, indeed, Joseph Sommers. But I think, young man, you should come inside out of this

March cold before we both catch our deaths, as my mother used to say."

Josephine Sommers opened the door wide, hospitably stepping back, and waved Jamie graciously into an entrance hall replete with lustrous black oak-paneled wainscoting, assorted Victorian bric-a-brac, what appeared to be an original casting of Frederick Remington's 'Cowboy' and a large central staircase that ascended into shadowy upper floors. A majestic newell post on the first step served as a mounting for a typical Victorian rendition of a Greek goddess of some sort sculpted from white marble and clothed in flowing garments except for one bare shoulder and breast. The goddess held aloft a globe, which served the practical purpose of illuminating the hall and staircase while providing the esthetic satisfaction of a popular museum piece.

"Now, take off that coat and come into the parlor, Mr. Stanner. I was just making a pot of tea—it's a bit past teatime, you know, but I always have my tea in late afternoon. It's not often, however, that I have a nice young man to share it with."

Josephine Sommers whisked Jamie from the spacious entry hall and drew back two wide pocket doors opening into a parlor surprisingly reminiscent of the Smiley family parlor at the Mohonk Mountain House, except for a few more contemporary touches. The wallpaper was an almost pea-green damask with highly ornamental floral bouquets in a deeper shade of green that invited one's touch to the raised velvet-like finish. Matching drapes, floor to ceiling, framed the graciously curved bay window that faced the gazebo extending from the front porch.

Directly opposite the parlor entrance was a beautifully veined, emerald green marble fireplace topped by a cream-colored, voluptuously curved mantel supported by miniature Corinthian columns. Large, oriental cloisonné vases of variegated colors were positioned in alcoves on either side of the mantel.

A loveseat and several Victorian chairs, some with arms, were upholstered in a gold brocade.

The walls were strategically decorated with oils of European grandeur—Arcadian landscapes, ancient castles and Byzantine churches, all in gilded frames.

Over the mantel was a bucolic scene filled with small children gamboling in a verdant pasture among contented cows against the background of a huge red barn and white farmhouse.

Period room that it certainly was, Jamie felt the parlor suggested the touch of a modern professional decorator of a definitely eclectic bent. He had the distinct impression that the entire room had been redecorated rather recently.

"My, what a beautiful room," he uttered rather banally. He compounded his prosaic comment with: "Looks like a picture out of *House Beautiful.*" Jamie had guessed right even though his pithy observations lacked pithiness.

Josephine Sommers smiled happily. "I'm so glad you like it, Mr. Stanner. As a matter of fact, I had the room redone not long ago. I got a little tired of my parents' taste for the dark musty excesses of the Edwardian age. So, after a mishap with my furnace, which decided to give up the ghost, sending great belches of black smoke throughout the house, particularly in this room, I got the nerve to brighten things up a bit since I had to replace practically everything in here.

"Parents, Miss Sommers? Did You say parents?" Did her use of the plural indicate her father was still alive after her birth? Did she know him? Or was she merely referring to his contributory influence along with Helena, her mother, on the household's furnishings prior to her arrival on the scene? After all, Joseph and Helena Sommers had owned the house before Josephine was born.

"Why, yes, Mr. Stanner." Her eyes fairly twinkled. "It is a common and well-established scientific fact that a child must have two parents, at least at the beginning of life. Although, these days, it would seem the role of the typical father is more and more being subordinated to that of a mere donor, a procedure that does not either mandate or guarantee continuity of his performance in the traditional role of forebearer.

"I'm happy to say that in my case, my father, a very loving man to say the very least of him, performed all the duties of fatherhood with aplomb.

"And, now, Mr. Stanner, please sit down. I shall pour for you a delicious variety of tea that was very popular with my parents when they visited a favorite place of theirs—and mine too, I might add. It's called 'Mohonk tea,' a special mix of orange pekoe and cut-black tea."

Jamie, if he had not been in the process of seating himself at the loveseat before which on a low cherry pedestal table an exquisite silver service was arranged, would probably have collapsed at that moment, more than likely sending silver service, teacups and saucers helter-skelter to the four corners of the Sommers parlor. His knees turned to rubber as he heard the word 'Mohonk' falling so close on the reference to Josephine Sommers's father as a loving man. Both instances virtually demonstrated a surviving Joseph Sommers beyond the November weekend of the 13th, 1904.

"Are you all right, Mr. Stanner? My word, you do look as though you've just seen a ghost." Miss Sommers was tantalizingly solicitous. The look she gave Stanner was open and expectant. "Have a drink of this lovely Mohonk tea. I'm sure it will revive you."

Stanner, confused, muddled from what he had just heard to the point of near incoherence, wasn't sure he could get a word out edgewise. He decided to be totally straight-forward.

"Miss Sommers," he began, haltingly. "I have a very strange story to tell you that involves your father. I'm not quite sure how to proceed, so I suppose I should start at the beginning."

Josephine Sommers replied with a faint Dickensian smile. "Why, of course, Mr. Stanner, that's always been a very good place to start, the beginning, that is."

Was she making fun of him? She was the very epitome of attention, sitting so primly with her teacup in her lap—smiling like the Mona Lisa herself. what was she thinking? Jamie wondered. He took a large sip of his Mohonk tea, the milieu of the Lake Lounge at the Mountain House flooding his mind as the hot tea invaded his senses, burning his throat, swirling into his nearly empty stomach. It warmed him immediately. He began to feel light-headed, almost as if he had downed in one gulp a double shot of Jack Daniel's, straight up.

Jamie began his story from the time he and Jennifer had left Connecticut on Saturday morning, February 26, 1993. He told her of the purchase of the signet ring, his experience on the trail at Eagles' Nest on the way to Sky Top, his encounter with the 'mystery woman,' his awakening as Joseph Sommers, the events of the next twenty-four hours in the life he experienced as Joseph Sommers, her very father—the arrival of Theodore Roosevelt, the conspiracy, all of it. He hardly paused. She never interrupted him but sat politely, her eyes riveted on his. A just visible smile never left her face but occasionally attenuated and then faded away again, like a ripple in a small pond at the mercy of an inconstant wind.

Afterward, he couldn't be certain as to just when it happened. Was it during his recounting of his first glimpse of the conspirator on the morning of November 13th just off the trail at Eagles' Nest? Was it when he spoke of the approach of the Roosevelt party deep in the labyrinth, the President boisterously leaping from rock to rock as the members of the party made their way to that point in the chasm to just below Eagles' Nest?

And did it really matter? For in one, swift, freeze-frame moment of time, Jamieson Stanner, once again, found himself on the edge of the cliff at Eagles' Nest—only he wasn't Jamieson Stanner anymore. There was no longer a Jamieson Stanner. Who had been Jamieson Stanner was now one Joseph Sommers and this Joseph Sommers was looking down the barrel of a pistol wielded by the man from whom he had only just wrestled an iron bar.

There is absolutely no vestigial memory in this Joseph Sommers of a Jamieson Stanner. There is only one mind, one memory, one course of action open to this man who faces imminent death in the next seconds.

There has been no 'break' in continuity to allow Jamieson Stanner to depart and return to 1993 to search in dusty archives and to follow a faint trail to Tarrytown to resolve the mystery of the disappearance of one Joseph Sommers. There is only the here and now of this Joseph Sommers in 1904 who is struggling with a madman on the edge of a precipice to prevent the assassination of a President of the United States.

The events on the cliff edge happen in unalterable order in a predestined trajectory of which the participants have no perception other than the semblance and substance of their own present reality as they play their roles out, not of the past, not of the future but of the exact moment of their occurrence.

And so, the pistol flies from the assassin's hand as Sommers executes a deft kick with his right foot, the weapon soaring upward in a half-circle and falling deep into the crevasse.

The assailant rushes at Sommers with an angry snarl. He loses his footing, hurtling headlong in a dive toward Sommers, who is standing perilously close to the craggy brink high above the yawning maw of the labyrinth. For stark seconds, the two men grapple on the edge, their momentum veering them both in an uncontrolled lurch over the rim of the crevasse, arms and legs windmilling in empty space, flailing in a vain effort to arrest the plummeting bodies.

In the brief flash before blackout, Sommers hears a shot fired from behind him on the rim of the crevasse and sees General Marcus Sidon, far below, stagger backward, clutching at his chest. Then, there is nothing. Sommers is unaware of a shot fired from the floor of the labyrinth up toward the rim. He does not see a body falling backwards away from the edge of the bluff. He does not hear the sickening crunch of another body hitting the sides of the rocky slabs on its death flight to the floor of the abyss. He does not feel the arresting boughs of the ragged but rugged hemlock, stubbornly, but fortuitously growing from a precarious ledge twenty feet down from the rocky pinnacle he has just left so unceremoniously.

The first thing Sommers hears as he struggles to free himself from an unconscious state into which he has been thrust is a mans voice. "Hold on, Chief—hold on. I've got a rope. Just hold on. Don't try to move."

The disembodied instructions come closer as Sommers regains groggy consciousness to discover his body clutched in the topmost branches of a tall, scraggly hemlock—a springy sort of cradle that, while having snared his clothing and broken his fall, is by no means a safe berth.

Sommers is alert now, awakened and cognizant of his survival, but helpless and vulnerable to further jeopardy, hanging as he is in the shaky limbs of an evergreen that seems to him hardly sturdy enough to support the weight of a brace of partridges.

A hemp rope with a loop on the end comes dangling down from above accompanied by further instructions from the cliff-edge. "Chief, can you hear me? Are you all right? can you fix the rope under your arms, Chief? We can lower you down from up here."

Sommers recognizes Agent Kenner's shrill tenor. "Take your time, Chief. Can you talk? Are you able to set the rope?"

"I'm all right, Kenner—yes, I think I can set the rope. I've about got it. Give me a minute. I'll have to push off the wall to clear the tree. Take up the slack, easy now."

Activity suddenly cranks up in the labyrinth below Sommers, excited voices overlapping. He recognizes the President's staccato commands. "Gently now—stretch him out—easy." Then, "Hm, can't feel a pulse. Try to stop the bleeding. Here, take my handkerchief."

Another voice, Kenner's, hails from above Sommers on the rim of the chasm—a shout that covers the voices from below. "Chief, we've got the slack." Sommers feels the rope tighten under his armpits. "Push out—see if you can clear the tree. Don't worry, we've got you."

Sommers manages to turn himself, facing the steep rock face. The hemlock branches scratch his face as he puts both feet against the nearly vertical slab and gives a strong shove. He swings out to the right, disentangling himself from the clinging limbs, seemingly reluctant to release their ward. "All right, Kenner," he shouts, "I'm free—lower away."

The rest is anti-climactic. Sommers, hanging like a Chinese puppet, is lowered nearly forty feet to the floor of the labyrinth, itself a haphazard crazy quilt of gigantic rock splinters and slabs lying in grotesque positions at all angles. Eager hands reach up to grab Sommers. Exclamations pour from the three men on the bottom—Roosevelt, Spring-Rice and Agent Sachs—Kenner and Meyers having raced around up Sky Top trail to effect the rescue from above at Eagles' Nest.

"Bully, Joseph, you're a sight for sore eyes. You came a close one, this time. You all right?" Roosevelt helps to loosen the rope around Sommers's shoulders.

"Yessir, I believe so, sir, thanks to one hardy hemlock and some kind of blind luck." Sommers rubs his arms and shakes his head, smiling broadly at the President.

Roosevelt is ebullient. "Sommers, that's the bravest act I've ever seen a man perform. We all thought you were a goner, for sure. I owe you my life, and you can bet your best saddle I'll make it up to you."

Cecil Spring-Rice comes over and shakes Sommers's hand. "I daresay, the President is right, Sommers. You are a courageous fellow. I doubt it would be an exaggeration to state that you have saved all of our lives. God only knows how we might have survived such a rock slide as you've thwarted."

Agent Sachs just smiles broadly and shakes his chief's hand. Sommers smiles in return. The relief he feels has as much to do with the fact that he isn't leaving Helena an early widow as it does to know he has cheated an horrific death. He can still feel the sensation of falling and blacking out.

Kenner and Meyers, somewhat breathless, having raced back down from Sky Top trail, emerge from the recesses of the labyrinth. Sommers embraces both. "I owe you two my life."

"Hey, Chief," Kenner blusters, "it could have been anyone of us up there."

Roosevelt, his face creased by consternation, speaks. "Now, gentlemen, I'm afraid we don't have any more time for ceremony. We've got ourselves two dead bodies down here and maybe one up there on the cliff. What about that, Agent Kenner? Did your bullet find its mark in the man that shot the General?" Kenner was an excellent marksman. He knew before he climbed up to Sky Top trail to rescue Sommers that he had gotten his man.

"Yessir, he's dead, sir—bullet through the neck."

"I see—Hmm, well, we've got quite a fine pickle here, haven't we?" Roosevelt walks over to a crumpled heap that had once been a living breathing man. For the first time, Sommers notes the conspirator he had grappled with. His face, turned up, is unrecognizable—a bloody blotch joined to a torso with limbs that seem to sprout at all the wrong angles. Blood had splattered over the surface of the rock that caught the impact of the man's body. Even to an experienced and hardened professional as Sommers, the sight is sickening. He turns away. Roosevelt doesn't seem deterred by any of it.

"Gentlemen," he states, "before we go marching off announcing all of this to the world-at-large, causing a panic on Wall Street, revolution in half of South America and God knows what else in Europe and the Pacific, what with the Japanese and the Russians already shooting the pants off of one another, we'd better sort out a few things here.

"We don't have a lot of time to decide how to handle all of this, but whatever we do—we're not going to go off half-cocked and place this nation in jeopardy by haphazardly announcing an unsuccessful assassination attempt on the President of the United States. I believe that kind of disclosure could have unhealthy repercussions and undermine confidence in the government and my administration. The world right now is full of tinder boxes waiting for a spark which could well ignite dreadful consequences. There are too many crazy anarchists running around as it is, ready to fan such a spark into a world-wide conflagration.

"Nosirree, we've got to get to the bottom of things here. Joseph, I suspect you've been working on something that led up to what's happened here. Suppose you quickly get us on board with what you know. I hope you feel up to it."

"Yes, sir, I'm none the worse, thanks to my men here." Sommers runs through his experiences of past hours following the dinner the previous evening—first, the conspiracy uncovered by General Sidon's wife, the General's complicity in a plot to steal the detonators, the secret meeting, his own discovery by the conspirators, the chase up to the Mountain House roof and down to the basements, his eluding of the conspirators and his rediscovery of them at Eagles' Nest as they prepared to unleash an avalanche of stone on the President and his party. The only thing Sommers leaves out is his extraordinary thrust into future time and his manner of awakening up on Sky Top trail near Eagles' Nest just prior to the President's beginning his morning 'scramble' through the labyrinth.

"Well, now." The President is incredulous. "It seems to boil down to a conspiracy to kill me, to make it look like an accident to throw everybody off the track, then to sell military secrets to some foreign agent representing God knows what foreign country." He pauses. "General Sidon, traitor that he seems to be, or, for that matter, was, is too important a man to just disappear." The President's mind is working feverishly. He has a scenario. "Gentlemen, if we are to uncover anything beyond what we now know, we are going to have to keep these events under our hat. Sommers, I'm going to detach you from the Treasury Department to report directly to me at the White House. You'll go undercover to investigate this whole business. Maybe you'll find something, maybe you won't. But if we blurt out all that's happened here today to the public, we'll surely force the foxes to go to ground.

"In the meantime, we've got ourselves three bodies to dispose of. The General is easy. He just had a heart attack, brought on by an unfortunate collision with an excessive amount of lead. I believe it to be in the best interest of protecting this country from further chicanery that we do not divulge otherwise. I've got a doctor up here with me, a long-time friend of mine, an old hunting buddy who once helped me drag a grizzly three miles back to camp. He'll attest to the General's heart condition. No one can deny the General did suffer a massive coronary. I can tell you, that bullet tore up his pumper like it was Swiss cheese.

"My only regret is that, under my plan, I cannot divulge to the American people the absolute blackguard General Marcus Sidon has turned out to be. I shall, of course, speak to Mrs. Sidon, acclaiming her courage for her part in exposing her husband for his villainy. No doubt, she may meet the news of the General's demise with, shall we say, not unbounded sorrow."

The men surrounding the President are speechless. Roosevelt, they are all aware, is nothing if not unorthodox, but this adventure upon which he is about to embark beggars comparison with any of his other escapades to date. It is nothing less than deliberate obfuscation of vital evidence in a criminal matter of the most serious nature, so thinks Roosevelt's close friend, Cecil Spring-Rice. However, he does not voice his disapproval. On the contrary, he shakes his head and smilingly says, as much in grudging admiration as in wonder at Roosevelt's bold scheme, "Theodore, you surpass yourself, I must say."

"Thank you, Springy. I knew I could depend on you." Roosevelt pumps his friend's hand mercilessly and turns to the others, none of whom in their subordinate positions would dream of offering any negative comment, whatever, as to the President's plan, even if asked, which, of course the President has no intention of doing.

"Now you men are sworn to secrecy on this matter. Not a word of this to anyone, not even your wives. The destiny of this nation may well rise or fall on how well you keep the faith until we've found the rest of the weasels responsible for this and nailed their hides up to the barn door." The President faces Sommers and takes a step toward him.

"Sommers, when I was here in '92, I remember a steep climb and a cliff a mile or two yonder off the Carriage Road to the southwest, there." T.R. points in a southerly direction toward the end of the lake. "Place called the Traps. Dangerous trail—fellow could fall off there in a dozen different spots just admiring the view, if he didn't watch his step."

Roosevelt's eyes suggest a distinct tinge of merriment as he spins out a bizarre plan to get rid of the two bodies of the conspirators.

"These rapscallions who were so set on doing us in are going to have a do-in of their own. It's going to turn out they got drunk, had an argument. One of 'em pulls a gun, shoots point-blank at the other, but before he drops, the victim lunges at the shooter, knocks 'em right off the cliff. So, we end up with a body on top with a bullet through his neck," the President points up to the edge of the chasm, "and another one piled up on the rocks below with every bone in his consarn body broken." The President waves toward the twisted, bloody corpse that was once a man, lying crookedly against the unyielding rocks that lay strewn across the floor of the ravine. "Somebody'll find 'em sooner or later."

The men grouped around the President are silent. They all know that T.R. is not looking for acquiescence from anyone of them. Cecil Spring-Rice is smiling and slowly shaking his head. He is used to Roosevelt's idiosyncrasies, but this one absolutely staggers even his heretofore well-stretched sensibilities. Spring-Rice was once quoted in a remark describing Roosevelt's unpredictable and often unilateral behavior as that of the workings of an adventurous, boyish mind that had just about reached the level of a six-year-old. It was, of course, a sidelong compliment to not only Roosevelt's perpetual mischievousness in dealing with the to-be-expected perfidy of the scions of government and big business, but to his unflinching confidence in his sole judgment of a situation that whatever course of action he would undertake would be the correct one.

Roosevelt looks around the small silent circle of men. "Now, I know what you men are all thinking—our President has spent too many hours out in the western noonday sun without a hat and his brains have frizzled. And you all might be right—to a degree. But, I've learned a couple of things in dealing with rascals like these fellows here. Sometimes you have to throw the book away, that is, if there happens to be a book about things like this."

Roosevelt's gaze shifts to the murky dawn breaking above the chasm. He pauses for a moment and smiles enigmatically. His eyes reflect a story teller's excitation.

"When an Indian hunts a buffalo out on the plains and all he's got is a bow and arrow, he doesn't just run out in front of the herd and wave his arms and shout, 'Hey, you there—you look like a good fat bull. Would you mind trotting over this way so's I can shoot you?' Nosirree, you know what that Indian does? He crawls on his belly, maybe for a half mile or more. He sneaks up on that buffalo just like a mountain lion slinks along through the rocks on the trail of a bighorn. You see, the thing the Indian and the mountain lion have in common is that they both like to eat. Neither one of 'em is keen about chasing wild game over the countryside for the sake of the exercise.

"Now, if we're to ferret out the rest of whatever villains are in this piece, we'll need all the wits we can muster. Sommers, that's where you're going to come in after we leave here."

The President's jaw clenches as in affirmation of a weighty decision having been made.

"In the meanwhile, we've spent enough time joshing around here like a bunch of washerwomen at the spring house. We've got work to do." Roosevelt takes a step toward Sommers and places a hand on his shoulder.

"Joseph," he addresses Sommers in a tone which mixes an almost brotherly affection with that of a kindly schoolmaster handing out homework assignments, "you take Agent Kenner with you and hustle down to the stables and hitch up a buckboard and get back here as quick as you can get. Just tell the stablemaster someone's not feeling too good—that'll be the General here, of course—and needs a ride back to the Mountain House—nothing more, understand?" Sommers nods his head as the President continues. "On the way, stop at the front desk and locate Dr. Elias Coover. Tell 'em the President needs a hand to drag a bear back to camp, and pronto." Roosevelt's face breaks into a wry grin. "He'll understand.

"In the meantime, you two men," T.R. addresses Sachs and Meyers, "get on up to the cliff there and lower down that other snake. And make sure you find that pistol." Sachs and Meyers take off through the narrow, wedge-like opening leading back toward the beginning of the labyrinth trail like two fugitives with a pack of bloodhounds at their heels.

"We'll load up the General here in the buckboard and get 'em back to the Mountain House under Dr. Coover's supervision. Cecil and I will offer our condolences to Mrs. Sidon. Then, we'll search out the Smileys, explain what happened."

The President cannot suppress a devilish wink and an even more devilish grin that spreads across his face, not dissimilar to the expression of a schoolboy fabricating a wild tale of his singular involvement in the capture of a runaway horse. No matter that his life had been in supreme jeopardy just minutes earlier, the President seems to be enjoying this episode as much as his famous charge up San Juan Hill in 1898 in the face of deadly Spanish bullets.

The mood is brief, however. His countenance takes on a serious aspect, the grin disappearing like the sun ducking behind a cloud bank. "We must keep things under control. In view of the General's demise and the diabolical nature of this whole business, we'll need to get back to Washington and see to certain arrangements—also put to immediate rest any rumors among the press as to what really happened here at Mohonk.

"Now, Joseph." the President is suddenly very solicitous toward Sommers. "How are you feeling?" T.R. does not wait for Sommers to answer. "Now I know you've had a damn rough day of it all so far, worse even than breaking a herd of wild mustangs from dawn to dusk. But, you and your men are going to have to bring that buckboard back here again and load up this pile of manure"—Roosevelt gestures toward the broken body of the assassin—"along with his cohort up there and get 'em over to the cliff at the Traps, as the plan calls for. You know what to do." Roosevelt reaches into an inner pocket of his tweed riding jacket, pulls out a silver flask and hands it to Sommers. "Hardly ever drink this stuff—good for emergencies, though, like this one. Nothing like a little Wild Turkey for snake bites. Too bad these snakes won't be able to enjoy it. Douse 'em up good, Sommers, after you get 'em over to the Traps.

"While you're down fetching the buckboard, we'll give these bodies the once-over for any identification or incriminating evidence. A disagreeable task and I doubt we'll find anything; still it must be done." Roosevelt turns and looks up toward the top of the cliff. Sachs and Meyers are just visible beyond the edge preparing to lower down the body of the other assailant.

"You fellows up there, don't forget to locate that pistol—and hustle it up. We don't want any early morning hikers wandering across our path." The President turns back to Sommers. "If I remember, Joseph, I believe you arranged to have management keep the trails closed off until 9:00 AM for our security."

"Yessir, that's correct, sir."

"Well, now, then," the President draws out his watch, "it's almost 7:30. We should have enough time, but just to be sure, leave one of your men stationed to block off the entrance to the labyrinth until this dirty business is concluded. Also," the President adds with a grim look at the broken body of the very dead and bloody assassin sprawled across an equally bloody rock, "you'd better bring back a couple of pails of water to clean things up a bit so's it doesn't appear as though we've slaughtered a bear or two down here."

"Yessir, this place could stand a little housekeeping," Sommers adds with a droll grin.

"All right then, Joseph, off you go. Best you and Agent Kenner take a moment and leave a message for Agent Yost. He's with Mrs. Roosevelt and the children still, I hope?"

"Yessir, that's his assignment, Mr. President, until relieved by me."

"Very well, Joseph. Fill him in on things quickly and tell him to keep mum. Have him convey to Mrs. Roosevelt that I'll be along shortly and that she is not to leave our quarters until I get back, understood?"

Sommers nods, motions to Kenner and proceeds back toward the twisted passage of the labyrinth.

"And, Joseph, bring back some blankets to cover the bodies. We don't want to look as though we've been picking up victims of a new outburst of the bubonic plague."

Joseph Sommers turns to look back, staring at Roosevelt's resolute jaw as he heeds the last instructions of his Commander-in-Chief in the smoky, early morning overcast that stretches foggy fingers down through the walls of the labyrinth.

"Are you quite all right, Mr.Stanner? For a moment there, I thought you had burned your throat. I do like my tea to be hot—almost scalding. I apologize if it is too hot for your liking."

Jamie looked up from his cup. How long had he been 'out'—adrift in another time warp, once again as Joseph Sommers? It had to have been less than a split second. He hadn't dropped the tea cup. Indeed, he had been about to gulp another swallow of the still steaming hot liquid when it had happened.

He had gone back—he had relived every moment in Joseph Sommers's life following the terrifying plunge over the precipice. He had experienced Sommers's remarkable escape from death. He knew everything now that had immediately followed the struggle with the assassins up until Sommers's hurried departure to fulfill Roosevelt's commands. He remembered the story in the *New Paltz Independent* about the two vagrants, discovered having done themselves in over at the Traps. Roosevelt's wild ploy seemed to have worked. But what role did Josephine Sommers play in the revelation? Was she aware of his backward passage? He was disturbingly off-balance. More than ever, he needed answers.

"Miss Sommers, I must apologize. I don't know what happened. I feel as if I—" he had trouble spelling it out; his mind churned as he tried to collect and draw rational meaning from the existential gyrations that left his senses swimming in a sea of unfamiliar currents, threatening to drown him unless he could reach landfall.

"A moment ago, somehow, Miss Sommers, I was back again on that day in the labyrinth, just as I was describing it to you, only I wasn't there as Jamieson Stanner, I was Joseph Sommers. I experienced every moment of your father's life during and for a short time after the assassination attempt on the President. It's all clear to me now. Your father wasn't killed in the fall from the cliff. He came back here to Tarrytown with Helena, your mother. You were born the next summer."

Josephine Sommers interjected. "That's quite right, Mr. Stanner. Yes, I was born on August 3,1905, to be exact, and my father, so my mother told me, went through the whole neighborhood handing out cigars to the men and chocolates to the ladies, he was so proud."

Jamie set the teacup down carefully on the table. Amazingly, his hand was now steady—unlike minutes before when Josephine Sommers casually discussed the attributes of her father and proceeded to serve Mohonk tea to her rubber-kneed and shaken guest. But Jamie's mind was meshing like an over-heated gear box. He was trying to sort out hundreds of questions to ask Josephine Sommers.

"Miss Sommers—why do I suddenly have the idea that you knew about me, even before I came here today? What gives me the impression that a drink of your Mohonk tea from that lovely teapot of yours sent me hurtling back into the past—1904, to be exact?" He paused. "You've been waiting for me to show up on your doorstep, haven't you?"

"Oh, my dear Mr. Stanner." Josephine Sommers's face was wreathed in a beaming smile that seemed to brighten all the corners of the parlor against the advancing twilight of the early March evening. "You do have an imagination, don't you?" She placed her teacup on the table and stood up. Jamie followed suit. Their eyes locked. For a brief instant, Jamie thought, Josephine Sommers, with her slightly quizzical expression, still smiling tantalizingly at him, looked exactly as Helena Sommers had on that magical Saturday evening in 1904 when he, as Joseph Sommers, was so coquettishly informed of his forthcoming paternalism.

Jamie was ready to swear that Josephine Sonmers could read every thought simmering in his feverish mind despite the somewhat epileptic characteristics of his present cerebral processes. The smile lingered softly on her face but her visage suggested she had something of great moment to reveal to Jamieson Stanner.

"Mr. Stanner, perhaps this is the time to show you something. Mind you, it won't explain the why and wherefore of your strange experiences, but it may fill a few holes in the fabric of your, may we say, recollections."

Moving to a large cherry secretary of Lincolnian proportions sitting imperiously in a rear corner of the parlor, she opened the massive roll-top desk and removed an elegantly finished wooden veneer box that appeared to have been designed to hold stationery and writing materials. She moved back to the tea table and sat down, turning to Jamie with an expression, so Stanner felt at that moment, as if she had just completed a very long journey. There was both weariness and happiness in her look, but now she was home and she was now, finally, it would seem, able to fulfill a promise made long years ago.

"Mr. Stanner," she began, "my father informed my mother and me, not long before he died, in the mid-forties just following the end of world War II, that someday, someone would come searching for what is contained in the papers within this keepsake. He said that the person would know to treat the information revealed herein with absolute confidentiality and that nothing of the facts of the account related here should ever be released to the public, no matter that all the principals might have long since passed away."

She opened the lid of the box and removed a somewhat yellowed envelope which she handed to Jamie. "It would seem, Mr. Stanner, that you are the man my father had in mind to receive this."

Jamie, his hand steady but his pulse racing, took the envelope. He turned it over gently. On the front upper left-hand corner was printed a return address—Office of the Special Deputy, The White House, Washington, D.C. The flap of the envelope was not sealed.

"May I?" Stanner was about to reach into the envelope.

"Of course, Mr. Stanner. It is for your eyes."

Jamie removed several pieces of neatly folded paper. The outside sheet seemed to be something of a letter, handwritten, displaying excellent penmanship, the script covering only one side. It was addressed: *To Whom it may concern.* It was signed at the bottom by Joseph Sommers and dated November 1,1945.

"Are you familiar with the contents of this envelope, Miss Sommers?" Jamie was surprised at the steadiness of his voice despite the fact the he could easily detect the sound of his blood coursing through his carotid artery. He must calm himself somehow. He didn't need a stroke to incapacitate him now that he was this close to resolving the awesome riddle of Mohonk.

Her voice was soothing and almost therapeutic as she answered. "I am, indeed, Mr. Stanner. I was very close to my father. He seemed quite concerned, that is, before he wrote this, about something that happened on the weekend of November 13, 1904 at the Mohonk Mountain House. He told my mother and me that he needed to explain something about that weekend that had haunted him over the years. He believed that someday, someone would come looking for what is in that envelope—and here you are, Mr. Stanner.

"From what you have told me of your experience at Mohonk, I believe there is no doubt that you are the one to whom my father was referring.

"Now, allow me to fetch a fresh pot of tea. I do not wish to distract you from the contents of those papers you hold in your hands." She picked herself up and waltzed from the room, teapot in hand, just as if it was the most natural thing in the world for her to be entertaining a man, her junior by some forty years, who claimed to have lived twenty-four hours in the life of her own father, ninety years in the past.

Jamie removed the additional sheets. They were typewritten, single-spaced and appeared to be a report of sorts. At the top of the first sheet was a salutation addressed to the 26th President of the United States—Theodore Roosevelt. It was signed by Joseph Sommers, Special Deputy to the President, and dated: April 15,1905.

Jamie's fingers were burning hot. Was it a chemical reaction to the paper or just the unnerving excitement generated in his system as he realized he was about to discover the final details of the mystery surrounding the life of Joseph Sommers—a mystery which had transcended nearly a century to engulf his own life, mind and soul and link him with a man who had lived 90 years earlier, a man with whom he not only shared the same initials, but a man whose life and being for something of twenty-four hours in 1904, he knew in the only way a man can really ever know of another man's life—by living it.

Jamie decided to read the letter first. It began:

> To you who shall one day read this account, I am bonded for all time. I know not who you are. I know only that you will, one day, come from a future time. You already came for short hours into my life at a most critical juncture, although, at the time, I had no knowledge of your existence. It was only later, when by some strange providential workings, I found myself cast upon your own distant shores of 1993, that I realized we shared a mutual destiny, indeed, it would seem, a juxtaposition of our very souls.
>
> I have no explanation for you as to why or how in the mind of God this crossover should have occurred and I do not doubt you are no more cognizant than I in understanding the nature of this perplexity. We both know, however, that it has happened and that somehow, within the contexts of our own times, there occurred a strange transcendence through which time, as we know it to be in our normal lives, was disengaged, creating an intersection through which our two lives merged. Perhaps it happens in other peoples, lives as well.

My words do not enlighten, I fear. The matter is beyond my grasp. It may well be that you will advance a better explanation of what I most certainly believe to be some substance of the Divine. It would have been, I believe, tragically remiss for me not to have shared with you my perceptions which have haunted my waking and often sleeping moments down through the years.

The enclosed report will help, I trust, to shed something of light on certain events that followed the astonishing weekend of November 13,1904, events, that once you learn of them, will enable you to place in perspective something more of that portentous period as well as lend some measure of comfort, if not rationale, to a troubled psyche.

In your service, I am,
Joseph Sommers
November 1, 1945

Jamie allowed his hands to fall to his lap, the letter still grasped. It was difficult for him to assess the sensations that possessed him at that instant. On the one hand, there was a quietude that had swept over him as he read. There was also an intense exhilaration. He had somehow stepped through the veil that separates man from the unknown voids that contemplation of death conjures. He knew that from that moment on, future life for him would encompass ever wider contemplations. He now knew there was an on-going of life beyond the narrow dimensions of three-score years and ten, the average life span the Bible assigned to a man within the meager measurements of conventional time.

The moment had come to read the report. Jamie gently folded the letter and placed it once again in the aged envelope. He drew out the report, unfolded it and held it up to the waning light of the candles that Josephine Sommers had earlier placed on the tea table.

It began:

Office of the Special Deputy to The President,
The White House, Washington, D.C.

Report to The President April 12, 1905
The Honorable Theodore Roosevelt
The White House
Washington, D.C.

My Dear Sir:

I have the honor of submitting to you and to your high office as President of The United States, the following final account of my investigation as Special Deputy regarding the "Mohonk Incident" as commissioned by you on the date, November 15, 1904, Washington, D.C.

I have investigated all possible connections between Brigadier General Marcus Sidon, USA, deceased, and certain foreign nationals or representatives in relation to the theft of highly classified U.S. ordnance developments from several U.S. Arsenals, in particular, the Sandy Hook Arsenal and Proving Grounds in New Jersey.

It has been determined that a case of the newly tested and approved time fuse detonators known as USA #46 S.Q. P.D., designed for use with high explosive shells of various calibers, had been removed from the Sandy Hook Arsenal by General Sidon, without proper authorization, sometime in early November 1904.

Some information regarding the development of this device is included in the 1904 year end report of General William Crozier, commanding officer, U.S. Ordnance Dept. U.S. Army. I quote:

"In connection with the routine work of this department, important experiments have been conducted, having for their object the development and completion of successful working designs of the 21 second combination fuse for mobile artillery, the centrifugal percussion fuse for all calibers of projectile above the 2.24 inch and detonating fuse for all classes of field, siege and seacoast projectiles to be charged with the service high explosive. An object sought in the investigation has been a time fuse that would enable the maximum effect of shrapnel fire to be developed at all ranges with the new field gun. Experiments with detonating fuses have been conducted during the year, resulting in the approval for manufacture of three forms of these fuses for major, medium, and minor caliber projectiles, respectively."

In a recent report by one of our Ordnance Department field agents examining information obtained (at least, as much as has become available, to date) regarding the latest Japanese explosive ordnance, it can be seen that the Japanese military have also developed a highly advanced detonator, which, since the outbreak of hostilities with Russia, has proved to be of paramount significance in the unusually successful operations against Russian forces, in particular, this past January with the fall of Port Arthur and Mukden. Japanese Naval sources, while unwilling to share with us the technology of these new explosive devices, have assured our field people that the use of the new detonators in their naval armaments will reduce the entire Russian Navy to scrap iron. Indeed, they welcome a confrontation with the Russian Navy and believe it will come this spring.

My sources indicate Russian agents became aware of this development in mid-1904 as a result of the devastation visited upon Russian forces by Japanese field guns and heavy artillery utilizing H.E. shells equipped with the new detonators.

It is apparent that Russian agents became 'friendly' with General Sidon sometime during this period. As a consultant to you in armaments and munitions development, he was, of course, privy to the latest U.S. ordnance technology. The General was, obviously, compromised in some fashion and entered into an agreement to supply information and, most damagingly, actual prototypes of the U.S. detonators, which, according to General Crozier's report, are even more sophisticated and technically superior to the Japanese models.

Although, regrettably, there is no tangible evidence to back up the charge, the agent who I had managed to have secreted within the Russian Embassy in Washington informed me that it is likely, based on snatches of surreptitiously obtained reports, that the assassination attempt on your life had its nefarious beginnings within the Embassy. How much, if anything, the Russian Ambassador, J.J. Korostovetz, Count Cassini and/or the Czar himself, may know of or be contributory to the conspiracy is highly speculative. My agent advances the opinion, not without some thread of credibility, based more on the lack of general knowledge among embassy personnel of such an attempt or conspiracy, that there were very few people directly involved, indeed, perhaps no more than the two conspirators we dealt with at Mohonk, an Embassy contact and, of course, General Sidon himself. It has the earmarks of a rather hair-brained scheme, inefficiently composed and, certainly, carelessly and unsuccessfully executed, I am happy to be able to say. Still, such wild and, seemingly, poorly planned undertakings sometimes succeed, as witness the appalling assassination of President McKinley, carried out by one madman, but with no evidence revealed of collusion with other anarchists of his ilk, despite the enormous investigatory resources that sought to make of the affair a world-wide plot.

Again, my agent is inclined to presume that a very small clique of radicals, anxious to ingratiate themselves with their superiors in the hopes of rising to positions of greater influence within the hierarchy of the Embassy and, perhaps, even to ascend to the inner circle of the Czar himself, devised this portentous blueprint. Whether the plan carried the approval of higher ups, we shall, perhaps, never know, nor may we ever really tidy up the loose strings and unquestionably decree an end to the affair.

The Russians believe your sympathies lie predominantly with the Japanese in the matter of the war and distrust your views on Far Eastern affairs in general, feeling that their national interests and the questions of territorial jurisdiction, particularly in relation to Korea, Manchuria and the Sakhalin Islands, are not being considered in an even-handed manner. Hence, the decision by some radical elements to eliminate you and any chance of your influencing the outcome of the Russo-Japanese conflict that would imperil Russia's long-range plans and self-interests for the area. At the same time, such deviants who authored the plan to quiet you permanently saw an opportunity, in liaison with General Sidon, to obtain U.S. ordnance, vis-a-vie the detonators, that would surely have impressed their own military people and given them a specific advantage in neutralizing the Japanese superiority which, up until the present, has resulted in devastating losses of Russian forces. Such losses, according to my sources, cannot continue to be tolerated if Russia is not to be ultimately and thoroughly defeated. If the conspirators were to enrich themselves in the successful execution of such a dastardly deed, then all the better from their point of view.

It is probably a fair consensus, although no direct evidence supports the theory, that General Sidon was targeted by one of the assassins (no doubt planned from the beginning) when it was quickly concluded that the assassination attempt was to fail. The General was not to be left alive to betray the identity of the plotters or the extent of the conspiracy.

Alas, as we discussed some of these issues prior to your departure for your hunting trip to Colorado, it would seem we have reached a stalemate on fingering other specific felons responsible for the Mohonk Incident, beyond the two who met their demise at the scene. I would agree with you, on the basis of our investigations to date, we have probably scotched, at least for the time being, any further attempt to jeopardize your health.

Although we have uncovered no further machinations beyond General Sidon's abortive attempt to pass military secrets to alien hands, security has been vastly improved at the Sandy Hook Arsenal and Proving Grounds and other U.S. Arsenals under General Crozier's command. Certain officers stationed at Sandy Hook who might have been involved with General Sidon have been transferred to less sensitive posts where they will continue to be observed and subject to scrutiny to ascertain any guilt, or for that matter, innocence in their future duty.

Regarding Major Hertzog, the General's one time aide-de-camp, although I never, personally, took a liking to the man, I believe, nevertheless, that I have done him an injustice in my judgment of his capabilities as an officer. In retrospect, I confess my observations of his duties in handling the many details and coordination attendant upon your visit demonstrate to me that his performance was superior and unflagging. However, as a possible suspect in the conspiracy, I assigned an agent to follow him religiously and to report any deviation or untoward behavior in his performance in the new assignment and station given him in the Quartermaster Depot at Fort Meade, Maryland. I am happy to report to you that he is performing his duties, according to his superior officers, in a diligent, energetic and thoroughly exemplary manner. Perhaps in the subservient position in the shadow of the General, he felt thwarted, due to his assignment to routine, fairly mundane tasks. I have no doubt that he must have picked up quite a lot of loose ends the General left hanging. In any case, it is my sincere belief, based on everything known about the Major, that he knew nothing of the conspiracy nor the General's compact with foreign agents in the theft of the detonators.

As reported to you earlier, I saw to it that an agent was placed in the Turkish Embassy on the odd chance that the Mohonk Incident might have been devised by them in conjunction with the Russians, or at least to determine if their participation might have been sought. Your expression of outrage of late in the world's newspapers as to the wanton killing of Armenians by the Turks in their on-going ethnic struggles has not exactly endeared you to the Ottoman government. Also, there is always the possibility of Turkish agents acting as intermediaries in the collection and dissemination of U.S. military secrets for whatever profit can be obtained from unscrupulous sources. A high-ranking officer at Sandy Hook, who did not wish to be identified, offered the information voluntarily during the course of the investigation that everyone in the world seems to want to get their hands on the latest U.S. military technology, particularly the #46 detonator. He believes foreign agents in Washington are as numerous as "flies in a milk house."

In light of these events, Mr. President, and in my advisory role to you, particularly in view of your mandate to me for comments and advice on improving security measures related to such matters, may I humbly suggest you might wish to expand the office of Special Deputy to include the employment of a more specialized secret force to deal more directly with the collection of foreign intelligence as it relates to the interests of U.S. national security.

And now, as I recently announced to you there might exist the possibility in the not too distant future that my health could force my early resignation, I regret to say that, indeed, that day has come. I must turn over the reins of this important office of trust and responsibility to which you appointed me last November. My doctor advises me that if I wish to see the birth of my first child, due this coming August, I can no longer delay an operation of some consequence. He advises me it is not serious yet, but will be in a short period if not attended to immediately. It would appear that my physical engagement with the conspirators, unhappily, in combination with my confrontation, happily, with that mighty sturdy hemlock, has taken some toll, after all.

I close, then, this final report with my wishes for your continued good health and prosperity and my heartfelt thanks for the opportunity of serving you in the interests of this country that we both love so well. May God bless you and protect you in the performance of your duties in the years to come as you continue to give to this nation and to the world the distinguished leadership for which you are so well known and loved.

Your servant in the cause of peace and justice,
Joseph Sommers, Special Deputy

As Jamie finished reading the report, he placed it along with the letter and the envelope down on the tea table. Josephine Sommers returned, as if on cue, with a replenished steaming teapot.

Jamie's eyes moved to acknowledge her entrance, but his body was immobile. He was all but paralyzed by the revelations he had just encountered. Although he had not a clue as to what he might have expected or what he would ultimately discover in this visit to the Sommers homestead, he certainly never anticipated reading a report written by Joseph Sommers to President Roosevelt some 90 years previously dealing with national security and aspects of international espionage. Nor had he ever envisaged a personal note from Sommers attesting to, clarifying and confirming every intimation of his experiences over the November weekend of 1904.

"Now, Mr. Stanner, I'm sure you're ready for a warm-up of delicious Mohonk tea."

Jamie was mildly surprised to note that, indeed, his cup was nearly empty. He recalled taking only a gulp or two. As Josephine Sommers poured the scalding liquid into Stanner's cup, he finally found his voice, weakened though it was by the disjointedness of straddling two worlds.

"Ahh, well, Miss Sommers, I hope another swallow of Mohonk tea won't send me back to 1904 again. I think I'd like to quit this regression business while I'm still ahead." His feeble effort toward a pun was met by a quiet smile and a touch of her hand to his own as she finished pouring the swirling mahogany beverage into his cup and took her place on the settee beside him.

"Mr. Stanner, I'm glad you finally found us. From your experience, you have, perhaps, learned something of the sweet mysteries of life. And as for the passage we euphemistically call death, well that, indeed, is another profound mystery—one for which, I daresay, you are not quite ready." Josephine Sommers smiled radiantly as if she had just endowed Jamie with all of the understanding he needed to fathom the remaining mysteries of the universe.

Jamie placed his teacup on the table. He had downed most of the hot tea with some apprehension as to where he might find himself after a swallow or two. He had traveled nowhere and abruptly sensed that there would be no more journeys. He reached over and gently clasped Josephine Sommers's hands.

"Miss Sommers, I am grateful to you. I can't adequately describe my feelings at this moment—peace, exhilaration, relief, yes—great relief that what I've experienced is not the product of an overworked mind. Strange—the questions of how? why? or what? has occurred here should press for answers, but right now all I can think about is that I'm not a candidate for Gestalt therapy. Thank you. I feel a strong bond with you, I confess."

"And I with you, Mr. Stanner. We shall meet again, I am certain of it."

Jamie drained the remaining swallow or two of his tea, set the cup on the table and stood up. Josephine Sommers followed suit. They walked slowly and quietly to the front door.

He turned to her as he put on his coat and grasped the doorknob. "Miss Sommers, may I ask you where your father and mother are—well—interred?" It sounded so gross to him, the request—like discussing the attributes of cremation as opposed to underground burial as a means of disposing of one's loved ones.

"Father and mother rest in their earthly forms in the Tarrytown cemetery upon the hill behind the old Dutch Church, Section 10C, to be exact. But, of course, they are not there. We really must stop thinking of graves as resting places. They are simply memorial grounds where, of course, we often go to seek solace and comfort, bound as we are by our earthly emotions and our primitive perceptions about the hereafter. While we are confined within these earthly perimeters, we do still seek connections with our loved ones. Such places as embrace our worldly remains are the only doorways to the beyond we seem wont to acknowledge. I used to visit my parents' graves. My mother died in 1955. But I no longer do so. I think of them now in much more pleasant climes."

"Miss Sommers, would—that is—I wonder if . . ."

Josephine Sommers smiled that radiant smile again, truly dazzling Jamie as he stumbled to speak in parting. "Oh, I know what you are going to ask me, Mr. Stanner, I can practically read your mind. Of course you may come to visit me and you may bring your friend Jennifer, as well—at any time you like—but," she paused, and at that moment, it seemed to Jamie that a barely perceptible flicker of light crossed her face, a reflection such as a mirror might throw for an instant, and then it was gone, "you must understand, Mr. Stanner, your friend may not—shall we say—see things as clearly as you do now about all of this. However, I'm sure, in time you'll be able to convince her of the glimmer of truth we have finally been able to share together."

"Thank you and good-bye for now, dear lady." Jamie paused

and smiled as he spoke in an apologetic manner. " Ah—Miss Sommers—ah—do you have a telephone? Could we—ah—is it too soon?—ah—I'd really like to bring Jennifer back tomorrow if that wouldn't be too inconvenient?"

"You may come anytime as you may wish, Mr. Stanner," Josephine Sommers quietly responded as she reached up to give Stanner a light kiss on the cheek. "But I'm afraid I don't have a telephone. In any case, I shall not be far from here. The neighbors will know where I am if you don't find me at home when you arrive."

"Good-bye again, Miss Sommers." Stanner impulsively put his arms around her and gave her a gentle hug. "I'll look forward to seeing you then. I can't tell you what this has meant to me."

"Nonsense, young man. Look to your future now, and my blessings on you."

Slowly, the big heavy door closed and Josephine Sommers, like a wraith, appeared to melt away into the darkly paneled foyer. The latch of the heavy portal struck the door jamb with a resounding clash of metal as the bolt slid home. The sound was jarring and unexpected—it made Jamie jump. It reminded him of the way the door to room 490 closed so finally that last time when, as Sommers, he had said goodnight to Helena, not knowing if he would ever see her again. Did all of this happen just now? If he were to ring again would Josephine Sommers come to the door as she did before?—or would the bell simply echo through the hollow, inner chambers of the Sommers mansion, unanswered by anyone—anyone living, that is?

Something on his left caught Jamie's eye as he turned toward the front of the porch. It was Josephine Sommers in the corner of the big bay window of the parlor. She had drawn back the curtains and was smiling and waving to him, the tea table candle in her left hand casting a warm pleasant glow across her face. God, Jamie thought, as he waved back after moving on toward the front steps, what a beautiful woman she was, even now in her late eighties. He felt a sudden tenderness toward her as he thought of Joseph Sommers holding her as a tiny baby and, later, walking with her in the nearby park as a tot. When she grew to become a beautiful young woman, would Joseph Sommers have cast judgmental glances at her many beaux that undoubtedly wore down the front steps of 33 Irving Street? What of this lovely lady could he know of her past? Did she never marry? Had she never left home? And what about Helena? Did her life continue as a vibrant romance with Joseph?

Helena outlived Joseph by ten years. What of those years? One day, he would find out about the lives of Joseph, Helena and Josephine Sommers, beyond Mohonk. He knew now that he had to visit the cemetery behind the little Dutch Church. He knew, somehow, that mystery would ever surround the lives of the Sommers family—but his connection with them could never be severed. He was part of them and they were part of him—forever. That's the way it was and nothing could change it.

As he climbed into his car, Jamie felt an irresistible compulsion to get back to Fairfield, Connecticut, to share all of this with Jennifer. She would have to cancel any appointments she had for tomorrow. He was determined to return with her to 33 Irving Street. Although he still had not the foggiest notion of the meaning of his experience, he now had proof of the reality of it all. There would be plenty of time, years, he thought, to sift through the metaphysics of the events and come up with something rational. For now, the evidence he had uncovered confirming the existence of Joseph Sommers and his family was unquestionable. What actually occurred at Mohonk on that apocalyptic weekend of November 1904 was no longer a mystery—no matter how blanketed the events had become in the 90 years of layered time since their occurrence. Jennifer would meet Josephine Sommers. She would read the letter from Sommers, written to an obscure 'Whom it may concern.' She would read the final report of Joseph Sommers, Special Deputy, written to Theodore Roosevelt, 26th President of the United States. The intersection with seemingly alien dimensions, the juxtaposition of past lives on present, as well as the reverse—the time expansion and contraction—none of this now was in doubt. It only remained to determine the meaning of it all.

Chapter Fifty-two

Jennifer, cooperative as she had tried to be when Jamie had returned and announced plans to revisit Tarrytown again the very next day, had been unable to cancel a previously scheduled meeting with some bank people regarding a series of appraisals for a group of foreclosed properties. It could have meant the bank scheduling another company for the work if Jennifer were to miss the meeting. Thus, departure for Tarrytown had to be delayed until a little after 1:00 PM.

Traffic had been light on the Merritt Parkway and they were now approaching White Plains on Rt. 287.

"It'll work out all right, Jen, although I would have preferred a morning visit. I'm not sure I'm up to another tea-time with Josephine Sommers." Jamie had related to Jennifer everything about his interview with Joseph Sommers's daughter, including his unnerving whisk back to the labyrinth on November 13, 1904.

"That sequence, Jen, from the time Sommers fell from the cliff until the plans Roosevelt worked out were implemented, probably took an hour or so. Yet, I was still holding the teacup in my hand and Josephine Sommers was asking me if the tea was too hot. I couldn't have been out of it—that is, out of 1993 and back in 1904—for less than a split-second in real time."

"Oh, Jamie, this is all so weird. I mean, I don't doubt what you're saying—what you experienced as Joseph Sommers, but it's still so hard to believe. This is real *Twilight Zone* stuff."

"I know, Jen, but you'll see. You'll see the Sommers house for yourself—33 Irving Street. You'll meet Josephine Sommers, face to face—the eighty-eight year old daughter of Joseph Sommers himself. You'll see and read the letter Joseph Sommers wrote to me. He didn't know my name, but he believed that one day I would show up at his house.

"I find all of this pretty tough to chew on myself, don't worry. But it's there—the letter, the report to the President. I saw it. I read it, and you will too—no matter what explanation someone may wish to make of it. I certainly can't, and neither could Sommers. He accepted it because, to him, it was real and it is just as real to me."

Jamie turned away from the highway for a glance at Jennifer. She smiled wistfully and touched his hand, which gripped the gear shift. He couldn't quite decide whether she was just humoring him or really struggling to make sense out of what she might very well still believe to be complete and utter nonsense.

"Look, Jen, just keep an open mind until we get to Tarrytown. If what I'm telling you is anything other than what you can verify with your own eyes, well, then we'll stop off on the way back at the Mid-Hudson State Hospital at Fishkill and you can have me committed."

"Oh, Jamie, please don't even joke about something like this. There has to be an explanation. Let's just get to Tarrytown and take things from there." Jennifer tried to make her voice sound reassuring, but it had that child-like quality that suggested she was the one that needed assuring. Jamie decided to take another tack to lighten things up a bit.

"Jen, think what a terrific story all of this would make if it ever got out—that President Roosevelt covered up a plot to assassinate him. The tabloids would eat it up. Naturally, no one with half a brain would believe it—it would ring about as true as the discovery of Elvis, alive and well in a secret love-nest with Princess Diane." Jamie's face softened. For a brief instant, he could see Helena's face before him, bright and beautiful, telling him, i.e. telling Joseph Sommers, that she was pregnant.

He recovered himself and turned, smiling, toward Jennifer.

"Of course, I could never allow that to happen—to let anyone know about all of this. I would be betraying a trust, to say nothing of needlessly damaging the reputation of one of the greatest presidents to ever sit in the oval office."

Jennifer remained silent. She really didn't know what to say. She was fast running out of ways to respond to Jamie. She was having enough trouble dealing with, what appeared to her as a frightening full-blown obsession that seemed to have taken complete control of him.

"There's the turn-off, Jen." Jamie directed the Subaru off Rt. 287 where the highway continued on across the Tappenzee Bridge over the wide expanse of the Hudson. He turned right at the bottom of the ramp to Rt. 9 north, which led into and through the village of Tarrytown. It was a few minutes before 3:00 PM.

"Won't be long now, Jen. God, I can hardly wait until we drive down Irving Street and you get to meet Josephine. You'll love her, Jen. She's a real sweetheart. She'll probably serve us Mohonk tea, even if it is a little early for tea time." He paused and winked at Jennifer. "If there's something in that tea that sparks time travel, at least maybe we'll take off together."

Jennifer leaned over close to Jamie and kissed him on the cheek. "I wouldn't mind getting lost in time with you, darling, as long as the clock stops while we're in bed together."

Jamie smiled. "Leave it to you to see the erotic implications."

They had made love the night before, after he had told her about his discoveries. Jennifer had been especially attentive to him. She had told him over and over again during their mutual love-play that she loved him, *really* loved him. He was touched by her movement toward him. It was unlike the way things had been before. There was a new ingredient. His heretofore gnawing insecurity about her inconstancy in her feelings toward him was fast diminishing. What was it that had changed her? He didn't know. Maybe he should go off in time more frequently, if it had such an effect on her. He was happy about the difference in her. He hoped it would last. He wasn't sure but, somehow, it didn't bother him too seriously, the prospect that it might not last. His insecurities about Jennifer no longer ruled him in the face of the revelations and experience of Mohonk. There were other contemplations in his life now. He knew he was not the same Jamieson Stanner who had wheeled into the Mountain House that cold, wintry afternoon such a little while ago. He would never be the same again. He didn't know what other changes would take place in his life. He certainly wanted Jennifer to be a part of it all but his life and his love would no longer be subject to her rhythms and whims.

"You okay, Jamie? I don't like it when you get too quiet. You looked just now like you were back in 1904 again."

Jamie laughed. "No, my love. I'm right here with you, feeling the heat from your warm body and wanting it next to me as usual. Look, Jen, there's Irving Street on the left, just ahead."

As he made the statement and looked ahead himself to the turn off North Broadway on to Irving, an uneasiness gripped him.

There was something about the trees that looked different—different than how they had appeared yesterday, anyway. As the car made the turn, Jennifer exclaimed, "My, this a pretty street—all these old Victorian homes. They keep them up nicely, don't they?"

Jamie wasn't looking at the houses. He was looking at the trees as they slowly drove down the street. They were all just as tall as he remembered them from yesterday. The limbs arched up and over, branches from both sides of the street meeting in the middle. But somehow there was a difference. They looked more gnarled. You could see where large branches had been cut, leaving gaping holes where power lines passed through. Here and there were smaller trees of far less girth, obvious replacements for those deciduous giants that had gained maturity and given inevitable way to storm and strife. Well—Jamie thought, maybe he hadn't been quite as observant as he thought on his first visit to Irving Street. He had been too excited, he imagined, about finding the Sommers homestead.

Now, he viewed the houses. He had been driving quite slowly. They were nearly half way down the street approaching No. 33. Jennifer was ohhh-ing and ahhh-ing, quite taken by the museum-like quality of the street. "God, Jamie, these houses are right out of a picture book."

Jennifer's impressions notwithstanding, he didn't think the houses looked as bright and fresh as they had the day before. He could see paint peeling from the clapboards of several homes. It was as if the houses he had seen yesterday might be compared to a case of brightly polished and waxed apples shining irresistibly in a supermarket display. The houses he was looking at now were like a case of unpolished, somewhat bruised fruit that, while still retaining something of their original color and appeal, were beginning to turn.

Jamie's attention had been so taken up by such observations and Jennifer's distracting chatter that he was completely unprepared for what met his sight as they pulled up to No. 33.

Jennifer was the first to say something.

"My God, Jamie. That can't be it. Are you sure you have the right number?"

He was sure. There couldn't be any doubt about that. The number was still visible on the front door, but the door itself had been secured by heavy planks nailed across the front.

The beautiful bay window from which Josephine Sommers had waved good-bye to him yesterday had been broken and plywood had been nailed up haphazardly. Glass shards from the broken window were scattered across the front porch. The whole house was drab, unpainted for God knows how long. That was obvious. More obvious yet were black smoke smudges and soot above all the boarded-up windows. Such signs required no deep speculation to conclude that a fire had ravished the interior—not since yesterday, but years ago, leaving a forlorn hulk, a skeleton of its former self standing on a lot, unkempt and overgrown with weeds and untrimmed scraggly bushes.

The attached gazebo was in even worse shape. Part of the roof had been torn off in some long-past windstorm. Rain had seeped through, rotting much of the structural beams supported by the once grand Greek columns. Several had fallen. Others leaned askew, threatening to collapse. Of the once splendid balustrade, many spindles were missing or broken. The railing still ringed the deck of the gazebo but now only in warped and twisted sections that would be prone to complete collapse given the slightest nudge.

"Jamie, all right, now—what's going on? What's the catch? I know you weren't in that house yesterday." She crossed her arms. "Where in the world were you?"

Jamie was dumb with disbelief. He thought he must be going out of his mind. It was just too much. He sat motionless, staring. He couldn't speak.

Without a word to Jennifer, he stepped out of the car on to the same bluestone sidewalk he had stepped out onto the day before. Jennifer was saying something. He couldn't hear just what. It didn't matter. He wasn't listening. He could hear nothing but the words of Josephine Sommers, as spoken in the Sommers parlor short hours ago:

"Of course you may bring your friend Jennifer to see me at any time you like, but you must understand, she may not, shall we say, see things as clearly as you do now about all of this. But I'm sure, in time, you'll be able to convince her of the glimmer of truth we have finally been able to share together."

The words echoed across the unkempt lawn of No. 33 Irving Street with its stubbles of uncut grass and litter from countless forays of undisciplined children and careless neighbors.

"She may not see things as clearly as you do—" Jamie was reaching for something. There had to be a meaning behind this. What was it? Why couldn't he grasp it? His body shivered suddenly, as if someone had just dropped ice cubes down the back of his shirt.

He walked slowly toward the house. He could hear Josephine Sommers speaking to him, once again, in the words of yesterday. *"I shall not be far from here. The neighbors will know where I am when you come, if you do not find me at home."*

Jamie had reached the front steps leading up to the porch. The house loomed over him. The gathering afternoon shadows that lurked in light-starved corners crept stealthily up the faded, smoke-stained clapboards and boarded-up windows, threatening to consume the structure in one pervasive final gloom of the winter evening.

But, somehow, to Jamie, the closer he came to the house, the less forbidding it became. He was now standing on the front porch. He could clearly see the unpolished and now rusty door ringer. The cold shivers that had swept over him at his first glimpse of 33 Irving Street bare moments ago had left him. He stood silently contemplating the shabby structure that had once been the Sommers homestead—or had it? What had happened yesterday? Was Jennifer right, after all? He wondered if the door ringer still worked. Without touching it, he could still feel the cool metal grasped in his hand as he had turned the ringer a matter of hours ago. He reached toward the ringer to repeat the exercise. As he touched the handle, a balmy current of air enveloped him, swirled around him. He felt a comfortable warmth in stark contrast to the raw March breezes that had prevailed throughout the afternoon.

The door ringer turned easily, setting off a ratchety bell-like frequency that echoed throughout the hollow interior, just as it had yesterday. But today there was no sound from within, no door opening a crack by a curious occupant. There was no Josephine Sommers to welcome him and urge his entrance into the warm parlor of the Sommers household. The planks nailed so thoroughly across the double entry doors were immovable.

Hold on, was it his imagination or was that the sound of a woman's laughter coming from deep within—a young woman? It was happy laughter. Could it be Helena? Could it be Josephine? It was musical. No, there was music—a piano playing softly touched by delicate fingers. It was a Viennese waltz similar to the strange night music he had heard at the Mountain House, drifting across the lake, coming in the open window of Room 490 in the Rock Building on that abstruse evening he had discovered Joseph's and Helena's room.

The music segued smoothly into a lively quick step and a man's hearty laughter merged with the woman's. Then, abruptly, the sounds were gone—all but one. It was a banging, the sound of a broken shutter somewhere swinging uselessly in the contrary shifts of light wind sweeping in from the Hudson River, warning of inclement weather to come.

There were other sounds now, though, behind Jamie. Jennifer was out of the car talking to a middle-aged man who was passing by, walking his dog.

"Jamie," she cried, "Jamie, please—come here and listen to what this man has to say about the Sommers house."

Jamie walked back, still stunned at the unacceptable phenomena of the deserted house, but he was convinced that, somehow, something was at work. He was sure it could all be cleared up if only he could reach into that distant corner of his mind where a tiny voice seemed to be saying, "It's all right. All of this shall be made clear in good time."

"Jamie, this is Mr. Heron. He lives down the street." Jamie nodded listlessly at Mr. Heron who returned the peremptory acknowledgment. "Please, Mr. Heron, tell Jamie what you just told me."

"Well, first of all, nobody's lived in that place for something like eight years. There was a fire—started by a faulty furnace. An old woman, must have been about eighty or so, died in the blaze."

"And just who, Mr. Heron, was that old woman who died in the fire?" Jennifer prompted.

"Her name was Josephine Sommers. Lived alone there after her parents died years ago. I never knew her. I've only been here for about four years."

Jamie turned back to look at the house. "What about the property? How come it was just left to rot? Who owns it now, do you know? Has it just been left abandoned?"

Mr. Heron reached down to placate his dog, a tan cocker spaniel. The animal was getting impatient to continue his afternoon romp. "Property's been tied up in litigation. The Sommers lady left it to the Village of Tarrytown to be used as a home for unwed mothers and abused women. Naturally, the neighborhood put up a squawk and it's been tied up in a zoning battle ever since. Talk now is that the town is going to tear it down and offer the lot for sale."

"I see," Jamie smiled to himself. He was remembering Josephine Sommers's comments about fathers these days, who didn't accept their paternal responsibilities. "Well, thank you, Mr. Heron. You've been very helpful."

Jamie turned to Jennifer as Mr. Heron proceeded with his charge down Irving Street. "Jen, I know you think I'm nuts, but I was here yesterday in this house and so was Josephine Sommers."

"Oh, Jamie, I'm scared. I don't understand any of this." She began to cry softly.

"I know, Jennifer, but you will—in time. I don't understand it either, but I know there's an explanation."

He took her face in his hands and tenderly kissed her tear-stained cheeks. "I just want to look around for a minute more and then we have just one more stop to make before we leave. Okay?"

"Okay, Jamie, but please, let me go with you. I don't like standing here while you go searching."

"C'mon." Jamie took her by the hand and walked toward the distressed gazebo.

He wouldn't have seen the object if a squirrel hadn't bounced out of a tree beside the now decrepit shelter just at that moment. The squirrel, searching frenetically for winter forage, raced over to a pile of leaves, scattering them wildly, scrutinizing the ground for nuts. Finding one, the squirrel chattered and scolded the two adults who were barely inches away from its feet, shook its scraggly tail in furious reprimand and with a burst of kinetic energy leaped for refuge up the trunk of the barren elm from which it had only just descended seconds ago.

Chapter Fifty-three

THE OBJECT WAS LYING flat on top of the leaves now. It was an envelope. It couldn't have been out in the weather for very long. It would have been decimated by snow or rain. Jamie reached down to pick it up. The flap was unsealed and the envelope was empty. He looked at the front, which was blank except for a return address in the upper left-hand corner.

In neat, officially looking type, it stated:

Office of the Special Deputy
The White House
Washington, D.C.

Jamie smiled and handed the envelope to Jennifer. It was acutely clear to him, finally.

"There you are, Jen. This is the exact envelope I held in my hand yesterday, given to me by Josephine Sommers. This is the envelope that contained the letter from Joseph Sommers and his report to the President—Theodore Roosevelt, dated April 15th, 1905."

Jamie's voice was calm and measured. "She came back, Jennifer. She had to come back. She had the instructions from her father to meet me and give me what was in this envelope. No matter what happened before yesterday or what happens tomorrow, nothing can change the fact that she came back."

Jennifer was speechless. She stared at the envelope, wide-eyed. Her eyes reflected both fear and wonder.

"It's all right, Jen. It's all right now. Don't try to understand it. Just accept it." Jamie reached down to kiss her reassuringly. "And now, I have one more mission to perform before we can get on with our lives."

Jennifer's voice was child-like, barely audible. She was overwhelmed. She didn't understand any of what was happening, but she knew that Jamie did. He espoused a new strength, an understanding that was beyond her. It frightened her and fascinated her. She knew now that she loved him—could never let him go. She didn't understand what was happening, but it didn't matter. She no longer felt like she was drifting. She knew she wanted to be with him for as long as she lived.

"Mission, Jamie? What mission? You have to take me with you. I'm not letting you leave me now, not for anything."

Jamie smiled and said, "This mission is right here in Tarrytown, Jen. Remember—I said we have one more stop to make before we leave? We're going to the cemetery where Joseph and Helena Sommers are buried. I suppose Josephine is there as well. That's what she meant when she told me yesterday the neighbors would know where she is if we came to visit. C'mon, it's not far from here."

Jamie gave a farewell look at 33 Irving Street and climbed into the car. The gray afternoon light was fading fast. It was now after 4:00 but he felt there would be enough time left before dark to accomplish the task he had set for himself. As he turned the wheel away from the curb, he looked back one last time at the Sommers homestead. The house was now quite dark and brooding. It was devoid of life, merely a shell of its former existence as a happy place with happy people, loving people. The Sommers family was long gone. There was no longer any real excuse for its being. It was now just an empty echo of things that had been. Jamie found himself wishing that the house would soon come down. It was sad to see it standing in that condition. The house deserved to be put to rest. Its purpose had long since been served. He turned back to the street. Jennifer gave him a pensive look and snuggled as close to him as she could get within the confines of the inordinately practical bucket seats.

As they made their way up Rt. 9 north toward the outskirts of Tarrytown, a rose-colored sky appeared magically in the west over the Hudson as the sun made a last ditch effort to burn through the cloud cover.

It wasn't far to the old Dutch church, a modest but venerable stone structure that had seen better times since its founding by the early Dutch Burghers who had migrated north from the downriver village of New Amsterdam in the late 1600's. There was a large sign just outside the front of the church which sought contributions for restoration, amounts pledged for which were recorded on a strikingly visible graph in the shape of a huge thermometer with ever rising temperatures depicted as amounts of gifts were tabulated.

The cemetery stretched on up a hill behind the church. It seemed that every square yard of ground sprouted a tombstone—some grandiose, others, just simple tablets, still others, eloquent with elaborately sculptured angels, mostly in weeping and mourning positions. There were cherubims and a variety of birds and other small animals, all cut in stone, perched in strategic poses, some gazing toward the heavens, others looking down on the lonely graves in sympathetic sorrow. There were even mourners and bystanders exquisitely carved from the granite surrounds, all in eternal vigil, dedicated in stony solitude and expectancy to that final Day of Judgment and Awakening when all souls should stand before their Maker to receive mercy and forgiveness for their blighted earthly lives or, in the alternative, damnation for sins and transgressions thought to be unforgivable.

Jamie thought of his boyhood, in company with his father and mother listening to visiting campground evangelists predicting hellfire for sins of every conceivable stripe and nature. The itinerant preachers emphasized hell and the awful consequences of sinful living far more than the rewards of virtuous lives in a bliss-filled heaven. Jamie often went home after such meetings on Sunday evenings, unable to sleep, imagining that he must be surely one of the worst of sinners and thoroughly fit for the fires of hell. Mother Stanner always assured him in such desperate moments that that was not the case and to go back to sleep secure in the knowledge that God had already chosen him for the Kingdom of Heaven and that all he need do for the rest of his life was to live virtuously so that he might be worthy of God's gift of eternal life.

Jamie was now beginning to believe that life and death might be far more complex than the sawdust trail preachers envisaged it. And yet, the paradox was that maybe the whole business was more simple than one could imagine. Certainly his experience of the Mohonk weekend had had its effect. But there was something that yet eluded him. He would only know the answer to the last riddle in his mind regarding his strange journey to the past, he believed, when he stood before Joseph Sommers's tombstone.

"There, Jennifer, there's Section C-10, right up ahead." Jamie put a comforting hand over Jennifer's. She was silent. She didn't know what to expect on this odyssey of Jamie's except that she had to see it through.

Jamie parked the car near the top, well past the sloping fields of monuments. Here the land flattened out into a shady vale presided over by a towering statue of General Ulysses S. Grant and a number of Civil War graves. Section C-10, surprisingly, was not 'wall to wall' with headstones. Jamie took Jennifer's hand and together they walked along a graveled path until they came to the edge of the vale. Across the tiny meadow, about forty feet from where they stood near a now barren sycamore tree, there were three stones set at equal intervals from one another. As they walked closer, they could see that the stones were uniform, simply-cut, modest memorials and each carried a brief inscription.

The first stone commemorated Joseph Sommers, 'Faithful and Loving Husband of Helena.'

The second was dedicated to Helena, 'Beloved Wife of Joseph.'

The third headstone, and no surprise to Jamie, was inscribed, Josephine Sommers, 'Loving daughter of Helena and Joseph.'

Jamie and Jennifer stood quietly hand in hand in front of the three stones.

"Jennifer, there it is—the answer to the mystery."

Jennifer had been looking at the stones but not really examining them. However, she began to feel a shivery sensation as Jamie took her gently by the hand and pointed to the date of Joseph Sommers's birth and death. Slowly, she began to read outloud, "Born January 15, 1867—Died November 10, 1945.

"My God, Jamie, he died on the day you were born."

"No, Jen. On November 10, 1945, Joseph Sommers passed on."

"Oh, Jamie, I don't know what to think, what to believe, This is awfully heavy."

"Perhaps you should look at the dates for Helena, Jen."

Jennifer began to shake visibly as she read the dates for Helena's birth and death. "Born April 20, 1872—Died June 9, 1955. My birthday, Jamie, my birthday. She died on my birthday."

Jennifer's face lost its color. Her eyes flickered and her body went limp. Jamie caught her and held her very close. He kissed her eyes and stroked her forehead gently. The color slowly came back to her cheeks. Her eyes fluttered and opened. Her body twitched slightly as the muscles responded to her awakening once again. "Jamie, Jamie," she cried softly. "What does all of this mean?"

"I don't know, Jen. We know only what we know. Perhaps, we've been blessed or cursed to know more than others. That will remain to be seen."

Jamie looked over at Josephine Sommers's headstone. "Just like Mr. Heron said, Jennifer." Quietly and slowly he read the dates. "Born August 3, 1905—Died January 15, 1985. That would be when the fire occurred, just about eight years ago."

Jamie lifted Jennifer's face close. He looked closely into her eyes. "And now, Jen, I have one last task to perform. Are you all right? Can you stand alone?"

"I'm okay, I think—shaky, scared half to death, maybe, but, yes, I'm okay—for now anyway, but don't move too far away from me." Jennifer braved a smile and kissed Jamie's hands as he released his hold on her.

Jamie reached into his pocket and took out a small container. It was a gift box for a ring. He opened the box and took out the gold ring it held. Jennifer didn't have to examine it to know that it was the ring she had bought for him in the Gazebo Shop at the Mountain House inscribed with the initials J.S.

Jamie knelt down on the hard, cold earth beside Joseph Sommers's grave. He took from another pocket a screwdriver, which he had removed from the glove compartment of the car as they had parked near General Grant.

Almost ceremoniously, he dug a hole about eight to ten inches deep near the headstone and, with one last glance at the ring, dropped it in and filled the hole with the little pile of dirt he had removed. He found a small flat rock nearby and placed it over the tiny burial site. He stood up and moved to Jennifer, placing his arms around her and kissing her very tenderly.

"It's finished, Jennifer. Now the rest of our lives are ahead of us—as well as behind us," he said with a wry smile.

Whether it was a sign, who could know, but just as they both turned for a last look at the three headstones, a stunning ray of burnished gold light rent the clouds behind them from the west and illuminated the three stones as if a theatrical spotlight had been turned on by some heavenly stage manager.

Jennifer turned to Jamie, a big happy smile now erasing earlier worry lines. "Jamie, I have to ask you something, right here and now. It can't wait."

"Okay, my love, so ask away."

"Jamie, will you—marry me?"

Jamie chuckled softly and kissed Jennifer in a long, deep, kiss.

"To quote a tired old cliché—I thought you'd never ask."

Slowly and silently, arms around each other, they walked back to the car, past General Ulysses S. Grant, standing tall, posed in his eternal vigil, from which he seemed to be saying, so Jamie thought irreverently, "I could sure use a drink!"

EPILOGUE

LATE AFTERNOON April showers had moisturized the air throughout the Rondout Valley. Beyond and below the Mountain House to the west, ground layers of emergent fog, like smoky tendrils, sifted the spring twilight into tones of russet, gray and blue. The distant Catskill ranges, blanketed in the deepening purplish haze, slowly lost their struggle to assert their dominant profile.

In the dwindling daylight, the western horizon came to resemble a vast and endless seascape, the demarcation of sky and land obscured by the descendent cloud banks merging with the thickening fog. Land islands, darkened by the verdant vegetation of forests, thrust up craggy humps through the swirling mists like the bony spines of monstrous sea serpents slumbering in the lower depths of watery chasms. It was a scene not unlike that of eons past when the deep waters of an inland sea covered the Mohonk lands and the territories of the Hudson Valley.

"Here it is, honey." Jennifer's voice, soft and reverent, came from just ahead of Jamie where she had stopped upon reaching a stony ledge overlooking the lake. She was kneeling beside a newly placed rustic cedar bench. The bench had been positioned in front of an ancient gnarled pitch-pine on a promontory of Pine Bluff that offered a dramatic view of the lake and the chiseled cliffs of Sky Top. The pine tree, crafted only by wind currents and the barely sustainable soils to be found in the cracks and rifts of the rock slabs, stood sentinel-like, in total effect—a giant bonsai, its trunk and twisted limbs curling protectively around the little bench.

"Isn't it just perfect, Jamie—the way it looks out over the lake?"

"Yes, they did a good job. I think Joseph and Helena would have approved."

Jamie came around the end of the bench to join Jennifer. He took her hands gently, kissing her finger tips. Jennifer lifted her hands and cradled Jamie's face, drawing him down to her as she reached up with a breathy sigh to kiss him.

They held each other for a few unspoken minutes, enfolded in the light spring breeze that caressed Pine Bluff. The needles of the pine tree quivered silently. Jennifer turned toward the bench.

"Think of all the people who will pass by and read the plaque in the years to come. They won't know anything about the story behind all of this."

"No, you're right, Jen. All the people who come to Mohonk in the future will have their own stories, their own mysteries, their own destinies—and all that we may know of them may be nothing more than what people will see here—names on a memorial tablet."

Jamie knelt and touched the raised letters on the bronze plaque and quietly read aloud the inscription:

IN MEMORY OF
JOSEPH, HELENA AND JOSEPHINE SOMMERS
"LIFE AND DEATH ARE ALL PART OF THE SAME GREAT ADVENTURE"
—*THEODORE ROOSEVELT*

"It's quite beautiful." Jamie stood up slowly, his voice almost a whisper. "We're all a part of it, Jennifer—for the millions of years before and the millions of years to come—we belong."

He paused and then reached into his jacket pocket. "Just one more thing we have to do."

He drew out an envelope, a bit crumpled and yellow from age. He laid it out flat against his palm. The envelope was without contents. On the front, in the upper left hand corner, there was a return address, clear and legible despite the antiquity of the paper. Jamie read the address aloud as he reached into his jacket and drew out a book of matches.

"Office of the Special Deputy, The White House, Washington, D.C."

He walked over to the cliff edge, Jennifer clinging to his arm. The wisps of breezes that usually flowed over and around the edge of the precipice died down abruptly to barely a sigh as Jamie lit a match. He touched the envelope to the tiny flame, which leaped to devour the dry, yellowed parchment, hungrily incinerating the bits and pieces as they fell away over the cliffside—charred sparks and ashes of the only remaining fragment of evidence of an event that might have altered the course of nations.

As the last remnants of the burning envelope disintegrated in the lake-side shadows creeping along the water's edge, the cry of an eagle soaring above from the direction of Eagle Cliff pierced the dusky sky.

"Hear that, Jennifer? Look—up toward Sky Top."

Jamie pointed to the majestic bird, gliding on the air currents flowing from the lake upward toward the Smiley Memorial Tower high above the jagged rock scrambles falling away from the hatchet-like features that, from the angle of Pine Bluff, resembled George Washington's profile.

"That's the first eagle I've ever heard or seen at Mohonk," came Jamie's excited voice.

The eagle soared gracefully over the lake, dipping a wing tip now and then, correcting for the shifts in the thermal currents. Another piercing cry issued from the bird as it wheeled abruptly and set off for Eagle Cliff directly opposite Sky Top. It finally disappeared in a sweeping arc over the tree tops.

"Oh, Jamie," Jennifer spoke in a hushed voice. "Do you think, maybe, he was trying to tell us something?"

"Well, Jen—I think if Teddy Roosevelt had had his way, he might very well have opted to come back as an eagle." Jamie gazed at the now empty sky, searching the heavens for another sight of the great bird. He stood quietly for long minutes and then let out a great sigh, smiled and waved at the horizon.

"Good-bye, Teddy—your secret is safe with us."

Jamie turned to Jennifer and held out his hand to her. Jennifer smiled and took his hand, squeezing softly. Very close together and wordlessly they negotiated the rock ledges leading down from Pine Bluff to Eagle Cliff Road and the entrance to the Mountain House. The eagle cried one more time from far away, a faint echo. Then it was gone.

AUTHOR'S NOTES . . .

In 1869, Albert Smiley, heeding the advice and counsel of his twin brother, Alfred, purchased, not far from the village of New Paltz, New York, a tract of land, a mountain top and a tavern, all of which was situated in an incredibly picturesque setting of the Shawangunk Mountains just west of the Hudson River.

This unique mountain top paradise, a scenic wonder that had even been the subject of a lithograph by Currier and Ives, would soon undergo a 'sea-change' under the tutelage of the Smiley brothers, devout quakers, that would turn it into one of the East's most famous summer resorts. The centerpiece would be a magnificent 300 room 'Mountain House' that slowly rose from the stark monolithic stone ledges along the lakeside. This rambling 'house' faced resplendent wooded heights across the lake that ascended to a promontory the Smileys aptly named Sky Top—a pinnacle from which six neighboring states could be viewed.

Peopled by a coterie of some of the most celebrated Americans of Arts and Letters of the 19th Century, the Mountain House soon came to enjoy an international clientele as news of the distinguished resort spread to most of the capitals of the civilized world.

Its eminence, not just as a family resort, but as an apex for the exchange of intellectual, cultural, religious and social issues, radiated far and wide, even to the doors of the White House.

Four United States Presidents walked the gracious corridors of the Mohonk resort, along with senators, congressmen, Supreme Court justices and other well-known public figures. World renown religious leaders, preachers and churchmen of every persuasion, to say nothing of many tycoons of American business, including John D. Rockefeller and Andrew Carnegie, all broke bread together in the great Mohonk dining hall.

During such prosperous years, the members of the Smiley family became known for their dedicated stewardship and humanitarianism. They sponsored annual conferences dealing with the welfare of the American Indians and gathered world leaders together at Mohonk to discuss and encourage the adoption of international arbitration among nations, a movement directed toward achieving true world peace. Such a movement influenced the establishment of the Hague World Court and Tribunal, the formation of the League of Nations and, ultimately, it would not be an exaggeration to state, the organization of the United Nations.

In 2001, the Mohonk Mountain House celebrated its 132nd anniversary of continuous operation still under the ownership and management of the Smiley family and their descendants.

Acknowledgments . . .

It borders on cliché to state that a writer never toils alone to produce a finished work—that there are, indeed, often numerous persons called upon for their wit and wisdom and expertise during the production process.

And so it has been with this author who received countless insights, input and support from the following individuals as he worked to complete the manuscript of *The President's Weekend.*

My everlasting thanks to:

Sherrie Murphy, my agent and longtime friend, for her prodigious effort toward finding a publisher. Many Smiley family members associated with the operation of the Mohonk Mountain House, including: Jane Smiley, past Mohonk Archivist, who searched historical records for facts critical to the authenticity of my story; Nina Smiley, Director of Marketing and her husband, Bert Smiley, the President of the Mohonk Mountain House Corporation for their review and approval of the finished manuscript; Rachel (Smiley) Matteson and Gerow Smiley, for providing important historic details in the operation of the Mountain House over the years. Maureen Stanton and Ralph Loanna, in particular, as well as all the other members of the household staff at Mohonk for their many assists in providing for my comfort at Mohonk while writing *The President's Weekend.* Kathleen Sheehy, Assistant Curator of the Sagamore Historical Society at Sagamore Hill, Theodore Roosevelt's home at Oyster Bay, N.Y., for her thorough evaluation and many welcome suggestions toward improving the authenticity of the manuscript. William F. Atwater, Director/Curator of the U.S. Army Ordnance Museum at the Aberdeen Proving Grounds in Maryland, for his expertise in authenticating details of military hardware for the author. Marion Ryan, historical and reference librarian at the Elting Memorial Library in New Paltz, N.Y., for her invaluable assistance in helping the author research local historical facts critical to the authenticity of the story. P.J. Belanger, my dear friend of many years who reviewed and enthusiastically approved the final draft of *The President's Weekend.* Monica Randall, a colleague of mine and published author who loves and has written wonderful ghost stories of her own, for her support and encouragement along the way. Suzette Hays forhelping me to 'locate' Peter Cooper, my publisher. Peter for his brilliant surgical-like touch in editing and his assistant editor Teal Hutton for her meticulous attention in proofing the final manuscript. My brother and closest friend, Robert Cameron Reed, for his editorial expertise as a professional librarian and grammarian, invaluable assets I drew upon frequently. Jeanette Mass, for her proofing and corrections of first printing. Janet L. Petitti, for typing and trascribing tapes of my initial text.And finally, my son, Cameron Francis Reed, a computer wizard who spent hours and hours formatting my rough drafts into a finished and polished manuscript, and who introduced me to the wondrous world of computers and word processing.

More great titles from

VIVISPHERE PUBLISHING:

THE LIFE OF THEODORE ROOSEVELT
W.M. Draper Lewis

BIRTH MARK
Bill Rowe and Peter Cooper

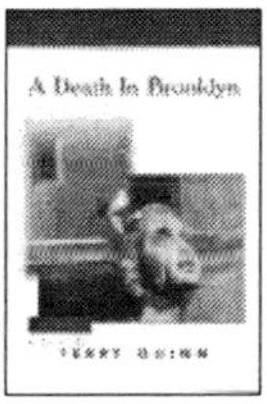

A DEATH IN BROOKLYN
Terry Quinn

DUET:
PARNASSUS ON WHEELS
THE HAUNTED BOOKSHOP
Christopher Morley

PSYCHIC FAIR
George O'Har

INFINITE DARKNESS
INFINITE LIGHT
Margaret Doner

MONTANA GOTHIC
Dirck Van Sickle

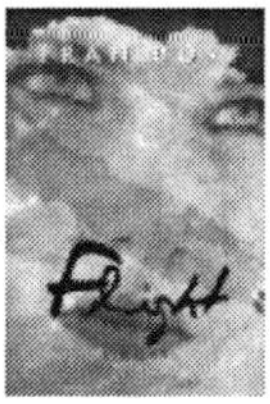

FLIGHT
Fran Dorf

MANHATTAN GOTHIC
Mel Arrighi